# The Coin of Kenvard

Joseph R. Lallo

ISBN: 978-1951240028

# Table of Contents

# ACKNOWLEDGMENTS

In this, the sixth full novel in the main Book of Deacon series, I would like to once again thank Nick Deligaris for his excellent cover illustration. I would also like to thank Tammy Salyer for going above and beyond to help make this story comprehensible. And most importantly, I would like to thank the readers who stuck with me this far. If not for you, the Book of Deacon Saga would have closed out as a trilogy and my writings would have continued only as idle scribblings in the back pages of notebooks. Thanks for all your support!

# Prologue

The Northern Alliance was an icy place. Even in summer, all but the southern fringe wore a heavy blanket of snow. In the freshly rebuilt palace of New Kenvard, that cold was a distant memory. Near as it was to the southern border of its land, the capital enjoyed that rarest of things for denizens of the Northern Alliance: a green summer. Even in the harshest of blizzards, though, the home of Myranda and Deacon would have been a place of warmth, happiness, and love. It was home.

Myranda turned the page in a thick book. By now, she knew the story by heart, but the daily ritual called for the book, and far be it from her to argue with tradition.

"'And so Gilliam raised his hands and conjured a rope of glimmering light,'" Myranda read in a spirited voice. "'He slid down the rope into the mysterious valley. Wind stirred the leaves of the five trees before him. They were massive, far larger than they had appeared from above. He heard laughter and coaxing voices from within the circle, but he saw nothing but ice and the trickle of a meager stream. It was a magical place. Of that, there could be no doubt. But what sort of magic?'"

As she spoke, an audience of two stared up at her from the floor. The first was Deacon. He sat cross-legged, and on his lap and wrapped in his arms was the second. A young boy, not yet two years of age. He had the vivid red hair of his mother and the keen, interested gaze of his father. He hung on his mother's every word as she read.

"'When he was near enough, Gilliam could feel the power of the tree. There was more to this valley than mortal eyes could comprehend. Finally, he would set foot within the ring. Finally, he would learn what was inside.'"

She snapped the book shut. "And so will we. Tomorrow."

"Nuh!" objected a tiny voice.

"Leo, today is a very important day. You've had your story, but you are a prince and you have certain duties," Deacon said. "You will have more of the story tomorrow."

"Nuh!"

Myranda sighed. "He's got your thirst for knowledge."

"Gilliam spins a fascinating tale," Deacon said.

"I'd not realized your former gray master was so skilled in storytelling."

"There are those who claim it was his only skill. Half of the lessons he taught in the early days were wrapped in some half-fabricated tale of his supposed exploits that he borrowed from myth or legend."

"Regardless of their origin, Leo can't get enough of them. Something tells me in a few months we'll be answering endless questions." She thumbed at the pages of the book again. "Father hasn't come for us yet. There's a bit more time. Perhaps one more chapter…"

"No, no," Deacon said, hefting the boy from his lap to turn him face-to-face. "Discipline, Leo. You are an heir to the throne of Kenvard. You must learn discipline. Sometimes that means having to wait for the end of a story. We have very important business this evening."

"*Nuh!*" Leo pointed a pudgy finger at the book.

"How about the game? Hmm? Would that do?" Deacon offered.

"Game!" Leo replied.

The little boy toddled a few steps away and turned, eagerly looking to his father now. Deacon fetched an egg-shaped bit of amber crystal from his pocket and clutched it tightly in his left hand.

"Look closely now. What is *this*?" he said.

Deacon stirred the air. Feathery wisps of light swirled together. They coalesced into a radiant form, a sleek, elegant dragon.

"*Myn!*" Leo said, clapping his hands.

"No, it is a *dragon*, and *Myn* is a dragon, but this is a different dragon. Myn is red, and this dragon is—"

"Myn, Myn, Myn," Leo insisted, pointing at the illusory dragon.

"No, no. This dragon is green. Not every dragon is Myn," Deacon said patiently.

A steady thumping beyond the palace wall made the ground tremble. The shuttered window darkened as something outside blocked the light. Myranda smirked.

"You knew it was going to happen," she said.

A soft scratch popped the shutter open. With a jangle of askew jewelry, a gleaming red reptilian snout poked inside.

"Myn!" Leo announced, pointing to the dragon who had heeded his call.

The dragon pulled her snout free and angled her great golden eye against the window to scan the inside.

"He is fine, Myn. Deacon is just playing the game," Myranda assured the faithful beast.

Myn glanced to the illusion Deacon had summoned. Her expression brightened.

"Garr," the dragon said. Though the creature had spoken at a near whisper, her deep voice echoed through the room.

"Gah! Gah! Gah!" Leo said.

"Please, Myn. Leo is supposed to answer on his own," Deacon reprimanded.

The dragon gave him a hard look, then haughtily pulled away and slammed the shutter.

"I think she likes our boy more than she likes you," Myranda whispered.

"I've never been very high on her list of affections." Deacon focused on Leo again. "But Myn was right. This is Garr. Garr comes from the south. From Tressor."

"Gah," Leo repeated.

"And what is Garr?" Deacon asked.

"Duck."

"No, Leo. Dragon."

"Duck."

"He is a dragon. Just like Myn."

Leo waddled over to the illusion and bent low to inspect it. After a few moments of consideration, he pointed at the green, scaled creature and looked Deacon in the eye.

"Duck," he affirmed.

"… We'll try another one. Who is this?"

The light splashed away and reformed, this time assembling into an elegantly dressed creature with foxy features.

"Ivy!" Leo peeped.

"That's right. And what color is Ivy's dress?"

"Boo."

"Blue is right!" Deacon said.

He leaned forward to his boy and gently pressed the gem into the toddler's hands. Rather than risk the boy dropping the powerful mystic focus, Deacon held Leo's hands on either side.

"Now, Leo. Can you show me *green*?"

"Geen," Leo said, looking his father in the eye.

"No. Feel the crystal and show me green."

Leo blinked at his father. He looked to the crystal. A candle flame of a glow flickered ever so briefly in the heart of the gem. It faded as quickly as it appeared. Leo tugged one hand free and pointed to the green cover of the book Myranda held.

"Geen."

Deacon laughed. "That's right, Leo. Green."

There was a knock at the door. It creaked open a moment later to reveal a finely dressed older man standing in the doorway.

"Is it time, Father?" Myranda asked.

"Carriages are already arriving at the gates," Greydon replied.

"Heavens. I must have lost track of time. Leo still needs to get dressed."

"Fah!" Leo said, dismissing his father for the far more important visit from his grandfather.

Greydon Celeste plucked his grandson from the ground. "Need I remind you that this is an official state ceremony?" he said, hefting the boy on one hip.

Myranda grumbled. "The crown?"

"At least for the introductions. It is protocol."

"So be it," Myranda said. "I will be along shortly."

Greydon nodded and pulled the door shut. Deacon climbed from the ground and brushed some dust from his trousers.

"It strikes me that I perhaps should not have been sitting on the ground in my royal finery," he said.

"Story time is more important than royal protocol as far as I am concerned."

She slipped the book onto a shelf of similar ones. Beside the bookshelf was a table set with two velvet pillows. One pillow, embroidered with the words *Her Royal Majesty*, bore a golden ringlet etched with a fine design and set with precious gems. The other pillow, meant to bear Deacon's crown, was empty.

"I never expected the most trying aspect of nobility would be the wardrobe." She donned the crown and frowned at its weight.

"One becomes accustomed to it in time," Deacon said, adjusting the ringlet on his head. He looked to Leo. "He's learning so fast," he said, his eyes sparkling with pride.

He rushed to a second bookcase and selected one of a dozen similar volumes. With a flourish of his fingers, he summoned a stylus to his hand and began scribbling fresh words on the page.

"He knows his colors very well. He hasn't quite got dragons and ducks straight, but one can follow the line of logic. Long necks, long faces. Wings." He flipped back a few pages. "It was only three weeks ago that he called every color pink. He'll be casting his first spell before the month is out, mark my words."

Myranda huffed a breath. "I am in no rush for that. He is enough of a handful without being able to command the forces of nature."

"It would help him get to sleep," Deacon said, jotting a few more notes down. "When I was a boy, I would exhaust myself each night trying to levitate this and conjure that."

Myranda considered his words for a moment. "Tempting… But come. We shouldn't keep the others waiting."

"I'll be along shortly. I just need to mark this down."

Myranda stepped from the room as Deacon scratched out a description of his boy's progress. As tended to be the case, even a hasty record of a very typical afternoon took line after line of words for him to record properly. His usually precise penmanship wavered a bit as he closed off one paragraph and began a second. A shudder in his hand traced a jagged line onto the page. He pulled the stylus from the paper. It was trembling in his grip.

"Not again…" Deacon muttered.

He shut his eyes tightly. The shudder in his hand worsened. Thin red veins traced from his fingertips to his wrist. They swept back and forth like worms held to a flame. Where they curled across his skin, the texture changed to something coarse and black. He summoned the crystal to his grip and held it firmly. The shifting change in his hand slowed and faded. His flesh eased back to its proper appearance.

Deacon pocketed the gem and twisted the silver ring on the ring finger of the afflicted hand.

"Deacon!" Myranda called.

"Yes! Coming. Mustn't shirk my duties." He looked to his hand and murmured, "Mustn't lose control."

6

# Chapter 1

"Now announcing, Queen Caya of and King Croyden of Vulcrest!"

The assembled crowd roared their approval as the pair of stately monarchs entered New Kenvard's freshly christened grand hall. The palace was still very much on the mend. Decades of decay and far too many battles had left scars that would take years more construction to repair, but if this hall was any indication, it would shine as one of the most elegant structures in the north. Once, banners depicting victories over Tresson forces had decorated the walls. Now, the tapestries told of the true enemy, the D'Karon. Freshly milled stone gleamed. The air was thick with the smell of fresh wood.

By far the greatest achievement of this place was the effect it had on those in attendance. Queen Caya enthusiastically clutched the hands of friends and well-wishers. Her handlers had long ago lost the fight to keep her distant and regal in her decorum. As recently as five years prior, only a small circle of the northern aristocracy would have been deemed worthy of a personal greeting from the crowned head of Vulcrest. Now there were representatives from Tressor bowing their heads to her. Elves from the Crescents gave bemused smiles as the queen clapped their backs. And most astounding of all, a white-furred malthrope stood at attention, barely able to contain her glee as she joined the other ambassadors.

"Ambassador Ivy!" Caya proclaimed. "I'd feared you wouldn't be able to attend."

"My boat arrived just yesterday. Myn fetched me so I could make it in time."

"I don't think I've ever seen an outfit like that."

Ivy took a step back and turned in a circle, revealing a sandy-yellow dress of simple but exquisite make. "Do you like it? The people of Den made it for me specially for this occasion. I begged them to send one of their own along with me as a proper delegate, but—"

King Croyden cleared his throat. "Perhaps this could wait until the banquet."

Caya rolled her eyes. "I'd thought he was a stickler for the rules *before* we put a crown on his head. Very well, very well." She continued down the line and found her place to one side of the blue carpet running the length of the grand hall.

"Now announcing King Terrance and Queen Tanya of Ulvard."

A more reserved ovation from the crowd greeted a stately couple. They were each twenty years older than Queen Caya, with silver-threaded hair and dour expressions. What they lacked in liveliness they made up for in dignity. This was a pair of nobles who looked the part of a king and queen. They marched along the carpet, offering little in the way of greeting to the dignitaries flanking it. After Caya's rousing entry, their appearance was somewhat glaring in its subtlety. A crackle of anticipation lit up the crowd the moment Terrance and Tanya took their place opposite Caya, as all in attendance knew who came next.

"And finally, announcing Queen Myranda and King Deacon of Kenvard, Guardians of the Realm. And Prince Leo, first heir to the reborn kingdom."

Again the people erupted in enthusiastic applause as the new monarchs appeared in the doorway. Myranda held her son in her arms and beamed at friends and subjects all around. Deacon walked beside her, pride radiating from his face.

"I do wish Ulvard had selected someone a bit more *vibrant* to lead their kingdom. It must be terribly embarrassing to hear such silence for their own leaders sandwiched between such adoration," Caya said.

"The guests are *supposed* to remain silent during the entry. It is intended as a sign of reverence and respect," Croyden said. "This boisterousness is your doing, you realize. Allowing such clamor when you were queen of the Alliance."

"Yes, Croyden," Queen Caya said. "And I am rather proud of it. But if you are so concerned with keeping to protocol, do feel free to save your lectures until the wine and cheese course."

Myranda and Deacon took their place at the end of the carpet.

The royal steward raised his voice. "The king and queen shall now speak!"

Silence fell swiftly and all eyes turned to the monarchs.

"Greetings to my friends, my allies, my family," Myranda said. "It is a great honor to welcome you to the restored grand hall of New Kenvard. The road of recovery has been a long one. Longer than any of us supposed. The hall was still in ruin when Prince Leo was born. When Queen Caya saw fit to formally dissolve the Northern Alliance and once again make Kenvard a kingdom of its own, the coronation took place in the shadow of the palace. Many grand occasions came and went, unable to wait for the resurrection of this hall. Now, we can finally celebrate a moment in the way the kings and queens of old intended."

Myranda signaled the well-dressed men to either side of the doors leading to the courtyard.

"Introducing Myn, Guardian of the Realm, heroine of the Battle of Verril!" the steward proclaimed.

The doors creaked open and Myn marched proudly inside. In lieu of the fine wardrobe worn by the other attendees, Myn's scales were polished to a glassy sheen. Her horns jangled with silver and gold chains. Most notably, a silk satchel hung from her neck. With the arrival of the majestic dragon, the size and scope of the grand hall suddenly seemed barely adequate. She marched gingerly along the carpet. Those less familiar or accustomed to the dragon faltered, backing away as she plodded by. She circled Myranda and Deacon and plopped down, head held high.

"The pouch," Deacon whispered.

Myn regally lowered her neck, presenting the satchel she wore. Myranda handed Leo to Deacon and unfastened the pouch from Myn.

"To my knowledge, there has never before been a ceremony of this sort to mark this specific occasion," Myranda said, tugging open the satchel.

"Any excuse for good friends and good drink!" Caya shouted.

The audience roared in approval.

"There is something to that. But before the wine flows, the business at hand. When the Northern Alliance formed, many became one. Three rich histories were set aside to battle what we believed to be a common enemy. Mistakes were made, and as the new shepherds of these kingdoms, it falls to us to correct those wrongs both great and small. Those we labeled as enemies when the Alliance was formed we now count as allies. Today, we restore another fragment of the identity we share as the people of Kenvard. I present to you the gold glint, freshly minted coin of Kenvard."

She pulled a handful of the gold coins from the satchel. One side depicted the face of Myranda herself. The reverse depicted the curve and point of the Mark of the Chosen, along with the reborn kingdom's name and its new motto.

"Wisdom, courage, honor. These are the principles by which I hope to lead. These are the principles that embody the spirit of our people. In the end, gold is gold, silver is silver, and copper is copper. We are all free to do trade with whatever coins we choose. But from today, we can carry the same reverence for these principles in our purses as we do in our hearts. Thank you all for coming. And I hope you all enjoy the celebration."

A riotous final cheer shook the room. Servants emerged with silver trays, and the festivities began in earnest. Ivy practically pranced from her place in line and tackled Myranda with a hug.

"Myranda, it's been too long!" she squealed.

"Too, too long," Myranda said, arms tight about her friend. "How have things been in North Crescent?"

"Later, later," Ivy said. "There's someone I've got to meet."

She turned and flashed a gleeful smile at the wide-eyed Leo. "Hello, little prince. My name is—"

"*Ivy!*" squealed the child, arms held out to her.

The malthrope gasped and covered her mouth. "He knows me?" she said, her voice cracked with emotion. "But I haven't seen him in over a year. Not since just after he was born."

Deacon held the boy out, and Ivy gratefully hugged him to her.

"We've made sure Leo knows all about the other Chosen. Stories every day. And illusions."

"I've read all about you in the little notes your father writes," Ivy said, nose to nose with the giggling child. "Have you missed Auntie Ivy?"

"Ivy," he repeated.

She squealed in delight. "I've got presents for him, can I walk him around to go get them?"

"Take Myn. She probably doesn't want to be cooped up in here," Myranda suggested.

Ivy let Leo slip to the ground and held down her hand. "Come on!"

The prince eagerly toddled along with the playful malthrope. Myn plodded carefully behind, head low to nudge the unsteady walker upright whenever he started to falter. As the unusual pair of "aunts" marched out the door, Caya stepped up, already with a drink in hand.

"Cheers to you, Myranda, Deacon. Kenvard has never had so fine a pair of monarchs, and a boy has never had so fine a pair of parents."

"Nor so fine a set of godparents," Myranda said.

"Flattered." She laughed. "Though Croyden rather wishes you hadn't given us the distinction. The queen of one kingdom serving as the godmother to the son of another smacks of the very sort of alliance we were trying to put to rest."

Caya elbowed Deacon in the ribs. "You'll have to have two more children to even things out with Ulvard and Tressor." She took another sip of her drink. "So, have you spoken with Tanya and Terrance yet?"

"As a matter of fact, I haven't," Myranda said, scanning the hall. "Where have they gone off to?"

"The king and queen wish to wait until they are formally presented during dinner before they mingle socially," Croyden explained. "Protocol."

"Protocol is for dull people who can't improvise," Caya said. "And that is precisely who the nobles selected to lead Ulvard."

"You would be better served to keep such opinions to yourself," Croyden said.

"Among friends is as good as in private, Croyden. And I am not impugning their leadership. Just their personalities. They'll be a fine king and queen. They're just a bit of a wet blanket."

"If you aren't fond of them, how did they come to be the king and queen? Surely you had a hand in their selection," Deacon said.

"Oh, the usual ways. Scribes dig up family trees and trace ancestry. A handful of blue bloods argue about who has a claim to the throne. Discussions, redrawn borders, promised marriages, and Terrance and Tanya came out with the crowns."

"I wonder how things might have differed if you'd let the Ulvardians select their own king and queen, as the people of Verril did with you."

"If we let the Ulvardians select their own queen, they would have chosen me again. Splitting up the Alliance was hardly a popular decision. But it was time. The Northern Alliance was always a military alliance. It sent the wrong message, keeping it together once the borders to the south reopened."

She gazed about. "It strikes me, there is one rather notable individual who seems not to be in attendance."

"Oh?" Myranda said.

"Ether. She's usually good for a memorable entrance."

"She will be along. Celia has not been well, and she wished to remain with her until she slept."

"Celia? … Oh, yes, yes. Her 'mother,' correct? I am sorry to hear that she is unwell. Lovely woman."

"It is really nothing to be concerned about," Deacon said. "She requested me to look into it personally. Little more than a nagging cold. I would have cured her, but Celia herself insisted it wasn't necessary."

"Ether has become *very* protective of her."

"Ah. I see. The only thing worse than having no one in your life to care about is the realization that once you *do* have someone to care about, you might lose them. She's existed since the dawn of time and only in the last few years has she learned the sort of things the rest of us learned with our first pets. I don't envy her."

"I'm proud of her. She is finally a part of the world she's sought to defend for so long," Myranda said. "Hopefully, she can learn to embrace the good times once she comes to terms with the bad."

"The sooner she learns that the better. To that end, let us find our seats, eh? I am famished."

#

The next few hours were, for the most part, a well-deserved escape from the everyday difficulties of resurrecting three kingdoms that had not had to function separately for more than a century. Music and dancing, good food, and plenty of good drink. Even Ivy's gleeful insistence on toting Leo around with her wherever she went was a relief. It was rattling at first. Myranda and Deacon found themselves taking turns anxiously realizing they'd lost track of their child, only to spot him chasing Ivy among the tables or balancing on her knee to make a mess of a thick slice of pie. Now Leo had dozed off in Ivy's arms while she dreamily walked him around the room, murmuring a soft melody. Myranda and Deacon had no shortage of people to help them take care of their son, but there was a special sort of ease that came from knowing that family was caring for family.

"Look at them," Myranda said with a smile, pushing aside the plate with the remnants of her dessert. "Thick as thieves already. I don't think I've had Leo go this long without calling for Deacon or me since he learned his first words."

"Surely you have a nanny for him," Queen Tanya said.

"Several. And nursemaids and servants and a dozen others. But I lost my mother quite young, and I'd believed I'd lost my father as well. We never know what the future will hold. I want as much time with my boy as I can get."

"Admirable," King Terrance said.

The tone he used suggested it was, in this case, a synonym for "I fail to see the relevance of this conversation." As tended to be the case, the seating for the feast was dictated not by friendship but by diplomacy. Myranda and Deacon were joined by Queen Caya and King Croyden representing Vulcrest. Ambassador Maka, a dark-skinned and silver-haired gentleman, represented Tressor in lieu of their monarchs. They, at least, were people Myranda easily counted among her friends. King Terrance and Queen Tanya of Ulvard showed little indication that friendship was anywhere on their list of requirements. They were amicable, but dedicated to the less jovial aspects of the gathering.

"If we could bring ourselves back to the topic of grain. I consulted our records prior to the separation of our kingdoms, and it would appear Kenvard provided us with a small but indispensable portion of our wheat and rye. I would very much like to formalize in the form of a treaty some manner of assurance that the supply will not be interrupted."

"If you have need of grain, King Terrance, Tressor has a ready supply," Maka said, his voice flavored with the accent of the southern tribes.

"That can be discussed, certainly, but at present I would prefer to reestablish prior agreements before sculpting new ones."

"Terrance, your dedication to diplomacy is admirable, but there is a time and a place," Caya said. "I have neither the facts, nor the figures, nor the inclination to work out trade agreements at the moment. We are here for two reasons. The first is to celebrate a milestone for Kenvard. So unless you're through celebrating, I suggest we keep the business talk to a minimum."

"As a matter of fact, I think it would be an excellent time to move to the next order of business. If that pleases our host, of course."

Myranda glanced about. As tended to be the case when Caya was involved, the evening had been a lengthy one. Most of the other tables were empty, as their guests from across the kingdoms had retired for the evening. At some point a number of the tables had been pushed aside, and Myn had slipped inside to flop down and consume astonishing quantities of mashed potatoes. Now she was dozing. As they watched, Ivy took a seat on the dragon's folded claws. Myn sleepily curled a tail around the malthrope. She sighed and leaned against Myn, the prince still safe in her arms.

"Now would be an excellent time," she agreed. "I would have preferred to wait until Ether arrived. These matters concern her. But better not to let business linger."

Myranda summoned some of her servants and instructed them to fetch her should Leo awake or Ether arrive. She stood and led the other monarchs into the hallway.

"The private meeting room is this way. I am told this was formerly the muster room, where matters of strategic importance were discussed among officers before orders were dispatched in times of war. It feels like a triumph to utilize it for a more peaceful purpose."

Two guards stepped aside and opened the door. The monarchs of three kingdoms and the ambassador of a fourth stepped inside. With the exception of Myranda and Deacon, each of the representatives brought an assistant. Those accompanying King Terrance and Queen Tanya carried a large cloth-wrapped box of some sort.

The room was comfortably appointed. A long table, large enough to accommodate twice as many people, stood in the center. There were refreshments, enough candles to provide ample light, and a fireplace to keep it warm. The guards shut and secured the door.

"Let's get down to it, then," Caya said. "I'm anxious to—"

"One moment," Deacon said.

He and Myranda turned to the fireplace.

"When were you going to announce yourself?" Myranda asked.

Two points of light flared among the flames. Gradually, a human form coalesced and stepped from the fireplace. Myranda and Deacon remained impassive. Caya and Croyden were irritated. The king and queen of Ulvard, and both of the servants, were beside themselves. The only person in the room who seemed genuinely delighted was Ambassador Maka.

The brilliant form faded until a beautiful woman stood before them. She was dressed in a manner that seemed precisely calibrated to very slightly exceed the elegance and extravagance of all in attendance.

"I was awaiting the proper moment," she stated.

"The proper moment would have been when you arrived. I am sure the other attendees would have been excited to have a fourth Chosen One announced," Myranda said.

"Celia was quite firmly of the opinion that arriving late would have been disruptive and rude," Ether said.

"What was her assessment of your plan to secretly infiltrate a secure meeting room during a gathering concerning the leaders of the entire continent?" Caya asked.

"We did not discuss it." Ether took a seat at the table. "I believe there was important business to discuss?"

Myranda and Deacon turned back to the others. The Ulvard royalty were still visibly rattled.

"King Terrance, Queen Tanya, I present to you Ether, the great shapeshifter, Guardian of the Realm. Ambassador to Tressor and the Crescents," Myranda said.

Ether gave a nod.

"If what you are presenting here today is indeed what we believe it to be, it falls under Ether's oversight," Deacon clarified.

King Terrance surveyed the room and, upon discovering the other royals were adjusting far more quickly than he, he rallied. "The case, please," he said, signaling his assistant.

The frazzled assistant placed a burlap-wrapped case on the table. Deacon stood and began to pull away the wrapping.

"Workers in the outskirts of Territal were expanding a stable when they turned up this case. I think you will agree that it matches the description of what you instructed us to be mindful."

Deacon revealed the box. The surface was unnervingly pristine for something pulled out of the ground. It was a glossy black metal with an oily sheen. Looking into it gave an eerie sense of depth. The top of the box featured spiderweb-thin white etchings. They traced out complex patterns interspersed with all too familiar runes.

"D'Karon…" Ether said. She rose to her feet and shifted to stone, smoldering eyes fixed on the box.

"You are certain?" Queen Tanya said, endeavoring to keep her gaze from shifting to the supernatural actions of the shapeshifter.

"There is no mistaking it." Deacon pulled on a pair of gloves and ran his fingers along the surface of the box. "Four of them have turned up in the years since the D'Karon were defeated. This is the fifth. If this is like the others, it contains a wand and a spell book. Each is capable of spreading knowledge of D'Karon magics. That is concerning enough, but tolerable. The issue is the ease with which these items can be used by the unskilled to potentially devastating effect. Even the box itself is a work of grim brilliance. I haven't worked out precisely how they have achieved it, but it prevents mystic power of any kind from escaping while it is shut, though it does allow a small amount of magic to filter in."

"Why, precisely, is that brilliant?" King Terrance asked.

"Keeping power from escaping prevents the box from being detected. This may as well be an inert piece of stone for all Myranda, Ether, or I am concerned. But it still allows the wand and book to slowly absorb power."

"Your instructions regarding the boxes suggested the D'Karon wanted them to be found. I distinctly remember your claim that the entirety of their purpose was to be found and used by those unaware of their danger to reopen the portal for a D'Karon return."

"The D'Karon have *just* been defeated. We have all done our very best to spread the knowledge of their treachery and of the danger they pose. It would do little good for these things to glow like beacons and draw others to them. If we've done our jobs, any who might find one will know to present it to us to be secured. They need time to pass, both to empower the artifacts within, and to let the memory of their attack fade. This rune here is the D'Karon word for 'seed,' and it is an apt name. They need time to put down roots and bear fruit."

He leaned forward and inspected the seam at the front edge of the box. His hand shuddered a bit as he ran a finger across the seam. He jerked his fingers clear.

"Has this been tampered with?" Deacon asked. "The others we've found were quite firmly sealed."

"We performed some minor investigations with our own mystics."

Deacon shut his eyes tightly. His fingers curled. "You have opened the box in the presence of the mystically adept. That was... inadvisable."

"The instructions regarding the treatment of these boxes were very clear," Myranda said firmly. "They are to be delivered to us so that we can store them safely, and they are *not* to be opened."

"It was an act of pure idiocy," Ether snapped.

"Now that is uncalled for," King Terrance replied. "We took all due precautions."

"You couldn't have taken all due precautions, because even *we* are still determining what precautions are necessary, and we have considerably more experience with D'Karon workings and teachings than you," Myranda said. "If you've opened the box, the artifacts inside have a greater charge than they would have otherwise. That alone is potentially disastrous."

"I will have to investigate," Deacon said.

Caya reached out and threw the cloth cover back over the box. "I agree, but I'd much prefer you do so while the leadership of the continent *isn't* gathered around a potentially lethal mystic artifact."

"Right, yes," Deacon said. "Naturally, that is wise."

"When and where will you investigate it?" Queen Tanya asked.

"As soon as possible and in a properly fortified workshop. We have a vault outside of the capital."

"We request that a member of our staff be present for the investigation," she said.

"Why?" Myranda asked.

The king and queen of Ulvard glanced at one another.

"Please understand that what I say now does not reflect any personal feelings or opinions. I am merely stating a dispassionate assessment of the facts at hand," the king said.

"Always an encouraging way to begin a statement," Caya said, swirling her wine.

He continued. "There are reasons for the people of Ulvard to believe we may not have an equal place in the actions of the north."

"The world is, of course, grateful for the actions of the Chosen," the queen said. "We all owe our lives and freedom to their great deeds."

"But seers and readers of the prophecy will agree that the Chosen represent the *world*. It would be reasonable that the people of Tressor would be concerned if it appeared the Chosen serve only the north."

Maka nodded. "It was indeed a matter that required some degree of discussion."

Queen Tanya continued. "Now it seems they serve only Kenvard."

"I serve no kingdom," Ether said.

"Be that as it may," the queen said. "Ivy acts as an emissary from the Court of Kenvard, and when not serving as ambassador to North Crescent, she makes her home here. Myn makes her home here as well. Naturally, you do, Queen Myranda. And now you insist upon being the sole guardians of artifacts of the fallen conquerors."

"Queen Caya, you and the Chosen have a history together," the king added. "Quite simply—and again, this is not a personal assessment, but a logical one—it is not a stretch to suggest that the division of the Northern Alliance was less the creation of three kingdoms and more an opportunity to expel Ulvard."

"Ether gave the others a weary look. "I have no interest, nor place, in politics. If you insist upon discussing petty nonsense, I will take the seed to the vault and take my leave."

She stepped toward the box. Myranda motioned for her to stop.

"No. It is a reasonable concern. If we are to work together separately as well as we did as one, then we must be transparent in our tactics and our aims. Queen Tanya, King Terrance, I invite you personally, or representatives of your choosing, to tour our kingdom. We will show you what precautions we have taken, and we will share with you the techniques we utilize to render the D'Karon creations safe. It was always our intention to share that knowledge when it was ready, but naturally keeping our fellow kingdoms involved in the process is not only fair, it is wise. The D'Karon ruled over the whole of the Northern Alliance after all, and Ulvard and Vulcrest have had to cope with their legacy to a large degree already. This is simply a very specific and very dangerous example of that legacy, and we will deal with it collectively. That education will begin with the storage of this very seed. Maka, Tressor is, of course, welcome to all the same knowledge I offer Vulcrest and Ulvard."

"I thank you, Your Majesty," Maka said.

The king and queen of Ulvard conferred with one another for a moment.

"That is acceptable," the king said.

A disruptive clacking sound drew all eyes to Ether. She drummed her stone fingers against her thigh. "Are we through with pointless gestures and empty words? Shall I do what should have been done at the outset?"

"Ether, I congratulate you on making it clear that you are not a diplomat of Kenvard, Vulcrest, or anywhere else," Caya said.

"Take the box and stow it in the vault, but inform those present to expect an official visit to oversee its handling," Myranda said.

Ether's solid form vanished into a burst of wind. The breeze curled around the box, securely wrapping it and hoisting it into the air. Rather than wait to be allowed out of the room, she and the box whisked into the fireplace and out the chimney.

Queen Tanya and King Terrance blinked uncertainly at the still flickering flames. It was clear they were far less accustomed to the casual application of supernatural might than the rest of those in attendance. As before, when they realized they and their assistant were alone in this reaction, they swiftly gathered themselves.

The king adjusted his clothes, tousled into disarray by the burst of wind. "I believe that concludes the official business?"

"I would say so," Caya said.

"Very well then. I believe the queen and I will retire. We are not accustomed to conducting the affairs of state at so late an hour."

"You will find members of my staff just outside the door. They will take you to your quarters," Myranda said.

The royals politely excused themselves. When the door shut, Caya pulled the crown from her head and thumped it on the table with all the finality of a laborer kicking off their shoes for the day.

"If that is any indication of how future summits are likely to go, I'm am going to have to insist upon stronger drink, and earlier in the day," she said.

"They care about their kingdom. I can't fault them," Myranda said.

"That's fine. I am perfectly willing to be the one to assign fault to them. I crowned them as the rulers of Ulvard a full six months before restoring Kenvard *specifically* because I had a feeling the process would be far smoother with you than them, and they've underscored that a dozen times over."

"We are all learning to adjust," Myranda said.

"You could stand to be a bit less overtly benevolent in your compassion and understanding, Myranda. It takes the wind out of the sails of an otherwise enjoyable airing of grievances."

Myranda laughed. "My apologies. Do continue."

"No, no." She waved her hand. "Diplomacy and all that."

"Are we through here?" Deacon asked, touching his fingers to his forehead. "There will be much work to be done in the days ahead. It has been a taxing day. I could use a bit of rest. My head is aching terribly."

"You could start by removing that crown of yours," Caya said.

"Not just yet," he said.

"We really should be going," Myranda said, standing. "Adorable as it would be to leave Leo to sleep in a heap with Myn and Ivy all night, it would be best to put him to bed."

Caya raised her finger. "Just one more point, if I may. For the purposes of official record, this is not state business, as I really don't need to hear from the good king and queen of Ulvard for being left out. However, have you had any rumblings about strange events here in Kenvard?"

"I've just mentioned having to collect my child from his babysitters, a malthrope and a dragon. Strange events are relative," she said.

"Point taken. I will be more specific. I have been informed that some hunters in the Dagger Gale Mountains were quite certain they saw, for a few moments at least, a flicker of a churning white wall to the north. The description was a bit too familiar to disregard out of hand."

Myranda froze. "Were they certain they saw it?"

"I didn't interview them personally." Caya cast a weary glance at Croyden. "That is evidently *beneath* a queen. But Tus spoke to them. He didn't mark them as certain of *what* they saw, so much as certain they saw *something.*"

"If something like the white wall happened again, we would be aware of it," Deacon said. "That was an event that threatened the whole of the world. There would be no doubt."

"Such was my assessment. But I am a woman well aware of my limitations, and chief among them is an ignorance of magic. This seems like a matter that could bite my people rather firmly if I were to ignore it."

"Quite so. Far too many rumors and legends involving the D'Karon have come true. No. You were right to let us know."

"As this has taken you by surprise, I suppose you haven't had similar events here," Caya said.

"I've heard no reports, but we've had our hands full. Maka?"

"Nothing of the sort. At least, nothing deemed serious enough for me to be made aware before this gathering."

"I hate to add yet another item to an already full plate..." Caya said.

Myranda nodded. "We will keep our eyes open. If we can manage to coax Ether to look into matters, we will."

Caya stood. "Then it has been a fine and productive evening. Congratulations on your thriving new kingdom, and give little Leo my best."

Myranda hugged Caya. "Always."

#

"This way," Myranda whispered.

In what may well have been the greatest and unlikeliest of her many heroic achievements, Ivy had managed to climb from atop Myn and carry Leo all the way to his room without rousing the sleeping child. Myranda led the way to his crib in the royal nursery.

"Such a cozy place," Ivy murmured, setting the boy down. "Though it seems awfully small for the prince of a whole kingdom."

"Let's just say those who built the palace had very different ideas of how the royal family should live than Deacon and I do."

The pair slipped back into the hallway.

"I believe this was once the maid's quarters. The intended nursery is in a different wing entirely."

"But how would you know if the baby needs you?" Ivy asked.

"As it has been explained to me again and again by the staff, the king and queen *don't* need to know when their baby cries." She adopted a very official tone of voice. "Your head must be clear and sound and turned fully to the needs of the kingdom."

"So who takes care of the baby?"

"Half the staff of the palace. This is our room here," she said.

Myranda opened a large door directly across the hall from the new nursery. This place, at least, was precisely the sort of quarters one would imagine for a royal family. Ostensibly, it was simply their bedroom, but it was nearly as large as the whole of the home they'd stayed in while the palace was being repaired. A comfortable sitting room served as the entryway for the suite. Furniture of the finest and most elegant sort filled the room. Beyond was the bedroom proper, with a four-poster bed large enough to fit half a dozen people.

Deacon sat at a desk in one corner, stylus in hand, hard at work. He still wore the crown.

Ivy crossed her arms. "How did I know, in a big, comfortable room like this, you'd be bent over a book?"

He looked to her and smiled. "Oh, Ivy. I am so sorry I didn't have the opportunity to spend more time with you during the celebration."

"You were busy, and so was I." She flopped onto one of the couches. "Leo is so *cute*! And smart, too. Did you see him play the drum I gave him?"

"I certainly heard it," Myranda said, somewhat less enthusiastically.

Deacon scratched out a few more lines.

"I feel as though I should be telling you all about what things are like in Den, but you've read it all in the messenger pads."

Myranda stowed her crown on its pillow and sat beside Ivy. "I've kept up on the official matters, but I'm sure there are little things, day to day."

"Mmm…" A half smile came to her lips. "It is strange. I've spent nearly two years there. Surrounded by people who look like me, after believing when we lost Lain that there were no more. And it is lovely. It is a wonder to see how they live. And it fills my heart to watch them grow. I can even see flashes of him in them, you know. But… it isn't home. *This* is home. They're talking with the elves to the south now. Things are calm. I think it might be time to stay here. At least for a bit."

"Well you're certainly welcome in the palace, or in our home near the edge of town."

Ivy clapped. "Oh, right here in the palace would be best. Where I can play with Leo."

She glanced in Deacon's direction. "And who knows," she said flatly. "Maybe if I stay long enough, I'll be lucky enough to catch Deacon relaxing for a few moments."

"You should know by now, books are where I feel most at home," Deacon said.

"You could at least take off your crown."

Myranda and Deacon looked to each other. Ivy flicked an ear.

"Is something wrong?" she asked.

Deacon set down his stylus and turned. "She should know," he said.

Ivy's expression hardened. "I should know what? Are you two hiding something?"

"This doesn't leave this room, Ivy. It is a matter that…" Myranda paused to gather her thoughts. "The kingdom has enough of a task ahead. They don't need to have undue concern for their king."

"Something *is* wrong…" Ivy said.

"Do you recall the affliction my hand suffered?" Deacon asked.

"Of course. It was sort of… which-way. It changed. But that's what the ring is for." She glanced to Myranda's ring. "*One* of the things the ring is for, anyway."

"Well… The ring hasn't been working quite as well recently," Deacon said.

"What's happening?"

"Increasingly often my hand continues to misbehave regardless of the ring. At first it required a moment or two of focus to will it away, and the tremors or minor shifts wouldn't return for weeks. In the last few months, things have changed. Even with the ring, keeping my hand steady requires constant focus. Rather than risk faltering during an official function, I took the time to place a similar but stronger enchantment on the crown. With it in place, my affliction is kept in check just as well as the ring managed in the beginning."

"But…" Ivy prompted.

"But today I had an episode. A minor one. But it does not bode well."

"So what do we do? What happens now?" Ivy stood. "Do you need me to get something? To do something? I am ready for another adventure if that's what it takes."

"It isn't dire, Ivy. And I've been making progress on what I believe will be a proper cure. But it will take time. And if the affliction worsens to a certain degree, I may need to step away to tend to it. For now, there are more important things to worry about."

"You've got to take some time to think about yourself sometimes, or you won't be around to handle the other stuff," Ivy said.

"If I don't deal with the other matters, there is no reason for me to be here," Deacon said. "Five D'Karon seeds we've found. Five. The D'Karon have only been gone for three years and we've found five of their seeds. Properly charged, each one has a wand with the power to give even a complete novice the means to cast D'Karon spells. That's to say nothing of the spell book with the teachings to perform some of their most complex and heinous rituals. In a little box, invisible to even *Ether*."

"We'll find them."

He shook his head. "We won't. Not all of them. At any rate, we'll never be sure. One and a half centuries of war. They had full access to the entirety of the Northern Alliance. And the people of Den were worshiping their teachings. There could well be seeds planted in North Crescent. Turiel was in the southern reaches of Tressor, and she'd been at work for the D'Karon since before their arrival. There could be hundreds of these seeds. They could have scattered them into the sea, hoping for them to wash up on the shore one day. And all it takes is one. One seed and enough time for it to grow and the door opens wide. The D'Karon return."

"All we can do is be vigilant. We watch for the D'Karon. We fight their workings. And we teach the world to do the same in the future," Myranda said.

"We've always succeeded before," Ivy said.

"It is charitable to say that *we* have succeeded. I have played my part, but *you* are the ones who succeeded. You and I, we won't be here forever. Someday this will be Leo's world."

"We will raise him right and make him ready," Myranda said. "We will make certain that he won't have to stand alone. He will have the *world* by his side if ever he must fight."

"What sort of parents are we if we let that happen? We hand over a world with smoldering embers somewhere within waiting to set it aflame?"

"Nothing is ever certain. We take care of the world, and we take care of our children. It is the best we can do."

Deacon looked to the wall, beyond which his baby slept. "We need to do better."

#

Myranda lay in bed. Ivy had retired for the evening. The palace was still. And yet, a light burned. Deacon was at his desk. Books had arrayed themselves around him, hanging in the air. His stylus worked of its own accord, jotting down notes as he read from this page and that. It was anything but rare for Deacon to work long into the night when something had seized his interest. There was something different this time. When she looked to him, she didn't see fascination and enthusiasm. She saw concern. Anxiety. Frustration. Deacon was a man of intense focus and dedication. It had served him and the Chosen well. But there were some riddles too complex for one man to solve. He was taking the weight of the world upon his shoulders.

When he approached the bed, he paused before the velvet pillow meant to hold his crown through the night. Not until he had his gem in hand did he finally lift the gold circlet from his head and set it down. She watched the flesh of the ailing hand. It seemed mundane, but a wizard sees more than what her eyes show her. There was something about his hand and arm, and flickers elsewhere. It was a tension, as if his spirit were a tightened muscle. He slipped into bed beside Myranda.

"It's getting worse, isn't it?" Myranda said.

"I can manage."

"You're pushing yourself. You won't be able to manage if you wear yourself out."

She clasped his hand, closing her own fingers around the gem. With her power and will joined to his own, she felt a bit of the weight shift to her. The tenseness eased. Deacon slid swiftly into an exhausted sleep. Myranda did not. For a time, she turned over the events of the day. Her son should have been her greatest concern. Beyond that, her kingdom should have dominated her thoughts. In a way, they did, because she did not want to imagine a world in which she had to rule a kingdom or raise a child without Deacon by her side.

This affliction was more than he could handle on his own. She could lend him her power, but a cure had thus far escaped both of their expertise. Deacon needed help, and there was but one place in this world where he might find it. It was hardly an easy path to recovery, but she wondered what the most difficult part would be: reaching those who might help him or convincing Deacon that he needed to go.

# Chapter 2

The next day, a brisk but pleasant breeze stirred the air. For a few weeks a year, the weather in Kenvard was temperate enough for the people there to enjoy the outdoors rather than simply endure them. Myranda made it a point to take full advantage. She, Deacon, and Leo ate their breakfast on a balcony overlooking the town. It was a glorious view, if somewhat obscured by Myn, who was just large enough to comfortably rest her chin on the railing and gaze at the trio.

Presently, Myranda and Deacon were fighting a three-way battle with Leo. Balancing the need to feed the boy, the need to prevent him from attempting to feed Myn his oats, and the need to prevent the staff hovering around from taking over proved to be quite the daily challenge.

"Myn, stop encouraging him," Deacon said as she flicked her tongue out to snatch a glop of mush the boy flung in her direction. "You don't even like oats."

"I am helping," Myn replied.

"Hep! Hep!" Leo crowed.

"I wouldn't have expected having a child around would help Myn pick up the language, but then, the two are siblings, in a way," Deacon said.

"Hep!"

Leo slapped his silver spoon into the bowl of oats. A healthy dollop of the stuff splattered Deacon, Myranda, and Leo, much to the child's delight.

"Queen Myranda, if you like, I could feed the boy," remarked Sadie, a young servant girl who, to her credit, was more concerned about being permitted to do her job than having to do it under the watchful gaze of a dragon.

Myranda swirled her fingers and flexed her mind, drawing the oats from her outfit and flicking them toward Myn. Deacon did the same for himself and Leo.

"Sadie, I have a full slate of tasks today, and this is the one I've been looking forward to. Thank you very much but I will manage."

Deacon dislodged a few flecks of oats from his crown, which he had donned moments after awaking.

"As a matter of fact," she added, "if you would please give us some privacy for a moment? There are family matters to discuss."

"As you wish, Queen."

The servants excused themselves. Deacon conjured a swirl of light to dance before Leo's eyes, which served as enough of a distraction for Myranda to sneak a spoonful of oats into his mouth.

"Deacon, how is your hand?"

"It is always better in the mornings. I likely could have forgone the crown, but I thought it best to keep my mind clear for the tour of the library and vault today." He glanced at the sun. "We should start preparing before much longer. I wouldn't want to delay Caya's departure."

"I worry that it is worse than you've said."

"I wouldn't lie to you, Myranda. You know that."

"But you haven't always been forthcoming."

"I suppose not." Deacon attempted to maneuver a spoon into Leo's mouth. The boy proved a match for his dexterity.

"It's already clear that the affliction is growing more difficult to control. My worry is that it might be spreading. You said you needed the crown to be clearheaded. Is the affliction affecting your mind?"

He sighed. "I am not certain. It is true that I've struggled with clarity more recently than I ever have before, but there is no reason to assume that it is a result of the same ailment. It could be as simple as fatigue from having to maintain constant focus to keep my hand stable. It isn't without its benefit. I haven't felt my mystic endurance improve like this since I was first learning magic."

"Regardless of whether it is fatigue or the affliction, it is only going to get worse."

Leo dipped his pudgy hands into the bowl and flicked a helping directly at Deacon's face. The oats stopped before they could touch him, halted by a hasty spell. They plopped back into the bowl.

"Let us be honest, between Leo and our subjects, we aren't likely to be overcoming our fatigue anytime soon."

"I can only split my attentions so much, Myranda. The cure to the affliction can wait, so it shall."

"But if you were cured, your mind would be sharper, you would be better rested. You would be better able to perform your other tasks."

He pinched the bridge of his nose. "I can't be certain I will be able to cure it. I am no white mage, and there aren't any such mages outside of Entwell who are more skilled than you or I."

Myranda took his hand. "Then I think you know what you need to do."

Deacon looked her in the eye, for the moment genuinely uncertain of her meaning. "I don't understand… You don't mean that I should return to

Entwell."

"I mean precisely that."

"Absolutely not!" he objected. "I am needed here."

"That you are needed here is precisely why you need to do this."

"Kenvard has a long way to go before we can afford to rest. We never know when another D'Karon seed will be found. And Leo needs his father."

"I'm not suggesting you go back never to return. I am suggesting you go home long enough to find a cure."

"I have their teachings. That is enough."

"A fresh perspective from a clever mind is worth *years* of studying texts, and you know it."

He shut his eyes tightly. "I can only go when the falls have relented, and I won't be able to return for months, when the falls relent again. You are asking me to leave at a fragile time in Leo's life and a crucial time in the life of a kingdom. And most importantly, they would not have me."

"You don't know that."

"I repeatedly violated their ways both before I left and with the very means I used to leave."

"It has been years, and you have saved the world from peril time and time again. They will welcome you with open arms."

"I cannot…" he snapped, fist wrapped tight. Deacon took a moment to compose himself, fingers pressed to his temple and pain in his expression. He took a breath. When he spoke again, it was with steadiness and logic.

"Myranda, I understand your concern, and I admit that a trip to Entwell, even if it takes me a year to return, might well be the fastest route to a cure. But let us look at this dispassionately. Either I am so thoroughly in the clutches of this affliction that I am impaired, or I am not. If I am not, there is no urgency in seeking its cure. If I am, it would be unwise for me to seek it in Entwell. The cave is treacherous. Even knowing there is no beast, and even knowing that I must contend with the flood, it is not a simple journey. My magic would be severely curtailed within the cave, and it is a maze. Unlike you, I've never passed through it. I was born in Entwell, and I transported myself instantaneously from within."

"I've thought of that. You need a guide."

"Myranda, you can't."

"That much I won't argue with. It will be trying to handle things without you. We certainly can't afford to send both the king and queen away for months."

"Who else is there? Lain is dead. Myn is surely too large to navigate the cave the same way she entered it."

"By my count that leaves just one person."

Deacon searched his memory. "Who else... No... Surely not *him*."

"He knows the way. And Caya was boasting about having recently caught him again."

Once again, Deacon was silent. His expression was troubled, but Myranda knew the look in his eyes. If nothing else, Deacon was willing to embrace wisdom when it presented itself. Myranda took up the spoon and managed to feed Leo a few more helpings.

"You truly believe this is necessary."

"Deacon, your body and spirit are at war with one another. You've subjected yourself to things no mortal has ever faced. The effects have lingered, and they are only going to get worse. I love you. I don't want to lose my husband, I don't want the kingdom to lose its king, and I don't want Leo to lose his father. You owe it to yourself, and all of us, to get help."

He nodded slowly. "For you, and for Leo, I will."

Myranda stood and threw her arms around him. "I knew you would come to your senses."

A bird fluttered down to peck at a fleck of oats that had failed to find its way onto an expensive bit of royal wardrobe. Like most of the residents of the capital, the birds seemed to have come to the conclusion that Myn wasn't a concern.

"Bud!" Leo observed, pointing a messy finger.

"Sparrow," Deacon specified, always quick to seize an opportunity to educate.

"Parrow."

"That's good, now what is Myn?" Deacon pointed to the dragon. "What sort of creature is she?"

"Duck."

"No, no. Leo, Myn is not a duck."

Myn pivoted her head to face Deacon. "Quack," she stated.

Myranda stifled laughter.

"Duck!" Leo asserted, vindicated.

"You really aren't helping, Myn," Deacon said in defeat.

"Come," the queen said. "Leo's had all he's going to eat. We've got to have a word with Caya. Considering how much trouble he gave her, it may be difficult to persuade her to part with your would-be guide."

#

The tour of the library and vault wouldn't be happening for a few hours, but preparations for travel had already begun. Royalty traveled with a considerable entourage. Organizing them for a journey even within a city or the neighboring areas took time. Dividing the various tasks among the assorted servants and guards was a task in and of itself. Myranda and Deacon were thus able to steal a moment to pull Caya aside to the private room off the great hall again. Myranda hadn't wasted words, jumping directly to the issue at hand.

"Desmeres? You want to talk to *Desmeres*?" Caya said, barely able to hush her mischievous glee.

"Specifically, we need to borrow him for a few months," Myranda said.

"A few *months*? I know you have a history with him, and not a very pleasant one. If you were anyone else, I'd guess some sort of torture was in store for him."

"Nothing of the sort. We need him to help guide us to something that can help Deacon."

"And it will take months? With your resources I wouldn't imagine it would take more than a few weeks to get anywhere in this world."

"We are hoping he can take Deacon to Entwell."

"Mmm. Homesick, eh?"

"That isn't the specific malady we are hoping to treat, but it is among them," Deacon said.

"I see. I won't pry, but I should be frank with you. He's given us a terrible runaround. The list of crimes he has committed are deceiving in their severity." She counted off on her fingers. "We shall discount his betrayal of our beloved Chosen. Heinous though it was, it must be set aside in an *official* sense because he was serving the Alliance Army at the time. But he has stolen priceless weapons from my very own honor guard not once, not twice, but six times that we know of. He has assaulted members of the Elite. He has defied orders. He holds the distinction of being the very first person to illegally cross the redrawn border between Vulcrest and Ulvard. His least official and most severe of crimes, from my personal point of view, was making a fool of my soldiers on countless occasions. If he were any other man, he would be rotting in a dungeon or dangling from the gallows."

"I'm pleased to learn you've been merciful," Deacon said.

"I am quite merciful, but in his case it was almost entirely self-interest. You spoke on his behalf after the incident with his hand, and that helped, but he's wiped that goodwill away. The fact is, I keep him around because he still does good work on weapons, though somewhat more laboriously these days. Genera does a reasonable job of keeping him in line, most of the time. And there is the fact that he is *technically* my father-in-law."

"Technically?" Deacon said.

"He wasn't formally introduced to his son until adulthood. Fatherhood is most certainly technical at best," Caya said. "Now, this *is* a royal family matter. If you dig deeply enough into Vulcrest's history I'm quite certain you could find precedent of justified execution of in-laws. I choose to forgo such filthy matters." She lowered her voice. "Unless he *particularly* vexes me again."

Outside, the sound of preparations was dying down.

"We'll be needed soon, so I suppose we'd best hammer out the details. First, the warnings. He doesn't strike me as reformed so much as run-down. I don't imagine he will be trustworthy."

"That much we've come to expect from him. Scrupulously honest and completely undeserving of trust," Myranda said.

"I would suggest it would be difficult to keep him in line, but if there is anyone in the world I trust to manage it, it is one of you two." She mused for a moment. "I suppose there is no reason *not* to loan him out. Provided you return him when you are through with him, of course."

"It will be no less than three months. We can't be certain how long it will be, but we hope not more than a year," Myranda said.

"Tolerable. And having him out of our hair should give my honor guard the opportunity to guard *me* instead of him." She held out her hand. "You have a deal."

Myranda shook it. "You are doing us a greater service than you know."

"How soon do you need him?" she asked.

"It can wait until the present tasks have been settled," Deacon said.

Myranda looked to him. "I would much prefer it happen sooner than later."

"I'll be more specific," Caya said. "You can travel a good deal more swiftly than I can. Will you need him before I return home?"

"Certainly not," Deacon said.

"Ideally yes," Myranda said at the same time.

Caya smirked. "While we are awaiting a consensus on the issue, I'll just have my scribe write up a writ of transfer." She clapped them on the backs. "Now let us get this tour started. I cannot *wait* to see what a library that was designed by Deacon and Myranda Celeste looks like."

#

The first stop on their journey didn't require much travel at all. The representatives from Ulvard, Vulcrest, and Tressor wove their way through the recently rebuilt halls of Kenvard Palace until they reached a formidable door with a pair of guards standing at attention. Though the wall was tall and the ceiling vaulted, the door itself was scarcely taller than Deacon himself as he stood before it.

"This is the first of three vaults we have created for housing things of great danger or great value. Our security precautions are many. The door is nearly a yard thick. Iron-wood plank, studded and clad with additional iron. It is braced from the inside. The brace is moved into place utilizing a complex mechanism operated by a specially made crank with only three copies. Two locks…"

As Deacon continued to list the security precautions, Caya tugged Myranda aside and whispered to her.

"You have a dragon in the courtyard. Was this all necessary?" she said.

"We are leaders," Myranda said. "A defense isn't a defense if only one person can use it. Ideally, you and the Ulvardians can utilize similar tactics to protect your own artifacts."

"Mmm," Caya said. "Our artifacts are, at present, protected by Tus, and I suspect he would be rather upset if I suggested we were to replace him with a particularly fancy lock."

"A particularly fancy lock and a few magic words," Myranda corrected.

"… Incantations specific to each person who might require entry," Deacon continued, his explanation having caught up with Myranda's implication.

As he had been describing the assorted means to keep the royal treasures safe, the guards had been disengaging them. Locks, cranks, and spells requiring the cooperation of at least three people finally rendered the door safe to open. Both men grasped the handle and hauled at it. Hinges groaned as the interior was revealed. Deacon held out his hand and summoned his crystal to his side. It cast light upon the assorted shelves within, loaded with chests and cases.

"This vault has an outer and inner room. As do each of the others we have built. This outer room is protected *only* by the defenses I have described. Such precautions are more than sufficient to ensure the safety of our jewels and other historic artifacts. But the second door is far more mystically augmented. At present, only Myranda, myself, and the royal scribe have the proper spells to release its wards. These wards are *extremely* important. The items contained within are of a potent mystical nature and could be terribly dangerous in the wrong hands."

"You keep dangerous mystic artifacts in your home?" Queen Tanya said.

"Are they D'Karon in nature?" King Terrance asked.

"No. Our D'Karon artifacts are kept in a more remote vault, with identical safety precautions save the addition of Ether among those capable of opening the door. The walls have been constructed and treated to ensure magic within remains within, and magic without remains without. Both are equally important in storing D'Karon creations. I shall detail the specific enchantments now, as the sooner you are made aware of proper storage and preparation, the sooner you will be able to store and care for D'Karon artifacts without our aid," Deacon said.

Queen Tanya tilted her head ever so slightly. "In a moment. Do you mean to say that you have *weapons* of incomparable mystic potency here within the palace? Weapons of your own creation?"

"Ulvard is entirely without mystic weaponry. That you have a mystic arsenal kept secret from us…"

"If I may. These are artifacts. With the exception of the Sword of the Chosen, none of them are explicitly weapons, and even in the case of the sword, that it is the shape of a weapon is incidental. Its importance is far more significant as a vessel and focus of power. But I certainly do not intend to keep this or anything else secret from my fellow royals. The full contents of the deep vault are as follows, in declining order of power. The Sword of the Chosen, a runic mirror of yet-to-be-determined provenance, seventeen highly refined focus gems…"

"Yes, yes," Terrance said. "A full record can be delivered at your leisure. The relevant point is Kenvard's disproportionate mystic capabilities."

"A concern that can be best addressed, as with nearly all other concerns, with knowledge. If you are content to have the details of the vault provided to you at a later time, then I see no reason to delay our trip to our city's library."

#

The second stop on the hastily scheduled tour of Myranda and Deacon's twin-pronged attack on the D'Karon legacy was the royal library. Like much of New Kenvard, it was reclaimed from the rubble of the ruined old city. As the other royals stepped from their carriages, Deacon took it upon himself to boast of their achievements.

"After essential buildings were restored, this library was the first addition to the city to be constructed," he proclaimed, spreading his arms before a building of gleaming, polished stone.

"I remember this part of the city well," Myranda said. "Before the Kenvard Massacre, this quarter of the city was devoted to the storage and distribution of weapons and armor for deployed troops. At the time, it was vital for our defense. The library represents a new and far more precious form of defense against the threat that the war has left behind."

"Forgive my confusion," said King Terrance. "Is a tour of the library truly necessary? I am quite familiar with libraries. We have one in Territal, after all."

"I think you will find this one a bit different," Myranda said.

She approached the building's heavy wooden doors, and a pair of servants stepped up and opened them. The whole of the procession filed through the doorway into the dim interior. The stark light of day pouring through the doorway made the place seem dark as night. When the door shut, white-blue light gradually swelled. Deacon smiled as he watched small rough-cut gems set into lanterns along the walls take on a soft glow. The light revealed a place still very much in progress. The building itself was complete, but it had yet to reach the tiniest fraction of its potential. Rows of shelves stood like soldiers along the rear of the room spread before them. The rest of the room was furnished with long tables and chairs. The chairs were empty, though each table had six books laid out. Pots of ink sat beside each book. Quills bobbed into the pots and wove their way through the air in an intricate dance. It was eerily like some manner of ghostly factory, dedicated to filling books as swiftly as possible.

"I have devoted my life to knowledge," Deacon said. "Knowledge is wealth. But it is wealth of a special sort. It is wealth that *grows* in value the more it is shared. My firmest belief is that nothing cannot be known. We need only seek answers, and, if we are clever and determined, we shall find them. What you see at the back of the room is my grimoire. It is, unquestionably, the greatest concentration of mystic knowledge in existence. It took a considerable amount of time and effort, but I was able to enchant a phalanx of quills with a spell I've long depended upon for my own purposes. Even at this scale, it will take months if not years to achieve my goal. But when it is through, five copies of each book contained within my own will have been recorded. One set shall be kept for our own people in Kenvard. The rest will be presented to Vulcrest, Ulvard, Tressor, and the Crescents."

Queen Tanya stepped up to the nearest of the books and gazed at the page. "'Terrax Mascill's Poison Touch'?" she said.

"Ah, yes. At present, some of the lesser aspects of the black magic disciplines are being recorded." Deacon marched to the back of the room and fetched a thick leather tome. "We have completed the white magic already."

"'Parkek's Blood Burn,'" King Terrance read. "These are spells in your personal collection?"

"I could hardly consider my library comprehensive without them. Look, here. 'Milliway's Soothing Balm.' This is a counterspell to the Blood Burn," he said. "For everything that can harm, there is a thing that can heal. That is why a properly stocked mystic library is an indispensable defense. If we understand the darkness, we can counter it with light."

"Is it wise to make the powers of darkness so readily available?" the king asked.

"Right now the books are merely being copied, and you'll note, the door is under guard," Myranda said. "When the collection is complete, the access to the books with the greatest potential threat will be limited to those with adequate knowledge to use them wisely."

"Access will be earned through understanding. And if something is properly understood, it is implicitly safeguarded against misuse," Deacon said.

"It isn't misuse that concerns me, King Deacon. It is the skilled and accurate use of a spell designed to destroy. We are presently at peace. Heavens willing, we will remain so. But if war is to come again, these dark spells in the hands of our enemies…"

"No one should use magic to harm," Deacon said. "But to hoard the most dangerous magics for fear of our enemies using them upon us betrays the intent to use them upon our enemies. Understanding is the solution. Truly understand the threat of the spell, and those too dangerous to be used with care and precision will never be used. And if a magic *is* to be used in anger, I would much prefer to know the tools that might be used against me. The best way to achieve this is by sharing them."

"You have an admirably positive view of human nature," King Terrance said, with no suggestion in his tone that he shared it. "I believe this tour is inspired in part by the very real and very firmly held belief that certain types of magic represent an existential threat to us."

"D'Karon magic…" Deacon said. "Yes, though it pains me, the tools of the D'Karon and those spells too close to them represent what I hope will be the *only* class of magic that must remain forbidden from wide distribution. But even *they* must be understood. Come, follow me."

He led them past the rows of drifting quills through the aisles of half-filled shelves to a peculiar book stand. It held a single book and stood beside a door far more heavily fortified than seemed appropriate for a place of knowledge. Indeed, it was a perfect match for the door to the deeper level of the palace vault.

"Beyond this door is a room set aside for the study of D'Karon magic. To date, we have yet to train any of Kenvard's mystics to a sufficient level of knowledge to, in my judgment, safely engage with their teachings. At present, only Myranda and myself are permitted inside. But that is not to suggest that no one else will ever be permitted into this room. In time I hope that each of our kingdoms would have a handful of dedicated masters who have devoted their lives to understanding the D'Karon arts specifically to devise counters to them. To that end…"

He plucked the book from the stand. "What we have here is the present state of my understanding of the weaknesses of the most dire D'Karon spells."

He flipped it open and drew his crystal to his hand. "This spell is used to dispel the miasma that dragoyles breathe." He held the crystal to the page, and several arcane shapes became illuminated. "We believe that a properly empowered set of sigils like these will prevent a weak D'Karon portal from being opened nearby, regardless of whether a beacon exists to anchor one.

"This book isn't yet a mature enough body of information to be of immediate use, but I am working every day to expand this information, and…" He glanced to Myranda. "Interruptions notwithstanding, I had hoped to have the first volume finished within the year."

He thumped the book back down and jabbed the cover with his finger. "*This* is our best defense against the dark times out from which we have so recently just clawed our way."

"Do you destroy the D'Karon information when a counter is found?" Queen Tanya asked.

"No. If we destroy it today, we might someday find ourselves without the means to study it if new threats arise."

"Then what is to stop a rogue person from utilizing D'Karon teachings in the future?"

"Terrance, please," Caya said. "He's spent the last hour listing off his endless precautions. I don't know if I have the constitution to endure another verse of that particular song."

Myranda nodded. "As leaders and keepers of this wisdom, that is our problem to solve. We have seen the vault. We have seen this book. They are only the *first* of our defenses. It will be the work of our lives to protect the D'Karon goods. But it is a challenge I happily take upon my shoulders."

"And you see yourselves as the only qualified keepers of these dangerous artifacts," Queen Tanya said.

"At this precise moment in time, I consider the *Chosen* to be the only qualified keepers," Deacon said. "But that will change. Soon your libraries will be stocked. Soon you will all have a copy of this book in its finished form. Soon people around the world will be working on learning and sharing knowledge. There will be other vaults to collect other artifacts safely."

"And thus other places where a rogue might use those artifacts," Queen Tanya said.

King Terrance nodded. "Yes, there seems to be something you are unwilling or unable to come to terms with, and that is the grim reality that there are some things that can never be controlled. Some knowledge must be wiped away."

"No," Deacon insisted.

"If the D'Karon magic remains in any form, it is a threat. We cannot preserve this knowledge and still be safe from it. There is no other way."

"That is *precisely* why we must always strive toward understanding. Even when those things we study seem dangerous. The most precious information comes at the greatest risk. It has always been the case. Lives are lost in the pursuit of knowledge all the time. But not nearly as many as lives that are lost to ignorance."

"Security, freedom, knowledge, peace of mind. They are frequently at odds," Terrance said.

"Of course they are, but of them, knowledge is paramount."

"You value knowledge greater than security?"

"Greater than security because without knowledge of danger there can be no security. Greater than freedom because without knowledge of where we can go and what we can do there can *be* no freedom, and *certainly* greater than peace of mind. There is no mind more peaceful than one shrouded by ignorance," he asserted sharply. "Wounds heal. People live and die. But some knowledge, if lost, can never be regained."

Deacon's fingers were white-knuckle tight about his crystal. It was flickering with a sickly glow. Myranda stepped to him and wrapped her hand about it.

"The point is, we are open with our methods, and we shall share them. This is something that we *all* must involve ourselves in." She turned to Deacon. "Why don't you take a moment to identify which books have been completed? Perhaps our guests would like to take them home and add them to their libraries now."

Her eyes darted surreptitiously to the smoldering crystal in his hand. "I wouldn't want you to be wringing your hands in idleness while we have the golden opportunity to give our neighbors the gift of knowledge."

Deacon glanced to his hand, then back to Myranda.

"An excellent idea, my queen," he said. "Come. Let me show you the volumes of white magic we have recorded, my friends. With these books and a few sharp minds, scores of maladies shall be a thing of the past."

#

Some hours later, after an interminable and overly formal farewell ceremony, the royals of the other nations were sent on their way. Myranda and Deacon returned to the palace.

"With the exception of some of the protocol-mandated chaff, I believe that was an exceedingly worthwhile ceremony," Deacon said, climbing the last of the steps to the royal quarters.

"Agreed. The D'Karon seed is stowed, the concerns of the other kingdoms have been addressed, if perhaps not wholly put to rest—"

A discordant rattling echoed through the corridor.

"— and Auntie Ivy has provided our son with a noisy new pastime," she said.

"Music," he mused. "It hadn't struck me that might be an interest of his."

"At the moment I would suggest 'beating things with sticks' is the far greater interest," she said.

"Even so. There are bardic magics that draw their power and focus from rhythms."

"You might have to entertain the possibility that he won't turn his mind to magic."

"Of course, but we can explore it. I don't believe we had a master of such magics in Entwell, but I feel certain we have information in our library."

"Perhaps you could ask about bards upon your return. We should start planning for your journey. Many preparations will need to be made. First a trip to Vulcrest to collect Desmeres. Then a trip down through to Ulvard. We will require travel papers for the two of you and the rest of your party…"

"We needn't rush things."

"You as much as asserted that wisdom was more important than saving lives while attempting to allay the concerns of our neighboring kingdoms a few hours ago."

"Tact and nuance have never been strengths of mine. I may have expressed myself somewhat poorly."

"And once you are cured, that will be less of a concern. We've discussed our plans for the kingdom at length. I can see to them in your absence, and with this ceremony completed, there aren't any ceremonies from which your absence will be glaring until the end of the year. We aren't likely to find a better time for you to take a sabbatical."

Deacon drummed his fingers against his side, keeping somewhat better rhythm than his son as he approached the door to their quarters.

"What will we tell the subjects? And the staff?"

"With the staff, we should be honest." Myranda sighed. "Ideally, we would be honest with everyone. But circumstances are such that we cannot afford to be perfectly open. Particularly not on the subject of Entwell. But there is no reason for dishonesty. You, Myn, and I will leave for Vulcrest. We will give the stated purpose as… a consultation about a prisoner with ties to the Chosen. No word of that is a lie. And when I return, we shall simply, also quite honestly, say that you set off to discuss a sensitive matter with some colleagues from outside the kingdom."

They opened the door to their quarters. Rather than one of their many servants overseeing the child, Ivy was crouched before him. A simple but well-built drum sat on the floor between them. The drum and its sticks were built in the unmistakable style of the malthropes of Den. Sadie the nanny was standing in the corner, watching the pair, ready to swoop in should she be needed.

"Mama! Dada!" Leo proclaimed when he spotted them. He started to climb to his feet.

"Wait, wait, wait!" Ivy said. "Show, show."

She tapped out a little rhythm on the drum with her stick. Leo savagely attacked the drum with his, giggling all the way. He looked to her expectantly. She repeated the rhythm and got a second "performance" in reply.

"See? He's learning. We take turns beating the drum. He'll be playing in no time." Ivy clapped. "I can't wait until his little fingers are long enough to play something like a flute."

"Very impressive," Myranda said, plucking Leo from the ground.

"I hope you don't mind. Ivy was rather insistent on spending more time with Leo. And I wasn't able to persuade Ether to remain in her own quarters either," Sadie said.

"Ether?" Myranda said. She raised her eyes and, for the first time, noticed Ether sitting silent and motionless beside the fireplace. "Oh! I'm terribly sorry, I didn't notice you," Myranda said.

She stood. "I imagine not. The child does command one's attention."

"He usually commands everyone else's attention, too," Myranda said. "I'm impressed he's left you alone."

Ivy smirked. "He's a very perceptive boy. He figured out what the rest of us did a long time ago." She leaned forward and scrunched her nose at Leo. "Auntie Ether is no fun."

"Are you through with your official business?" Ether asked, unwilling to engage with Ivy's taunt.

"For now. Did you want to speak with us?"

"I believe *you* wanted to speak with *me*."

Myranda thought for a moment. "Oh! Yes, there was a matter. I am sorry, Sadie, we need the room for a moment."

"Of course, Your Majesty."

The young servant slipped from the room. Deacon took Leo from Myranda and set him on the ground to toddle around the room, hand in hand with his father.

"I wanted to ask you, Ether. Have you felt anything unusual recently? Anything reminiscent of D'Karon magic or any unexplained bursts of power?"

"Nothing. I would have summoned you if I had."

"Queen Caya suggested there was a curious event in Verril. Sightings but little in the way of proof. From what she described, I imagined I would have felt something, but if you haven't felt it either, it seems this may have simply been a handful of people letting their imaginations get the better of them. Still…"

"I will be vigilant," Ether said.

"That's all that I can ask. As it happens, if we are able, Deacon, Myn, and I may be heading north soon. Time permitting, we can look into the matter directly."

"We haven't made a firm decision in that regard," Deacon called as he helped Leo to climb on his bed.

"Kings and queens are *busy*," Ivy observed. "Say… are you taking Leo with you?"

"No," Myranda said. "It will only be a few days before I return, so—"

"Let me watch him!" Ivy squealed. "Let me watch Leo, it'll be great! I can sing him songs. I can read him books. We can play games. I want to try hide-and-seek. They have another name for it in Den, and it seems like it'd be so much fun in a castle. Ether could help too!"

The shapeshifter turned to Ivy. "I have no interest whatsoever in playing nanny to this child."

"Ether, you'll love it. Look at him! He is adorable."

"I have little use for most of humans. What value is there in spending my time with an incomplete one?"

"It'll be fun," Ivy repeated, a bit more forcefully.

"I have Celia to look after."

"You told me all about it last night. She has the sniffles."

"She is mortal. Mortals are frail and near death when in good health. When ill, they are nearer to death. This is the least I can do."

"I'll tell you what. Why don't you go back and *ask* her what she would rather you do? Should you stay and watch her sniffle or help keep an eye on the heir to the throne of Kenvard?"

Ether gave the malthrope a withering stare, then turned back to Myranda. "Do you have further need of me? For duties beyond childrearing?"

"No, Ether. Thank you, as always, for your vigilance."

Ether nodded stiffly. She took a respectful step away from Leo and, as before, burst into wind to make her exit.

Ivy waited for the breeze to die down and flicked her ear. "She'll be back," she said slyly.

"You're so sure?" Myranda said.

"The one person in the world whose opinion she seems to trust is Celia, and what do you think she's going to tell her to do?" Ivy trotted over to Leo and gave him a tickle. "This is going to be such fun!"

"We haven't even decided when, or if, the trip is going to happen!" a flustered Deacon replied.

"What is the trip about, anyway?"

"My hand is becoming a bit more difficult to keep stable," Deacon said. "It may be helpful to seek aid in a proper cure."

Ivy furrowed her brow. "More difficult… You mean even more difficult than before? You just said you had an 'episode' a little while ago."

"It has continued to dominate my thoughts, and those of the queen."

"This isn't some minor thing, like you've been saying, is it? This is more than you can handle, isn't it?"

"Sometimes. It really isn't—"

"And you can fix it but you haven't yet?"

"I can *likely* fix it *more quickly*, but it will take months, and—"

"Just go and fix it! Nothing is more important than your health. You have a son who depends on you," Ivy scolded.

Myranda smiled. "That makes two of the divine protectors of our world who agree. Shall I have a word with Myn and see what she thinks?"

"We can ask Ether, too. She'll tell you to go get help right away just to disagree with you," Ivy added.

Deacon shut his eyes and twisted his ring for a moment. "Very well. I yield. May I at least have a few hours to prepare some notes and gather some things for the journey?"

"Absolutely. We'll leave after supper."

Ivy squealed in glee. "I'm going to go make a list of the songs we're going to learn."

She bounded off. Deacon sat on the bed and gave Leo his finger for the boy to climb to his feet. Though Deacon was looking Leo in the face, his gaze was distant, lost in thought.

"You're doing the right thing," Myranda said.

"That certainly seems to be the consensus. But it is difficult to embrace that fact when it means hiding away for months. At least, if we are swift, I may reach Entwell before the blue moon. It would truly be an honor to be a part of another one. I wonder what the focus will be, now that Ether has been summoned? We shall see, I suppose." He shook his head and swept Leo off the bed. "Your father has something to take care of, Leo. I'll be gone for a while. Let's make the most of today."

He sat and perched his boy on his knee. "We've got stories to read, games to play." He sighed. "But maybe a lesson first."

"Guh," Leo opined.

"I know, I know. But lessons are important, even when they're not wrapped in stories. And lessons aren't only for little boys growing up. We're all learning lessons, all the time."

Leo industriously attempted to unfasten the buttons of his shirt.

"I want a lot of things for you, Leo. I have so many hopes and dreams for your future that for the first year of your life I didn't know what to hope for most. But I think I know now. So listen close. If nothing else, this is what I wish for you and what I believe you should wish for your own children should you have them. May you grow into the sort of person wise enough to recognize the flaws in those who came before you. May you accept them for what they are, and may you choose not to pass them on. If enough of us do that, the world can only get better."

Leo blinked at Deacon. After consideration, he made his addition to the conversation. "Book now," he said.

Deacon smiled and tousled his hair. "That's my boy."

#

Ether whisked across the countryside, the wind of her elemental form curling and mingling with the chilly breeze of spring. The sensation of her mind and body spreading through the rivulets and eddies of nature was an odd reminder of just how much the last few years had changed her. There was a time—most of the world's existence, in fact—when this communing and combining with the primal forces was her default state of being. Now she spent most of her days focused into the form of a mortal.

By any true measure, she was more in touch with the world when commingled with the elements. But in a way she was only beginning to grasp, being among the mortals, among the creatures, made her feel far more like a part of the world than she ever had before.

She coalesced into her human form once more, boots sinking into the wet snow that lingered in this more northerly part of the land, then knocked on the door of a simple home.

"Celia, I have returned."

"Come in. Please, come in," called a voice rough with illness.

Ether pushed the door open and stepped into the cozy little home. A small fire burned in the hearth. Celia sat in a chair beside it. Her face was a bit pale, eyes and nose rimmed with red. Though ill, she was in no visible discomfort or distress. Her face brightened as Ether stepped inside.

"Ah! I hadn't expected you back so soon! I trust the ceremony went well?"

"As you suggested, I entered discreetly rather than interrupting."

"Good, good. Tell me all about it. How did things go?" She took a hand from her tea. "Nothing not meant for my ears, mind you. I know things far above my station are discussed in places such as these."

"Nothing of interest. The king and queen of Ulvard postured, fearful that their place in history is as meaningless and unremarkable as it appears."

"Ether, that isn't very nice."

"There may have been a disturbance to the north. It is unlikely, but I have been asked to keep watch for indications of danger."

"And have you been?"

"I am ever watchful." She stepped forward and placed a hand on Celia's head. "You are still suffering from your illness. Have you been resting?"

"Nothing but. It has been ages since I've gone so long without doing a proper load of laundry. I fear I am beginning to go a bit mad. That's why I was hoping you would have some interesting stories to tell me about the ceremony."

"Nothing interesting happens at ceremonies. Humans who believe themselves to be towering figures in their worlds dress themselves in bright colors and shiny stones. They draw lines on a bit of parchment and call them borders, as if through the stroke of a brush they can shape the land. They declare these things to be against the rules, as though their opinions could alter the course of morality and righteousness. It is foolishness and spectacle."

"But the food and wine are lovely."

"So I am told," Ether said. "I was too late to partake."

Ether stood and raised the nearby tea kettle to test its weight. Finding it empty, she lifted the lid and drew her mind to the task of shifting air to water to fill it.

"You wouldn't have been if you'd listened to me when I told you I was perfectly able to care for myself."

The shapeshifter stepped onto the hearth and shifted to flame, kettle still in hand. Crackling flames licked about the black metal, gently heating the water and chasing away a bit more of the cold lingering in the room.

"And what of the prince?" Celia said.

"They continue to take great pride in his every motion and utterance," Ether said.

"New parents," Celia said. "I remember when Emilia took her first steps. From the way I crowed, you'd have thought she was the first baby ever to walk."

Steam hissed from the kettle. Ether set it on the table and returned to her human form to gather the ingredients for tea.

"I didn't think it possible, but Myranda and Deacon are even more protective of the child than they are of the rest of their kingdom. A full palace of servants to keep it safe while they travel."

"Perhaps you'll have a child one day. You shan't understand until then."

Ether prepared tea with the wooden and mechanical motions of someone who had never had to do so for herself. "Others grasp the lunacy more easily. Ivy insisted on joining the army of caretakers."

"Oh, Ivy is back from her trip? She seemed so lovely when I met her."

"She dotes on the child as though it were her own. She even suggested

I should join her in caring for it."

Celia took the tea and warmed her hands on the cup. "And when do you begin?"

"I have you to care for. You are unwell."

Celia's expression became more firm. "Ether, do you mean to tell me that you have been asked by the queen of Kenvard to help care for the prince, and you shirked that duty to prepare tea for an old washerwoman?"

"They don't need my aid."

"*I don't need it either,*" she said. "This isn't the first time I've been sick and it won't be the last. Now Myranda is the queen, and more than that, she's your friend. She's asked you to help her, so you help her."

"Myranda did not ask me to watch her child. Ivy volunteered to watch her child and encouraged me to do the same."

"Ivy volunteered you?" Celia tipped her head. "You two didn't get along for the longest time, as I recall."

"She is a trying individual, and if not for her value to the world, I doubt I would have tolerated her presence."

"And she feels the same about you?"

"Quite vocally."

"Then it is even more important that you go and lend a hand."

"I don't understand."

"Then go to her and listen to what she has to say and you *will.*"

"She made no indication that she had anything to say, Celia. It was simply another of her endless, infuriating quirks."

Celia didn't reply. She simply sipped her tea and gave Ether a look that the elemental had come to understand took the place of the sort of things other people she'd dealt with might shout in anger. Perhaps it came from her years without hearing, but Ether had never met someone who made such effective use of silence as Celia.

"You are certain it will have some value for me to see to the child."

"There is always value in spending time with a child."

"And you are certain you will not succumb to your illness in the absence of my care."

"Quite."

Ether released a harsh breath.

"Something wrong?"

"Ivy suggested I ask you what I should do. I suspect she anticipated this response."

Celia grinned and took another sip. "Clever girl. You can learn a lot from her."

#

True to his word, within hours Deacon had made his necessary preparations. It was a tribute to both the capabilities of their staff and Myranda's capability to command them that by sunset the whole of Kenvard was prepared for an unplanned absence of the crowned heads. Myn crouched in the courtyard for Myranda and Deacon to load a few bags on her back.

"Myn, Myn, Myn," Leo said. "Fye! Fye!"

"Yes," Myn said simply. "I will fly."

"I will see you soon, Leo!" Myranda said, hoisting Leo up to give him a hug and a kiss.

Deacon held his head to his boy's, jostling his crown slightly. "Don't forget your father now." He looked to Ivy. "I made a special pad, extra-large. Make sure to leave it clear. I'll send messages for Leo every night. If the book enchantment works through the mountains, the pad should too, if a bit slower."

"We'll draw you pictures!" Ivy said, taking Leo.

The king and queen climbed to Myn's back. The great red dragon lowered her head to address the boy. "Be good."

"Duck!" Leo said, raising his hands.

"Dragon," Deacon corrected.

Leo poked the end of Myn's snout.

"Duck."

Myn gave Ivy a bemused look.

"We'll draw pictures of ducks and dragons," Ivy said.

Myn nodded and spread her wings. Ivy hurried to the edge of the courtyard and held Leo tightly, ready for the dragon to leap to the skies. Myranda and Deacon each tipped their head, then glanced in the same direction.

"One moment, Myn," Myranda said, patting the beast's back.

A stiff and persistent wind stirred the courtyard. It selected a dusty patch of stone and resolved itself into Ether's form. Ivy opened her mouth to speak.

"You needn't say anything. I do not need to hear you gloat," Ether said.

Ivy laughed. "It is going to be fun, Ether. You'll see."

The shapeshifter turned to Myranda. "Do not dawdle. I suspect your absence will be interminable."

Myranda and Ivy both laughed. She and Deacon waved and Myn took two long strides before leaping into the northern sky. Ether turned back to Ivy.

"This is a terrible idea, and you are entirely to blame."

Ivy paced toward the door. "It is going to be great. You and I together, working toward a common goal. Just like old times!"

"In the old times we were constantly at one another's throats because you were insufferable and I had yet to develop a tolerance for such foolishness."

"That may be true, but *I* certainly enjoyed it." She hefted Leo. "They left us with a list of things that they want to make sure to do every day. We'll have to feed him, obviously. Tomorrow he'll have a bath. Every afternoon and every night there is a story, or at least part of one. He likes walks outside when the weather is nice, and the rest of the time can be whatever we want! Games. Art. Music."

"How can an infant have such a busy schedule when my own days are virtually empty?"

"Because he's got a mommy and daddy who love him and want him to grow up big and strong and smart and happy. And you've spent eternity looking down on everyone." Ivy bounced Leo up and down. "Leo, who am I?"

"Ivy!" he crowed. "Ivy, Ivy, Ivy."

"And who is that?"

Leo pondered the question. "… Feep," he decided.

"That is in no way my name."

"It *is* cute, though. So what do you want to do now? Sing a song? Read a book? Myranda said Deacon usually makes illusions to show the story. You could do that part."

"I am a Guardian. He is the child of a Chosen One, and as such a creature of great importance for this world. I will watch over him and keep him from harm. That was sufficient for the *world*, it should be sufficient for him."

"Suit yourself, but you're missing out." She held Leo in front of her and booped his nose with hers. "Come on, Leo! Auntie Ivy is going to read you a story, and Auntie Feep is going to stand there and be no fun like always."

"I am *not* Auntie Feep!" Ether said, walking briskly after them. "This is a terrible mistake…"

Joseph R. Lallo

# Chapter 3

A woman paced through the streets of a small town not far from Verril. A heavy fur cloak hung about her shoulders, its rich, plush hood framing her face. The day had been a long one, but she'd done her work well. Now she was looking forward to some hot tea, some hot soup, and a few well-earned minutes of venting her frustrations to a friendly ear. As she approached the entrance to her modest but comfortable home the door opened and two heavily armed men stepped out. She gave each of them a friendly nod and a half smile.

"Tavers. Merritt. Fine to see you," she said.

Both men touched their fingers to the brows of their helmets, as if to doff caps to her.

"Evening, Miss Genera," said the first soldier, presumably Tavers.

"I trust everything is well with him?"

"He hasn't made a fuss today." Merritt indicated the curls of black smoke from a thick chimney sticking up from the rear of the roof. "He's got his hands full, I'd say."

"Three days of good behavior in a row. At this rate people are liable to believe he's properly reformed this time," she said.

They stood beside her as she pulled the large brass key from within her cloak. She slid the cover for the lock aside. The mechanism released a solid click, and she pushed her door open. When no one rushed from within, the soldiers bid her a cheerful good evening and she slipped inside.

The air in her home was hot and dry. Not warm, genuinely hot. She smiled at the wave of heat and hung her cloak. She didn't mind the heat. Given the fact that her outfit, with the exception of the cloak, was designed more around its appearance than its utility, she spent most of the day just a bit too chilly. A baking-hot home helped ease that away. After a full day at the edge of shivering, it felt good to wipe a bead of sweat from one's brow now and again.

"Desmeres?" she called.

Rhythmic whooshes of air, the pumping of bellows, stopped.

"Genera?" he called back.

"Who else would it be, love? Have you eaten?"

"The day has gotten away from me. I've not had lunch yet, let alone dinner."

"I'll put the tea on if you put the soup on."

"Certainly. I'll need just a few minutes more with the forge."

"Just be sure to make it a few minutes and not a few hours."

She paced to the kitchen. It shared a thick stone wall with Desmeres's personal workshop, and thus was a good deal warmer even than the rest of her home. Genera tugged some bone pins from her hair and shook it loose. She filled a kettle with water and set it on an odd strip of metal poking through the wall. Desmeres, for all his faults, was terribly clever. A slab of metal that ran through the wall to the forge meant while he was at work, she needn't start a fire to cook or boil water. One could simply place it on the sizzling-hot metal and wait a few minutes.

Now with some time on her hands, she kicked off her elegant but impractical shoes and tucked her toes into a pair of fur-lined slippers. Book in hand, she sank into her favorite chair and lit a lamp for a few minutes of reading. The now familiar sounds of huffing bellows and clacking hammers slipped into the back of her mind as she let the words on the page weave into her thoughts. What stood out, to a distracting degree, were the far softer sounds from the outside.

A stiff, irregular breeze rushed against the walls and roof loudly enough to reach her ears. Soft conversation on a usually silent street came next. This city was in the shadow of the Dagger Gale Mountains. No one lingered in the streets for polite conversation. She set the book down and turned to the door. If someone was talking outside her door, they were talking to the soldiers. That seldom boded well for her or Desmeres. The resounding knock on the door came as no surprise a moment later.

"One moment," she said irritably, snatching the key from the shelf beside the door. "You know, if you have business with me, you could have mentioned it before I got comfortable."

She rattled the key in the lock with a bit more theater than was really called for. When she tugged the door open, her eyes widened and the key dropped to the floor.

"Y-your Majesties…" she gasped.

Plastered with snow, Myranda smiled at her from the doorway. Deacon stood behind her, and peering in behind was the large and unnervingly curious face of Myn.

"May we come in?" Myranda asked.

Genera shook herself from her moment of shock. "Oh, of course, of course. Inside, please."

Myranda and Deacon shuffled in, stomping snow from their boots onto the floor of the mudroom. Myn poked her head through the doorway as if to survey the suitability of the place before giving the trembling Genera a snort and nod. When the dragon withdrew her head, Genera shut and locked the door.

"If I'd known… a royal visit… I am terribly sorry, you weren't announced," Genera said.

It took a great deal to fluster her, but having to shift from a cozy night in to hosting the freshly crowned royals of a neighboring kingdom managed it quite nicely. She hurriedly took their cloaks and coats, then busied herself preparing seats and further tidying an already extremely neat sitting room.

"Please. You have a perfectly lovely home. I hope we haven't interrupted your evening," Deacon said.

"As though I could have a more important activity planned than hosting the king and queen of Kenvard. *Desmeres! We have guests!*"

"Guests?" Desmeres called back. "I was under the impression that was not permitted."

"These particular guests warrant an exception, and I need you here right now!" she barked. "Er, Your Majesties, tea?"

"If it wouldn't be too much trouble," Myranda said.

"The kettle is already on," she assured them, hurrying to the kitchen.

Deeply ingrained hostess instincts took over as she fetched a pair of trays and four delicate cups from the cabinet. Piece by piece she assembled artistically perfect arrangements on the tray. Teacups, honey, brandy, cheese, jam. She sliced bread and set it on the slab of metal to crisp it. There was no shortage of enormously influential and powerful individuals she'd served over the years. But this was the first time she'd hosted them in her own home, and, it was fair to say, the first time she genuinely respected and admired the powerful figures in question.

"I imagine you are here for Desmeres," she said.

"Chiefly, but you shall be a part of the discussion as well," Myranda said.

"What we intend to ask of you and Desmeres will represent a considerable interruption to your life," Deacon added.

"He hasn't done anything I don't know about, has he? Not since he popped over to Ulvard for some special ore without permission, at least?"

"Not to my knowledge," Myranda said.

"So this isn't a *punitive* interruption, then?"

"No, certainly not," Myranda said.

A door in the kitchen, vault-like in its thickness, slid heavily open. Genera felt a brief wave of relief at not having to handle her royal guests alone. The relief vanished in a hot jolt of realization that turned out to be an instant too slow to be of any use.

"Hold Dowser!" she yelped.

When the crack of the opening door was wide enough to allow it, a whirlwind of scampering paws and flapping ears burst through. A rolling, excited howl filled the home. The creature rushed out, ran a sniffing ring around Genera with enough speed to flare her skirt, then launched into the sitting room. Not until he'd slid to a stop in front of Deacon did the blur of a dog remain stationary long enough to be properly observed. Dowser was a vulbaka, an enormous breed of scent hound. At two years of age he was still a big gangling, but he managed to be nearly face-to-face with the seated king. A shaggy coat hung down over his body and flopped over his eyes. His ears dangled comically long. He jutted his nose into Deacon's face and snuffled a few times, then bayed joyously and dove atop him, burying the king in eager doggy and threatening to dislodge his crown.

"Dowser, down!" Genera ordered.

The dog raised his head, then sullenly slinked from Deacon's lap and sat on the ground. The upwelling of enthusiasm had covered Deacon with dog hair with remarkable efficiency.

"My apologies. He really is quite well trained. He just sneaks his disobedience into the space between commands," Desmeres said, stepping into the room. "A letter-of-the-law rather than spirit-of-the-law sort of dog. I imagine he takes after his trainer."

The half-elf looked weary and haggard. He was glazed with sweat and smeared with soot from working in his shop. Time took less of a toll on him than most, but in these last few years there was one rather significant change that was difficult to ignore. One of his hands was flesh and bone. The other was certainly not. Dark nuggets of skillfully shaped metal had been formed into the tips and segments of fingers, as well as the major parts of the palm. Thin bits of chain connected the segments in lieu of joints. Overall it gave the look of an artfully designed puppet's hand. Fine lines etched into the back of the false hand glimmered almost imperceptibly, betraying its mystic nature.

"How is it serving you?" Deacon asked.

Desmeres raised the hand and snapped its fingers, flaring the glow of the enchantment. "The dexterity is satisfactory, but the feeling is less than ideal. A bit clumsy. Not that I can complain." He lowered his hand and snapped his fingers again. Dowser trotted over and heeled beside him. "I don't imagine you've come here to check on your handiwork."

"No, I'm afraid not. We have a rather significant favor to ask of you."

"Well, I've got a meal to prepare, so—"

Genera set down the trays. "Desmeres, you have an audience with royalty, you will sit here and hear what they have to say. Besides, you don't make a meal half as well as you craft a sword, and I am not having the king's and queen's memories of their time in my home hinging upon your best attempt at soup."

The frazzled woman nudged him out of the way. He gave her a bemused look as she set about preparing a meal.

"Well then. I suppose I am listening," he said.

#

A kingdom away, Ivy, Sadie, and Ether were having a bit of trouble with suppertime. Leo sat in a sturdily built chair with ribbons tied about his waist to hold him in place. A meal was set before him, torn-up pieces of bread, meat, and fruit scattered on a tray. From the size of the circle of debris around him, Leo had been far more interested in hurling them about than actually feeding himself.

"*Whoa,*" Ivy exclaimed, leaning aside as Leo hurled a slice of apple.

It whisked past her and upset an overfilled bowl of grapes, dumping them over the table and onto the floor.

"Are the pieces too big? Maybe the pieces are too big," Ivy mused, pinching a piece of meat with her claws to delicately split it up.

"The child has teeth," Ether said.

"But he doesn't know how to *use* them yet. You have to be careful. Children are just learning things."

"Mama," Leo said, holding up a bit of apple as if as an offering in exchange for his mother.

"Mama will be back very soon," Ivy assured him. "You should eat a nice big meal so you'll be strong enough to play all day when she does, all right?"

"Dada," Leo countered.

"Dada will be a bit longer. Look, apple! You love apple."

Leo considered the fruit, then held it out again. "Myn."

"Myn will be back with Mama," Ivy said, her cheerfulness beginning to flag.

"Why don't you just allow the nanny to feed him? It is her role, is it not?" Ether asked. "She is watching from the doorway, no doubt ready to descend upon this sorry state of things as soon as you give up."

"I want to try. And you're supposed to be helping too."

Ether stood. "Very well. The solution is simple enough."

She stepped from the room. A gentle breeze fluttered the edge of the lace tablecloth on the adult table. The soft click of returning footsteps drew Leo's eyes to the door, where Myranda stepped in.

"Leo, my child," she said. "I have returned. Have you not been eating your meal?" The faux queen took a seat beside Leo and picked up a piece of bread. "Eat," she encouraged.

Leo eyed her critically. He extended a hand and took the bread, then set it down and pointed. "Feep," he accused.

"No, child. I am your mother. And I am very cross with you that you have not been eating."

He rather dramatically turned his chin up at her. "Feep."

The queen stared at him evenly. "Perceptive child." Her disguise faded and she appeared as Ether once again.

"Wow," Ivy said. She leaned closer to Leo. "That's very good. She used to fool *me* all the time. She even fooled my friend Lain a few times. Did Mama and Dada tell you about Lain?"

"Lain," Leo repeated.

"Lain was a very smart person," Ivy said.

"Brilliant," Ether corrected. "This world has seldom seen a sharper mind."

"You're sort of named after him, you know. You see, Lain didn't have a name. Not really. Lain was what people called him because of how smart he was. He took all sorts of tests and learned and practiced for a long time. One day he proved he was *so* good at what he did, the people who taught him called him Lain, since that's the name they used for the best of the best at what he did. But that wasn't the only thing people called him."

Ivy casually handed him a bit of meat as she spoke. He took it, staring in interest as she continued the story. "When he first met your mama, he wasn't trying to be a friend. He was trying to catch her because bad people wanted her. And she was very smart, just like you. He knew if he said who he was and showed what he was, she would be afraid. So he acted different. He tried to be as nice as he could." She tapped him on the nose. "As nice as he really was, once you got to know him. And when he was pretending, he used a different name. Leo. Just like you. Leo was the first name your mother knew him as."

Leo sat with his eyes fixed on Ivy, waiting for the next bit of story. He absentmindedly took a bite of the food, too enthralled to be stubborn. She smiled.

"Ether, maybe you want to try?"

Leo turned. "Feep?"

"We are telling stories about Lain?"

"We're telling any sort of story."

Ether sat in sullen silence for a moment. "Many years ago, before you, before your mother, before anyone you know, I watched over the world. And in those days, though I did not know his name, I knew of Lain…"

#

The shapeshifter was unaccustomed to telling stories, and it showed. Her story wasn't about any one thing. It wasn't a story of a heroic act, or even of one of the less noble things Lain had done in his life. It was simply a story of how he was, where he was. A moment in time. It might not have held the boy's attention sufficiently to distract him from his insistence upon ignoring his meal if not for the one bit of storytelling Ether could do that Ivy could not. When she could not or would not find the words, she simply demonstrated. She changed herself. She conjured swirling wisps of wind to dance through the air, flickers of flame and whorls of dust that she cast into shapes to play roles in her tale.

When she was through with her somewhat aimless story, Ivy took over. The malthrope made up for the missing magic with her enthusiasm and flare for performance. Eventually, seemingly to his own surprise, Leo had all but cleaned his plate.

"There, see? Was that so bad?" Ivy asked, freeing him from his seat and bobbing him on her knee.

"I've spent my time on more worthwhile endeavors, but this was more tolerable than I'd anticipated," Ether said.

"I was talking to Leo, but I'm glad you weren't being *tortured* by your time feeding a cute little prince." She bobbed him some more, then glanced to the doorway. "We must be doing a good job. The nanny stopped watching us."

"Feep. Do. Do, do," Leo requested.

"Do what, child?" Ivy asked.

"Just swirl something up for him. He likes that," Ivy said.

Ether curled her fingers through the air, and a streamer of dust from the ground rose up and wove itself into a churning, complex pattern. Ivy held Leo close as he clapped and reached for the mystic display.

"Why are we doing this, Ivy?" Ether asked.

"We're doing Myranda a favor."

"She did not ask for it and did not require it. And I certainly did not need to be involved."

"Yeah, but…" Ivy's ears lowered a bit. "I don't think you're ready to understand yet."

"We have nothing better to do than entertain a child. I believe we have time enough for you to test my understanding."

"It is going to sound stupid."

"Then it would bear little distinction from anything else you say on a day-to-day basis."

Ivy gave a derisive laugh. "Very funny. I can't quite explain it, but I miss this."

"You've never watched Leo before."

"Not *this*." She indicated herself and Ether. "*This*."

"Ivy, there are few people in the world with whom I have a more antagonistic relationship than you."

"I know. That's what makes it stupid. But the back and forth. It's… I don't know… like sisters. I've been thinking a lot about family. Families are *so* important in Den. Malthropes usually have *huge* families. Twins are very common, and the whole village comes together to raise all the kids. It's lovely, really. And they accepted me in a way that I never could have dreamed of. But still… I'm no stranger to finding my own family. You, Myranda, Myn, Deacon. Lain, when he was here. And all the people that helped us. You're all my family now. And this place… Kenvard is where Aneriana was born. And that means it's where *I* was born, even if that's not who I am anymore. It would make sense if I just moved to Den. And I'm sure they would be glad to have me. But if I have a place in the world… I want it to be *here*. I want it to be with Myranda, and Deacon, and Myn. And *you*. And I want to be there for Leo. I want to be Auntie Ivy. I want to spoil him with cake and get into mischief with him. You can't say you don't want the same."

"I most certainly can."

"Then why are you spending all your time with Celia? She made her way just fine without you, and you made your way just fine without her. But it seems like the two of you have gotten along so much better together."

Ivy leaned down to fetch a wooden ball from the floor to give to Leo. "We all had an important job to do before. People are always talking about having a purpose. Maybe our world-saving days aren't over. But someday they will be. Someday we'll have to decide for ourselves what we want out of life. And when that happens I want to be surrounded by people I love, who can be there for whatever comes next. And I want that for you too. Even if you think everything I say is stupid."

"I do not think everything you say is stupid. Merely the vast majority," Ether said.

Ivy turned Leo to face her and held him up. "You hear that, Leo? Progress."

"Foh!" Leo announced.

He hurled the wooden ball. It whisked past Ivy's ear and knocked into the overfilled bowl of grapes, tumbling it across the table and onto the floor.

Ivy stared at the spilled fruit.

"The bowl was already spilled…" Ether said, voicing the very thing that had seized Ivy's thoughts.

"Did someone come in and replace it?" Ivy supposed. "They couldn't have. We'd have noticed."

"Perhaps the child did it? Levitation and manipulation are simple mystic accomplishments, and he is the child of two rather gifted mystics."

"I'm pretty sure Myranda and Deacon said he hasn't done any magic at all yet. Could his first trick have been that complicated?"

"Possible, but unlikely." Ivy turned to the scattered fruit. "Curious…"

#

It hadn't taken Myranda and Deacon very long to lay out what they required of Desmeres. After such debate among themselves, Myranda had streamlined their position quite capably. Nevertheless, Desmeres was slow to indulge them.

"I am not even certain I can do what you are asking of me. I passed through the Cave of the Beast but once, in the opposite direction, nearly eighty years ago," Desmeres said.

"Lain was able to lead Myn and I through the cave with little trouble after a similar amount of time."

"Granted. And though it pains me to diminish myself in any way, I am by no measure Lain's equal," Desmeres said.

"I have confidence in you, even if you do not. Regardless, it is safer to go as a pair than alone, and doubly so if one of you has prior knowledge of the cave."

"It might also help to have a fellow Entwell native with me when I arrive," Deacon said.

"Ah, yes. Because of your less-than-acceptable escape route. Tell me, if you were able to transport yourself from there to here, why can't you transport yourself from here to there?"

"That required the aid of Azriel. I may have the power to cast such a spell, and I may have the focus, but I haven't got the power *and* the focus to achieve it again."

"Couldn't Myranda help?"

Deacon held up his hand. "The very malady I am attempting to remedy was caused by the malformed spell that brought me here. I shall not risk Myranda or anyone else on my own botched techniques."

"And what do I receive in exchange?" Desmeres asked.

"Complete forgiveness of any misdeeds against Kenvard, a strong advocate against misdeeds committed against the other kingdoms, and perhaps a clean conscience," Myranda said.

"Oh, I've wiped my conscience clear, thank you."

"The white wizards back home can certainly restore your hand to flesh and bone," Deacon said. "A task that would require a fair amount of research for either Myranda or me to perform."

Desmeres cocked an eyebrow. "Now *that* might be worthwhile. I

55

assume you have permission from my current keeper?"

Myranda produced the writ Caya had prepared.

"I see… Isn't the queen still in your very kingdom?" he asked.

"On her way back."

"That you had to beat her here underscores the immediacy of your need, I imagine."

"Quite so."

Desmeres raised his voice. "What say you, Genera? Should I—"

"You've been asked by the king and queen of Kenvard to come to the king's aid. The answer was yes a half hour ago!" she snapped.

"I would be risking my life."

"For a good reason, and you are a difficult man to kill."

"I will be away for months."

"You've disappeared for weeks at a time before."

"You would have to look after Dowser while I am away."

She leaned into the doorway. "I shall endure the hardship."

He looked to Myranda again. "Before I give my final answer, what happens, hypothetically, if I refuse?"

"We would find another way," Myranda said.

"But Deacon's journey through the Cave of the Beast is, at this point, an inevitability," Desmeres supposed.

"It seems so," Deacon said.

"Then I suppose I have no other answer but to agree," Desmeres said. "It would be a terrible thing to let you wander about in that cave without a guide. You could get into mischief were you to take a wrong turn. When would you want to leave?"

"As soon as possible. I took the liberty of arranging for transportation prior to coming to your door. We will have carriages and provisions ready for us, courtesy of Queen Caya, within the hour."

"Within the hour? Are we leaving so soon?"

"As soon as possible," Myranda said.

"Not that I am complaining, but why are we traveling by carriage rather than having Myn drop us off?"

"Because the new king and queen of Ulvard are less willing to waive the formalities than Caya. They would prefer a dragon not soar through the skies of their kingdom without time enough to 'prepare the populace.' As if Myn hasn't been a common sight in the Northern Alliance for years. As it is, even with you traveling via carriage, I will be working with Caya's people for days more to finish the proper permissions and declarations to allow you to cross through Ulvard. I intend to do so while you are in transit."

"Supper is nearly finished, if you would do me the honor of sharing a meal before you leave, Your Majesties.”

“Of course. I’ll have to see to Myn, briefly. But I would be delighted,” Myranda said.

“It will be interesting to learn more about you, Genera,” Deacon added. “Knowing Desmeres as I do, this is the calmest and most upstanding I’ve seen him. I can’t imagine we have anyone to blame but you. And owing to the tasks of resurrecting a kingdom, I’ve scarcely had the opportunity to speak with you for a few moments on our prior meetings.”

“Considering the circumstances of those meetings, I doubt the impression would have been as positive. As for Desmeres, he’s matured quite a bit on his own. But it wouldn’t be far from the mark to suggest the largest part of my trade is knowing how to handle unruly men.” She glanced aside briefly. “Though I’ve never anticipated discussing such things with royalty.”

“It should make for engaging dinner conversation,” Desmeres said. “Now let’s eat.”

Joseph R. Lallo

58

# Chapter 4

Several days had passed with Deacon and Desmeres taking turns at the reins. Deacon was dressed simply, save for his crown, which he still wore beneath a large hood. Desmeres was a bit less dedicated to keeping a low profile. In his case, his was not quite as infamous among the subjects of the kingdom. He'd had the questionable judgment of making his enemies at the very top. Myranda had evidently done her job, as when they reached the border crossing, the patrols allowed them through with little more than a gruff reference to "the men the runner was going on about."

Now they were trundling somewhat unsteadily into the heart of Melorn Woods, headed toward the mouth of the Cave of the Beast. There was only a short distance left to go, but there was no telling how long it would take, given the density of the forest and Deacon's lackluster skill at guiding the horses.

"You can snap the reins a bit to get more speed out of them," Desmeres said, climbing through a hatch from the inside of the carriage to sit beside him in the driver's seat.

"There isn't much of a road here. I don't want them to strike anything," Deacon said.

Desmeres held out his hand. "Give me the reins. Novel as it is to have the king of Kenvard as my personal driver, I was under the impression there was some urgency."

Deacon handed them over. Desmeres snapped the leather straps a bit.

"The horses have eyes, you see. They won't run headlong into a tree unless they are particularly spooked or particularly dim."

The carriage rattled along the uneven forest floor for a few seconds.

"May I be frank, Deacon?" Desmeres asked.

"I've never known you to be anything but frank."

"Why are you trusting me with this?"

"You are trustworthy."

"I am most certainly *not* trustworthy. I've betrayed the Chosen, I've stolen from three different monarchs. I am definitively untrustworthy."

"Let me clarify. You are a self-interested man with very specific motivations and aims. This task serves those aims, so there is no danger of betrayal in this case." Deacon looked to him. "You are predictable, which is as good as being trustworthy in this case."

"That's an assessment that requires a level of social insight of which I did not imagine you capable."

"As with most things, I am relying upon the insight of advisers."

"So Myranda is the one who has me figured out."

"Chiefly. Though I must say we both had our doubts about that after visiting your home."

"Oh?"

"The first unexpected matter was that you *had* a home. My experience with you to date has chiefly been crossing paths with you as you danced between strongholds, safe houses, and lairs of collaborators."

"These last few years have been a tumultuous time for me. I have had deeper roots in the past."

"And then there was the matter of Genera."

"If you intend to speak ill of Genera, you are going find me far less cooperative with his little errand."

"I wouldn't think of it. She is a match for your wit and capability. You are well suited for each other. I simply hadn't envisioned you allowing yourself to find happiness with anyone. You are self-destructively driven. I would have expected you to become restless. To sabotage yourself before you could settle down and become comfortable. Proof, again, that my social insight is lacking."

"Don't discount your insight. This little arrangement was not lacking for attempted sabotage, either purposeful or not. Genera is remarkably adept at shrugging off foolishness and speaking to the heart of the matter. I tell you. Youth and beauty are far too eagerly sought. Wisdom, my friend. Experience. They belong on the list, and youth is a small price to pay for them, so long as you can tolerate discovering just how many mistakes you've made along the way."

"I am pleased to say I was blessed by the love of a woman who has them all."

"We can't all earn the love of a demigod."

The rode on for a few moments more, but a turn of phrase bounced about in Desmeres's mind until it found its way to his mouth again.

"Self-destructively driven." Desmeres held up his hand and clacked the fingertips. "Sometimes there are worse things than a little self-destruction. Losing the hand hasn't been all bad. If you spend your life with potent tasks demanding your full attention, occasionally you find yourself without the time or inclination to think about anything else. Honing the shape of metal is meditative, but directed. It takes ages to do it properly, but if you seek to work to the level I do, a single errant swipe of a file could cost you the weapon. As I learned to work with one hand, or one and a half as the case may as well be now, I had time to think about these purposes of mine."

"It is worthwhile to look upon where you've gone, and where you are going."

"I let good things slip through my fingers, Deacon," he said. "I let opportunities pass me by. Don't get me wrong. Someday I'll do what I set out to do. Someday I'll make the finest weapon this world will ever have the good fortune to behold. And I will see to it that the weapon finds its way into the hands of the proper warrior to prove it so. It just shouldn't have taken the loss of my hand to realize that there is more to a great warrior than skill. There's more to a weapon than how well it is used. But if it is used for good, I don't just need the right weapon. I need the right hero."

"You've already armed the Chosen with your creations."

"True, but... I am not certain I can explain it. The Chosen were destined to fight for the defense of their world. They didn't *choose*. They were *chosen*. I fully admit it may be a crooked view of the world, but I want more than that. A man who cannot work is not lazy. One must have the means to work and choose not to in order to be a layabout. The same goes for heroism. The Chosen had but one path to follow. They could have failed, and if they had, we would have been consumed by darkness. But they could not turn away. Show me a person with two roads before them. One leads to safety for themselves, the other leads to triumph over evil. That choice is the last piece."

"Interesting... And how does one find such a hero? The greatest challenge of this world has come and gone."

"Bah. Evil always lingers. Choices like that are made a dozen times a day. But to find the one who would make the proper choice *and* would have the skill to wield one of my weapons properly... as with everything else in my life, if I can't find one, I may have to make one."

Deacon turned to him. "It is difficult to cut through your flowery language sometimes, but it sounds suspiciously like you've just suggested you wish to have a child."

"The thought has crossed my mind."

"Two more thoughts should cross your mind, then. The first, putting the weight of your *own* ambitions on a child is a terrible way to bring them into the world. And second, you already have a son. He's the king of Vulcrest."

"There is a boy who, by virtue of Trigorah Teloran's slavish devotion to elven tradition, bears my name. Everything else he has become has been in spite of me, not because of me. Though he is, at least, evidence that I make for excellent breeding stock. But you have a boy of your own. How has that changed matters?"

"Night and day, Desmeres. Before and after. That boy is the rising sun, casting everything into stark contrast. You talk about drive? Purpose? Leo is everything. His happiness, his future—I would challenge the gods to give him the life he deserves. I would remake the world to keep him safe."

"There's more to life than safety."

"There is. Doubtlessly so. No so long ago I asserted that very thing to the new king of Ulvard. There is so much to learn. So much to understand. But Leo is a child. He is *my* child. And so many of the people of this world are *like* children. They are unprepared for certain challenges, certain dangers. What is the use of learning if we ignore the most important lessons? Some things can only lead to sorry, to ruin. It is up to us to glean what we can of them, and to use that knowledge to keep the path to enlightenment open while keeping the path to destruction closed until people are wise enough to calculate their own risks. There is more to life than safety, but without safety, life is uncertain."

"Precisely, and thus the two roads, and thus true heroism."

Deacon shut his eyes tightly. He pressed his fingers to his head and shuddered a bit.

"Something troubling you?" Desmeres asked.

"I'm… it is nothing serious. Just a flare-up. It rattles my focus a bit."

"I'd expect to see the mountains crumble before your focus started to flag. I've never seen someone with their mind wrapped so tight so often."

"Mmm…" He gritted his teeth. His crystal flashed and smoldered. After a second or two of a vaguely pained expression, he relaxed. "I apologize," Deacon said. "What was the topic of discussion?"

"You were championing safety at the expense of freedom. I was firmly of the belief that freedom is more important."

The rumbling carriage hit an uneven piece of forest and rocked. Deacon took the reins from Desmeres and tugged at them, slowing the horses a bit.

"On that point, we shall have to disagree."

They continued along the road, a bit less jostled by the rough ground. Desmeres slipped a hand into his coat.

"I hear you've got your own coins now." He revealed a copper coin. "I spent a great deal of my time outside Entwell working out how to get more of these. Another purpose of mine. When I was handed this coin, it was the currency of the Northern Alliance. Now it's just the currency of Vulcrest."

He turned the coin over in his hand. The copper was clearly quite new, but it didn't take long for a patina of green to begin coloring it. The milky hue drew the finer details of the coin into stark contrast, with the tiny crevasses holding the color while the rest was polished by handling. From the red gleam of the high points of the coin, it was handled quite a bit.

"Quite the clever choice," he said, flipping the coin facedown to reveal its back. "The Mark of the Chosen on the back of each coin. And you've kept that alive with your own currency, correct?"

"It seemed both proper to honor the Chosen and wise to engineer a means to ensure a mark is seldom far from hand."

"Quite so. The burn of the mark is a fine test of one's intention for the world. I don't suppose you have any of the new coins on you?"

"I've learned that royalty is seldom called upon to pay directly for anything, but for the purpose of this trip I am carrying a few."

"Good. I'd consider keeping one handy if I were you. You never know when you might need it."

#

Myn spread her wings and soared through the sky, dipping in and out of the sea of clouds that blanketed the north. Myranda held on tightly, shut her eyes, and let her mind wander. Of all the things that had come from finding her place as one of the world's defenders, this was among her most cherished. There was such freedom in taking to the sky, either with Deacon and the others or even alone with Myn as she was now. Puffs of flame sent warmth surging through Myn's body. Myranda needed to summon the merest twist of magic to turn the icy wind into something brisk and invigorating. In this moment, it was precisely what she needed.

A queen and a warrior are two very different things. She'd never truly felt at home on the battlefield. The throne was, perhaps, a better fit for her. It was not without its trials. Difficult decisions and frustrating clashes with strong personalities filled her days. But today, at least, she had removed a heavy weight from her mind. Deacon was on his way to his people. She had no doubt he would return healed of his ailment and ready to rule by her side with a clear mind and an even hand. This dose of freedom was her reward for the achievement, which had taken *days* longer than she'd intended thanks to the endless requirements of the Ulvard Crown. And best of all, she was headed home to her son.

She leaned low and rested her head against Myn's neck. "We've been through so much together," she mused. "In a way, it started with you."

A realization trickled into her mind. "Dip below the clouds for a moment, would you?" she said.

Myn released a delighted little sound and tucked her wings. She sliced through the air in a graceful twirl, prompting Myranda to hold tighter.

"Easy!" she said with a laugh. "We're not showing off for anyone."

The dragon spread her wings again and burst through the bottom of the clouds, trailing streamers behind her. Myranda gazed down from the dizzying height. Ravenwood spread out beneath them. To the west, the Rachis Mountains rose up. Myranda scanned across the icy slopes.

"Yes… Yes, we're not so far from where I first met you. And there, down below. I think I see Wolloff's Old Tower."

Myn curled her head to gaze at it. "What is wrong with it?" she asked.

"Oh, there's nothing wrong with it, I was just… that's… that's odd…"

Myranda's eyes weren't as sharp as the dragon's, so it took her a moment to realize that the shadow-shrouded little clearing with its rickety tower jutting out didn't look quite like the forest around it.

"Let's have a look," Myranda said.

Myn cut her wings once more and eased into a slow spiral toward the place where Myranda's journey into the mystic arts had begun. As they wheeled closer, the oddness of the clearing came into far starker focus. All but the southern fringe of Ravenwood was tucked into the Low Lands at the heart of Vulcrest. As such, the forest was well within the stretches of the kingdom that never truly shed its layer of snow. This time of year the best the thick wooded lands could hope for was a gray, slushy, incomplete thaw. For the most part, that was precisely what the forest showed. Tall pines sent globs of wet snow tumbling to the forest floor in the gusts of wind off the mountains. But the wizard's tower was quite different. Myranda could see hints of green in the shadows of the surrounding trees. When she drew nearer still, little points of color revealed wildflowers. By the time Myn was flapping her wings to slow for a landing, the air itself was warm and heavy with the scent of spring. Elk and rabbits, eager to partake in this unexplained but welcome bounty, dashed from the clearing when Myn's great claws crunched into the grass.

"This is astounding," Myranda said.

Myn lowered her head to drink from the cool clean brook. Myranda shut her eyes, trying to focus on what her mystic senses told her about the place. The tower had always been a particularly potent mystic focus. It straddled a meeting of several ley lines. Myranda had, to her minor embarrassment, never truly understood the nature of ley lines, but she knew that gathering mystic powers to a task was far simpler here. Beyond that faint warmth and clarity in the back of her mind, she couldn't detect anything in the least supernatural at work in the clearing. It was as if the circular patch of forest with the tower at its center had changed its mind about its favored climate.

Her concentration shattered as the door to the cottage wrapped about the tower's base pulled open. A portly and exceedingly irritable man in dingy white robes and a pointed hat stormed out along the gravel path leading to the door.

"Is this your doing?" he barked.

"Wolloff! What are you doing here?"

"We move the books out, we move the books in, a great big stir about soldiers coming this way and that. When the whole commotion is through, I decided to move back in. I only *just* get settled, and I wake up to find flowers and grass where snow should be. Now is it your doing or not?"

"Had I known you were here, I would have asked you the same question," Myranda said.

"I'm a white wizard! Why would I go messing about with the seasons? Which this *isn't*, as I've lived here off and on for *years* and it's never looked this way that I can remember," he snapped.

Myn thumped up and lowered her fearsome face to his. "Be nice," she instructed.

Wolloff gave the dragon a hard look. "Don't think I don't remember the little whelp you used to be."

The comment did not soften Myn's expression. Wolloff pointed at Myranda.

"And don't think I don't remember the young rebel you used to be. All the respect in the world to you, Your Majesty, but if you're tinkering with my little piece of the world, I'll thank you to remember where the border is. This is Vulcrest."

"*Be nice,*" Myn rumbled.

"Myn, it is fine. Why don't you go have a meal?"

Myn sidled a fair distance along the clearing in order to keep Wolloff locked in her gaze for as long as possible. She lingered, took a whiff of the air, and dashed off. Myranda shifted her focus back to the wizard.

"Wolloff, this is not my doing. What could have caused this?"

"I don't know what *could* have caused it, but I know what didn't. This isn't magic that did this. Not directly, anyway." He stomped his foot, sending a blossom of dandelion seeds into the air. "This hasn't got the shape or the will of magic to it."

"I agree."

"Of course you agree. I taught you well and you learned well. This is something deeper than magic. To every means of observation available to me, this is what this patch of forest thinks it ought to be doing."

Myranda gazed at her surroundings. "Caya spoke of a curious event to the north. But it was brief and unconfirmed. This is unmistakable."

"Unmistakable, yes. And nefarious."

She took a breath of the fresh air. "It doesn't seem worrisome to me."

"It is unexplained and it is happening to my tower. That's quite nefarious enough for me."

"When did this happen?"

"Yesterday or the day before. I'm not certain. I may have lost a day studying it.”

“I am going to have to look into this.”

“Indeed you are.” Wolloff removed his hat and wiped sweat from his brow. Having vented his frustrations, he seemed a good deal more composed. “I… I suppose it would be proper to thank you for the invitations to the ceremonies of late. And to apologize for my absence.”

“No need to apologize. There are so many of them. And if you’d been present at the coin ceremony, you might have missed this change.” She paced to the edge of the clearing, where the snow patchily returned, along with the chill in the air. “I’m not certain if I should be sorry that Deacon isn’t here to tug at this riddle or happy he isn’t here to be distracted by it.”

Myn thundered back into the clearing. Her time in the lap of luxury hadn’t dulled her hunting skills in the slightest. Her satisfied grin was tinted with her recent meal, and she faithfully dropped a second elk, in its entirety, at Myranda’s feet.

“Staying for supper then, are you?” Wolloff asked.

All the freedom and ease of her flight began to erode. She’d seen enough of the dark and unexplainable in her life that even something so innocuous as a bit of lovely unexplained weather was enough to set off cascades of concern in her mind. Her instinct screamed at her to call Deacon back, to rally the troops and find what this was about. She stifled those feelings. It needed to be investigated, certainly. But Deacon would gladly give up his chance at recovery to tangle with this puzzle. And more to the point, if this *was* something threatening, she wanted to be with her son.

“Have you been given one of Deacon’s pads?”

“The ones where everyone can spy on what one another is writing?”

“That is one way to put it.”

“I haven’t.”

Myranda paced to Myn’s side and pulled one from her things.

“This is mine. I have others at home. Keep it, and if something happens that we need to know about, make a note of it. We will do the same for you. I have to get home.”

#

Deacon and Desmeres stepped from the carriage in front of the Cave of the Beast.

“If Myranda has done her diligence, and I have no reason to suppose that she hasn’t, then someone will be along to collect the horses tomorrow. Will they be well enough here?” Deacon asked.

“Better than we’ll be,” Desmeres said, staring down the mouth of the cave. “This is not a pleasant place.”

They shouldered their provisions.

"Let's not waste time," he said. "We won't know if the cave is fully passable until we have made it a fair distance inside. In the best case, we can make it through in two or three days. It won't be the best case, because I'm working from seventy-five-year-old memories, and the cave is seldom obliging. But we should move quickly. On the off chance the cave is clear or soon will be, it will save us several months of waiting if we're able to take advantage."

He sparked a small, dim lantern to life. The light was a curious one, with a comically large reservoir of oil and scarcely a candle's worth of light. It was clearly the sort of thing meant to last for ages.

"As I am the one with the expertise, such as it is, I am going to lay down the law right now," he said, pacing into the darkened interior.

"Of course."

Desmeres pointed to the trickle of water running from the mouth of the cave. "The water is flowing. That is not a good sign. It means there is at least some flooding in the cave."

"That stands to reason."

"There will be no exploring. This mountain is a honeycomb of passages. Thousands of them, branching and looping upon themselves in confounding ways. As far as I know, the safe routes through the cave can be counted on one hand. Trust me when I tell you, we will not be finding a new route through. So do not question my instructions."

"I bow to your expertise."

"Especially now, with the walls and floor slick with water, death waits at every corner. Your magic won't save you. If we keep walking, within the hour it will take everything you have to conjure even the simplest effect."

"So I've been told."

"Do not deviate from the path I lay out." He turned to face Deacon. "Because we are going to get turned around, even with my guidance. I will lay out a plan. This water flows from the heart of the cave. For the first half of this trip, only two directions matter. Forward, and upward. Forward is against the flow of the water, and upward is self-explanatory. If you head with the flow, you are heading in the wrong direction. If you head downward, eventually you will find a flooded chamber and have to turn back."

"Understood."

"And this is the most important. If we are heading forward, we do *not* head left. I don't care if we are running from a cave-in. Left is death."

"You are certain?" Deacon said.

"What did I say about questioning me?" Desmeres held up his false hand. "The last time I ventured in that direction, I lost my hand. A great many things have been lost there, and as far as I am concerned, they can stay lost.

Now let's go. Slow, steady pace. Forward. Upward."

In just the space of the briefing, they had moved beyond the light from the mouth of the cave. The meager flame and the smolder of Deacon's crystal were their only illumination. In the flickering glow, Desmeres caught glimpses of the wizard's face.

"You are smiling."

"This is a fascinating place," Deacon said.

"The next few days will disabuse you of that opinion, I can assure you of that."

#

Leo toddled through the palace. The little boy had an uncharacteristically serious look on his face. Ivy stalked low behind him. The pair looked like they were on the hunt.

"What do you think? Any guesses?" Ivy whispered, angling her ears this way and that.

"Nuh. Guh, guh, guh," Leo opined.

He teetered forward. The little boy turned a corner, heading for the long hallway with the doors to his room and that of the king and queen. Ivy caught him and righted him as he attempted to take the turn far more quickly than his posture would allow. The boy moved as though his legs and his head were only vaguely aware of each other's intentions.

It had taken a fair amount of persuading, but Ivy had talked the rest of the staff into leaving them be during the evening. They tended to distract Leo from the very important business at hand.

He tottered to his doorway and stopped.

"Is she in there?" Ivy said suspiciously. "She could be *anywhere*, you know."

Leo entered his bedroom and peered about. A single candle lit the room. He surveyed the many toys, some made of cloth, others of wood. After deep consideration, he pointed to a specific toy soldier in a set of six on the top shelf.

"Feep," he accused.

Ivy stood and plucked the soldier from the shelf. "You're sure?"

"Feep."

The malthrope eyed the toy. "Well?"

All watched the carved and painted piece of wood. After time enough to sow doubt in Ivy's mind, the figurine shuddered and then burst into a rush of wind.

"Ha, ha! That's three out of five," Ivy taunted as the disguised shapeshifter returned to her human form.

"I do not understand how the boy can identify me..." Ether said,

68

crouching to inspect him. "You are more focused than you appear."

"Feep," Leo said with a poke to her chin.

Ivy picked him up. "Three out of five. You know what that means. You watch him tonight."

"I never should have made the wager."

"But you did and I won, so *you* watch him tonight."

"Why would you have *me* watch the boy? You *like* watching him."

"You should have some time with him. After all. I'm Ivy, you're Feep. You should at least spend time enough for him to learn your real name."

"If he can identify a perfectly disguised elemental, he should certainly be able to master something as simple as a name. I suspect the boy is doing it on purpose."

"Then you should be friendly enough for him to not want to pull your strings anymore."

Ether shook her head. "If I am to watch the boy, I should select one of his stories. He seems to like them better than my own."

"Don't be long. It's past bedtime and Myranda is going to be back soon. I don't want us to look like bad aunties. Even if an auntie *is* supposed to let the nephew break the rules."

Ether whisked away.

"Just a few more minutes and then stories and bed. What do you want to do until then?"

"Go!" Leo said.

He toddled out into the hall again. Ivy followed.

"Where are you going? There's nothing over there," she said.

He teetered and wheeled with purpose toward a small dead end of a hallway. There were a few of them scattered along the wall. For the life of her, Ivy couldn't work out what they'd initially been designed to do. They didn't lead to any rooms. The only distinctive feature at the end of each was a large wall with a smooth surface. Rather than a showcase for some manner of art or history as she would have expected, which would at least give some reason for the alcove, it was precisely the opposite. The wall was kept clear and clean, making the absence of decoration almost glaring. Leo stopped in front of it.

"Go," he said, pointing at the wall.

"There's nothing there, Leo. It's a wall. Why do you always come here? That last door we passed was to your room. Let's head back."

"Dada. Go."

"Dada won't be back for a while. Let's go see if Auntie Ether picked a book yet."

"Go!" Leo snapped.

Ivy grumbled. "This is the only time you're not any fun. And that *includes* when you make a mess." She leaned heavily on the wall. "Look? See? Not a door. There's nowhere to go." She placed her sensitive ear to the wall. "I can hear the wind on the other side. Even if there were a door, it would just lead outside."

"Go," Leo said.

He stepped up to the wall and pressed his little hand to it. Compared to the shove Ivy had given, it was nothing at all. Nevertheless, the moment his palm touched the wall, the smooth section hinged open. Ivy snatched him from the floor in a panic, fully expecting the section of wall to swing out over the courtyard below. It didn't. Instead, it revealed a large, comfortable room. Initially dark, crystals flared to life to reveal what appeared to be a small workshop. A simple counter, something of a desk meant to be used standing rather than sitting, was covered with pages and half-written books. That was all Ivy could see from the doorway, and given the impossible location of the room, she wasn't going to venture any farther with the toddler in her arms.

"Auntie Ether!" she called.

"I am looking for a short tale. Myranda seems to have stocked this place with tales that will take hours to read," Ether called.

"Auntie Ether, we need your help right now!"

To Ether's credit, the tone in Ivy's voice was enough to summon her to their side in the time it took for a gust of wind to rush down the hallway. She hung in the air beside them, swirling in place with a piercing glow for eyes. The eyes narrowed as she observed the impossible room before them.

"What is this…" Ether said.

"I don't know, probably just a Deacon thing, but I'm not taking chances there's anything awful and magical going on. The D'Karon had things under this palace for a while, and even though they rebuilt it, there's no telling—"

Ether raised her hand to silence Ivy. The wind tightened and intensified until she shifted to stone. Her heavy, thumping footsteps took her through the doorway. The shapeshifter surveyed the contents of the room while Ivy struggled to keep a very squirmy Leo from slipping free.

"It is nothing. The only spells in place are those that allow the room to exist and for the gems to glow."

"So it's safe?"

"As safe as any other library."

Ivy gingerly stepped inside. Ether's assessment seemed sound. Ignoring its location and well-hidden entrance, the room looked to be nothing more than a small study.

"I guess Deacon made a little cozy place for him to be alone with his work sometimes," Ivy said.

"Stick!" Leo shouted.

Ivy looked to the ground. The boy was holding his hands out for a stout painted stick.

"Not alone," Ether said.

She snatched up the stick and presented it to Leo. He grabbed it and proceeded to bat playfully at Ether. Still in her stone form, the stick clacked harmlessly against her.

"Easy there. You don't want to hurt Auntie Ether. When she's human, that'd hurt her."

"Book!" Leo said, now waving his stick in an ostensibly less violent way. He still managed to thump Ivy squarely on the head.

She pushed the stick aside and set him down. The books he was reaching for were like any of the others that utterly surrounded Deacon in his daily life. Ether selected one. Leo immediately settled down. He clutched his stick in both hands and waited patiently.

"It would appear he wants to hear from these books," Ether said.

"Deacon doesn't read him bedtime stories from spell books, does he?" Ivy nuzzled Leo's cheek with her nose. "That seems like something your daddy would do."

"This is a memoir. A transcription from the book he was forever scratching away at," Ether observed.

"Book!" Leo encouraged.

"I don't know if you should read it. That's probably pretty private."

"Deacon has seldom indicated anything resembling personal boundaries or shame regarding his life. And the boy has plainly been read to from these books."

"I suppose…" She hugged Leo a little tighter and flopped onto the floor. "Even so, I should listen for a while, just to make sure it's the right sort of story for him to be hearing."

Ether opened the book to a page marked by a blue ribbon. "'Myranda did not so much as stir until midday, when I reluctantly woke her and informed her that the ceremony would be starting soon. When she left her hut, there was a feeling of anticipation permeating the village. People rushed to and fro. I led her to the courtyard where the elder's hut had been. It was now entirely missing, and in its place, there was a rectangular marble altar…'"

#

Desmeres grazed his false hand along the wall as they crested a slope in the cave. "The feeling is almost gone in my replacement fingers. I'm surprised the hand still works," he said.

"I endeavored to make the animation spell a relatively simple one, both to ensure it wasn't too taxing for you to maintain and specifically to ensure it would continue to function in adverse conditions. It was really a very fascinating puzzle to—" Deacon began.

"It was an observation, not an invitation," Desmeres said.

"Ah. Forgive me. Myranda is rather indulgent when it comes to my enthusiasm on matters such as this."

"Perhaps her greatest sign of divinity is her patience." Desmeres indicated the crystal in his hand. "How is the cave treating your ailment? I understand it takes a degree of effort to keep it under control."

"I am handling it well enough. Mystic focus is growing more difficult, but the very effect that is weakening my grip on the affliction seems to be weakening the affliction as well."

"Would the cave itself be able to cure you, then?"

"I very much doubt it. Like the crown and the ring, it would at best dampen the effects." He tipped his head and shut his eyes. "It is a curious feeling to have my magic fouled in this way. I feel… fuzzy. It is a bit like being inebriated, but in a strictly spiritual sense."

The gentle lapping of water echoed through the cave. The slick floor started to slope treacherously downward. After a short distance, rippling water filled the path ahead.

"As I suspected, still flooded. There may be a clear path higher up in the caves, but this is the most certain path I'm aware of. The important question is whether the water is rising or falling."

"Is that not obvious by simple observation?"

"Not in the short term. It takes quite a while for the cave to flood to this level. The emptying is somewhat swifter, but not the sort of thing visible to the naked eye."

He dropped his heavy pack on the ground and tugged a rope from it. He tied a knot in the rope, affixed one end to the pack, and threw the other in the water.

"We'll check back in a few hours. That should give us an idea of which way the water is moving: toward the knot or away. Until then, this is as good a place as any to make camp."

Deacon nodded and set his pack down to prepare a moderately dry place to sit upon.

"So. The cave is as good as being drunk for a spell caster. Interesting. You strike me as the sort of man who could benefit from a bit of inebriation. Step out of yourself for a while. It can do you good," Desmeres said.

"It is fascinating, but unwise. I wouldn't expect you to understand the folly of that statement, though."

"Oh?" Desmeres said, leaning against the wall. "Indulge me. We've got nothing but time at the moment."

"There are endless reasons. First is the simplest. We train all through our lives to achieve a depth of focus and a precision of control. Stripping *all* of that away, even temporarily, would be unnerving."

"You are speaking to an artisan who had one of his hands lopped off in this very cave. I assure you, I can fully embrace that concern. But I live on. And it's revealed a few things about me that I would consider worth knowing. You've never been the sort to turn up his nose at a lesson."

"Fair." Deacon gave him a thoughtful look. "As I recall, you weren't very forthcoming about how precisely you were injured."

"That was by design."

"It was a very clean cut."

"Indeed. We are discussing you, not me. What other reasons do you have for wanting to hold so tightly to the mystic focus that the vast majority of humanity never even approaches."

"How to put it to words…" Deacon stroked his chin. "When we train, we build strength. The more your spirit channels and harnesses magic, the greater its capacity for further magic. This isn't implicitly so, of course. Some spirits are more able to harness greater power from the start, and there are those who suggest that some spirits will never rise to the heights of others regardless of training. But those who have devoted their lives to serious mystic practice will find themselves with tremendous power at their disposal. Power brings danger. Focus allows us to harness it, but also allows us to direct it. To erect walls to keep ourselves from overstepping ourselves."

"Mmm. I see. A mean drunk, in this context, could be *very* ugly."

"Indeed. Less of a concern within the cave, as the same influence that strips away the control would leave the power toothless."

"Then what are you worried about?"

Deacon lowered his head. "Perhaps this is a personal point, not a universal one. But losing control, *allowing* myself to lose control… it would feel like stepping off a cliff. Like once it was gone, it would never return."

"Afraid of what's lurking below the surface?"

"I have practiced control and discipline since birth. My earliest memories include the constant half-aware flex of my mind. The person I am, the real me, is controlled and measured. Deacon without control isn't Deacon."

"How do you know it would be bad?"

"Were you present in Verril during the final battle?"

"By that time I had made enough poor decisions regarding my allegiances that it seemed wise to put some distance between myself and the Chosen."

"When Myranda and the others continued north to Lain's End, I remained behind to defend the capital. It was well beyond my capabilities, but I'd kept a small quantity of a very potent potion for restoring mystic power. Caya contributed to me consuming an… *improper* dosage. Gray magic, combined with that much power… some of the things I'd done were a hairbreadth from truly horrific. A whisper less control and there wouldn't be a Castle Verril anymore."

"Point taken." Desmeres glanced to the water. He readied his own bedroll. "I don't know about you, but a long ride and a short hike has got me exhausted. If this water is rising, we'll need to fall back and wait. If it is falling, we'll want to move quickly to take advantage once it is clear enough. Either way, we'd be better served by a rest."

#

Ivy sat in a veritable nest of comforters and blankets snagged from her own room. Leo had proved much happier and more manageable in Deacon's secret room than in his own, so Ivy had decided it was better to cuddle up with him there than fight with him elsewhere. She yawned widely and continued reading from the book.

"'I cast a spell or two to be absolutely certain that there was no longer any danger, and as the moon rose dimly behind the clouds, we marched on. The infectious joy Ivy had felt had done more for us than a night of sleep ever could, so there was no need for further delay. The mood was considerably brighter now. Forgoing the bow as she walked, Ivy plucked the strings merrily, a smile on her face.'"

She shut the book. "I remember that day. It feels so strange to read about it from the pages of a book," Ivy mused.

"Book," Leo said with a yawn of his own.

"I think we've had enough. That's a happy moment, and there weren't very many of them in those days. I don't want to leave you with something that will give you nightmares."

Leo looked up at Ivy. "Book," he repeated after careful consideration.

Ivy smirked. "I guess I *did* say that aunties are supposed to spoil their nephews and break the rules. But let's see if we can find one that's got something shorter."

She looked up to Ether, who had been standing at the worktable through Ivy's entire shift as storyteller, leafing through some of the notes and incomplete books.

"Have you found anything else Leo might like?" Ivy asked.

"These are mostly incomplete spells and musings on how to complete them," Ether said, scanning a fresh page. "Musings of other sorts as well."

"Are they really that interesting? You've been reading them all night."

Ether set the page down. "I have been trying to make sense of them. For all his faults, and they are innumerable, Deacon has always had a remarkably clear understanding of magic. At least, magic as utilized by mortals. His focus is gray magic, primarily nonelemental. I question the logic when, as my mere existence illustrates, elemental magics are superior and represent the fundamental workings of nature. But he conjures useful effects." She tapped the page. "What he suggests here is… to put it lightly, deranged."

Ivy covered Leo's ears. "Hush, that's his father you're talking about."

"The boy can't understand my words yet."

"He is brighter than you think. Now be nice." She uncovered Leo's ears and turned him around. "Auntie Ether's just joking about Dada. She probably just doesn't know what he's talking about with his magic."

"*He* doesn't know what he is suggesting. The words are written as though he's grasping at smoke, attempting to make sense of some *new* interpretation of things that are already fully understood. Listen." She snapped the page. "Earth, fire, wind, and water are the fundamentals of the physical world. But there exist other aspects that do not fit neatly within them. If my own expertise so routinely manipulates the world without relying upon the four elements, then surely there must exist other elements. Perhaps deeper elements."

"It makes sense to me." Ivy paused. "All right. It doesn't make *sense* to me. But I can see why he would think that sort of thing."

"It is drivel and blather," Ether said. "The words drive deeper and deeper into abstractions, absurdly supposing each of them is somehow its own element. He talks endlessly of 'acquiring samples' of these elements. There is a full page musing on 'a curious new twist of the spiritual landscape that warrants investigation.' He seems to think that—"

"Wait!" Ivy's ears perked up. "Something's happening. I hear horns. There is an alert."

Ether flashed to her wind form. "I shall investigate."

#

Hours had passed. While Desmeres had managed to fall deeply asleep, Deacon was having difficulty doing the same. It wasn't for lack of exhaustion. His mind, muddled as it was by the effects of the cave, simply wouldn't allow him to sleep. As he tended to do when unable to sleep at home, he'd set his mind to unraveling this riddle and that. This, as always, had quite the opposite effect. The concerns that had sent him here clashed with the concerns that had kept him from coming here. He saw the faces of the people who had made him the man he was today drifting in his mind. He heard their voices condemning him for his violations of Entwell's most sacred beliefs. He saw the face of his son, his mind painting nightmarish tableaus of the boy finding a D'Karon seed and summoning the invaders again.

The one valuable outcome of his churning mind was the experimental discovery that he could fully relax his will for the first time in ages and not worry about the affliction's effects. The ring's and the crown's enchantments were still mercifully effective, and the scrambling effect of the cave itself was enough to take up the rest of the slack that the affliction had gained. In a way, the rest for his mind was far more refreshing than a few hours' sleep would have been. It left him with enough of his wits to truly assess and analyze the cave.

As confounding and complex as the influence of the cave was, it wasn't completely random. He let his mind's eye open wide and took in the dazzling patterns of magic and will. Here and there he could feel echoes of other minds. Some seemed to be his own mind reflected back at him. Others were quite likely the spirits of those who had fallen to the cave and never found their way to the great beyond. They were trapped here forever, or at least until a means could be found to free them. It was a chilling thought, but he soothed his existential terror with the knowledge that such a thing must have been extremely rare, as countless people had lost their lives to the cave over the years and he could feel only a handful of things that might once have been spirits. Indeed, there was truly only one that he could state with any certainty was not a stray thought of his own twisted into a new shape.

Presented with this new fascination to sink its teeth into, his mind tugged and pulled at the distorted will. He couldn't tease out an identity, but as the hours ticked on, he became increasingly certain of its location. Of course, it didn't matter how certain he was. If he didn't confirm, it would only ever be a simple guess. And if this truly was a lost spirit trapped for eternity in the cave, it would be a horrific thing to knowingly leave it here to its fate worse than death.

Finally, his curiosity got the better of him. He stood and fought a weak glow into the heart of his crystal. This would have to be investigated, even if it meant heading out on his own. He paced back along the slick stone to find the source.

A small part of Deacon's mind nagged at him, reminding him of dangers and urging him to return. This small part was drowned out by the combined voices of curiosity and duty. Aside from a brief pause every fifty steps to scratch a mark into the wall to follow back, he dedicated himself fully to the search for this trapped will. If there had been no walls, it would have been simple enough to pinpoint a direction and head directly for it. But every new tunnel twisted and distorted the view in his mind's eye. He may as well have been trying to focus on a single pebble on the floor of a rushing river.

He ventured deeper and deeper, tracing his way through coiling tunnels. The nagging voice became louder. He was a long way from Desmeres now. He'd left himself a means to find his way back, but he wasn't sure which way he had truly gone. There had been backtracking, climbing, sliding. The will was stronger now. He was close. His single-minded focus on the slowly approaching will wasn't broken until he heard the soft skitter of spidery legs.

Deacon froze. Their journey thus far had been through the section of the cave subject to cyclic scouring by floodwater. Beyond the odd centipede or beetle, there was nothing alive here. But what he heard in the tunnel ahead was far too large to be one of those. He tightened his grip on his gem and pulled his struggling focus together into a point powerful enough to stoke the light in the gem's heart.

A pair of eyes gazed at him from the darkness, reflecting his own light back at him with a golden tint. The eyes were small, set too close together to be anything as worrisome as a bear or a dragon. Deacon felt for his gray blade. He'd brought it with him to the cave, but to his dismay he discovered he'd left it behind in his pack along with his pads, his books, and everything else he'd deemed indispensable for such a journey. A sharp chatter reverberated up the tunnel. The eyes rose higher in the cave. Far higher than something with so small a head should be able to manage. They twisted, flipping upside down. A leathery rustle joined the skitter and chatter. Finally, it reached the edge of his light. The thing was long, curling. Its head was canine, but its body was clearly serpentine. Wings somewhere between those of a dragon and a bat spread in an intimidating display. Tufts of feathers topped the wings, as if the creature itself couldn't decide if it was bird, bat, or dragon. Long, chitinous legs clung effortlessly to the ceiling as it clambered toward him. As horrid as the abomination was, it was familiar.

"Mott?" Deacon called out.

The thing stopped, eyes narrow and mouth wide. He recognized his name.

"You are Turiel's familiar," Deacon said.

Now the eyes widened and brightened. His own name had been notable, but the name of his master was another thing entirely. It was a source of curiosity, interest. The thing folded his wings slightly and deftly dropped to the cave floor, pivoting as he fell to clatter toward Deacon with a dizzying dance of legs.

"How did you get here. What is this about?" Deacon said.

He kept his gem tight in hand. The presence of the monster raised a thousand questions. At the moment, the greatest of them was how precisely the beast was still alive. Mott had at least begun his "life" as an extension of Turiel's will. Deacon was personally responsible for coaxing this beast's creator through a portal of uncertain stability. Deacon had been operating under the assumption that Turiel had fallen, but her death should have ended Mott as well. Yet here he stood. How? Why? And perhaps the most crucial questions at this moment, did this creature recall what Deacon had done to Turiel, and did he hold a grudge?

Mott clacked closer, ears back and eyes narrow. He extended his neck until his pointed nose could sniff at the intruder. His posture, if such a thing could be properly interpreted for so mixed up an anatomy, slipped from hostility to cautious curiosity. Deacon risked shutting his eyes to focus again. Mott was most certainly *not* the will he had been searching for. The thing may as well have not existed in his mind's eye. But he was on the right track. The residue of a mind was stronger here. Almost strong enough to have a familiarity, but he couldn't place it.

"Is Turiel here? Is that why you are here?" Deacon asked.

It chattered, almost pleasantly, and tapped in a circle around him.

"If she needs help, I am willing to help her. No one is beyond redemption," he said.

Mott tapped his many legs in excitement. The cold tip of his tail coiled around Deacon's wrist, and the beast clattered back in the direction Deacon had come, attempting to lead him away.

"No, no. It is this way. I can feel it," Deacon said, pulling back.

The tail tightened. Mott's chatter took on the edge of a growl. He tugged more firmly. With eight legs, the creature could pull with remarkable strength. Deacon resisted. He'd come this far seeking to help someone trapped in this place. He wouldn't leave without at least finding out who or what they were. Another tug at the beast burned through the last of the benefit of the doubt he had earned. Mott's ears pulled back. His lips peeled into a snarl.

Deacon pulled his blurred mind together and attempted a spell to repel the beast as Mott lunged for him. What should have been a shield sputtered and faltered. A shimmering disk of magic coalesced before the monster, but a snap of his jaws shattered it into flares of white and blue light.

The monster's long body lashed and constricted around Deacon. Without a proper weapon, magic was his only recourse. He peppered the scrambling creature with flares of flame, flashes of light, and anything else the wizard thought might slip beneath the influence of the cave. Each was at best a distraction. The many limbs and long body of the beast made him seem to be everywhere at once. Legs clawed and scraped at his arms. A tail ensnared his legs. He held up an arm to shove at Mott, only for the monster's jaws to clamp on to his wrist. The writhing mass of monster overbalanced Deacon, and he hit the ground hard. The crown fell from his head. The gem slipped from his grip. Both clattered down along the tunnel ahead.

Without the steadying influence of the crown, Deacon could feel the chaotic whims of his affliction surge. No crystal meant no light. He could not see what was happening, but he could feel it. The hand clamped in Mott's jaws started to change. His fingers curled and writhed bonelessly. Spiny protrusions emerged. Then came the smoldering glow. Whatever his hand had become, it was threaded with something intensely hot. The shifting hand sizzled against Mott's tongue, and the monster recoiled. In the weak glow of his afflicted hand Deacon reared back and drew his desperate mind into the proper shape for one of the simpler spells he could muster. He drew upon the endless, silty moisture clinging to the walls of the cave and doused Mott liberally in the dank water. A second twist of his frazzled mind managed the briefest burst of complex magic. Deacon knew the spell was far too sophisticated to survive the influence of the cave for long, so he funneled all the strength and focus he could muster into it. His gambit paid off. The water dousing Mott glimmered and shifted, turning to a thin layer of stone that wholly encased the beast. Deacon's spell faltered just as the last patch of water changed to slate gray.

Mott was still, now looking like little more than the work of a particularly disturbed sculptor. He was still alive inside the shell of stone, or at least he was still animated. It was hardly a permanent solution. Deacon couldn't be sure how thoroughly the stone had shifted, and thus how long it would be able to hold the deceivingly strong creature. Gods willing, it would hold him for a good long while. Deacon would have to trust it would be enough. He couldn't afford to waste the time to kill a beast that didn't truly live. Without his crown he was tasked with controlling his chaotic affliction himself, a task that would have been difficult enough even *with* his crystal.

He wrestled his hand into something resembling humanity. Through some combination of the well-designed enchantment and more than a little bit of luck, the ring had not been destroyed by his hand's transformation. It gave Deacon an anchor of sorts to center his focus on. For now, he could fight his way past the cave's influence and his own flailing spirit, but it was only a matter of time before this spell faltered like all the others. He needed his crown or his crystal, and he needed them now. Already he could feel the thorny influence in his mind. Swirling chaos eroding his thoughts. Between keeping his body human and keeping his mind sharp, he had barely enough of his intellect left to stay on his feet.

Deacon staggered down the tunnel. The floor was treacherously smooth. A gold crown could slide a long way down a slope like this, and his egg-shaped crystal was probably still rolling. It didn't matter. He had no choice but to venture deeper.

#

Myranda shook her head and wiped some weariness from her eyes. Myn had flown well into the night. The wizard herself had nearly dozed off more than once, but now she felt invigorated by the sight of her beloved city in the distance below. The palace was better lit than she'd expected it to be so late

79

in the evening. Little points of light traced their way across patrol paths and along walls. They moved quickly, too. Horsemen had been deployed.

"What is happening…" Myranda said.

She felt Myn tense beneath her. The dragon thrust her wings and launched south with renewed speed.

"What? What is it? What do you see?"

"Attack," Myn murmured, her voice a throaty growl.

Myranda squinted into the night. Far to the south, too far to be within even the farthest reaches of the city but too near to be their nearest neighbor, there was motion on the ground. Myranda's night vision was too weak to make it out with any detail. She shut her eyes as Myn surged toward the motion and focused her mind. What she saw, scanning with her mind, was nearly as weak and ill-defined. There were soldiers. Not human. Nearmen. They were heavily armed, and in numbers great enough to overrun the city.

She didn't waste time wondering how they could have appeared. Questions could wait until the city was secure. A streamer of fire erupted from one of the towers of the palace. At first Myranda feared it was another sign of attack, but it soon resolved itself into the vengeful, fiery form of Ether. She streaked out over the city and down along the field. In her light, the first wave of New Kenvard's soldiers could be seen, charging to meet the foes.

Myn dropped down to charge along the ground. Ether sizzled through the air beside her. The wall of inhuman troops loomed closer. Closer.

And then it was gone.

The foes vanished without fanfare, without light or sound. One moment Myranda could hear the stomp of their boots, the next the field ahead was empty. Neither Myn nor Ether was willing to trust her eyes. The elemental continued forward to where the soldiers had been and flared her fire brighter. A brilliant orange-white glow illuminated the field. Myn cast a long shadow, and the approaching friendly troops spurred themselves faster. The force that had brought them here was gone. But not without a trace.

Myranda hopped from Myn's back and gazed down. "That was not our imagination. And it was not illusion," she said.

The field was churned up with boot prints. There *had* been attackers here. She turned. Less than a mile separated the footprints from the edge of her city. If they had been real enough to trample the field into mud, then their blades and bows were real as well. What would have happened to the city if they had reached it? And why *hadn't* they reached it. She needed more information. More answers. But one question needed to be answered before all else.

"Is he safe?" Myranda called to Ether.

"The boy is with Ivy, deep in the palace. Nothing seemed out of the ordinary there," Ether said. "What was this? I don't feel any residue of magic.

Anything that could have conjured so vast a force and whisked it away should have been astonishing in its power. The field should still be reverberating with the intensity of it."

"I don't know. Has anything like this happened here before? Anything at all out of the ordinary since I've been gone?"

"Nothing." Ether dropped down and shifted to human. "No… There was one thing. Curious but not threatening. The boy knocked down a bowl of fruit twice, but none of us observed it being righted in between. I fail to see how this could be connected."

"It isn't clear to me either," Myranda said, climbing back to Myn's back. "But unexplained things have been happening all over the three kingdoms. It can't be a coincidence. Ether, I want you to go to Tressor. Be diplomatic, but firm. I want you to find out if anything like this has been happening there."

"Yes. Wise. I shall return with the answers," Ether replied. She shifted to wind and burst skyward.

"Come on, Myn. I need to see Leo. After this, I need to see for myself that he is safe."

"We need Deacon," Myn stated.

"By now he's in the cave. It will be difficult to reach him." She shut her eyes tightly. "We will find a way to reach him if we have to, but if there is any way to solve this without him, I intend to. It was difficult enough to persuade him to seek a cure. If he is pulled away, I worry it will be years more before he will risk leaving again."

#

Deacon held his healthy hand to his head and tried his best to split his already taxed mind between keeping his ailment in check and illuminating his path. As crucial as it was that he find his crown, the crystal would be easier to find and more useful. He had so far managed to keep his hand flesh and blood, though what sort of flesh and what sort of blood was varying moment to moment. It was unsettling, but nothing he hadn't had to deal with before. The truly disquieting thing he had to cope with now was the more recent symptom of his illness. The one he'd kept to himself for fear of what Myranda might say if she knew. He could feel his thoughts betraying him just as his hand did. It was nothing so sinister as madness. At least, not *proper* madness, he told himself. He simply felt his mind shift from the sharpened instrument he'd made of it through years of discipline to something… else. Something equally honed, equally potent, but playing by a different set of rules. As though it was a mind borrowed from some other Deacon, some version of himself that had followed the same path, but in a different world. What worried him most wasn't that it felt like a violation. It was that it felt so very natural. It was insidious.

Not until he was ankle deep in water at the end of the slope did Deacon

81

finally find his crystal. He reached down and plucked it from the dank water. The blunt edge it brought to his focus was enough to wholly restore his hand and smooth the wrinkle in his mind to something he could more easily tame. He raised the crystal high to light the cave around him. If he was lucky, the crown had made it this far as well.

What he saw struck him as wrong, somehow. Debris was piled here. It certainly could have been a cave-in. The ceiling was jagged and crumbled overhead. But it seemed too thorough. The pile of stones before him was mounded perfectly, like someone had endeavored to piece the bits of fallen roof into a wall.

"So. Finally, *you* have come."

Deacon turned to seek the source of the voice. There was no one. "Who is there?" he shouted. His voice echoed and folded upon itself.

"Don't tell me you don't know me."

The reply had no echo. And, he realized, it was in his own voice. He wasn't hearing it with his ears. He was feeling it in his mind. His panic had distracted him from the very thing that had brought him here in the first place. Now that he at least had the crystal, he realized that the will he had followed this far was now right in front of him, trapped on the other side of the stones.

And he finally recognized it.

"Epidime," he said coldly.

"Is it that time already, Deacon? Our time?"

Deacon took a step away from the wall. Epidime felt weak. He was dimmer in Deacon's mind's eye than even a mundane human would be. There was no risk of him forcing his way into control, as he'd done so many times before. At least not at this distance. And he wasn't drawing any closer.

"You… you're trapped here, aren't you?"

"I am. By Desmeres, of all people. Not even a Chosen One. A grave injustice."

"A fitting prison for you."

"An effective one, I must admit. And I cannot place all the blame on the treacherous half-elf. My curiosity was to blame. It was bound to get the better of me one day. This mountain was the piece of this world I couldn't properly investigate. Irresistible for a lifetime student like myself. But then, I don't need to explain that to you."

"Now that I know you are here, I can take the proper precautions to keep you here."

"If special precautions were necessary to keep me here, do you think I would still be here? I am defeated, Deacon. Finally at your mercy. So now is the time."

"What time are you talking about?"

"Don't tell me I overestimated you. You have questions. Minds like ours always have questions. And you are in the presence of the only source you will ever have for some of the answers you seek."

"I don't need to know anything that badly."

"Oh no? Then answer me this. Why have I never taken you as a host? You aren't one of the Chosen, but you walk among them. No mark to save you. I've gone to the effort of taking *Lain*. I've sought Myranda. But you? I had you at my mercy, and there were only words. You may think me a scoundrel. You may think me a demon. But I pray you never think me a big enough fool to miss that opportunity without a good reason."

"I don't need to know."

"You do. You always need to know. It is a thirst we share. To know. Always to know. But if I must appeal to something that truly matters, I have a question for *you*. How complete are your memoirs? I know you have sought to record every nuance of the end of the Perpetual War. All the exploits and challenges of the Chosen. But you haven't, have you? You can't know *everything* that happened, because you cannot know what happened behind the closed doors of the D'Karon. You cannot know the hearts and minds of people now lost to the world. There is only one source of such knowledge now. I swam in the thoughts of some of the greatest mysteries of your world. I plotted and planned with D'Karon you defeated. Every gap in your story lurks in my mind."

"... The story is complete enough."

"And what of your son?"

*"What do you know of my son?"*

"Only what drifts on the surface of your mind. You're working too hard to keep yourself stable. You can't shield everything from me, even in my present state. You fear for his safety. You specifically fear what those like me may do to him. Ironic."

"My only fear is that he might one day face an evil such as you."

"The seeds. You've found some, haven't you? But perhaps, not all. Perhaps I know where they are. Perhaps I am the only one who knows where they all are."

"We will find them. We will find another way."

"You are already working on a way, aren't you?"

Deacon shut his eyes tighter and tried to shield his mind, but every bit of effort he put into blocking Epidime's gaze into his thoughts allowed his affliction to rebound. The D'Karon continued.

"Is that how it happens? Is that how it begins and ends? With you tinkering with things even your mentors didn't know to warn you against? You know your way is treading on dangerous ground. But you know it could work.

You are missing pieces. And I know where to find them."

"You are lying."

"Who would know if not me? I have traveled so many worlds. Scoured them for all there was to know. Everything I know could be yours. Or even just the bits and pieces you need to make your world safe."

Deacon gritted his teeth. His mind was swimming. "You are trying to manipulate me. Why would you help me?"

"Does it matter? Think of what I'm offering you."

"No one in their right mind would trust you, even in your weakened state."

"Fortunate for us both that you aren't in your right mind. You wouldn't be here if you were."

"I'm still sane enough to know what should and should not be done."

"Deacon, I can give you insight into the D'Karon. I can give you insight into so much of your world that has been hidden to you. I can give you truths that no one else knows. And I am the only one who can give you these things. I am knowledge distilled. Lie to yourself if you must, but we both know that I represent *precisely* what you have been searching for. You can have the remaining pieces to your most precious riddle. You can, once and for all, protect your son, and his children, and every generation to come from the same tragedies that nearly wiped out the people of this world. I know how the door opens. I know how the door closes. There was a time when you sat, helpless, waiting to be interrogated by me. Now the roles are reversed. Ask your questions. Drink deep of my fountain of knowledge. If you fail to do so, you condemn your child to a life of uncertainty."

The wizard felt his mind shudder and curl. It wasn't Epidime's doing. He'd gone too long without the crown, and the cave wasn't sufficient to completely unravel the affliction. The longer he tried to hold it at bay, the wearier he became. The wearier he became, the deeper the chaos wove into his thoughts.

"I see the plan in your mind. I see the gaps that need to be filled. They are plain as day to me. And if nothing else, believe me when I tell you that a 'healthy' mind will never stumble upon them. If you truly wish to give your world the safety you seek, know that a sane and rational Deacon, free of this affliction and free of my insight, will never take the steps that must be taken. Choose now. And choose wisely."

Deacon's fingers wavered. His grip on the gem loosened. His strength of mind was flagging. He needed clarity. He needed relief.

He needed to know.

# Chapter 5

Desmeres groggily opened his eyes. It was disorienting to wake from a particularly exhausted rest at the best of times. Buried deep in the complete darkness of a treacherous cave was far, far worse. He felt for the darkened lantern and fiddled with the flint until it sparked to life. With the dim glow smoldering, he raised the lantern and took in his surroundings.

"Ah… Yes… the Cave of the Beast. Too much to wish for that this whole foolish enterprise was a dream."

He held the lantern down to the flooded tunnel. The water had receded greatly. It hadn't simply dropped a few turns down the rope. The rippling surface was nearly beyond the glow of the lantern.

"Good news," he said, turning to where Deacon had set down for the night. "We are in luck. Cave is draining, not filling. Another few days and we might be able to risk… Deacon?"

Desmeres tugged at the luxurious blanket atop Deacon's bedroll. There was no one there. He gritted his teeth and smashed his false fist against the wall of the cave. The metal digits sparked against the stone. He transferred the lantern to the false hand and pressed his other fingers to the bedding.

"Cold. He's been gone for some time. That idiot! How can someone with such an intellect be so astonishingly stupid?" He climbed to his feet. "A *child* would know not to wander off."

He pulled his pack to his back, leaving the bedding in place. "I should have taken some sort of a precaution against this. The whole reason I agreed to lead him was because it was far too dangerous for someone like him to be set free in the cave, and then what do I do? Leave him free to wander its tunnels."

A sparkling gash on the wall of the cave drew his attention.

"He was smart enough to leave a path, at least."

He quickened his pace. A few long strides took him to the first place where the cave split off into others. Another mark indicated which path Deacon had taken. The draining of the cave meant that it was mildly less slick than it had been hours before, affording him a bit more speed. He traced the path backward until he came to a particularly large cluster of intersecting tunnels.

One by one he searched the mouths of the different passages and found no mark. With each eliminated path, he grew more certain of what he would find. Sure enough, when all of the tunnels leading in one direction had been eliminated, he found the mark on the opposite side. A thin rivulet of water trickled near the mouth of the small tunnel, with its descending slope heading off to the left of the flow.

"Don't go left. I *ground* it into him," he growled. "*Deacon!*"

His voice echoed through the tunnels. Desmeres rummaged in his pocket and wrapped his fist around the copper coin. He let the mark press firmly against the flesh of his hand.

"Deacon, I know where you went!" he shouted, continuing along the path. "It is the one place that your curiosity and my luck would conspire to send you."

He continued on his way, shouting at each intersection. Sometimes he was simply shouting in hope of a reply. Other times he was shouting for little reason beyond venting his frustration at fate's unwillingness to allow things to go smoothly.

"I couldn't tell you what you would find, because you would have sought it out. I couldn't let you come here alone, because you might have stumbled upon it. Was I a fool to suspect when we'd gone *past* the danger you wouldn't retrace your steps just to fall into its jaws? Evidently so. If fate has torturous plans for you, one would think it would have the decency to leave me out of them."

He stopped, in part to scan the walls for the next mark, in part to listen for a reply. He was far more familiar with this section of the cave, having so recently and so notably returned. There was a considerable distance to go before he reached Epidime's chamber. He was only a few branching tunnels from the main path. In many ways, this section was the major crossroads of the whole tunnel system. It was likely more lives were lost here than any other part of the cave. One could not reach this point without a considerable amount of climbing. Half of the tunnels from here dropped sharply into jagged pits or into slick-walled chasms filled to varying degrees with water. Those who reached beyond this section at the wrong time of year unknowingly faced the threat of rising waters blocking both their way out and their way forward.

The faint scrapes Deacon had left behind would be easy for him to find, as he knew roughly where he'd left them. Desmeres was having a terrible time spotting the one for this section of the cave. There was every chance Deacon had taken a wrong turn here and met some unfortunate end. He was considering this, and grappling with whether he should feel sorrow or relief, when he heard something approaching.

"Deacon?" he called.

In reply, the scratching, scampering sound quickened. It was plainly no human charging in his direction. Desmeres pulled his hand from his pocket and slipped a dagger from its sheath. There was no preparing for what came next, however.

Mott burst from the darkness, body lashing and legs slashing. Fragments of his freshly broken stone shell still clung to him. He struck Desmeres hard, driving the half-elf back to the wall. Desmeres regained his footing and swiped his blade. It cut neatly through two of Mott's legs. They fell to the ground and twitched. Mott recoiled. He snagged the sliced away extremities with his jaws and tail and hobbled back to the tunnel entrance he'd come from.

"What is that thing?" Desmeres hissed, wiping blood from his cheek where the creature had made superficial contact.

He knew better than to assume it would die from its wounds, or that it would keep its distance. If he'd known something like that lurked in the caves, he probably would have thought twice about setting up camp in so open a place the previous night. Better to kill the thing now before it got the chance to do the same to him.

Desmeres edged forward. He saw its eyes catch the light of the lantern first. When it didn't strike, he edged closer until it was fully lit. The thing had its head low and its wings flat. It watched him suspiciously. When he inched a bit closer, it spread the wings and chattered out a threat. This was the first full look he'd gotten of the thing. In addition to the haphazard anatomy, it also crackled with lingering bits of stone.

"There is no world in which nature creates something like you," Desmeres said. "Tell me Deacon didn't make you."

The monster held its ground. As Desmeres tried to work out how best to dispatch the thing, his eyes caught something else. Just above the creature's raised wing, a fresh mark had been carved into the wall.

"Deacon came this way," he muttered. "I don't suppose you killed him? He's a friend, but death might be a mercy as opposed to what will become of him if he crosses paths with what's left of Epidime."

When he mentioned the D'Karon name, the monster's eyes took on a sharper, more penetrating look. It twisted its head around and aligned the disembodied leg in its jaws with the twitching stump. Tendrils of black knitted the cut together. A similar curl and alignment with its tail restored the second leg.

"I can see I'm going to have to cut you into far smaller pieces," Desmeres said.

Mott chattered a challenge and scrambled forward. Desmeres thought he was ready for the attack. A quick turn and jab should have been all it took to drive his dagger through the skull of this mismatched creature. This time, however, the thing did not attack in a frenzied scramble. It moved with purpose and guile. Though it was a mass of limbs and coiling body, every bit of the thing was narrow and spindly, leaving little for Desmeres's blade to bite into. A skilled slash of the blade missed the body and carved a long gash in the thing's wing. It shrugged off the attack and clamped its jaws around Desmeres's false hand, locking his grip around the lantern. The end of its tail coiled around his knife hand. Thus entangled, it flapped its wings and scrambled its legs to force him back.

Desmeres tried to fight against the thing, but its strength was inhuman. He stumbled backward. His back struck the wall. He slid along it, boots slipping and stumbling. Then, with a single startling step, he ran out of floor.

Both man and monster pitched off the edge of a precipice. Desmeres tried to wrestle a hand free to perhaps grab hold of something, but the beast ensnaring him held on tightly. He struck the steep slope of the cliff face. The lantern flew from his grasp. Another sharp blow produced a squeal of pain and a hideous crunch of chitin from his attacker. Finally, they splashed down into icy water. This was finally enough to separate the horrid thing from him. Desmeres flailed about in the inky frigid water. With all his equipment weighing him down and a hand made from animated metal, it was all he could do to stay above water. The darkness was complete, his lantern having landed some distance away.

In what felt strangely like fate was toying with him, Desmeres's blind paddling took him to a shallow stretch of the crevice, a place where at least his feet could touch the slippery stone. He got a firm foothold and painfully worked his way up the slope until he was on moderately dry land.

He gasped and sputtered for more than a few moments, retching cave water up and blinking away the red and blue sparks that crowded his otherwise useless vision. If the water hadn't been so cold, he probably would have been doubled over in pain. As it was, he was half numb. His pack, though waterlogged, was intact. The lamp had either finally sunk or been carried around a bend, as the only hint of light came from the threads of enchantment that animated his false hand.

Desmeres ran the thumb across the tips of the metal fingers. A rapid metallic click filled the cave. Bit by bit the threads were illuminated, casting a weak blue glow around him. The slope he'd dragged himself onto was the mouth of a tunnel. Water was sheeting out of it, suggesting a cavern farther up the slope was draining through it.

"Take stock," Desmeres croaked. "What have we got? Rudimentary light. And perhaps some torches that I can light if I can dry them out. The rest of my equipment, less the bedroll. Deacon had the pads, so I have no means to communicate. I don't know where I am, but with the cave still draining, I at least have the trickle of water I can follow to the heart of the cave, and from there a fighting chance to find my way back to a path I recognize."

He trudged a few unsteady steps along the slope. "Of course, I *am* a creature of this world who betrayed the Chosen." He wormed his hand into his drenched pocket and felt for the coin. "No burn from the mark, but that doesn't mean there isn't some higher being up there who is still holding a grudge for my slight against their avatars."

Behind him, a few distant splashes separated themselves from the rest. Desmeres shut his eyes and took a breath.

"I must have angered one of the trickster gods," he breathed. "Who else would conjure up this sort of torturous end?"

He turned and snapped his false fingers again. The light pulsed and he saw Mott's pathetic, half-broken form haul itself onto the slope. Twisted, fractured limbs slowly straightened and healed. Gleaming eyes locked on him. Desmeres realized his blade was not listed among his assets. Constant clicking and snapping of his false fingers kept the beast visible. Its eyes measured him as it stalked painfully toward him.

He gave a glance upward and addressed the unnamed powers that were who saw fit to taunt him with this fate. "The least you could do is send me out with some sort of message," Desmeres said.

Mott stopped briefly, as if to wait to see what he had to say. The pause didn't escape Desmeres's notice.

"Oh, so you can understand me, eh?" he said, backing slowly away. "Further evidence someone sent you."

The abomination kept pace with him. If talking would keep the thing distracted, he would keep the words flowing. He didn't know what he would do with the time it bought him, but it would be nice if he could use his mouth to get himself *out* of trouble for once.

"The way you piece yourself back together, you're someone's masterpiece, I'll bet. Maybe that's what sent Deacon after you, hmm? He heard something and just had to investigate the nameless horror. He was from Wizard's Side. They were all a bit off on that side of Entwell. Anyone who would willingly submit themselves to the whims of Azriel for a final test—"

Mott's head snapped up. He charged forward, closing the remaining space between them in a flash. Desmeres flinched and held his false hand up in defense. It was the only part of his body likely to withstand those jaws without serious injury. For a moment he remained motionless, hand held up. The impact that should have come never did. Desmeres cautiously snapped the fingers of the hand. A pulse of light revealed Mott inches away, expression serious, eyes locked on his.

"Heard something that piqued your interest?" Desmeres said shakily.

The thing didn't react. It was waiting. Desmeres tugged the last few minutes from memory. The name Epidime had produced a reaction, though hardly a promising one.

"Deacon?" he offered.

Nothing but a tip of Mott's head.

"Azriel?"

The thing tapped its legs in place, suddenly brimming with barely restrained enthusiasm.

"Why in the *world* would you know who Azriel is?"

Mott clattered in a circle around him and hopped in place.

"Do you want to find Azriel?"

The response was a squealing chatter. It didn't convey much meaning, but the absence of violence was as close to an affirmative as Desmeres was likely to get.

"You'll understand if I am not confident you can be trusted, since you just tried to kill both of us. If you want me to help you, you are going to have to earn a little trust."

Mott scrambled back a bit and tipped his head sideways. His eyes darted. Finally, he turned about and launched into the darkness. After listening to some splashing and scratching, Desmeres snapped his fingers a few times to reveal the beast had returned, not with something useful but innocuous like his lantern, but with his blade. He raised an eyebrow and gingerly plucked it from the thing's jaws.

"Handing me my knife... I can think of a few better ways to prove you're not an enemy, but point taken. One last test."

Desmeres clumsily fished the coin from his pocket. He touched the Mark of the Chosen to Mott's snout. There was no flash of light, no sizzle of flesh.

"... Well, either your soul is pure, or you don't have one. I don't imagine I'm going to get any better evidence than that. This way."

#

Myranda looked over the pages of her pad. Deacon's innovation had permitted a handful of key people across the world to deliver each other messages without the delay of runners and travel across kingdoms. In truth, only Deacon, Myranda, and Ivy used them with any regularity. But now the stylus had been scratching out messages without pause for over an hour. After she'd ensured that whatever unexplained foe had come and gone wasn't showing any signs of return, she'd sent out a message to all with a pad to tell of any unexplained phenomena, great or small. Replies had come quickly, and in huge quantities. There were far too many replies for her to sift through reliably. That didn't stop her from trying. At the moment she had no better option.

She raised her head at the sound of someone in the doorway. It was Ivy. The two hadn't spoken properly since Myranda had returned, beyond a brief handoff so that Myranda could attempt to get Leo to sleep while Ivy joined the soldiers to ensure the city was secure. Since then, Ivy had been bouncing back and forth between Leo's room and the windows to watch the horizon.

"Has he woken again?" she asked, already on her feet to see to her child.

"No, no. He's still asleep. Now *I'm* the one who can't sleep. But I'm not sure I should be. What's going on, Myranda?"

"I don't know." She gestured to the notes she'd transcribed from the messenger pad. "I've gone through as many messages as I can, but there isn't much of value there. I hadn't appreciated just how many tiny, meaningless curiosities happen each day. All I can do is try to think of how Deacon would deal with it. No one can make sense of hordes of words like he can. I've sorted them into piles. These are innocuous, things that could be a trick of the eye or a drunken delusion. These are more worrisome, things many people saw and could agree upon. So far, there have been only three reports of something of the scope we saw. The would-be attack on Kenvard, a flight of dragoyles over a lake to the northeast, and a glimpse of some black carriages rumbling into the Rachis Mountains."

Ivy looked over Myranda's record of the unusual happening a few hours earlier. "Did this feel… I don't know how to describe it. Did this feel *familiar* to you?" she asked.

"I've faced waves of nearmen many times," Myranda said.

"I know, but this felt… I don't know… *deeper* than that." Ivy sat down beside Myranda. Her expression was distant. "I don't remember much from before you found me. A little bit of the D'Karon generals trying to 'train' me. And before that, I only really remember flashes. It could just be that I'm back in Kenvard now. Maybe the feeling of home combined with the look of those soldiers from the window. It felt so much like the only real memory I have from when I was Aneriana. Those awful things rushing through the gates… And there was something else. I could barely see them in the distance, but something about the nearmen looked wrong. Different from the other times we fought them."

Myranda drummed her fingers. In the heat of the moment, she'd been more concerned about what the warriors could do than how they looked. She tried to recall their appearance, bathed in the orange light of Ether's flame.

"Yes," Myranda said. "I think you're right. Follow me."

She marched to the stairs and down to the courtyard, Ivy in tow. After the long flight, Myn should have been sound asleep. The great creature had a shelter of her own in place of one of the palace stables, but it was empty.

Instead, she had planted herself in front of the palace steps, eyes fixed on the southern horizon, faithfully watching for any new threat.

"Myn," Myranda called.

The dragon turned and lowered her head.

"Your eyes are sharper than mine in the darkness. Do you remember the color of the attackers' uniforms?"

"Red," she said.

"Red. You are *certain*."

"They wore red," Myn said, raising her head again to watch the horizon.

"But the D'Karon soldiers always wore blue. They were posing as *our* soldiers," Ivy said.

"Not always," Myranda said. "This happened once before. A massive attack, approaching the city of Kenvard from the south, in Tresson armor."

Ivy covered her mouth. "The massacre…"

"Caya mentioned glimpses of the white wall. You said the bowl spilled twice. Any of the dragoyle sightings. And the fact there is never any residue of magic afterward. Could these all be glimpses of the past? Flickers of what was?"

"How *could* it be? What would that mean?"

"I don't know… But there is a great deal in the recent past between the Northern Alliance and Tressor that we can't afford to have repeat. And New Kenvard has borne the brunt of the years as well. If this is the threat I think it is, we need to solve it before things get worse. We've worked too hard to put the past behind us for it to rise again."

#

A night watchman grumbled and tugged his leather hood a bit farther over his head. A cold, miserable rain was falling. The spring weather and the relatively temperate location of Territal had convinced him he didn't need to worry about warm clothing, but now that he'd been soaked through the cheap uniform he'd been given, he was wishing he'd invested in an overcloak. Or at least in some brandy.

"Head down to Territal, they told me," he grumbled to no one in particular. "Ulvard will be its own kingdom again. There'll be plenty of places to earn some legitimate money."

He flicked his hood to shake the water from it. "What do they need me outside the archives for?" he grumbled. "There's nothing worth taking. Just documents and the bits and pieces of our 'history' that no one cared enough to add to the royal collection."

The rain trickling down his face washed some of the grime from his forehead into his eyes. He was still rubbing them and cursing at the awful stinging sensation when he heard the odd clapping sound echo like a cracked whip.

"Hmm? Who goes there?" he said, blinking madly and reaching for the grip of his cudgel.

When his vision cleared, he didn't spot anyone. Just the same soaking-wet, dismal gray stone of a forgotten corner of Ulvard's capital. Even so.

"Probably just a bit of stone falling," he reasoned as he coaxed some more light out of his lantern.

He trudged along his patrol route, lantern held high.

Obviously, he was alone. The hour was ungodly, there were no homes in this part of the town, and the only place with doors still open was a lackluster tavern with watered-down ale. He peered down the cobbled street. It was empty, and it had been for the last few hours. No one could be here, because he would have spotted them minutes ago coming down one street or another. But things still didn't feel right.

"It's ghosts," he grumbled. "Here I thought the last guy was a drunk. Seeing things when he said he saw the Alliance banners flying again over the door. It's ghosts. Playing tricks on us. Convincing a poor workingman he's seeing and hearing things that aren't there."

The watchman stopped and peered at the sheltered entryway he'd left behind when he finished his short patrol circuit. A trio of wet footprints led to the door to the archives. And the door was ajar.

He gritted his teeth and slipped his cudgel free. "Blasted thieves trying to get me tossed from the job before I get my pay," he barked. "Who goes there!"

He rushed to the door and threw it open.

The wet footprints led deeper into the darkened archives. He raced after them. Wall after wall of shelves with sturdy chests and crates stored assorted items too valuable to dispose of but not impressive enough to display. He followed the trail, weaving deeper until a figure became visible at the end of a narrow passage between shelves. He was illuminated by a dim amber light, too steady and constant to be a lantern or candle. In one hand, he held a bit of enameled blue armor. In the other, he held the source of the light, a bit of glowing crystal.

"Whatever you've got, drop it! In the name of the king and queen!" the watchman ordered.

Whoever the thief was, he was unconcerned by the threat. He simply tugged open a bag and dropped the bit of armor inside. It vanished through the opening of the bag and failed to bulge the rest of the pouch, as though the satchel remained empty despite what the watchman had seen.

"I block the way. You will not leave with what you've taken!"

Now the figure looked to him. The watchman's mind took a moment or two to comprehend what he was looking upon. He *had* forgotten his brandy, and thus he hadn't been drinking, so he had little reason to be imagining what stood before him. It had to be real. But it made no sense.

Fortunately, he didn't have to grapple with it for long. The crystal rose high, a flicker of purple spread into a swirling portal, and the thief stepped away. Another soft clap flashed arcane power through the aisle. The force of it disrupted the contents of the shelves and dazzled the watchman. When his vision cleared, the thief was gone.

He stepped forward to investigate. The opened crates were all military garb for high-ranking officials of the former Alliance Army. Generals. There was no telling which he'd been rummaging through or what had been taken, just that it was a piece of equipment.

"What's going on here!"

The watchman jumped and turned. A robed man, his head hidden beneath a cavernous and drenched hood, stood behind him. The watchman recognized the outfit as one of the curators of the archives. If he was here so late at night, he wasn't one of the senior curators, but any one of them would gladly relieve him of duty for failing to prevent whatever had just happened from happening.

"There was a… I saw a…"

"Out with it!" the man snapped.

"I saw King Deacon steal something and vanish!" the watchman yelped.

"The king. Of Kenvard."

"Yes. He came and there was a clap of magic and he was gone. He stole something!"

The curator's hand disappeared under the hood to palm his face. "Why do they send the drunkards to the archives? First the banners and now this."

"I saw what I saw, sir."

"I am not going to go to my superior and tell him that the king of our sister nation came and left without a trace to steal—what? A random buckler from dress armor? I am going to have to catalogue everything and… listen to me. I have no interest in dealing with this now. Your shift ends at dawn, yes?"

"Yes, sir."

"You get outside, and you make sure no other 'rogue royals' show up to steal anything. Tomorrow I'll go through this. If I find something missing, we'll be discussing it." He turned to pace away. "You'd best come up with a better story by then, or else I would suggest you make yourself scarce."

The watchman tightened his fist around the lamp and trudged out to the cobblestone street again. He lingered for a moment or two, considering actually completing his shift. But he'd been all but dismissed already. If he was going to be thrown out on the street for being unlucky enough to see yet another of the ghostly events that seemed to plague this place, he was at least going to take advantage of the rest of the night to down some watery ale and figure out where he could hide out for a few weeks after he was blamed for the theft.

"This is what I get for looking for honest work," he grumbled, marching away.

# Chapter 6

Days later, Desmeres blinked at the point of light ahead. After squinting his way through the darkness for so long, his mind wasn't immediately willing to interpret the sparkling light in the distance as anything other than his imagination. Mott, on the other hand, lacked any imagination whatsoever, and thus was fully able to embrace it as reality. As such, he coiled his tail around Desmeres's wrist and sprinted for the distant ember of sunlight. Thus, Desmeres's triumphant return to his birthplace came not in a proud emergence from the cave, but in an undignified slide into the smooth basin of the currently dormant falls.

Mott disentangled himself from Desmeres and hopped to his many feet. He sniffed the air and glared at the people around the end of the basin. Unsatisfied with what he found, he chattered at Desmeres.

"How many times do I need to tell you? Those noises you are making don't *mean* anything to me," he growled. "But if you are looking for Azriel, unless things have changed, you'll find her in the crystal arena. It's on the north end of town, you can't miss it."

The abomination tapped gleefully around him, then flapped his wings and launched from the basin. A flurry of exclamations in different languages rang out as the absurd accumulation of disparate parts screeched by them. A rope ladder slapped down against the side of the basin, and one of two yellow-robed youths around the rim climbed down to meet him.

"Welcome, traveler. This must seem very strange to you, to find something like this here," the wind apprentice began. "You have reached—"

"The Belly of the Beast. Entwell Num Garastra. I am well aware; this is a return, not a discovery. I request a room in Warrior's Side, a hot meal, a warm bath, and an audience with the elder and as many of the masters as can be mustered. As soon as possible, and in that order."

"Of course, of course. Welcome home, traveler." The apprentice called to the other at the rim. "A returning warrior! Prepare a place for him!"

When it became clear that Desmeres did not require any immediate aid, the apprentice took a step away and muttered some arcane words under his breath. A gust of wind, guided with poor precision by the aspiring wind mage's will, plucked the yellow-robed man from the basin. He clumsily set down beside his fellow lookout and, between the two of them, helped to haul the rope ladder up while Desmeres held on tightly.

Desmeres felt a strange warmth in his chest at hearing such a symphony of dialects above him and found himself strangely moved by the sight of Entwell opening out before him. He'd never fancied himself nostalgic, but this *was* his home of many decades, and the place that had given him the skills and drive to make of himself what he had.

"When were you last here?" asked one apprentice.

"When did you leave?" asked the other.

The questions flowed continuously as they led him to the southern half of the village. This was, after all, a place dedicated to learning. Newcomers were a rare chance to inject new teachings, or simply fresh news of the outside. They interrogated him over things as innocuous as how his jacket was made to as complex as the precise nature of the enchantment that animated his hand. He didn't bother to answer any of their questions. There would be time for that later. The journey through the mountain hadn't been an easy one. He was in no shape to be racing back to the entrance before the falls began again. So he would be staying here for months. More than enough time for them to learn their fill of the decades he'd been away. But there was one point he felt worth making before they left him to his privacy.

"That thing that came through with me? I assume it went into the crystal arena. If it comes out again, keep an eye on it. It helped me navigate the cave, but I get the distinct impression it is about as faithful as a stray cat."

#

Myranda shielded her eyes against the wind. She'd gotten little sleep in the last few days, and Myn had gotten even less. The stylus of the messenger pads hadn't stopped moving, with accounts of unusual happenings pouring in at all hours of the night. Most were of no concern, easily explained away. Some were strange and possibly related, but harmless. So far there had been nothing truly dangerous. But from the moment she became aware of the possibility that history was repeating itself, Myranda knew that it was only a matter of time before she would have to make a trip to the Tresson border.

The sun was just beginning to break through the clouds when she reached the stretch of land separating Kenvard from its neighbor to the south. Decades of battle and spilled blood had scarred the land terribly. A proper battle had not been fought in years, but flora and fauna had yet to reclaim the worst of the damage. A small contingent of soldiers stood at attention along the border. One among them was distinct. A great green dragon towered over the soldiers. A rider in unique armor that matched the shade of the dragon's scales was astride the beast. At the first glimpse of the dragon and rider, Myn showed something besides tireless vigilance in her expression for the first time in days. The dragon mount waiting patiently at the border was Garr, and Myn was *very* happy to see him.

"Keep to our side of the border, Myn," Myranda said. "The soldiers will be tense. We don't need to give them a reason to take up arms."

Myn dropped down to the field and trotted the last few hundred yards. She heeded Myranda's request and held her ground on the north side of a clearly marked point on the side of the road. As she fidgeted and shifted in place, eyes bright and fixed upon Garr, Myranda stepped forward.

"Your Majesty," said Grustim, Garr's Rider. "You needn't have come personally."

"Speed was important and I wouldn't have asked Myn to carry anyone but me. I grant you and your troops permission to cross the border for the purposes of this discussion."

Grustim gave a respectful salute and climbed from Garr's back. The dragon stepped across the border and took his place beside Myn. She practically fell atop him, curling her neck and tail against his.

"What has happened?" Myranda asked.

Grustim pulled an official proclamation from his satchel and handed it to her.

"From King Aamuul. We have withdrawn the bulk of our soldiers from the border. Six of our watch posts have reported seeing troops massing to the north. Initially, alarms were raised, fearful that hostilities might have resumed without clear cause. Three of the watch posts subsequently spotted Tresson soldiers meeting the northern troops in battle, despite the fact that no sizable forces had been dispatched. In one case, the flag of the contingent was one of a long-disbanded battalion. We suspect magic."

"It isn't magic. At least not directly. We have had flashes of our history replaying itself as well. No hint of mystic influence precedes or follows them. Has any blood been shed?"

"No fresh blood, but in the case of one of the battles that recurred entirely on our side of the border, black blood from the fallen nearmen lingered. And an outpost we had withdrawn from, on your side of the border, was destroyed."

"I give you my assurance that this is not our doing. We are seeking answers, and we shall share them as soon as we have anything. Tell me, is there anything else unexplained that you can share?"

"Minor events. Unconfirmed. In the Southern Wastes, a traveling merchant who had died six years ago was spotted. The owner of a small rakka plantation believed some sort of wild brute armed with a scythe was attempting to enter his home, but it vanished without a trace. A harvest celebration briefly coalesced and vanished in a field outside the capital."

"No one has been hurt yet… Good. I will be instructing any and all of my soldiers to withdraw from any ground that was hotly contested during the war. It is my advice that Tressor do the same. You have my word as a sovereign that I have ordered my troops to stand down."

"I will deliver the message personally. You should be made aware that Dragon Riders have been dispatched to keep watch over the border."

"I will do my best to ensure Vulcrest and Ulvard clear the border as well. I will *not* see hostilities begin again."

#

Some hours later, Desmeres felt a measure more like himself. A hearty meal of bread and stew filled his belly. He'd washed way the grime of the cave, and a few moments with a gaggle of white mages had taken care of his minor injuries. In that time, he observed what had become of his old home. In most ways, it was staggeringly unchanged. The faces in Warrior's Side were new, but with the lingering familiarity that suggested they were the children of people he'd known. He'd nearly forgotten how thriving and varied this place was. The air buzzed with fairies. Stout dwarves and lithe elves walked the village in roughly equal numbers. But there were some differences. And chief among them was the preponderance of apprentices. A gray-clad young dwarf woman came to the door.

"Desmeres Lumineblade?" she asked. "The newcomer?"

"Not new, but recently returned," he corrected.

"The elder will see you now. We have gathered the masters, as you have requested."

"So quickly?"

"Yes. We've been expecting newcomers for some time now," she said. "My name is Grimma Shattershale, by the way. Gray apprentice." She led the way.

"Why, may I ask, have you been expecting newcomers?"

"There have been some events here. The elder will inform you of them, no doubt. But suffice to say, we have a vague awareness of some events of tremendous importance that have transpired in the world beyond the mountain, and thus the conclusion of the Perpetual War. It would stand to reason that the absence of war would mean renewed interest in the Cave of the Beast."

"The people of the three kingdoms have got their hands full untying themselves after the war. I suspect they'll need another few years to sort themselves out. And that's assuming something truly horrific hasn't been happening since I entered the cave."

"Is that a possibility?"

"If Deacon found whom I think he found, it may be an inevitability."

The elder's hut loomed ahead, and from the look of the audience that had assembled, the village was expecting something significant to come of this meeting. Wizards and warriors alike had assembled around the circular courtyard with the hut at its center. They kept the courtyard itself clear. As a former resident, Desmeres didn't need to be told why. The highest masters tended to punctuate their points of view rather energetically with whatever mystic flourish they found appropriate. It could be harrowing for those too close or unprepared.

Grimma remained at the edge of the courtyard as he approached the door. If Desmeres had been a mystic, he would have been humbled and awed by those waiting for him within the hut. He was barely a novice in the world of magic, and he could feel the hairs on his arm stand up in the presence of such potent wizards.

A dragon, barely the size of a large dog, stood in stately judgment. He was draped in a charred red sash. He, at least, was familiar to Desmeres from his time here. It was Solomon. Beside him, a yellow-robed fairy fluttered with crossed arms and a smug expression. If she had been the wind master when Desmeres was last here, he didn't remember her. The blue-robed woman beside her could have been confused for a human, but something in the flow of her hair and the shimmer of her skin and leggings suggested her present form was not her natural one. Desmeres very much suspected she was a creature of the sea. The dwarven earth master gave Desmeres a particularly harsh look, but all looked to the elder to begin the proceedings.

The stately woman with wizened features gazed upon Desmeres from her chair. It was too simple to be called a throne, but the air of dignity and wisdom of the elder herself elevated it to her station. She measured Desmeres, thin lips turned down in a subtle frown.

"Desmeres Lumineblade. Welcome home," she said.

"Thank you," he said.

"As I recall, you were already quite adept at your chosen specialty." She turned aside to an attentive young man at her right hand. "Has he achieved full mastery?"

He consulted a heavy book. "Full mastery in weaponcraft. But not highest mastery. That title was in contention between Croyden Lumineblade, Gurk, and Mrun."

"I see. Desmeres, then I have the bittersweet task of informing you that your presence here permits you to contend for the position of highest master of weaponcraft, as your father has, regrettably, passed on."

"Has he…" Desmeres's expression dropped.

He put his false hand to his chest. His relationship with his father had never been a warm one. Few of those raised in Entwell had strong bonds with their birth parents. The village as a whole raised each child. The first master a child apprenticed to was often the greatest parental figure in an Entwellian's life. Even given the fact that Croyden Lumineblade *was* the master Desmeres had apprenticed under, the older elf hadn't entered his mind in years. Croyden's most lasting impression upon his son had been the fact that Desmeres's illegitimate son shared the same name. But Desmeres had elven lineage. He'd known from birth that he would outlive most of those he knew. It had a way of tempering one's attachments to those more mortal than he, while at the same time placing the immortal family and friends at a separate level. He'd convinced himself his father would always be there, somewhere, ready to resume their relationship should their paths cross again.

It struck him in that moment that his mother was certainly gone as well. He was over a hundred years old, and she was only human. The new faces he'd seen in the town flickered through is mind, finally hitting home as those who had taken the places of people he had known. The cold, hollow feeling of loss must have shown on his face, as when the elder spoke next, it was with the rare tone of compassion rather than a decree.

"If you need some time, we can reconvene," the elder said.

He shut his eyes. "No… No, I came here for a reason. And though that reason may have changed, it is no less important."

"Admirable devotion to a cause. Precisely what we would hope to instill in our people. You stand in the presence of the highest masters of their respective magics. Ayna for Wind, Calypso for Water, Cresh for Earth, Solomon for Stone, and Vedesto for White. What do you wish to ask of us, and what do you wish us to know?"

"What do you know of the outside world in the years since Myranda Celeste came and went?"

"The great event of our era has come and gone. The convergence of the Chosen. The end of the Perpetual War," the elder said.

"Yes. We learned that the war was the work of a race of creatures called the D'Karon. The Chosen united and pushed them back, thanks in no small part to the help of Deacon."

The fairy wizard scoffed. "Don't mention that name here."

"Oh hush," the woman beside her scolded. "You heard the man. He helped save the world. With the devotion he showed Myranda, I knew he would be invaluable to her. Tell me, Desmeres, did he remain with her?"

"They are married and have a child," Desmeres said.

The mermaid swooned. "*Oh!* I knew it! They were a *perfect* couple. Tell me, what is the child's name?"

"Master Calypso, I imagine Desmeres has more pressing news than that to deliver. You can wait until he has spoken," the elder said.

"How such a childish mind could have risen to highest master of water magic is beyond me," the fairy muttered.

"It is called having a heart, Ayna. And don't pretend you haven't got one." Calypso turned to Desmeres. "My apologies, continue."

Desmeres took a moment to gather his thoughts. "This will take some time to properly explain."

#

For the better part of an hour, the masters and the elder listened as Desmeres attempted to summarize the most significant years in the world's history. He spoke of Lain's death, of Deacon's affliction. He described the means the D'Karon used, and the legacy they had left. Bit by bit he traced out the terrible danger each of the D'Karon generals represented. Most of all, he told of Epidime.

"He inhabits the bodies of hosts. Few are powerful enough to resist him. When he takes a host, their mind is open to him. He is cruel, unfeeling, and he has an unquenchable thirst for knowledge. He feeds his curiosity through any means available with little regard for consequences for any but himself. He is aware of this place, and there is nothing he wants more than to reach it. I lost my hand in my attempts to trap him in the Cave of the Beast. When Myranda finally convinced Deacon that he should return here to treat his affliction, they came to me in hopes that I could guide the ailing wizard through the cave. I agreed, precisely to ensure he would not stumble upon Epidime. While I slept, he wandered off. I do not know for certain, but I believe he may have crossed paths with the D'Karon. If he did, I fear for the safety of this world. We need to find a way to contact those beyond this place and send help."

"This is precisely the sort of action such an impulsive, impetuous young wizard would take," Ayna raved.

"He left us without notice. Without time enough to replace him with a gray wizard of equal skill," Cresh said in his own gruff language. "Gray magic is a lesser magic, but isn't without its use, and we've had to rebuild ourselves from his incomplete writings."

"But he did it to save the life of a Chosen One! And to aid in the defense of the world," Calypso defended.

"He attempted to interfere in the prophecy," Ayna said.

"He took his place in the prophecy," Solomon rumbled.

"He had no respect for the prophecy! Let us not forget, he was already deprived of apprentices after compelling Hollow to speak while no one else was present," Ayna said.

"Who but someone with a place in the prophecy could compel Hollow to speak?" Solomon countered.

"That is not for us to say," Cresh said.

103

"No, but if there is anyone among us who has insight into such a matter, it is Hollow, and he spoke for Deacon."

The voices and tempers were beginning to rise. Desmeres didn't need to be told what to do. He'd witnessed some of the more animated "discussions" that the wizards had gotten into during his youth.

He slipped outside and headed for the edge of the courtyard. Vedesto followed. Either he lacked the passion for the subject at hand that motivated the others to debate it so vigorously or he was not compelled to impress the others with a showcase of his craft. Things continued to get more heated as Desmeres reached what seemed to be a safe distance. Coiling flashes of light colored what little of the interior he could see through the open door. Shouting voices in a half-dozen languages firmly established conflicting points of view. Desmeres took his place beside Grimma behind a piece of cover. Like many of the apprentices, she was taking notes and listening intently to the shouting voices.

"Very impressive," she remarked, as though the shuddering walls of the hut and the wailing wind were of little concern. "You knew Deacon?"

"Well enough," Desmeres replied.

The ground beneath their feet trembled.

"I was not lucky enough to be in a position to apprentice under him before he left. I hope to become a gray master. In his absence, that would make me the highest gray master. Without a dedicated master to apprentice under, it will take a number of years of learning strictly from books before I can even begin to learn the lessons Deacon added to our knowledge, and they are voluminous."

"I imagine it was disruptive to lose him."

"Particularly due to the fact that he hadn't finished transcribing Gilliam's teachings."

A spire of stone splintered the edge of the hut. It eagerly fanned to flame in the screaming wind. Grimma simply raised her voice.

"He included some of his assessments, notions, and clarifications on Gilliam's teachings, you know. He is a visionary."

"Too smart for his own good, it would appear."

"*Enough!*" barked the elder, his voice carrying with supernatural strength and clarity.

The elements themselves heeded the command. Wind died away. Stones sank back into the earth. Fragments of earth and splinters of wood rose into the air and found their way, piece by piece, back from whence they came. In the silence, as if the tumult had been ended specifically so that the village would be able to hear it, the distant hiss of falling water resumed.

"Desmeres, enter," the elder called.

"Good luck!" Grimma called as Desmeres hurried back to the hut.

The final bits of char were healing from the walls as he stepped through the doorway. The brief but intense debate had left the wizards somewhat disheveled but none the worse for wear.

"We have considered the circumstances. While Deacon's affliction is a result of his own violations, we do not feel as though he should be left to wither. Were he to have made the journey with you, of course he would have been treated. He would have been assessed, and were he found to be of sound mind, we would have allowed him to resume his role among us."

"Against my protest," Ayna remarked.

"If you can be taken at your word, we similarly acknowledge the very real threat that could be posed by Deacon if he were to be subverted by Epidime. And the whispers of magic that we have felt through the mountain carry the intensity and aspect of things you have described. However, the falls have begun, and more to the point, the falls were due to begin within hours of your arrival regardless of your claim. There is no reasonable, expedient, or safe means for us to send anyone to render aid until they relent several months from now. You are free to request the expertise of any and all of our residents in devising a means to communicate with those beyond Entwell in the meantime. When the falls next relent, we will call upon our residents for volunteers to leave Entwell and render aid."

"A great deal of damage can be done in a few months."

"Perhaps so, but until we devise a method of communicating with those beyond the mountains, we cannot be certain Deacon has even been subverted. In the absence of a certain threat, I will not ask our people to risk their lives."

"Deacon uses pads to communicate. He had intended to bring one here to keep in contact with Myranda and his son. Unfortunately, it was in his pack, not mine. Could such a pad be created here?"

"Perhaps. It would require a level of gray mastery that he took with him. You are welcome to pursue such a solution, but it is likely that linking it to the other pads will not be a trivial challenge."

"Surely Azriel would have some insight."

"Azriel may have some insight, but she has chosen to withdraw from her active roles in Entwell for an indefinite amount of time of her choosing. As our founder, her centuries of service have more than earned her that right, and we grant her the solitude she has requested."

"Surely under the circumstances she could be disturbed," Desmeres said.

The wizards, who had centuries of mystic experience and unfathomable power among them, collectively shuddered at the prospect.

"You are welcome to attempt to do so," the elder said. "But if Azriel does not wish to have visitors, she will not have visitors."

"Then I suppose that creature who scrabbled out of the cave with me has been banished from the arena?"

"Ah… yes… The *creature*. I note its absence in your account."

"I do not know precisely what it is. I encountered it in the cave, and it seemed quite motivated by the prospect of being taken to Azriel. It didn't react to the Mark of the Chosen, so I supposed it was safe to bring here. Not that I would have had much of a choice, as the blasted thing pieces itself back together as though death is an afterthought."

"I see. Well, the beast hasn't left the arena, but that by no means implies it was well received." The elder looked to the doorway. "Ah. White Master Vedesto has returned."

Vedesto marched briskly through the doorway. "I wish to address the matter of your missing hand and its potential restoration."

"Why wait until now?" Desmeres asked.

"I consider it unwise to administer healing *before* a debate of this sort, as there are frequently a number of injured parties afterward. To heal someone beforehand is a pointless duplication of effort."

"I note the black master was absent as well."

"We are presently without a master of black magic, for similar reasons."

"Are we through, Master Desmeres?" the elder asked.

"Until I seek an audience with Azriel, I imagine so."

"Then I bid you peace. Though I leave you with a bit of advice, as one who has never had to face our arch mage. Wait until your hand is restored. It is best not to do business with Azriel, particularly against her wishes, if you are not fully recovered."

Desmeres turned to Vedesto, who held a milky-white gem over the false hand. "Are you confident I can be given a flesh-and-bone hand again?"

"In time," Vedesto said.

"How long will it take?"

"If you follow my instructions, and we do so properly? Three weeks."

"That will be a very long three weeks if Deacon is compromised."

"Then you are welcome to ignore my advice," the elder said. "But I do not imagine it will be of any benefit to you or anyone else to upset Azriel."

Desmeres scanned the faces of the wizards. He'd faced some terrible things in his life, and in general he did so *far* better equipped than he was now. Perhaps, regardless of duty, discretion was the better part of valor.

"I suppose we'd best begin the treatments, then," he said.

"A wise decision," Vedesto said. "This way."

Desmeres paced beside the white wizard. "And to think," he mused. "I remembered this place as safer and more civilized than the outside world."

"Proof that you have been away for far too long," Vedesto replied.

#

A few minutes later, Desmeres was in his hut, reclining on his bed while Vedesto and a small contingent of the same white wizards who had seen to his lesser injuries investigated the unusual condition of this newcomer. The white master spoke about Desmeres, rather than to him. It couldn't be more clear that the half-elf was less a patient and more the subject of a lecture.

"The prosthetic is animated utilizing simple levitation and manipulation magics. It is fueled through runic bindings, here and here, that draw upon the spirit of the attached individual."

"I wonder if perhaps you could refer to me as something more significant than 'the attached individual,'" Desmeres said. "I would have greater confidence in this entire enterprise if you at least maintained the illusion that you saw me as a living, breathing being."

"Of course you are a living, breathing being, Master Desmeres. As white wizards, your status as living and breathing is a precondition to our success. Now if you would excuse me, this will go a good deal more swiftly if you refrain from interrupting."

"My apologies. Please, continue," Desmeres said.

"Thank you. You will find that the cut is exceedingly clean, rare for a weapon of war."

"It was one of mine, and thus the clean cut is hardly surprising," Desmeres said.

Vedesto gave him a look that neatly emphasized the previous request for discontinued interruptions with little more than a twitch of his eyebrow.

"I'll leave you to your work."

Desmeres sat in silence as the finer points of removing his false hand, crafting a new hand, and affixing it to his arm were laid out with worrisome dispassion. As the apprentice white wizards parroted back Vedesto's teachings to prove they were listening, Desmeres noticed a familiar face waiting patiently at his door. It was the highest master of water magic, Calypso.

Vedesto gave the land-bound mermaid a look that delivered a characteristically dense amount of warning and meaning.

"When you are finished, Vedesto. I wouldn't dream of interrupting," she said sweetly.

"As it happens, you have timed your visit well. I am through here. For the day, at least."

"Lovely!" she said, stepping aside for him to leave.

Desmeres sat up in his bed. "Highest Master," he said with a nod of deference.

"Calypso is entirely sufficient, I assure you. I wished to thank you personally for braving the Cave of the Beast on behalf of Deacon. He is a dear friend."

"You are very welcome, though I would prefer not to claim that it was exclusively for that reason. I do need a hand, and there were a number of regrettable actions in my past that could stand to be redeemed. I noticed you were one of only two voices to speak unambiguously in favor of Deacon."

"As I said, he is a dear friend." She smiled and leaned a bit closer. "I take no small bit of pride in having nudged him and Myranda together. They were made for each other, don't you think?"

"They are a fine couple. Your words must have been particularly compelling, in light of the largely positive ruling of the elder."

"She is far softer of heart than she would have you believe. And it helps that righteousness was on my side. But I don't want to waste your time with idle chatter." She paused. "That is utterly untrue. I would *dearly* love to engage in a great deal of idle chatter, as few in this place seem to appreciate a good bit of conversation. Unfortunately, as you've impressed upon my colleagues, time is of the essence."

"That it most certainly is."

"You were originally of Warrior's Side, am I correct?"

"Yes."

"As a full master, you must have had *some* degree of mystic training."

"Runes and potions."

"Ah, I see. Nothing that would have required a test from Azriel."

"The popular opinion is that I should be thanking my lucky stars for having escaped her scrutiny."

"It isn't an exaggeration to say that passing my final test for full mastery was one of the more harrowing moments of my life. And I am one of the few people who navigated the Cave of the Beast by way of the sea. I understand the dry portions of the cave are largely free of wildlife. Not so of the portions dipping down into the water." She hugged herself. "Try attempting to piece together an air-for-water spell in a cave that is actively attempting to unravel your magic while the tunnel is draining away what little water is left to breathe, only to discover a great eel is sharing the tiny pool you're huddled in."

"And facing Azriel was worse than that."

"Considerably."

"Why?"

"Because the cave, the water, and the eel had to obey the rules of reality, and Azriel does not. Worse, within the crystal arena, I was intellectually aware that there was nothing she was capable of that I was not, and yet she was still able to make a plaything of me at her whim. She is a being of terrifying knowledge, an astoundingly swift thinker, and she does not allow anything to get between herself and her task, up to and including the death of her student."

"… I see."

"Her recent desire for privacy is responsible for a significant influx of Warrior's Side students pursuing serious mystic studies. The simple promise of not having to face her to reach full mastery of mystic arts has been quite compelling. I say all of this so that you will not underestimate the gravity of the following statement. I am willing to accompany you to seek council from Azriel. Even knowing she has specifically requested solitude."

"Really?"

"Really. And as soon as possible. I am not confident I'll be able to overrule my better judgment for much longer."

He stood. "So be it. It is probably best I move quickly, before Vedesto attempts to stop me or my own good judgment speaks up."

The pair trotted toward the western side of the village, along the mountains.

"I should confess," Calypso said. "Like you, I am not being perfectly selfless in this act."

"What else could be motivating enough to face Azriel when the others wouldn't?"

"She is acting very strangely, and I'm keen to find out the reason. More specifically, I am keen to find out the reason *before* Ayna does."

"Do you have a rivalry?"

"She certainly thinks so. She has found a way to cultivate a universal rivalry with everyone in Wizard's Side. I delight in finding ways to infuriate her."

"That seems awfully childish."

"I've got to have my fun *some* way. And if you'd spent any time with Ayna, you'd know she can stand to be tugged down from the pedestal she's placed herself on. Don't look a gift horse in the mouth. It's earned you a chaperone, hasn't it?"

"Trust me. These last few years have taught me not to take any bit of good fortune for granted."

#

Calypso and Desmeres approached the edge of the crystal arena. It felt odd to Desmeres that he'd never, in the thirty years he'd called this place home, been this close to the arena. The place was a natural wonder that had

109

been made all the more wondrous by the careful work of dozens of arcane artisans over the years. A large ice-smooth expanse of focusing stone spread out before them, easily as large as the elder's courtyard. Carved spires rose up around its edge, curving inward like fangs. In essence, it was like a massive head to a wizard's staff and had very much the same effect for those within its influence.

He felt the transformed mermaid beside him reach for his hand.

"Forgive me," she said, slipping her fingers into his grip. "I need to borrow just a bit of your courage."

"You don't need to do this."

"Unless you've been practicing your focus and conjuring, you'll want me with you. Are we ready?"

"From your descriptions, I'm not sure it's possible for me to *be* ready."

"Good. That's the right state of mind. Here we go."

They each took a step forward. His boot came down on the smooth crystal. Aside from an odd warmth fluttering in the back of his mind, nothing changed. He may as well have stepped onto mundane stone.

"Was something supposed to happen?" Desmeres asked.

"Yes. Something rather significant was supposed to happen. Azriel is ignoring us." Calypso tightened her lips for a moment. "This is going to be the thing that annoys her. And it is precisely why I had to come along."

She squeezed his hand a bit more firmly. "Hold tight now, and don't worry about holding your breath. You won't need to."

"Why would I have to hold—"

The end of his sentence was lost in a heart-stopping torrent of cool, clear water. It curled around them like a whirlpool in reverse, spiraling up from the center of the arena and swiftly consuming the pair. He'd expected it to hit him like a hammer to the chest. It did not. Instead, when the water reached him, it obligingly slowed, drifting gently but swiftly up along his body until he was wholly immersed. He blinked and tried to focus through the swirling water. The solid ground beneath his feet dropped away, and he was drifting in a sudden sea that had formed around them. The village was gone, replaced by an endless midnight-blue void of fresh water. He looked to his chaperone. There was a look of trepidation on her face, and her legs had been replaced with a glittering emerald tail.

"You can speak, Desmeres. It's only water for the purposes of locomotion. If I'm going to be knocking on Azriel's door, I'm going to do it in my natural habitat."

"You could have warned me," Desmeres said.

She tugged a little harder and thrust her tail, dragging him downward.

"I did warn you. I told you to hold tight. Now come. Azriel will be down here."

"How do you know where she will be?"

"Because when I envisioned this sea and brought it to reality, that's where I put the door to her cottage. Remember, in the arena, reality is clay to be shaped by the prepared mind. And whoever has the greatest capacity for concentration has the greatest influence."

She swam down and down, dragging Desmeres behind her. A sandy sea floor rose up out of the void. She skimmed along it, eyes searching.

"She's started paying attention to us," Calypso said. "The hut isn't where it should be. That means she's moved it. Do me a favor. Shut your eyes and try to envision a comfortable country cottage ahead of us. Just out of sight."

Desmeres did as he was told. Any explanation would draw upon magical techniques he'd barely understood seventy years ago and had long ago discarded.

"Good… Good… That will do. Yes. Here it is."

He opened his eyes. The precise cottage he'd envisioned wavered in the distance before them. Despite the fact that they were now swimming toward it with all the speed Calypso could muster, it didn't seem to be getting any closer.

"Just the door now. The door is all we need. Focus on the door," Calypso instructed.

Desmeres squinted at the door and tried to hold it in his mind. The rest of the cottage blurred, as if somehow sinking into a haze that hadn't claimed the door. They gradually drew closer. The door didn't seem to be retreating, but it managed to remain just beyond their reach for nearly a minute. Finally, they reached it. The door was stationary before them and, aside from existing in the absence of the rest of the cottage, it was entirely mundane. Calypso pivoted and fluttered her tail to bring them to a stop before they could collide with it.

"Knock," Calypso said.

He nodded and held up his false hand to do as she instructed.

"You, Calypso?"

The voice came from behind them. The mermaid swept them in a circle to find a woman of advanced but uncertain age standing before them. Her black robe rigidly refused to billow in the water. To look upon her, one would suppose she was on dry land while both Desmeres and Calypso were at the bottom of the sea.

"I thought I had made it clear I did not wish to be disturbed," she said. "I am quite certain it was only a few days ago that I left instructions with

Solomon after his hunting trip.”

“You have been undisturbed for two years, Arch Mage Azriel.”

“Two years, you say?” The duration puzzled her a bit but didn’t seem to be troubling. “Even so. I have much to do, I don’t have time for matters such as these.”

A half-heard sound echoed around them. It was just at the edge of hearing, more of an animal’s call than anything resembling a language. Azriel tipped her head.

“Is he, now?” Azriel replied, clearly addressing the unseen source of the sound. “Mmm… I suppose that is deserving of some degree of consideration.” She addressed Desmeres. “You are here about Epidime, correct?”

“I am. I imagine there are a dozen ways you could have learned about that, but I’m curious which it is.”

“Mott told me. He also told me you helped lead him here. He is very appreciative.”

“Mott. That would be the… *thing* from the cave.”

“Correct.”

“So those chatters and chitters *do* have meaning?”

“Certainly not. They’re simply sounds. But there are thoughts that inspire them, and the proper mind can easily interpret them. That isn’t terribly important. What is important is that you have left me in something of a quandary. There are matters worthy of discussion, but to discuss them properly would require me to abandon the very reason for my solitude.”

“Are there secrets to be kept?” Desmeres said.

“There are.”

“As it so happens, a great deal of my life has been spent honing the skills of keeping secrets.”

“Mmm… You were the one who set off to locate Lain, weren’t you?” Azriel said.

“One and the same.”

“You may well be capable of keeping the secret, then. Calypso?”

“I will treat your privacy with the utmost of discretion.”

“You are a highest master. A truth seeker. What I have hidden is something that, when I am satisfied, shall be made known to the others. But despite your assurance, I think perhaps you will be unable to hold your tongue.”

“If you wish for me to leave, I will. But I entreat you to allow me to stay. I’ve given Desmeres my word that I would act as his chaperone.”

“Far be it from me to force you to go back on your word.”

Azriel turned. The world around them turned with her. In the time it took her to pivot in place, the blue void resolved itself into a cozy, warm, dry cottage. Calypso was no longer by his side. Instead, Azriel held an open-topped glass orb in one outstretched hand. It was a bit larger than a melon, and swimming within it was Calypso, barely the size of a guppy. Azriel placed the fishbowl with its reduced occupant on a table.

"You will remain here while I have a word with Desmeres. If I decide you should be a part of the conversation, you shall join us."

Desmeres cast a look in Calypso's direction. Her arms were crossed and her expression was stern, but she gestured for him to follow without her.

The next room was larger but more dimly lit. It was a sitting room. Two large, stuffed chairs were set before a roaring fire. One chair was vacant. The other occupied. A pale hand rested on the arm, and Mott's long tail flopped off the side. A third chair wove together, rising up from the floor to complete a half circle along with the other two.

"Take a seat," Azriel instructed.

Desmeres paced to the freshly conjured chair and sat. He looked to the occupant of the middle seat. It was a terribly pale woman of a similarly advanced but similarly uncertain age. She was dressed in a simpler set of gray robes, with long black hair accented with two stark white streaks from her temples falling down past her shoulders. She had a serene look on her face and was lovingly stroking Mott under the chin. The beast may as well have been in heaven.

"So this is the boy who brought my precious Mott to me," the woman said softly. "You have my gratitude."

Mott chattered happily and coiled his tail around her leg.

"This little devil has been looking for me for ages, but he was just telling me about what he's been up to, and I suspect that is why you are here." She held out a hand. "I am Turiel, by the way. I am Azriel's younger sister."

"Turiel," Desmeres said slowly. "Yes. I believe I've heard of you. You are the reason the D'Karon came to this world. And you tried to bring them back."

"I am. Not without regrets. I was misled and I let myself be blinded to the truth." She patted Mott's neck. "In my feeble defense, I lived for centuries believing the D'Karon were saviors brought here to bring us out of the darkness. A lifetime of soul-deep belief is a difficult thing to shake."

"Thousands upon thousands of lives were lost because of you," Desmeres said. "That is indeed a very feeble defense."

"I only summoned the D'Karon here to teach me the strength to seek vengeance for Sister Dear," Turiel said. "If we are tracing blame to its root, she is closer to the source than I."

"I founded Entwell, and thus provided training for Myranda and Lain, provided aid for Myn, and facilitated the summoning of Ether. My role is inarguably on the light side of the prophecy."

"You could have sent word to me that you were unhurt," Turiel countered.

Desmeres could feel the world around him beginning to strain. The wood and stone of the cottage creaked as though a storm was whipping to life outside. Given how hostile the elder's discussion had become, it seemed wise to mediate this particular disagreement.

"It so happens the difficulty of communication to the outside is the precise reason I am here," Desmeres said. "I am told if anyone is capable of conjuring one up, now that Deacon is on the other side of the mountains, it is you."

The sisters both looked to him with a measure of irritation in their gazes, not pleased at the interruption. Turiel was the first to speak.

"This is about Deacon, isn't it?" she said. "Not just because he is the one who could most quickly work out the means of communication. You are concerned about his state of mind. As well as the population of his skull."

"Very much so."

Turiel ran her fingers through her hair and gazed into the fire. "I've had very little direct contact with Epidime, whom my little Mott here had taken it upon himself to keep locked away. There was a time that I'd hoped against hope he might, if briefly, choose me as a host. It was not to be. But I am *quite* familiar with his ways, at least with regard to the understanding the other D'Karon had of them. And I am not certain you *truly* have anything to worry about."

"Then you aren't familiar with Epidime's ways at all. He is a truly fearsome, chilling being."

"Oh, quite so. I have no doubt of it. But we are talking about the potential for *Deacon* to be taken, yes? We shouldn't assume that Epidime would do so." She put her fingers to her chin. "Or perhaps he wouldn't *need* to do so? It is difficult to articulate. You see, I crossed paths with Deacon a few times. In a very real way, I have him to thank for finally delivering me to my dear sister. And I can assure you, the boy was not well."

"We were hoping to bring him here to be cured."

"Oh, that would have been a sight to see. White wizards trying to untangle those knots." Turiel grinned at Azriel. "Always interested in preserving life, as though it were any preferable to death in the grand scheme of things."

"What does his condition have to do with Epidime?" Desmeres asked.

"Everything, I suppose. That sickness, that creeping stain on him. It would have *fascinated* Epidime. Some things are better observed from without than within. But then, Epidime is all about deep, intuitive understanding, so perhaps he *would* wish to look out from the inside? I don't know. By all accounts, he was more cautious than you might imagine. Always focused on things he or others had set in motion. But I'm babbling. I should come to a point. Epidime is concerning, yes, but you were right to be concerned about Deacon's illness. As something of an expert in matters of apocalyptic import, that is the matter that should be addressed above all else."

"Regardless of what our greatest concern is, we will need a means to contact the outside world to warn Myranda and the others," Desmeres said.

"Mmm. Azriel can speak to that more effectively than I. Were it me, I would simply suggest opening a D'Karon portal and hopping out to see to things personally. I could have sworn I felt someone zapping about with them not so long ago, but then 'not so long ago' spans years for me, nowadays. While she discusses the matter, I'd rather like to see that knife of yours."

"Why?"

"I believe I have a solution for Deacon's illness, but it requires a proper tool for applying it."

Desmeres wasn't fond of the idea of handing over his weapon to a woman who was responsible for the near death of a world twice over, but he wasn't in a very strong bargaining position at the moment. He slipped it from its sheath and handed it to Turiel. She gently nudged Mott from her lap and set the blade down in his place. While Mott yawned and clattered away to investigate the rest of the cottage, Turiel began to stir and prod at the blade. It flickered and wavered at her touch, seeming one moment to be no more substantial than a reflection in a pool of water, the next quite solid again.

"You wish to open communications to the outside world, correct?" Azriel said. "There is inarguable value in such a thing. Both in terms of delivering warnings and in collaboration. To a minor degree, there has been *some* communication already. I believe the stylus in Deacon's hut is still scratching away. Marking down his exploits and musings. But that is one-sided. And therein lies the dilemma. Within Entwell and beyond Entwell, a trained mind can see at a distance, link minds, and otherwise select a target and exchange information without very much effort at all. But these mountains will block all but the simplest or most overwhelmingly powerful spells. Deacon's stylus scratches away because the link is a simple one and was established before he left. If you *had* brought one of his pads, prepared on the outside, it likely would have functioned without difficulty. But establishing a link that didn't exist before? It would at the very least require cooperation from those on the outside. And to coordinate that cooperation, we would require the very means of communication we are seeking to create."

Turiel held the blade up to the light of the fire for a moment. "This is very nice, young man. Very nice indeed. You made this?"

"I did."

"You should be proud to have created something of this quality at such a tender young age."

"I am a century old."

"Still just a pup," Turiel cooed, setting the blade in her lap to continue her work.

"We should also consider the possibility that Deacon, if he is subverted, will be expecting this. With the amount of intrinsic difficulty in establishing a link of communication, it would require no effort at all to block or intercept said communication. If Deacon, or someone with access to his expertise, does not *want* us to communicate with the outside world, we will not. Certainly not with methods he prepared personally."

"So what would you suggest?" Desmeres asked.

"My sister's assessment of a portal is one possibility. However, given that the chaotic nature of the portal that deposited Deacon led to his current predicament, and given that the portal that delivered Turiel to me required the single most potent mystic focus in all the world as a target to bring her here safely—and even then it required some intervention on my part—I think it is safe to say we will *not* be transporting anyone. The swiftest and most certain method would be to send someone through the cave. They could bring a pad and stylus, or similar communication device of *our* creation, and thus open both a means of communication and a thread to copy for *further* communication devices to be created on your side. And whatever messenger brings the pad would be far more capable of ensuring the message is delivered, and might even be able to render aid."

"But the falls have begun."

"That isn't an insurmountable problem to solve. Merely a very challenging one."

"You should certainly send someone. And when you do, they should take this with them," Turiel said.

She handed the dagger back to him. The weapon had no outward signs of having been altered, but even Desmeres's untrained mind could sense an influence. Turiel had added an enchantment to the weapon.

"What have you done to it?" he asked.

"I have prepared it to deal with Deacon's issue."

"In what way?"

"I understand death in a way that few people do. Thus, I understand rot. And when the rot begins, there is only one thing you can do. Cut away the damaged tissue."

"You are suggesting that the proper way to cure Deacon is to kill him?"

"No. I'm telling you to cut away the part that is rotten."

"And how do you expect me to do that?"

"With that blade." Turiel turned to Azriel. "Not the brightest fellow, is he?"

Further assessment by Turiel or objection by Desmeres was interrupted by a soft clinking sound followed by a crackle and whimper.

"What is that scamp up to?" Turiel said.

Desmeres and Azriel hurried from the room. He slipped the blade into its sheath and nearly crashed into Azriel as she stood with hands on her hips at the scene playing out before her. Mott was on the table. He'd coiled his tail around the fishbowl and had two of his spidery legs clacking about, chasing the tiny Calypso. Rather than allow herself to be menaced, she'd frozen Mott's jaw shut.

"Mott!" Azriel shouted. "You are a guest here, and we do not treat ourselves to other guests."

Mott turned to her, ears and head drooping. He unwrapped himself from the bowl and clattered dejectedly to the room to seek solace with Turiel.

"My apologies, I am unaccustomed to having so many guests at once without some manner of a structured activity to occupy them," Azriel said.

She lifted the bowl and handed it to Desmeres. He tried to ignore the fact that the unfathomably powerful wizard who had escorted him here was now sulking in a container small enough for him to hold without much difficulty.

"I do hope you have found this visit fruitful. My advice is to create something in the vein of Deacon's pads here in Entwell and send it along with a messenger as soon as possible. I am confident the people of Entwell will be able to oblige, but if you prefer, I believe I can work up a procedure for their creation. It should be an engaging exercise, and I quite likely can achieve it more quickly than our current crop of gray wizards."

"That might be best."

"Excellent. Will there be anything else?"

Desmeres was tempted to take this opportunity to make his exit. Thus far he'd escaped any of her more unsettling whims, unlike Calypso. But there was a lingering point of concern. He glanced down at the bowl.

"Forgive me, just a moment more." He looked to Azriel. "And this matter is something I think you would prefer if we discussed alone. Just you and I."

"As you wish."

The bowl in his hands became somewhat heavier. He glanced down to discover that what had once been a bowl of water was now a perfectly round orb of solid glass with Calypso's tiny form frozen in the center like an insect in amber. When he looked up, he found the door to the adjoining room had vanished.

"What did you wish to discuss?"

He spoke quickly. Though he imagined whatever Calypso was experiencing at the moment wasn't life-threatening, he very much doubted it was pleasant.

"There is the matter of your sister. What is to become of her?" he asked. "By many measures, she has the bloodiest hands in our world's history. To spend the rest of her days pleasantly chatting with her sister in a cottage tucked away from the world hardly seems fitting."

Azriel shut her eyes and crossed her arms. "She has much to answer for. I am neither inclined, nor qualified, to judge her or to absolve her. If she can be redeemed, it will be a long road. But it is a road that should be taken. Justice will be served, and my affection for her should not shield her from the consequences of her actions. But my sister and I have been apart for many years. Forgive my selfishness, but I wanted some time with her before whatever must be done is done. For this reason, I am trusting you to keep her presence here a secret. And I believe I can trust you in that."

She tapped his head. "Just by coming here, you give me a far clearer view of your nature than you might realize. You are not trustworthy, but in this, you can be trusted." She tapped the glass orb. "Calypso, not so. Too much curiosity, too much duty. Does that satisfy you?"

"It doesn't satisfy me in the slightest, but it answers my question."

"Quite understood. Give me a day or so and you can send someone in to collect the proper spell to create one of Deacon's pads, or something suitably similar. Until then, I bid you farewell."

Her final words were still reverberating through the air when Desmeres suddenly and startlingly found himself standing on the glassy surface of the crystal arena once more. The orb had vanished from his grip, replaced with the fishtailed form of his mermaid chaperone cradled in his arms. The sudden weight of a full-sized mermaid sent them both toppling to the ground. Calypso untangled herself from him. A gasping breath and a few hasty spells later, she crawled from atop him with a fresh pair of legs and helped him to his feet.

"I swear she is harder on wizards than warriors," Calypso said shakily as she tugged him from the surface of the arena. "It is a sign of respect, but it is difficult to embrace it when you are dodging the jaws of a massive abomination while on display like a pet. Do we have a solution?"

"I'll fill you in with what I can, but I certainly hope time isn't of the essence, because it seems the only way we are getting word to the outside world is via an old-fashioned messenger."

"I see. That… that is disappointing. But still, we mustn't give up. Life isn't life without some worthwhile challenges."

# Chapter 7

Ivy plucked the strings of her violin with her claws. It had been her hope that she could get Leo to keep some sort of beat with the drum she'd given him. Alas, his enthusiasm could not be contained by the structure of any normal song. Ivy decided to simply fill the space between beats with the best approximation she could muster of a pizzicato tune that might accompany such a din. It served the purpose of keeping Leo distracted. In many ways, this made Ivy the most successful at her assigned task.

Myranda had returned from the front. The stream of messages had slowed considerably, though what messages did come through told tales of gradually more worrisome events. This at least provided enough of a gap in the flow of information for Myranda to jot down her own message informing them of the developments at the front. Since then, she'd been doing her best to make sense of what the events might have in common. She and several scribes had worked their way through the information, and now she was making use of a room in the palace she'd unsuccessfully attempted to avoid having rebuilt. The war room.

Freshly painted lines and labels separated a large table into a map of the three kingdoms and Tressor. Troop markers had been repurposed to label the locations of the unexplained events. Now, while Ivy and Leo filled the air with their cacophony, Myranda attempted to find patterns.

"Is this noise a problem?" Ivy asked. "It's the only thing that keeps little Leo from calling for Deacon."

"Ivy, if you ever have a child, and I hope that you do, you will learn just how effectively a parent's mind can inure itself to a racket."

A gust of wind threatened to knock the latest markers from their place. Ether stepped into the room a moment later.

"What have you found?" Myranda asked without taking her eyes from the map.

"As with the last three events you sent me to investigate, I found no trace to physically or mystically imply something had occurred. It is clear to me that most of these reports are due to imagination and panic."

Myranda plucked a marker from the map and set it aside.

"However, as I returned, I spotted another. In the Rachis Mountains, the mausoleums where the black carriages left their cargo."

Ivy shivered. "The place where the dead came back to life. We just read through that part of Deacon's account."

"It was that precise event, save one significant difference. We weren't there. The ruined husks rose. The great stone structures fell. Every attack I had hurled that day landed, I simply wasn't there to throw it. And before the battle could come to the same end as it did the first time, it all vanished, returned to the stone rubble we left behind."

"So the events are still brief. That is a small mercy. I suppose it is good news that there aren't echoes of *us* included. This is troubling enough without the appearance that we are actively engaged in such matters," Myranda said.

"It further illustrates that what we are seeing are not perfect recurrences. It is not truly a moment of another time, but some sort of living memory."

"A living memory that can open the same scars as the original moment." Myranda rubbed her eyes. "Tell me you see something I don't."

Ether looked over the table. "It all appears random to me," she said.

"Why in the name of the gods did this have to occur at a time when Deacon isn't here? He would have been giddy with delight attempting to solve this riddle." She looked to Ivy. "Have you tried the pad recently?"

"I wrote him letters in the big pad. And Leo scribbled."

Myranda gazed at the map. "... Perhaps there's too much information..." She turned to her scribes. "Is there anything remaining that we cannot confirm?"

They consulted the copious notes and, using hooked sticks, plucked away a handful of the markers. Only seven markers remained. Myranda darted her eyes across them.

"Castle Verril. Kenvard Palace. Bydell... I know these other places. There. That is where I rescued you from where the D'Karon were holding you. And that is where we found Ivy. If we include the sighting of the white wall, that was where Lain fell... They're all beginnings and endings for us."

"But what of Wolloff's tower? You've swept items from the map based on arbitrary criteria. You are seeing patterns where you wish to see patterns."

"Perhaps. But without anything more useful to draw upon, I can at least test if the pattern holds."

She raised her hand to will a handful of white markers into the air. One by one she dropped them down in all the places she recalled significant wins or losses during their journey through the Northern Alliance in the final days of the D'Karon. Several landed beside the remaining markers. One of them was alone. It was a small lake quite far from any cities.

"The place where we lost Myn," Myranda said. "It is too far from a city to have been easily observed. Ether, I want you to go there. If you find evidence that that horrid day has played itself out again, let me know. If not, remain there for a time. As useful as it would be to know that we've worked out a proper pattern, it would be far more useful to discover we were able to predict an event."

"As you wish," Ether said. She whisked into her wind form again and slipped away.

"Wow," Ivy remarked. "She must really be as baffled as we are. She did what you asked without even dismissing it as a waste of her time." The malthrope looked to Leo. "Now I'm worried…"

#

Desmeres paced toward the lake near the oceanside cliffs at the eastern edge of Entwell. Following the latest somewhat uneventful treatment from Vedesto, he'd returned to his quarters to find a note from Calypso requesting his presence there. For lack of a proper method to get her attention, he crouched by the lakeside and selected a smooth stone. A practiced motion sent the stone skipping across the surface. He watched the little ringlets produced by the stone ripple in ever-expanding circles across the lake's surface. When they'd nearly died away, and Desmeres was considering selecting a second stone, a new ripple appeared. It was wedge-shaped and moved toward him with purpose. Calypso broke the surface of the water and came to a stop just beyond the shore.

"Excellent! You're through already. Come! I think I have something," she said.

"Come? You wish me to join you in the lake?"

"Don't dawdle," she snapped.

She turned her back on him and motioned with her hand. He interpreted it as a beckoning motion for him to follow into the water—something he had no intention of doing. As it turned out, the motion wasn't intended for him, but for the water itself. A swell of crystal-clear lake water lurched past the bounds of the shore and drenched him. As it washed back into the lake, it dragged him along, plunging him into the water. Unlike when the water had swept upon him in the crystal arena, this was in no way illusory. He was actually dragged beneath the surface, blinking to focus his eyes and fighting to hold his breath. Calypso took him by his false hand and dragged him downward. As she swam, she gushed with words, far too excited to share her thinking to wait for him to reply.

"I've been waiting for you. Frankly, you are the only one I can discuss this with, at least for now. I've been puzzling over our little problem. I think I *may* have an answer to the question of how we are going to get word to the outside in a matter of days instead of a matter of months. It's really been a

123

fascinating riddle, and the answer I've got is so simple it just *has* to be the proper answer. A proper answer is *always* the simplest one available." She glanced in his direction. "Oh, my word. Water-for-air first."

She touched the pendant around her neck with her free hand. Warmth rushed across Desmeres's body. His held breath suddenly felt wildly insufficient. He coughed out his lungful of air and, in a uniquely terrifying sensation, felt cold water pour in to replace it. A few panicked spasms shook him before he realized that what he would normally classify as drowning had instead taken the place of breathing.

"I'm told that is a bit uncomfortable for the first time. I wouldn't know. Mermaids have been doing air-for-water for so long, we tend to take our first breath of air *long* before we're making any memories. It is like learning to walk, in a way. Perhaps learning to talk would be more accurate."

They reached the strangely out-of-place hut at the bottom of the lake. It wasn't unlike the other huts of the village, save for the fact that it was entirely stone and entirely submerged. Now that the dizzying journey was over and he'd had a moment to come to terms with his aquatic adjustments, Desmeres took a moment to appreciate his surroundings. Beautiful marbled patterns of light shifted along the floor of the lake. A stunning statue of a familiar dragon joined a handful of other statues scattered around the hut.

"Make yourself comfortable," Calypso said, nudging him into the hut. "I'll try to lay it out as plain as I can. It is really *quite* simple."

She tapped a small crystal dangling from the center of the ceiling. A soft aquamarine glow illuminated the single central room.

"I'd considered all the 'obvious' options. Deacon escaped via a portal. A small but crucial issue with that tactic is that it is in violation of our ways. I say this is small because things change, and they should change. It is entirely possible that if presented in a logical and dispassionate light, the elder would give her blessing for such a thing. There remains, however, the more substantial problem, and that is that no one here but Azriel is likely to be able to achieve the desired effect. Even she required aid, and I am quite certain if she had been willing to perform that task, we would not be having this discussion. So we move on. Is there a way to leave this place other than the cave?"

She swirled the water. Crystals began to form, and slowly an icy replica of Entwell formed before her. "You once called this place home," she said. "Have you ever found yourself in the discussion about its isolation?"

Desmeres experimentally tested his voice, now that he was breathing water, and found it to be operational, albeit with a bit more effort.

"I was somewhat single-minded in my time here."

"As many tend to be, but among wizards it is frequently a matter of debate as to whether Entwell was *created* specifically for isolation. In looking into this, I have become quite convinced that it is straining the bounds of the imagination to suggest that it is not a place crafted precisely for the purpose of giving people a sheltered harbor from the rest of the world. The cave, we have established, is complex and floods regularly. Even the mechanism of the flood is downright baffling. Then there is the fact that the mountain has a confounding effect of mystic focus. Then there is the matter of going *over* the mountain. To date, only the Great Elemental has succeeded. I believe you called her Ether? Lovely name. Perfectly suited. But the same horrid convolution of mystic focus combined with biting cold and astounding winds make passing over the mountain nearly impossible. The oceanside cliff has the same problem and leads to a sea that could chew the best of boats to splinters. Thus, there is no benefit in speed or safety in facing the mountain or cliff. The cave remains the best option. And that is when it dawned upon me. The cave, while flooded, is *not* impassable. A would-be traveler simply needs to satisfy certain vanishingly rare criteria.

"The first, they must be capable of spending *days* completely submerged in water, and that ability must be either nonmystic in nature, the result of an intrinsic mystic quality, or the result of a spell simple enough to escape the effects of the cave. Second, they must be able to exist *outside* of water for days at a time, for similar physical or nonmystical reasons. Third, they must be able to survive the cave's hazards. And fourth, they must be able to navigate the cave. There is no single person here who satisfies all these requirements. But it is possible for us to assemble a team who could."

She put her palm to her chest. "As you might imagine, I am speaking principally of myself. I can swim the flooded cave. I arrived here in that very manner. And though it will require repeated applications and a fair amount of effort, I know from experience that the air-for-water spell *will* slip past the cave's influence. Lamentably, I will *not* be able to conjure legs for myself. Again, experimentation has proved that a shapeshift spell will unravel in moments in the cave. A shape change might work, so long as it is applied outside the cave, but doing so would strip me of the intrinsic connection to air-for-water that would allow me to survive both the flooded and dry portions of the cave. This means I will be left with my arms and tail when the time comes to make the trek through at least the last third of the cave. It won't be *pleasant*, but I am confident I could survive a few days of such travel. But this is where I fall short. The cave is still a terrible maze, and I don't know the way. I could find my way, perhaps, but I doubt I could do so reliably as a mermaid dragging herself along stone."

"You came here from the sea, did you not? Couldn't you return the way you came?"

"I could. It would be difficult, but not impossible. But it would leave me in the Crescent Sea. I would then have to travel far enough north or south to escape the mountain's influence, then climb an entire mountain. It would take ages, even with my skills, and time is of the essence."

Desmeres sighed. "I suppose, if you could cast the same spell you've cast to bring me here, I could lead you back and help you traverse the dry portion of the cave."

"But I can't. Water-for-air is a *far* more complex spell to cast on a non-mer creature. The cave would unravel it. But there *is* another group of residents here who can make the trip with my help."

"Who?"

"Fairies. A fairy alone couldn't cross the flooded portion of the cave. Not even a water fairy. But once clear, they could absolutely navigate the remainder. Most of them found their way here *precisely* because of their ability to flawlessly and efficiently navigate anyplace with an unbroken connection to the outside world, thanks to their intrinsic mystic connection to wind. And that same connection allows them to survive for *ages* without the need for fresh air. So if I could carry one in some sort of airtight container until we reached the dry portion of the cave, they could help me and direct me to the exit. Once clear, I would be able to conjure a set of legs and carry any message or equipment to Myranda or the other Chosen. It can work, Desmeres. I am certain of it."

"You would be willing to risk your life, dragging yourself through a cave like that?"

Calypso flashed a smile. "I relish the challenge! Even if it wasn't to help a friend and potentially save the world, I think it is long past time Entwell had an ambassador to the outside, and a chance to see your world is not one to be missed. I'm embarrassed I didn't take it upon myself to attempt it *ages* ago."

"But what about the fairy you need to help you? I wasn't aware they could forgo fresh air for so long, but I seem to recall they are not fond of being cooped up in small spaces."

"Heavens, no. It is torturous for them. It would take a very, very dedicated and brave fairy to willingly subject themselves to such a thing. I have precisely the one in mind. And we won't even have to ask her."

#

Later that afternoon, Calypso stood in the shade of a large tree not far from the elder's hut. Desmeres leaned against the tree with his arms crossed. Buzzing filled the air. One by one, the many fairies of Entwell flitted into the shade of the tree. Most wore yellow robes, signs of their place among the discipline of wind magic. A few blue- and red-robed fairies appeared as well. There were even a handful of fairies in simple petal-like dresses, those who had forgone training or had yet to choose a focus. All told there were fifteen fairies, nearly the entirety of Entwell's fairy population. One rather notable figure was absent.

Calypso thanked them for answering her call. She laid out the plan she'd discussed with Desmeres with her usual speed and enthusiasm. Fascination and excitement rippled through the group of fairies as she explained why they needed to leave the place. That excitement died away at the very moment she held up the accommodations for the flooded portion of their voyage.

"I know it is a great deal to ask of you, but if you are to survive the cave, you will have to be sealed inside this jar for at *least* a day. Possibly three or four."

The canister she held had been whipped up by Solomon. It was just a bit more spacious than the sort of jar that would hold preserves during the long northern winters. The sides were crystal clear, and the top was stopped with a dense black bit of cork. The fairies peeled away, one by one. The thought of being contained in such a way, sealed away from their precious wind in such a tiny space, was more than they could bear. Only three of the fairies remained when all was said and done. Two of the wind fairies and one of the fire fairies. They whistled and trilled their way through a discussion about who, if any, might be able to endure such a trial.

They'd yet to reach a conclusion when the wind around them began to whistle with a gale force. Calypso shot Desmeres a knowing grin. He shook his head.

"Unbelievable..." he muttered.

"Calypso, this is nothing short of an *outrage*," Ayna screeched, darting into the shadow of the tree. "This is precisely the sort of underhanded, condescending act that you would stoop to."

"Ayna, please. Calm down."

"Do *not* tell me to calm down. I will take this to the elder herself. You propose an unprecedented act, something that will forever etch the names of those who would achieve it into our history books, and you do not contact me? You propose a trial that *requires* a fairy, a fairy who by any measure is the *key* to the trial's success—and you do not immediately bring it to me for assessment?" The fairy pointed at the now departing fairies in yellow robes. "You *insult* me by seeking out my own underlings? Those fairies haven't even reached mastery. They haven't even earned the right to study under me, but you would allow *them* the honor of this mission rather than me?"

"You are the highest master of wind magic. You are an indispensable part of Wizard's Side," Calypso said.

"Hah! You attempt to soothe me with your praise. While this is, of course, plainly true, if you believed it, you would disqualify yourself as well."

"I am our only mermaid. I have no choice but to volunteer. But there are many fairies. You can, and should, remain."

"Enough! I forbid any but myself to have this honor. Entwell's first ambassador to the greater world? The first to traverse the Cave of the Beast in its entirety while flooded? Not to the comparatively effortless seaward opening of the cave, but to the Melorn Woods entrance? It is crime enough that I would have to share that right with you. I will *not* be passed over."

"Very well, Ayna. If you insist. I will understand if you need time to prepare."

"I can be ready within the hour. I need only a quantity of nectar or a few drops of honey. I shall collect it directly and select a master to take my place in my absence." She darted forward and poked a finger in Calypso's face. "I do not want to waste my time waiting for you, so I suggest you gather your things as well."

She darted off again. Desmeres stepped forward and leaned close to Calypso, so as to avoid being heard.

"In a lifetime of manipulating people to achieve my goals, I have never seen a creature so easily bent to one's whims," he said.

"We all have our weaknesses. And I'll tell you something. I truly believe if we'd had more time, she might have volunteered herself for the mission even without the appeal to her contrariness. I've butted heads with her endlessly over the years. She can be all the things people accuse her of, but beneath it all, she has as fine a heart as any in this place. She just takes pains to protect it." She clapped her hands. "But if you will excuse me, there is much to do. I'll need to inform my temporary replacement, I'll need to gather some supplies. There are still the Deacon pads to be created, and…"

"And there is this," Desmeres said. He tugged the sheathed blade from his belt and handed it to her.

"What is this?"

"One of the points of discussion that you were not privy to involved the precise assessment of how best to cure Deacon. Perhaps of the affliction he came here to be rid of, perhaps of Epidime's influence. This blade is it."

Calypso slipped it from the sheath. She gently touched the blade and shut her eyes. "It is heavily enchanted… I'm… I'm not familiar with one of the enchantments. It feels… necromantic in nature. You aren't suggesting Deacon be *killed*, are you?"

"I am not suggesting anything, but Azriel seemed satisfied that this weapon was a solution, and so I present it to you."

The mermaid resheathed it and clutched it tightly. "Then I shall deliver it. But let us all hope it never tastes blood."

#

They'd prepared themselves as quickly as they could. Now Calypso lingered at the base of the falls, basking in the cool mist as she prepared for the journey ahead. Ayna had yet to appear. A lesser fairy might be having second thoughts, but Calypso knew Ayna would never dare do something that would even imply weakness. She would turn up. It was just a matter of when.

Because the falls had begun, no one was on lookout at them. Calypso was alone with her tail drifting in the basin of the falls as she checked herself over.

The ways of mermaids were largely a mystery to the people on dry land. Thus, the gear she wore came as a surprise to the handful of students to whom she'd said goodbye.

This was hardly the first time a mermaid had been called upon to brave dry land and a cave without the benefit of magic. There were outfits designed specifically for such challenges. It had taken a visit to some of the other mystics, but she'd been able to assemble the proper ensemble in little time at all. In place of her artful red and blue bodice, she wore a sturdy leather chestplate. Her glorious emerald tail was hidden by an apron of sorts, belted in place along its front. That would protect her tail and torso when the time came to drag them across the stone. Stout leather mitts with metal barbs at the fingertips would give traction and protection when she was beyond the edge of the water. A strong but light stick with a curved end would help her steady and haul herself upright if she needed to, and plenty of rope would give her the means to cross gaps a creature who was nimbler on land could easily vault over. It wasn't the most elegant of garb, but simply wearing it gave Calypso the feeling of adventure and accomplishment. It had been so long since she'd left her comfort zone, she relished the opportunity to test her limits.

She pulled some cords tight on her pack. Mermaids mostly had to concern themselves with keeping things wet when they left the water, but the sealskin sack she'd bundled should do equally well at keeping the goods she was meant to deliver dry. She had everything she needed. She was ready.

"Right on time," Calypso said as a buzzing wove into the hiss of falling water.

Ayna arrived. If Calypso had been given a week to dream up how her fellow master would have chosen to equip herself for the journey, she wasn't certain she would have come close to what Ayna had chosen to bring. For as long as Calypso had known her, Ayna had dressed in one of two ways. When she was particularly dedicated to making an impression, she would wear her yellow master's robes. All other times she was almost lost inside a fancy blue and white dress that looked to have been made from flower petals. Now, Ayna was dressed in something quite different.

A tiny jacket, too expertly tailored to her size to be anything but the handiwork of someone similarly tiny, had been laced shut with tiny threads. She wore leggings made from a sort of thin but tough material, and even had little booties on her typically bare feet. She almost had the look of a rogue in her snug clothing that balanced maneuverability with stealth and protection. She carried a pack about the size of Calypso's thumb.

"Where did you get an outfit like that?" Calypso said.

"That is neither your business nor your concern. Are we prepared?"

"I believe so. Are you not bringing your focus gem?" the mermaid asked.

Ayna glanced to the glass jar beside her. "My travel accommodations will be cramped as it is. I am confident any mystic feats will be well within my power without it. If a gem is necessary, I shall make use of yours."

"Are you sure? I can carry it for you."

"That will not be necessary. Now"—she glanced to the jar again—"is there a plan?"

"Not much of one. The first bit will be tricky. As I recall, the entrance of the tunnel might have a few air pockets before we reach a solidly flooded section—particularly so soon after the falls begin. But when we are into the submerged sections, things will be smooth until we reach the dry section."

"And how long will we be submerged?"

"One or two days."

Ayna shut her eyes. "So be it."

She buzzed to the jar and dropped her bag through the mouth. After a steadying breath, she dropped down inside. Her little boots clinked against the glass. The enclosed space made the soft flutter of her wings take on an odd humming tone.

"Be swift," Ayna said, doing her best to not sound as though she were pleading.

Calypso slipped the stopper in place and eased it tight. Ayna huddled down as the jar was sealed. Face stricken, she braced her feet against the side of the glass to keep herself steady and hugged herself.

"Be swift," she murmured again.

Calypso slipped the jar securely into a netted harness and tied it to her wrist.

"Here we go. Hold tight!"

The mermaid exhaled and leaped into the churning water. Once immersed in the bracing, frigid pool, she took a deep, refreshing breath. From the first instant of being immersed, Calypso was reminded of just how invigorating a properly lively body of water was. She let the thundering current curl around her, working her powerful tail to tame it. She dove deep, pushed with her free hand off the glassy bottom of the waterfall basin, and surged up along the sloped tunnel.

Darkness descended quickly. She touched her fingers to the gem about her neck and sent a twist of magic through it to provide some light. With each rhythmic beat of her tail, the influence of the mountain grew stronger and the light grew fainter. By the time Calypso was near enough to hear the slap and ripple of water in the first air pocket, the gem was already barely as bright as a candle. No matter. Her eyes were sensitive enough to make do with that for now.

She gazed at the polished stone of the oft-flooded tunnel. It curled upon itself, dipping down. She remembered that section of the tunnel from her arrival many years ago. It was the *only* part of the journey that she remembered clearly. Assuming it hadn't changed, it would be simple enough to traverse. A smile brightened her face.

In fact, it would be *fun*.

"This is going to be a little rough, but it'll be over soon," Calypso said.

Ayna's reply was a barely audible murmur of acknowledgment. Calypso redoubled her efforts. She pumped the sealskin-wrapped tail for all it was worth. When the moment was right, she tucked the jar by her side, streamlined her body, and launched from the water.

Slick with the water as she was, her speed sent her gliding across the stone that had been scoured smooth by so many years of constant flow. She zipped along the glassy tunnel, side-to-side slaps of her tail keeping her speed up, and well-timed swipes of her clawed glove helping her maneuver. She crested the slope of the curved stone and began the rapid slide down the other side. Digging her claws in, she pivoted to take the slide tail-first, peering over her shoulder to navigate in the dim light. The journey to where the water again claimed the tunnel was a brief one. She plunked down into it, turned about, and continued her swim.

"Are you all right?" she asked, holding up the jar.

Ayna's hands had joined her boots in bracing against the glass. Her glow was bright, brighter than Calypso's own gem, and her expression was stricken.

"Easy, Ayna. Easy. It will be fine. I promise you."

"Just swim. Just swim," the fairy said.

Even muffled by a layer of glass and some rushing water, the fairy's voice had the near-shriek of unbridled anxiety. Calypso had known it would be a difficult trip for her, but it wasn't clear until this moment just how difficult it would be.

"There will be other air pockets along the way. Would it help you to be let free to recover a bit?"

Ayna looked sharply at her through the glass. "I don't need your patronizing. Just *swim*."

"I'm not trying to patronize you," Calypso said, taking a turn and holding the jar up to decide where to head next. "You are in distress. I am trying to help you."

"It won't *help*!" Ayna said.

Calypso made another turn. "Why won't it help? I know that fairies don't like to be cooped up, but I don't know *why*."

"Just swim," she rumbled.

"I can swim and talk. But if you help me understand why you're scared, maybe I can help you calm down."

"I'm not *scared*," she snapped. "You couldn't possibly understand. You aren't a fairy."

A half-dozen replies flitted across Calypso's mind as she used the anxious fairy's glow to navigate. Making the proper choices, at least in this section of the cave, was relatively simple. Water-smoothed stone had a way of betraying the direction of the water's flow. A quick scratch across the surface was enough to let her know which way the floodwaters shifted, and thus which direction the dry stretch of the cave was. But making the proper choice of how to deal with Ayna was trickier. Calypso's instinct told her to be kind, to be gentle. But she'd known Ayna long enough to know she was far more liable to shift toward anger than toward serenity. And anger was an improvement over being beside herself with stress.

"I see. I thought you were a master. A teacher. I suppose everyone has their limits when it comes to articulating complex concepts."

"Stop it."

"When this is over, if you need help in putting your notions to words, I can lend a hand."

"I know what you are doing."

"Deacon always had a way with words, perhaps he could—"

"It is *not beyond my capacity to explain*!" Ayna snapped. "I am a fairy. We *all* are children of the wind. And I am a master of wind magic, so my connection with the wind has been honed to a needle point. The wind is a part of us. We feel it like an extension of ourselves. The motion of wind is like another sense. It connects us, to each other, to the rest of the world. I am stopped up in a jar. I am cut off from the wind. I have gone from knowing my place precisely, being one with a world-spanning flow of energy, to being trapped. Isolated. And it won't matter if you let me free in a vast cavern. If it doesn't connect with the rest of the winds, it is just a bigger jar."

She shut her eyes and shuddered. "The last time I came through this cave, I was restrained like this, in the possession of scoundrels who treated me like a tool. And now I am back again. Cut off. Alone."

"Well now you're here with me. I'm not a scoundrel, and you're not alone." She held the jar up to her face. "So things are looking up."

# Chapter 8

An icy form stood like a lonely sentry on the frozen surface of a lake. At Myranda's behest, Ether had been whisking through the three kingdoms to survey the supposed sites of curious events that had plagued the world in recent days. There was little here to suggest such an event had already happened. Now she waited, senses alert, to see if one *would* occur.

There was wisdom in Myranda's request. To observe one directly, from beginning to end, could indeed provide useful insight into their nature. And though it was a stretch, the locations along the journey of the Chosen were as good an indicator as any of those sites that might suffer an attack. Before arriving here, she had taken what had become a very familiar, and very comfortable trip to Celia's home. It was important to her that the woman be safe. Her health had improved, and the place had yet to see any flicker of disturbance. With that concern set aside, Ether was free to enjoy the solitude and vigilance that had defined so much of her existence. As a statue of ice, she watched the sky.

She remembered this place every bit as well as Myranda and Myn did, though not for the same reasons. For them, this place was a black stain in their memories, a place where they very nearly lost one another. At the time, Ether had yet to have truly embraced her allies and hadn't come to see the value and essential truth of emotion. Looking back upon that moment after having experienced the sort of loss that was all too common in the life of a mortal, she almost felt a pang of guilt for her callousness over the apparent death of Myn. She had changed more since that day than she had in the thousands of years before it. She had grown as a result of her alliance, her *friendship*. She never could have predicted such a thing, and a part of her feared what might have become of her if she'd not allowed it to happen.

The moment of self-reflection was cut short as a new sensation crackled through her mind. Something was happening. She focused all her senses upon this curious new feeling. There was no hint of magic behind whatever was twisting the world around her. No will guided the change she detected, no focus aided it. This was something more basic, more fundamental. It was closer to a sudden shift in temperature than a spell or curse, just a part of the world changing in a very natural way. But it was a part Ether had never supposed could misbehave in such a way without an outside force. *Time* was shifting. The fabric of the landscape was twisting, curling and drawing together. She swept her gaze across the sky. Black forms became visible. Dragoyles. She crackled herself free from the surface of the lake and changed to flame. She'd not been thrown back in time. Her place in the world was every bit as solid and secure as it had always been. It felt more like the past had curled upon itself, overlapping the present. This warranted further experimentation.

She streaked toward one of the dragoyles. Moments before impact, she shifted from flame to stone. Her solid body tore through the stony black hide of the beast. It released a stricken squeal and plummeted to the surface of the lake. She shifted to flame again and hung in the air.

"So they are solid, and they can be attacked. Valuable information. If they can be attacked, we can defend ourselves. I have no memory, fresh or old, of my own secondary interference in the battle, so it would appear that doing so will have no impact on events that have already occurred. Valuable information as well."

She hung in the air and gazed at the swarming monsters. There was a very specific moment she was waiting for. The moment that had marked this place as a tragic memory. She knew it took place in the air above the lake, so she did not allow her eyes to waver. In time, the telltale motions began to coalesce. They swarmed and gathered about an empty patch of ground, then an empty patch of sky. The monsters were undeniably focused on something, but that thing was not visible. It simply did not exist.

"Fascinating… The dragoyles behave as though we are there. The ice breaks as though Myn's tiny form smashed through. But we are absent. Does this phenomenon only effect the D'Karon creations, perhaps?" She let her gaze shift to the field below. "Perhaps it has to do with…"

The speculation vanished from her mind as her eyes set upon a sight that seared her very soul. A figure sprinted across the snowy field. It was no dragoyle. It was no working of D'Karon magic. It was something much more important to the world. Much more important to her.

"Lain…" she breathed.

He moved precisely as she remembered. She could even feel the smoldering, restrained point of power and light his spirit traced across the world as he moved. She was trapped in the raw emotion of seeing him, living and breathing, after all this time. Then, at the edge of her consciousness, she felt the crackle of change once more.

"No… *No!*"

She streaked toward him, but already she could feel the layers of existence sliding back into place. Before she could reach the ground, he was gone. Her fiery form shuddered and trembled, fingers clawing at the air where he had been. She pulled her body together into a human form and dropped down onto the snow. At her feet, the footprints Lain had left remained in the snow. She crouched and touched her fingers to them. For a time, she let herself dwell upon the feelings the mere sight of her lost ally had stirred up in her. But she couldn't wrap herself around the pain of the old wound forever. There was work to be done in the here and now. If she was to protect the world from these events, she had to make sense of what all of this meant. She had to inform Myranda. Her job here was done.

#

Back in Kenvard, Ivy paced through the halls of the castle. In her heart, she knew that her presence here had been important. She'd kept Leo safe, kept his spirits up, and thus allowed Myranda to devote herself fully to the task at hand. But there was still the lingering sense that all of this was beyond her. She'd always had a place in the other threats to the world. She could beat back the forces of darkness if they had form. She could talk sense into minds too blinded by years of war and fear to see the value of peace. But these events felt smoky, unreal. There was nothing she could do. Myranda still struggled with what they meant, and she was one of the most clever people Ivy had ever known. If it was beyond her dear friends, it was well beyond her. At this precise moment, even her dubiously heroic role as a babysitter was uncalled for. Myranda was waiting for more information, and thus had allowed herself to take the reins of the child's care for the time being.

Ivy should have been sleeping. She'd gotten precious little rest in the days since these disturbances had begun occurring. But she couldn't bring herself to lay her head down. Her mind was too stirred up. And so she paced, waiting for either exhaustion to claim her or a useful job to present itself. Her aimless journey had taken her to the royal vault. It was interesting how a disaster could shift the priorities of an entire kingdom. On any other day, the vault would be under constant guard. As it was, every available soldier in Myranda's command had been placed on lookout and defense, lest history repeat itself in a more violent way. The vault, home to some of the kingdom's greatest treasures, paled in importance to the safety of its people.

She smiled softly, proud of her kingdom and its priorities.

The smile faded from her lips. Something wasn't right. She squinted at the space between the vault's doors. Deacon had been quite proud of them. Rather than a simple external brace or even a complex lock, these doors were braced from within. Potent enchantments were layered atop spells that Deacon himself had devised to turn away would-be thieves. But as she gazed at the entrance, she noticed two things that worried her. In the tiny crack between the heavy doors, she saw no brace. And she knew from prior trips past them that the potency of the magic was such that even her own untrained mind could detect it. But the warm, fuzzy sensation of the spells was completely absent from her mind.

She tilted her head and sniffed the air. There weren't any worrisome scents, but there was one very strong and very familiar one that seemed out of place. Ivy placed her hands against the heavy doors and threw her weight against them. They swung sluggishly open.

"What is going on?"

She slipped through the crack between the doors. The vault had no lighting of its own. It should have been completely dark. Instead, a soft amber glow, too steady to be a candle's flame, glinted off the many polished relics and heaps of coins in the vault. Ivy crept forward, muscles tense. She didn't want to raise the alarm unless she had to. The guards were elsewhere for a reason.

The first chamber of the vault was filled with the mundane treasures of the palace. There was gold enough to handle the finances, mostly freshly minted Kenvard coins. Some of the recovered gems and jewelry from the days before the Northern Alliance had formed were kept safe there as well. To the rear, a second, equally secure door led the way to the artifacts with value beyond sentiment and rarity. That door was open as well, and she could hear someone moving about inside.

Ivy charged in. "Who goes there!" she barked.

A frazzled figure turned to her. It took Ivy a beat to realize just whom she was looking at.

"*Deacon!*" she squealed.

He was dressed as he had been when he'd left for his treatment, but the outfit had seen better days. His clothes were layered with multiple shades of grime, ranging from the general haziness one accumulates from a lengthy journey along the sloppy roads of the north to the gray silt of the Cave of the Beast. His hair was ragged and unkempt. He looked like he'd had a rough few days.

Ivy didn't care. She pounced upon him, wrapping him in a tight hug.

"Deacon, I'm so glad to see you! Things have been bad. None of us knows what to make of it. I don't know if you knew about the weird events that were happening all over the place, but they're getting worse, and none of us can figure it out. All I can do is keep Leo busy and hope we untie the knots before someone gets hurt."

"It will be all right, Ivy. Myranda has it all in hand. I'm sure she does," he said softly.

Ivy took a step back. "Are you healed? That was what this was about, wasn't it? It's only been a few days. How did you even make it there and back again?"

"It is a long story, and I am sorry to say I don't have time for it right now."

"Have you seen Myranda? You've got to tell Myranda you're back. She's been trying to get in touch with you. Why didn't you answer?"

"My things are still in my pack, and my pack is still in the cave," he said.

"Then come! We'll see her now. You can help us with what we're working on, and we can help you with whatever *you're* working on." Ivy tugged his hand to lead him toward the door.

He resisted. "Ivy, please. I don't have time to explain. I need to do this myself."

"Don't tell me you don't have time to talk to your wife and see your son," she said, hauling him a bit more forcefully.

She staggered back, nearly knocking into a shelf carefully arranged with locked-up mystic artifacts. She'd not lost her grip on his hand. Her fingers had simply passed through, as though his hand was no longer there. Ivy looked down. Where Deacon's hand should have been was a strange white silhouette, something of a reversed shadow, featureless and without substance. He shut his eyes. The gem in the other hand pulsed. Flesh wove its way back down his hand, restoring it to solidity.

"Deacon... where is your ring?"

"There is too much to explain, Ivy. I promise you, this will all be over soon. I just need some more time."

Her eyes drifted to his face. A bit of desperation colored his features. Then she looked to his hair.

"Deacon, where is your *crown?* You need help. Something is wrong."

She turned to head for the vault door. Deacon raised his hand and pulsed the gem again. The door to the inner vault slammed shut, sealing them inside.

"Ivy, please, don't make me do something I'll regret," he said.

The malthrope turned to him, expression fierce.

"Did you just threaten me?"

"No. I just... it is more than I can explain. I don't even fully understand it myself. But I have found a way to ensure the D'Karon will never find their way in again. No one will. I just need to change a few things."

"If it needs to be done, we will all help you. Why would you hide it from us?"

"Because it's dangerous. And it's..." He shut his eyes tightly and twisted his head aside. "If I do it, I will know an essential truth about this world that no one has ever dreamed off. To reveal such a thing should be valuable enough to ignore the dangers. And the security in the future will offset any of the risk now."

"Deacon, there's something wrong. I can feel it. I want you to come to your senses. You are sneaking through your own palace. You've given up the things you were using to keep your hand under control."

"I needed a new perspective. A new angle. I needed to think differently. And I needed new insight as well. I needed to know what… I just needed to know. And I learned so much, so quickly. I have answers, Ivy." His hand shifted briefly, blurring to a new form and back again. "It doesn't matter, I can't ask you to understand. No one can understand. But for now, I need the affliction. I need the chaos. It is what was missing. And I need this."

He held out the crystal to a heavy wooden case in the rear of the vault. Sigils and runes etched over the box flared away, burning like tissue paper. Nails slid from their places, planks lifted away, and the contents of the box drifted free. It was a damaged sword. Deep gashes marred every surface, but despite the long, rough road the weapon had taken, its brilliance and grandeur was not subdued. It was the Sword of the Chosen, bejeweled and emblazoned with the mark. The blade remained straight and true, paired with a sheath made far more recently than the weapon itself.

Deacon didn't take the sword in hand. He willed a length of the cloth wadding from the case to wrap it tightly, such that only the strap of the sheath remained exposed.

"Deacon, put that back. That is dangerous. And only evil people ever seem to want it."

"I will return it when the job is done."

Ivy planted her feet and tightened her fists. "You will return it right now, or I will take it from you."

"Ivy, please," Deacon said, his voice pained and pleading. "You have to trust me. I don't want there to be violence."

"Then put the sword back and come see Myranda. There have been too many times I've faced people who seemed to be friends but were something else. I know Deacon better than I know almost anyone, and he would *not* raise a weapon against one of the Chosen. This is your chance to prove to me you are the man I think you are. Put. The sword. Back."

Deacon held his ground. His expression was stricken. Something inside was tugging him in a dozen different directions. Ivy watched and waited. She wanted to give him every chance to do the right thing, but she couldn't afford to let him make the first move. He turned his head, eyes sweeping across the many items in the vault. There were other weapons and armor, but also things scavenged from Kenvard's past, things of mystic or historic importance that Deacon himself had expressed a desire to gain a better understanding of when time and circumstances permitted.

When he looked back to her, there was something new in his gaze. He still looked tortured, still desperate. But now he looked less like a man worried he might have to do something he didn't want to do, and more like a man who knew he'd already done something wrong.

Ivy narrowed her eyes and made her move. She dashed toward him. If she could bash him against the wall, dizzy him, she could perhaps knock the sword or his crystal away. Her shoulder struck him, but she didn't feel any of his weight behind the blow. What appeared to be Deacon uncoiled into a web of glimmering mystic threads. They curled and wrapped about her like a sprung trap, entangling her feet and sending her to the ground.

"Ivy, I'm begging you," Deacon said, fading to visibility two steps from where he had appeared to be. "If you have ever trusted me, trust me now."

"You don't get to demand my trust when you are trying to tie me up," Ivy growled, a flare of red in her eyes. "You're not Deacon. Not the Deacon I know."

"I had to stop pushing the change away. It was happening for a reason," he said. "It was showing me that there were other ways to think. I needed *every* insight. When the job is done, I will set it aside. But I have been too sane for too long. A problem that cannot be solved by a sane mind can sometimes be solved by madness."

Ivy growled. Another surge of red aura erupted around her. The mystic bonds seared away. She clambered to her feet. "You have a *child*," she barked. "You have a wife. You have a kingdom. You are needed. Stop this, now!"

"I intend to stop it all."

Ivy knew she had to end this soon. The frustration and helplessness she'd been feeling was combining with the betrayal of seeing Deacon act this way. A temper she'd been keeping under control for years was in danger of flaring out of control. It didn't matter how powerful a wizard Deacon was, if she lost control and let the rage take her, there was every chance she would kill him. Even if something had changed him, she didn't want that to happen. If there was even a chance that this was the friend who had given her a place in his home, she didn't want to risk taking his life.

Her nostrils flared. She breathed in a whiff of the air and angled her ears. She wouldn't be fooled by another illusion. This figure before her was certainly her foe. She launched toward him again. He backed away, pressing his shuddering, shifting hand to the face of a full-length, polished silver mirror that was among the collected artifacts. He made no attempt to dodge. She struck him full force, expecting to ram him into the mirror, but instead they both tumbled forward. With him wrapped in her arms, the pair was off-balance.

They teetered for a half-dozen steps before they spilled to the ground and continued to slide.

Finally, the pair struck the far wall. Deacon wrestled free and sprang to his feet. Ivy hopped up a moment later. The room seemed wrong now. It was pitched, as if built on a slope. And the entrance was on the wrong side. *Everything* was on the wrong side. In the time it took for her to grapple with her new surroundings, Deacon rushed toward the mirror, now on the far wall. His hand chattered and jittered as he pressed it to the polished surface. The mirror rippled like quicksilver. He crouched and dove through. Ivy sprinted after him, but the moment he was clear, the ripples died away. She slammed hard into the mirror. It rattled in place, and the entirety of the room trembled with it. With a slow, ponderous slide, the view in the mirror pitched toward the ceiling. The floor tilted along with it. It felt like the entire room was tumbling along with the mirror, but only Ivy was affected. She scrabbled along the tilting floor until the slope was too much for her and she plummeted to the far wall.

Deacon appeared in the mirror again as Ivy righted herself. The frustration and confusion had pushed her to the very brink of transformation, but even in her furious state, she'd worked out the mind-bending answer to what had happened. She was in the mirror, somehow, and Deacon was outside. She watched helplessly as he reached down and grasped the frame. Again the world pitched to follow the tilt of the mirror. Deacon stood it against the wall. She charged up and beat on the surface, but it was no use. Where it had once been a door, now it was a window, simply a way to glimpse the real world while she remained in this reflected facsimile.

She pressed her hand against the surface. "Deacon, let me out of here!" she shrieked.

"I just need time. Myranda will be able to help you. I'm sorry. Please believe me, I am truly sorry. I just need time."

She hammered at the mirror, rattling her world as he backed away. She could see doubt and regret in his eyes. Deacon rummaged in his pocket and revealed a freshly minted coin. It was different from those that littered the floor. It had a weight, an aura that made it seem somehow more substantial. With eyes shut, he gripped the coin tightly in his afflicted palm. The tiniest hint of relief came to his face.

"And I still have time..."

#

Calypso dragged herself forward and slid along the slick floor of the cave. The most uncertain part of the journey was behind her now. They'd reached the dry section of the cave. Ayna had taken some time to calm down and get her bearings once she got out of the jar, but she'd soon worked out the shortest path to the fresh air of the outside world. The only trouble now was actually reaching it.

The mermaid hauled herself up to the top of a short slope.

"It's down this way for quite a bit," Ayna said.

"No turns?"

"Gentle ones, but you won't encounter another tunnel for some time, so you needn't worry about taking a wrong turn."

Calypso grinned. "That should make things a bit faster."

She dug her gloved fingers into the crest of the slope and heaved herself past it. She'd fortunately taken the precaution of assembling an outfit that quite resembled what passed for mermaid armor. During the downhill portions of the trip, she could simply let her gloves drag along the wet cave floor to control her speed.

Ayna buzzed down and alighted on her head, riding the mermaid like a glorified sled. "This is a horribly undignified way for a mermaid to move," she remarked.

"It isn't so bad. We call it 'seal sliding.' When I was a little girl, me and the other mermaids would find a nice smooth stretch of shore along the base of the cliffs and challenge each other to see how far up we could slide." She smiled a bit wider. "I was *very* good at it."

Their slide took them to a low-roofed section of the tunnel. Calypso lowered her head, and Ayna dropped down to lie atop her head to avoid being scraped across the roof. With the little creature's prone form atop her, Calypso could feel a bit of a tremble when they came particularly close. It happened rather frequently. Ayna proved better at conjuring light in the confounding mystic environment of the cave than most mages could, but she could still only manage a dull glow that gave them precious little notice of the changing shape of the tunnel.

"How are you holding up?" Calypso asked.

"I am not the one flopping like a stranded fish," Ayna said. "Just focus on moving quickly. I don't want to spend a moment longer in this cave than I have to."

"If you think you can give me reliable directions, you are welcome to make your way to the mouth of the cave ahead of me."

"You'd never make it without my help."

They slipped along for a time.

"Tell me something, Calypso."

"Anything. I am an open book."

"Why did you decide to make this foolish journey?"

"I thought I was fairly clear about that. Deacon needs our help, as does possibly the rest of the world."

"You always say it that way. Deacon first, then the rest of the world."

"Deacon is my friend. A threat to the world is a little difficult to come to terms with, but a friend is a friend. Even if the world wasn't at risk, I would have made the trip."

"I don't know if I should count it as foolishness or bravery."

"It needn't be one or the other. One can be brave *and* foolish."

Ayna buzzed her wings and huddled down as a bit of a stalactite swept by. "At least bravery is a part of it." She paused. "At least a *friend* is a part of it."

"What do you mean?"

"I don't know that there is a single person in Entwell, and thus the world, whom I would have risked my life for."

"That's perfectly reasonable."

"And yet glory is reason enough for me."

"Hardly a rare motivation. Is this something that worries you?"

"No! Am I not worthy of such glory?"

"Of course you are," Calypso said wearily. "But you certainly seem introspective about it."

"… What worries me is that I suspect the reciprocal is also true. I don't know that there is a single person in Entwell who would risk their life for me. Deacon was gone for years, and the last things he did before he left were as near to crimes as we have in Entwell. And yet still there were voices in his favor. Still you list him first among the reasons for braving the Cave of the Beast. Mine is not a life that has lent itself to friendship."

"Bah. You've got a friend in me."

Ayna was quiet for a long while. Calypso wondered what she would see if she were able to glimpse the expression on the fairy's face.

"Slow yourself. Be ready to stop quickly. There is a chasm ahead," Ayna said after the long silence.

Calypso dug the clawed tips of her gloves into the stone and brought their journey to a crawl. Sure enough, the long uninterrupted slide came to a stop just shy of a yawning crevasse that split the tunnel. It was wide enough and deep enough that neither the far end nor the bottom could be seen clearly.

"Which way now?" Calypso said. "As if I didn't know."

"Across. This is the last major obstacle before the exit."

"You know how it goes, then."

Calypso pulled herself to a sitting position and twisted her pack around to the front. She pulled a coil of rope from inside and began to feed out a length. Ayna buzzed out and hung before her, counting out the loops.

"I have a friend in you…" Ayna mused. "I suppose you do not subscribe to the mystic tenet of spiritual purity through honesty."

"Are you calling me a liar? Because that is grounds for a duel."

Calypso snickered.

"We are forever at one another's throats. That is not a sign of friendship."

"I'm usually just trying to get a rise out of you. Friends tease one another all the time. It's something you'd likely be more aware of if you had more of them."

"That's enough rope," Ayna said.

The fairy pulled a length of thread from a tiny pouch about her waist. Calypso tied a loop in the rope's end. Ayna fastened her thread to the end of the rope. She buzzed out over the chasm. As she drifted farther away, darkness swallowed everything but the fairy herself. It was disorienting, looking out to see the tiny creature glowing in the midst of endless black.

"What in our time together in Entwell would lead you to believe I needed or wanted a friend?" Ayna asked, her little voice echoing with the distance.

"Everyone needs a friend," Calypso called. "And I could always use another."

Ayna reached the far side and planted herself. With a bit of effort, she began hauling the end of the rope across. It was slow going, but even mystically dampened as they both were, a fairy was deceivingly strong. When it reached her side, Ayna looped the rope over a bit of stone sturdy enough to serve as an anchor.

"Test it," she called.

Calypso pulled at the rope. It held firm. Next came what had become the most trying part of the entire journey. Calypso set about climbing the rope.

"Mermaids," she huffed. "Are *not* meant for mountain climbing..."

She pulled herself forward, hand over hand. Her tail looped over the rope, such that she hung below it. Until now, she'd been climbing walls in this way. In those cases she'd found that when the slope or shape of the wall allowed for it, she could brace her tail fin against the stone. It wasn't as useful as a pair of legs, but it did about as much good as a single foot. In this case, it was of no value. The rope was the only thing to hold on to. Calypso's arms shook with exertion.

"It is remarkable," Calypso huffed. "One forgets just how heavy one is when there is no longer a pool of water to lighten the load."

Ayna buzzed down to meet her. "You are struggling," she observed.

"Nothing," she panted, "that I can't handle."

A crackle of stone echoed through the tunnel. The rope sagged a heart-stopping inch or two.

"The rope..." Ayna said.

"That was my side." Calypso redoubled her efforts. "I knew I should have practiced my knots."

Another crackle and the rope sagged further. Ayna flitted down and bumped into the curve of Calypso's tail. She buzzed her wings like mad attempting to lend a tiny bit of aid.

"Not that I don't have considerable faith in your strength, Ayna, but I'm not sure you are going to do much good."

"We are near the mouth of the cave." She grunted. "The influence is weaker here."

A breeze started to form, curling up along the wall. At first, it did little good at all. The loosening rope continued to sag, and Calypso's arms continued to tire as she tried to reach the far side before one end or the other of the rope fell free. Moment by moment the breeze grew. Calypso could feel a good deal of the weight taken from her grip. Her speed increased while sliding herself along the rope. It had sagged such that the second half of the journey had her fighting the slope of the rope.

Behind them, the rope came free. Calypso squealed and held on tightly. A precarious dangle turned into a terrifying swing. The mermaid pivoted and flailed her tail, slapping it against the wall to keep from being bashed free. Her gloves began to slide. Arms weary from dragging herself through the heart of the mountain were not up to the task of supporting her entire weight. She gritted her teeth and squeezed as hard as she could. Ayna caught up with her and threw her little weight against Calypso. The wind whistled and swirled.

"Climb!" Ayna grunted.

The focused wind tightened. Calypso felt some of the strain lessen. She hauled herself upward. The play in the rope suggested the top must be near, but with Ayna below her trying to add her own meager wings to the task of lifting the mermaid, the way forward was shrouded in darkness. Calypso didn't know she'd reached safety until her trembling hand reached forward and found a stone ledge rather than more rope. She grabbed on tightly, hoisted herself up, and tumbled inside.

Calypso collapsed, exhausted. Ayna landed atop her. Both were gasping for breath, slow to recover from the exertion and exhilaration of the near disastrous crossing.

"Well," Calypso gasped. "That was… something. I think thanks are in order. You may have just saved my life."

Ayna nodded and straightened her wind-ruffled outfit. "You choose your friends well."

#

A short slither down another incline brought them to a moderate-size stream trickling out of pores in the stone. Calypso required little guidance to navigate from that point forward, able to simply slide along the water. Ayna took full advantage of this fact by darting well ahead of her, eager to be free of the cave as soon as possible. As Calypso sloshed closer to the cave mouth, the confounding pressure of the Cave of the Beast began to ease. She likely could have taken a moment to cast a transformation spell and provide herself with legs, but the seal slide, at this point, was considerably faster.

Before she knew it, she spilled out into the frigid breeze of Melorn Woods. Ayna had perched herself on the sign labeling this place as the Cave of the Beast. She was taking long, slow breaths, relief evident in her tiny features. Calypso shut her eyes and touched her amulet. Magic stirred and swirled. The straps of the armored apron unfastened themselves. A bit of transformational magic gave her a pair of legs to stand on. She stood and rummaged through her bag. The legs were simple enough to conjure. Producing a pair of leggings as well was a bit of a challenge. She'd never bothered to produce footwear along with them, so she'd toted boots along with her.

"We've done it," Ayna said. "The first to cross the Cave of the Beast during a flood."

"Another feather in what is becoming a very crowded cap for you, eh?" Calypso said.

"I am running out of challenges worthy of my skills." She glanced to the mermaid. "Though thanks are of course in order for your aid."

"And vice versa. We are a fine team."

The mermaid curled her fingers and tugged at her soaking-wet armor. The layer of water clinging to her pulled away as though it had been nothing more than a silken veil. She threw it to the ground with a splash.

"I have your things, if you want to bundle up," Calypso said.

"I used to call this place my home. It isn't *pleasant,* but I am quite capable of enduring it."

"Well then. No sense wasting any more time. You can travel far more quickly than me. Do you need to see the map again?"

"I am a fairy. I can find my way."

"Very well, then. You know what to do."

Calypso held out a small satchel containing one of the pads they had crafted. Ayna conjured a wind to carry it behind her.

"Do hurry after me. I very much doubt I shall have the patience for diplomacy."

With that, Ayna whisked off in the direction of New Kenvard. Calypso lingered for a moment, gazing off into the forest before her. In the rush to reach this place, it had been lost upon her until this moment that she'd never been to a place like this. She'd spent many years in Entwell, more of them than she cared to count. Though she still had her youth due in part to her mystic prowess, it was safe to say most of her life had been spent honing her skills in the lake in Entwell. The years before had been spent in the Crescent Sea, mostly near the cliffs of the Eastern Mountains.

She had prepared herself as best she could for this entirely new world. Her mystic endurance was such that she was quite certain she could maintain her human appearance for as long as was needed. She was quite accustomed to cold temperatures. Compared to the iciness of the northern stretches of the Crescent Sea, the snowy forest was nothing to worry about. But she wasn't ready for the odd bit of anxiety she felt, knowing she had never been so far from water, and would only be getting farther.

Fortunately, that anxiety was nothing compared to the giddy thrill of exploring a new world and having a task beyond academics to pursue. She shut her eyes and let her mind drink in this glorious new landscape. Behind, there was the strange, obfuscating haze that had shielded Entwell from the rest of the world. To the west, north, and south, the world opened out with dizzying, endless detail. But one thing stood out more than anything else. A small point of piercing light a stone's throw from where she now stood. She opened her eyes and turned to where the point had been. A dusting of snow had painted the forest a fresh shade of white. She brushed at some of the snow at the base of the sign Ayna had rested upon. Beneath it was a cloth sack. A stiff bit of parchment, seemingly unaffected by the snow, bore a simple message written in a shaky hand.

*To be delivered to Queen Myranda Celeste. Not to be opened by any hands but the queen's.*

She shut her eyes again. The reason the bundle had been so bright in her mind's eye was a potent enchantment layered over it. The spell had the unmistakable signature of Deacon's handiwork, though with a shade less precision than she knew him to be capable of. Even if the label hadn't warned against it, Calypso wouldn't have attempted to open the bundle. The spell would prevent it.

"I don't like that you've left something for someone else to deliver, Deacon," Calypso said, tucking the package away. "It implies you wouldn't make it back to her, or you couldn't face her. But she'll get it. That I promise. And at least I know you're alive."

#

Myranda stood beside the mirror in the vault, palm against its polished surface while her other clutched one of Deacon's transcribed spell books. Ivy was still trapped within the mirror. She was slumped against the polished surface as though it were a sheet of glass. The creature didn't appear to be hurt, merely in an exhausted sleep. The reason for her exhaustion was clear. While the reflection she was trapped in had clearly once been a replica of the vault, now it was a charred, shattered ruin. Ivy must have lost control. As horrid as it was to find her trapped in this way, it was also a mercy. If she'd transformed in the true vault, it would have been an incalculable loss to the kingdom.

The queen finished casting the spell. Ripples spread across the surface of the mirror and Ivy slipped through. The sudden motion stirred her, and after a snort of confusion, she realized she was free and scrambled from the mirror. The polished silver calmed behind her and once again reflected the contents of the room.

"Myranda. Myranda, he was here!" Ivy said, eyes still bleary from her exhaustion.

"Who? Who was here? Who did this to you?" Myranda said.

"Deacon! He was just here." She wrapped Myranda in a tight embrace. "Thank goodness you found me. I was afraid I would be trapped here in the vault for who knows how long."

"The door was wide open. The first person to happen by raised the alarm and sent for me to investigate. Did you say Deacon was here?"

"Yes. It… it was him. *Physically* it was him. It smelled like him, and it sounded like him. It even acted like him, a little. But I don't know how it could really be him. He stole the Sword of the Chosen. I tried to stop him, and he trapped me there." She wiped her eyes. "How long has it been? When did I last leave you?"

"A few hours, at least."

"Then he could be anywhere… Myranda, he's in trouble. He *is* trouble right now. He didn't have his crown or his ring. His hand was crazy. And he… he didn't look like he could think straight. Worse, it seemed like whatever was wrong with his mind was something he *wanted*. He was talking about a fresh perspective or something, and how the risk was worth it, because of some truth he was seeking."

Ivy grabbed Myranda by the shoulders, a flare of blue surging as a new thought seized her. "Is Leo all right?"

"He's fine. Ivy, are you *certain* about all this?"

"I don't want it to be true, but I saw it with my own eyes."

Myranda surveyed the room again. The spells protecting this place were as near to impenetrable as they could manage, and they'd been entirely unraveled when she'd arrived. There were perhaps three wizards in the three kingdoms who could have dispelled them, and Myranda and Deacon were two of them. Nothing but the sword had been taken.

"We've got to find him," Ivy urged. "He's not totally gone. He could have fought harder and he didn't. You saw what he did to me. He didn't want me dead. He just wanted me out of the way. Whatever happened to him, Deacon is still Deacon. If we find him, maybe we can stop it before something worse happens to him."

Myranda shut her eyes and focused her mind. As she had so many times before, she spread her mind far and wide. She always seemed to be searching for someone, something. Today, at least, she didn't need to hide from anything. She could freely peer into the world around her. There was no sign of Deacon, but she could feel other things. Terrifying things.

She opened her eyes. "Ivy, did you see how he arrived? Did you see how he left?"

"No. He was just here, and I was already trapped when he left. Why?"

"I can feel the residue of a D'Karon portal."

Ivy's expression sharpened. "They're back…"

"We don't know anything yet." Myranda turned to one of the handful of servants who had anxiously watched as she rescued Ivy from her impossible predicament. "Go to my quarters and fetch my casting staff. I need to investigate this further."

Myranda marched into the hallway as her staff person hurried to comply.

"What are we going to do if it *is* the D'Karon?" Ivy said.

"If it is, then we will do whatever we must. But we mustn't jump to conclusions. We have enough to worry about without adding imagined dangers on top of everything else."

"I need to get my blades. I need to have them ready. And I need…" Ivy's ears perked up and pivoted toward the nearest window. "Ether is back."

By the time Ivy was through talking, the whistling gale of Ether's approach was loud enough for Myranda to hear as well. Shutters burst open, drapes tore from the window far at the end of the hallway. The swirling form of Ether tightened into her human form and dropped down in front of Myranda. The look on her face was intense and spoke volumes.

"You've found something as well," Myranda said simply. "Very well. Follow me. It seems we have much to discuss."

#

Ether had been as terse as she could manage in relaying her findings, but the words had still struck Ivy nearly as hard as the experience had struck the shapeshifter.

"He was there… you saw him," Ivy said.

"An echo of the past, but it was him," Ether repeated.

"I wish I could have seen him…" she said. "Even if he wasn't real. I have so many memories of him, but I still worry they will fade. Just to see him once more."

Ether shut her eyes. "Do not wish for it. It is a fresh pain in an old wound. A reminder of loss."

"Even so. I'd rather one last sharp memory than nothing at all."

Myranda marched onward, leading the others toward her chambers. Her casting staff was in hand now. She was not immune to the pain Ether and Ivy were enduring. The knowledge that these disturbances could give her a glimpse of things long thought lost, that it could confront them with friends and foes from the past, was a revelation both terrible and wonderful. But she shoved the possibilities and consequences aside. There was simply too much to do to allow herself to be distracted. Better to focus on the facts and the clues.

"Where are we going?" Ivy asked.

"Deacon's study."

"The big one in your room, or the secret one in the wall?"

"You found the one in the wall?"

"Leo led us there. We spent a lot of time there while you were gone. I hope that wasn't *bad*."

"No. No. It was never meant to be a secret," Myranda said. "It was only meant to be somewhere that he could work in privacy if he desired. And I granted him that privacy, as he would for me."

"Not Ether," Ivy pointed out. "She was reading his notes. At least all *I* read were his memoirs, and I'm in them, so that doesn't count."

Myranda gave the shapeshifter a look. "You read from Deacon's notes?" she said.

"They were not secured in any way. It was hardly an invasion of privacy," Ether said.

"They were in a room that could only be opened from the outside by Deacon, myself, and our son."

"And your son opened the door," she said.

"Setting aside the impropriety, did you find anything that might indicate something like this was happening?"

"My readings were not comprehensive, but there was certainly evidence of unstable thinking. He was speculating about the very makeup of our world, things that were lunacy to consider."

"I'll have to read them for myself."

The group reached the same dead end that had been so useful for keeping Leo amused in Myranda's absence. She pushed the gateway open and stepped inside.

"Show me," she said. "Which books hold the writings that concerned you?"

Ether plucked the pile of notes from their place and spread them out before Myranda. She scanned the pages, and as she did, she felt a creeping, sour feeling in her chest. The words of each sheaf began as she had come to expect Deacon's notes. Wordy and complex but brimming with enthusiasm. Often they would reference things on the previous page, tackling them like some sort of riddle despite the fact that he had clearly written them himself. Then, sometimes after a few sentences, sometimes after several pages, there would come a single word. "Alone."

The writings that followed that word became increasingly erratic. They were less like a brilliant wizard working at the mysteries of magic and more like an outsider proposing answers to questions no one asked. They weren't dangerous, they weren't ravings. They walked step by step away from the way Myranda knew things to be and closer to some strange, half-demented musing of the way things might be. And each time a new sheaf began, the words of the Deacon she knew were more convinced of the merit of the madness that concluded the previous page.

"Alone…" Myranda said. "Whatever was causing this, he wouldn't allow it to occur unless he was alone." She looked to the corner of the room, where the little nest of blankets Ivy had fashioned was still curled up. "He wouldn't do it while Leo was with him."

"He didn't have the ring and crown on," Ivy said. "Maybe taking them off makes him… different?"

"The affliction was in his hand. It was growing worse, but it was only ever a physical thing."

"Then why would he choose a crown for further treatment, rather than a second ring?" Ether said.

"He needed more material to enchant," Myranda said. "We'd even tried it as a second ring, but it did very little good."

"Then why not a bracelet or a bracer? He chose to put the new treatment on his head," Ether said. "Read this page and tell me if these are the words of a sound mind."

Myranda returned her gaze to the page.

"'Earth, fire, wind, water. The mystical elements. Alchemical fundamentals. These are the basis for all else. Or so we have come to believe. There are clearly things beyond. Pure white magic. Pure black. The gray magics. My specialty. There must be fundamental magics deeper. Mana? Perhaps, but that is less an element and more a force. There are many forces. But what lies beneath the other elements? Earth, fire, wind, water. They make up our surroundings, our bodies. Everything. But they are the colors of the canvas. What is the canvas?'"

She turned the page.

"'What exists in the absence of those things? Time exists. A force? Space exists. A substance? Connected, as with air and fire. One feeds another.

Truth exists. Are these the deeper elements? Abstract to the mind? Must they be abstract? Are things possible because they exist within these elements? Can they be rendered impossible if they do not? Do not lock the door. Remove the door. Is this the way? But how?'"

Myranda gazed at the area below. Complex sigils were traced out in groups, variations of the same shape, like he was trying to work out which was the correct one.

"It doesn't sound any *more* confusing than Deacon usually sounds," Ivy said.

"He is suggesting that things like truth are fundamental forces that shape our world," Ether said.

"He is suggesting that *time* is something that may be able to be manipulated with magic in the same way that fire and wind are," Myranda said. "This is why you were concerned. We are seeing disturbances in time, and we're seeing Deacon musing about the malleability of time. So you suppose Deacon is responsible for these disturbances."

"He is musing about the nature of time, and time is rebelling against us. Why search further for a cause?"

Myranda drummed her fingers on the desk. "It would surely take an enormous amount of magical power to achieve an effect like this. I would have noticed if he had been experimenting, and he wasn't."

"Maybe he didn't do it, but he already will do it," Ivy said. "He... will have done it? He already did it, but not yet? I'm not sure how to say it."

"No, I understand," Myranda said.

"You do?" Ivy said with a cock of her head.

"If you throw a stone in a lake, the ripples will reached the shore even though that isn't where the stone landed. We could be seeing the ripples through time of something that will happen."

"Yes!" Ivy said. "That's what I mean."

"But he doesn't seem to have made any progress toward something like that," she said. "Through all of these pages 'No effect. No effect. This may be beyond the grasp of known magics.'"

"But if anyone could figure it out, it's Deacon," Ivy said.

"It may be folly to ask it, because logic is seldom necessary for a lunatic, but what possible reason would he have for toying with the past?" Ether said.

"If you don't know the answer to that, you haven't been paying attention," Ivy said. "There's a lot of things in the past that could use changing."

"He can't change the past and he knows it. He taught *me* that. The past is what got us here. It isn't a bridge that we can cross and cut down behind us.

It's a tree we're perched in the branches of. Try to make a change and it all comes tumbling down," Myranda said.

"… You're good at explaining things," Ivy said.

"I attacked one of the creatures from one of the time echoes. I certainly didn't do so in the first instance of that moment, and nothing changed. Not my memory, not even the surface of the lake. It shattered just as it had when the beast was still whole. If he imagines he can change the past, he is wrong," Ether said.

"There is no sense speculating on what he is trying to do. His mind clearly isn't where it should be. What we need to figure out is how he intends to do it, how we can stop him, and how we can set his mind straight again. Now both of you, help me go through this. All of it. We need to know why he needed the Sword of the Chosen. We need to learn the source of the D'Karon portals. Everything. From this point, we don't dismiss anything. It could *all* be part of the same thing. And we need to get to the bottom of it."

Myranda took a breath. When she spoke again, her voice had an edge to it, and she avoided looking her friends in the eyes.

"And what we've speculated here… that Deacon is doing this? It doesn't leave this room."

"If Deacon is a threat, others should be warned," Ether said.

"I won't see this world turn against Deacon until we are certain of what he's done and that we cannot stop him ourselves," Myranda said. "He is still my husband. He is still our ally. He deserves the benefit of the doubt."

Ether grasped Myranda's shoulder and turned her to him. "Myranda, we have a duty to this world, not to Deacon. If circumstance warrant it, are you willing to do what it takes to stop this?"

She shot Ether a sharp look. "We've fought beside each other often enough for you to know better than to ask me that question. This will be stopped."

"But… if the time echoes are happening, then doesn't that mean we *don't* stop him?" Ivy said.

Myranda slapped down another sheaf of notes. "I intend to find out."

#

Desmeres paced to the southernmost edge of Entwell. Beyond Warrior's Side, the mountains curved back to claim the stretch of level land that held the village. It was a rocky place, too narrow and precarious to be used for sparring or to build a place to live. A use had been found for it, nonetheless. This was where the people of Entwell honored their dead.

He walked past the urns holding the ashes of those who had fallen. Each was set into an alcove carved into the wall. A small plaque had been affixed with care to the space below the urn, proclaiming the name, the family, and the

154

accomplishments of each. There was no separation between the apprentices or the masters. Those who served for a century, teaching others and building the works of Entwell were side by side with those who had fallen to the cave but were brought through by the other members of their party.

That there were so few urns here, despite more than four hundred years of history, spoke of just how few had made it to this place, and how many of them were of a race so long-lived that they still remained. As he reviewed them and shivered against the cold wind from the sea, Desmeres swept his eyes over the names. He recognized many of them. Most of his life, by a wide margin, had been spent traveling the north. He was perpetually in motion, never anywhere long enough to make friends. All were associates, people he had found. People with whom he had struck deals and made alliances. But he'd spent his first thirty years in Entwell. He had memories of these people. And so many of them were gone. He found his mother's urn first.

A grind of stone caught his attention. When he turned, he found the elder was approaching. She was alone, a rarity for someone of such advanced age and towering importance. Desmeres stepped aside to allow her to pass, but she stopped beside him.

"It is good to see you here, Desmeres. So few in Entwell take the time to reflect upon the past." She turned to the urn before him. "We fix our minds on the future and what we can make of it. But the past is where we stand when we do it. It is worth taking a moment and seeing if there is anything more to be learned from time to time."

She brushed some salty debris from the plaque. "She lived to be ninety-eight. A good life for a human," the elder said.

"A long life, at least. I don't know that she had a good one," he said. "I wasn't here for most of it. The plaque says she was an honored and skilled alchemist."

"She was a fine woman. She added much to our understanding. She died fulfilled and content."

"Then she was better than I." He narrowed his eyes. "I don't know that I could find fulfillment in a thousand years. I've crafted my entire worldview around keeping it out of my grasp."

"It is never too late to change."

"A century is plenty of time to become set in one's ways…"

He continued forward, idly clacking the metal fingers of his yet-to-be-replaced hand. Some distance farther, he encountered his father's urn.

"And what of Croyden?" he asked. "He should have had centuries more. He should have had as much time as he desired."

His father's urn was nearer to the ground. He crouched to investigate it. "Poisoned… My father was poisoned?" Desmeres said.

"A mishap with a treatment for one of his blades, as I recall. A vial fell into his forge, and he was gone before we could help him."

Desmeres searched for the proper words. None seemed to exist. The first notion that seemed like it was worthy of breaking this silence was a simple one.

"So his final blade was left unfinished?"

"I believe so. It will be among his things."

"I would like to finish it."

"By all means."

He stood and dusted off his knees. "I've got a lot of work to do. And it feels strangely like I'm running out of time."

"No better way to find the motivation to get it done."

The pair turned back, marching toward Warrior's Side. As they approached, it became clear that something curious was happening in the heart of Entwell. Desmeres could feel a thick, intensely arcane quality to the air. If it was potent enough for him to feel it, it must have been truly monumental.

"Are the wizards having another debate in your absence?" he said.

When he turned to the elder, her face was serious.

"I recognize that spell. No one casts it like that anymore."

The pair hurried forward. Warrior's Side was nearly empty, the residents having already rushed to the center of the village. Desmeres and the elder reached it to find a familiar scene playing out. Intense magic curled and lanced out from the elder's hut. Apprentices and masters alike scattered to avoid the blasts and whorls of wind and stone. Pieces of the oft-destroyed hut in the center of the village burst to fragments as some manner of mystically enhanced debate raged on. But when the walls had fallen and those responsible were revealed, the elder froze in place.

"Elder Tavvic," she uttered. "He has been dead for two hundred years."

Without the hut to obscure the view, other aspects of the battle became clear. It was just as much an elemental battle as any such disagreement tended to become, but some of the elements were being conjured without an apparent source. Fire, in particular, roared from thin air.

"Everyone! Keep back, stay safe, and observe! Protect the rest of the village, but let this event play out. We need to learn," the elder said.

The wizards, masters and apprentices alike, formed a ring around the raging argument.

"Solomon would have been in this discussion. He is absent now." The elder turned to where the gray dragon had planted himself at the edge of the courtyard. "Or at least, not in place."

Styluses scratched out records of what was occurring. Scribes rushed to the elder's side to record her words.

"Only the dead," she observed. "Only the dead are appearing in the echo."

She shut her eyes, slipping deep into focus. Desmeres knew the look. She was experiencing the moment with a depth and precision that nonmystics could never hope to achieve. Whatever was causing this, the world was about to get the most thorough, precise insight into its workings one could ever hope to achieve.

#

Hours of poring over Deacon's endless notes had failed to yield any real insight. Working through them had genuinely been like trying to pick apart an argument between two people who didn't feel the need to fully articulate themselves. Deacon while alone, presumably Deacon without the crown, knew everything that his sane counterpart knew, so the thread connecting two lines of reasoning was often buried in subtext or entirely unspoken. A few things had become well established, however. The first was that Deacon was quite certain he would never be able to achieve his goal until he found some missing piece that, as of the pages written hours before his departure, continued to elude him. The second was that despite what the ripples of time might imply, he wasn't seeking to change history. Time was only ever mentioned in passing. Everything reduced to the repeated refrain, an oscillating musing between "remove the door" and the ill-defined "alchemy of existence."

In a way, it was a relief that he'd not planned some sort of dangerous tampering with time itself. In another way, it was terrifying, because that meant these ripples were unintended. It meant something had gone wrong or was going to go wrong.

With nothing else to draw upon, Myranda had moved Deacon's notes into the royal dining room. It was a smaller, more intimate space than the banquet hall that served as the setting for the royal family's day-to-day meals. Now the long table was arrayed with the different pages. Ether stood at one end, considering the words on some of the more recent writings. Myranda was staring, unseeing, at one of the earlier pages while her mind worked.

"Mama," Leo proclaimed, rousing Myranda from her trancelike musing.

She turned to him. Ivy had been taking her duties as an aunt very seriously, even amid this potential disaster. While they worked, she had been feeding him an impressive amount of sweets. His face was smeared with sugar and cream. Myranda pulled a napkin from the table and wiped his face.

"Dada," Leo said, trying to escape the unwanted cleanliness.

"We're trying to find him, Leo," Myranda said softly. She gathered the boy up on one hip and took her staff in hand with the other.

"Dada," he said, reaching for Myranda's staff.

"Do you want to look for him?" she asked. "He would be very proud to know you tried. Come. We've made no progress trying to think as he does. Perhaps it is time for a more direct approach again."

"If Deacon does not want to be found, he will not be found," Ether said. "He knows that you will search for him. He was the one who taught you how."

Myranda took a seat on the floor and set Leo on her lap. "Then let us hope he taught me well." She wrapped her arms around Leo and positioned the head of the staff where his questing hands could reach it. "Be calm. Just think of him," she said.

Remaining calm was not among the child's skills at this stage of his life, but Myranda did her best to ease her mind sufficiently for the two of them. She didn't bother looking for Deacon directly. If that had had a chance of working, she would have found him in moments. This search would be subtler. She let her mind flow outward, bit by bit. First she saw the soul of her son. It was small but intense. Wild and untamed. It was raw potential. She saw the complex whorl of Ivy's soul, radiant and colored by the worry and frustration of the impossible puzzle they sought to solve. There was Ether's soul. Tortured but controlled. Beyond, there were glimmers of her subjects, less powerful but no less complex. Her view expanded, the points of light forming clustered galaxies. First the capital. Then nearby cities. She could feel her son's influence on her focus, chaotically tugging it this way and that, less a participant in the search and more a spectator to it.

Further her mind spread. There were tremors and twitches in the darkened landscape between the clusters of souls. Too small for her to pinpoint. She couldn't be sure what they were, if anything. The world beyond the physical, the spectral realm, was lively and vibrant. Deep focus always revealed more twists and whorls of power and complexity. Some were the result of wizards and arcane creatures tugging at the threads of reality. Others were as natural as the weather. Sometimes it was obvious. At a time like this, differentiating the workings of will from the natural state of things required a keener and more experienced mind than hers. And the one she would call upon to render aid was the very man she was trying to find.

"Dada," Leo murmured.

Her view shifted again, drawn roughly by the influence of her boy. For an instant, she could see the familiar shape of Deacon's soul. It was gone in a flash, but in the time she could see it, it burned itself into her mind. The soul was curled, twisted. Like a page that had been tossed into a fire and snatched out again, it was singed and blackened in places. When it vanished, Myranda felt another hint of the D'Karon magic she'd hoped would be gone from this world forever. He'd vanished not because he had hidden himself, but because he had passed through a D'Karon portal. And now there was no sign of him.

"He's using their magic…" she uttered.

"No…" Ivy said.

"Where is he? If he is using D'Karon magic, he must be stopped," Ether said.

"I don't feel him anymore. He's gone beyond my means to detect him."

Ether stepped up and wrapped her hand around the gem. Her power and focus joined with Myranda's own, but the two were not in harmony. She saw further, but less clearly. There was still no sign of Deacon, but now there was a new point of powerful light. It was familiar, and what's more, it was aware of her. When her focus turned to it, it turned its focus to her, and the point of pristine yellow power sliced across the landscape toward her.

"What is that?" Ether asked.

"Who? It… it feels like someone from Entwell. It's been years but… if feels like Master Ayna," Myranda said.

"Ayna? I read that bit from Deacon's notes just the other day. Isn't she the awful wind wizard?"

"She isn't in Entwell any longer. She is coming here. And at the speed she's moving, she'll be here shortly."

Indeed, the increasingly common sound of wind rising to unnatural levels of speed and power howled from outside the palace. Myranda handed Leo to Ivy and paced to the nearest window. Though New Kenvard was in the midst of the short section of the year with pleasant temperatures, out of habit she left the windows shut tight. She pulled aside the drapes and opened the shutters just in time for a ball of gleaming yellow light to dart inside. The wind howled in as well, swirling the pages from the table.

Myranda held up a hand. The pages obediently ceased their stirring and settled back to their original places. The ball of light faded to the buzzing, exhausted figure of Ayna. She held a satchel a bit larger than she.

"Queen Myranda," she said with a rare bit of deference.

"Highest Master Ayna," Myranda said in return.

"Your palace is not as simple to find as I would have hoped, and I place the blame for that squarely upon your shoulders. You are a peerless wizard, and your home should be a beacon of mystic might."

She wavered a bit, nearly dropping the satchel she carried. "I require honey. Now." After a moment of consideration, Ayna made a diplomatic amendment. "Please."

#

Ayna sat on the edge of a bowl on the table. Myranda had filled the dip

159

in the stem of an overturned goblet with honey. Ayna chose to forgo dignity in favor of efficiency as she plunged her hands into the warm golden syrup and gorged herself. The Entwell-made pad was open before Myranda. She'd etched out a message of greeting with the stylus and was awaiting a reply. Ivy, still in charge of Leo, was fighting a pitched battle to keep the little boy from attempting to snatch Ayna from the table like a doll. It all might have been an adorable reunion, if not for the brief but devastating warning Ayna had added to the growing mound of concerns.

"Epidime…" Myranda said.

"Indeed. Such was Desmeres's suspicion."

"If Epidime was trapped in the cave, why didn't Desmeres *tell* us?"

"It is not my place to plumb the depths of a schemer's mind."

Myranda turned side. "Deacon didn't allow himself to be taken by Epidime. He wouldn't."

"He need not *allow* himself. It could have been against his will. And it would explain his otherwise inexplicable behavior. And his use of D'Karon magic," Ether suggested.

"Deacon was not taken by Epidime," Ivy said firmly.

"There is no time for sentiment," Ayna said. "If there is the *chance* he was taken—"

"He was *not* taken by Epidime," Ivy repeated. "I saw him take a coin from his pocket while he was in the vault. He held it in his hand. The coin has the Mark of the Chosen on it. If he was taken by Epidime, its touch would have burned him."

"You were on the verge of a rage transformation. Are you certain you can trust your memory?" Ether asked.

She stomped her foot, a gleam of red in her eye. "I know what I saw."

"Certain or not, the risk was deemed sufficient to engineer a means to escape Entwell despite the current state of the cave. This, naturally, required my own expertise," Ayna said.

"Did you come alone?" Myranda asked.

"No. Calypso joined me, but her mobility is inferior to my own. She is still traveling. She shall be along sometime later."

The stylus rose from beside the pad and positioned itself over the page. Two messages were traced out. The first was in bold, clear, elegant script.

*Myranda! Calypso. What aid is required?* the mermaid wrote.

The second message was traced out far more slowly, as though it was a struggle for the words to reach the pad.

*Myranda, I apologize. I thought you would be safer if you were not tempted to take on Epidime again. I see now it was not my choice to make.*

The words were Desmeres's. Myranda took the stylus.

*Desmeres, save your apologies. There is work to be done. The rest can wait. Everyone, I want to know everything. Every last word that we know about what is happening and where.*

When she released the stylus, Calypso wrote a reply.

*Too much to write. Will see you soon, and bring you a package I believe Deacon left behind. Ayna, tell her what we know, and remember the dagger.*

"Ah, yes," Ayna said. "I was not privy to the discussion, but Calypso and Desmeres sought council for the means to create the pad, among other things. Included in that discussion was the assessment that the surest way to cure Deacon's affliction would be to kill him with the dagger Calypso is presently carrying."

"Kill him?!" Ivy said, covering Leo's ears.

"I don't know that those precise words were spoken. There were metaphors and euphemisms regarding trimming rotten flesh or something of that sort, I'm told, but I think it should be clear to a rational mind that a dagger can have but one use when it comes to curing a man who has taken leave of his senses."

Ivy glared at Ayna. "You really live up to your reputation."

The fairy grinned. "I am pleased my reputation precedes me even beyond the borders of Entwell."

"You're just Ether from before she grew a heart," Ivy jabbed.

"I helped *summon* Ether, I'll remind you," Ayna said.

"What does that have to do with anything?"

"I am merely reminding you of my importance and value, and thus the degree of respect I believe I am owed."

"Enough," Myranda snapped. "Social graces aside, we need all the help we can get."

The stylus rose again. It was the slow trace of a message coming from Entwell, but this hand was much steadier and more precise. The writing began with a simple label. *Elder.*

*We have experienced what I suspect is another instance of the events plaguing the rest of the world. I shall record my assessment of the nature of the event.*

Symbols followed, mystic runes Myranda had never seen before. "What is this?" she said.

Ayna flitted over to the page. "Ah. Yes. Very wise. She is writing down a spell to communicate the *sensations* she experienced," Ayna said. "That could prove helpful indeed. Ether has experienced one of these events directly. There is value in contrasting the experiences."

"We shall have to cast the spell when it is complete, yes?" Myranda said.

"We will."

"Do you feel confident you will be able to do so? From what little I've seen, I must admit ignorance to spells of this sort."

"This is… it is a rather dense bit of gray magic," Ayna said. "It was not my focus."

"Ivy, take her to the library. Deacon's writings are there. I trust you will be able to find the proper techniques in those pages."

Ayna's expression soured. "I suppose so." She flitted up. "Though it pains me, I will expose myself to the coarse thinking of this rogue wizard in order to do my duty to the world."

She and Ivy hurried from the room. Myranda continued to work through what she'd learned.

"If Deacon is using D'Karon portals, as he appears to be, then he can move quickly. But he can only select places the D'Karon designated as anchors, and we've been working to dismantle them. That narrows things down. We should focus on finding him. We have myself, Ether, Ivy, Ayna, and Calypso. All of us with at least some experience in distance-seeing and tracking. Myn, Ayna, and Ether can move enormous distances quickly, and working together, either Ayna or Ether could help Myn carry others with similar haste. If we spread out, there are few places on the continent that will be beyond our reach. But it won't be enough to know where Deacon is. We will need to know where he is going and what he will do when he gets there. Back to the war room. We'll need the map and every one of our minds."

#

"Ah, perfect," Calypso said, trotting out of the edge of Melorn Woods.

She'd been able to devise a reasonably expedient way to travel, and thus had reached the edge of the forest far more swiftly than she'd anticipated. It was a rather taxing method, however, and moreover was quite likely to cause a stir. Magic wasn't as prevalent out here as it was in Entwell, so she didn't want to risk concerning the locals if she could avoid it. Now that the pad had been delivered, she was far more interested in keeping an eye on it than focusing on keeping her speed up anyway. It was a welcome bit of luck that she'd stumbled upon a small, strangely isolated tavern of some sort on the thinning fringe of Melorn Woods. The map labeled this region as part of the vast Low Lands, though, to the best of her map-reading abilities, she noted the tavern itself wasn't labeled. That was no surprise, however. The map she worked from was so old it still showed the borders from before the Northern Alliance had been formed. Rare was the establishment that survived a century and a half of war.

The Coin of Kenvard

Calypso stepped in from the cold. The interior of the tavern was dark and smelled strongly of smoke and charred meat. All eyes turned to her. Even after literally dragging herself through a cave and gallivanting through a forest, she was downright pristinely presentable compared to the majority of the dozen or so patrons within. The mermaid paused and searched her memory.

"The Northern Alliance. Either Crich or Varden," she murmured to herself. "Desmeres spoke Varden. It is as good a guess as any." She cleared her throat. "Hello! I am pleased to meet you. I wonder if perhaps I could trouble any of you for a warm drink and a warm meal?"

"I think you'd best be on your way," said a scrawny older man behind a rather makeshift bar at the far end of the room.

Calypso waved off a cloud of pipe smoke. "There doesn't seem to be another establishment for quite a distance. Do not worry. I was informed that goods and services are exchanged or bartered for here. I'm afraid I couldn't bring myself to ask Solomon to give up any of his gold, but Cresh provided me with quite a bit of silver."

She pulled a heavy pouch from her bag and revealed the glittering contents. "It isn't coins, but shape shouldn't matter *that* much."

The already focused attention on the newcomer sharpened, shifting from irritated curiosity to predatory hunger.

"Really, ma'am, this isn't the sort of place you think it is," said the barman.

"You shut your mouth," barked a lanky fellow beside the door. "We should be hospitable. Feed a hungry traveler."

Calypso was slightly taken aback by the overall disposition of the thin man. Different wizards developed their magic in different ways. Deacon was rather oblivious to the deeper emotions of those around him. Calypso, no doubt due in part to her predilection for socializing, was quite the opposite. As her mystic mastery grew, so too did her insight into the thoughts and intentions of others. It wasn't mind-reading, but she was more likely than most to see through a façade. This fellow had erected a rather substantial one in the space of a few words.

"If it is too much trouble, I can see to myself," she said.

"No, no. No trouble," he said, shutting the door and dropping a brace down. "Not much of a choice here, mind you. A slice of whatever the hunter dragged in, brown bread, and a bit of ale."

"I prefer fish, but I'm sure meat and bread will do. I'm not one for ale, though. Is there no water?" she asked.

"Hah! You can have water if you like. The well's not too far off."

"Lovely. I'll have a place to sit, a bucket of hot water, a bucket of cold, and a plate of whatever you serve."

"Two *buckets*?" the barkeep said.

The lanky man turned to the tender. "You heard her!" He led her forward. "You just sit over here. Right by me."

Calypso sat at the table beside the man and quickly set her pad down where the stylus would be free to move.

"What brings a lovely thing like you to a place like this?" he asked.

"Unfortunate business, I'm afraid. I understand there have been some unpleasant events around here recently?"

"Mmm," rumbled a man in the corner whose face was primarily beard and eyebrow. "Madness. Or so they say. People seeing things. Troops are moving."

"Oh. Poor thing," said her gracious benefactor. "Let me guess. With all this danger and uncertainty, you're looking for somewhere safe to hide, right?"

"Quite the opposite, in fact. I mean to help. I don't suppose any of you have any useful information."

One of the men in the far corner began to answer. The "helpful" fellow silenced him. "Plenty of time to discuss that after you've eaten."

The tender produced a bucket of cold water and a loaf of bread first.

"Thank you. Pardon me for *just* a moment."

She took the bucket and upended it over her head, dousing herself. Those nearby backed away, baffled and bemused. She sighed in relief.

"My apologies, but that was *badly* needed." She picked up the bread. "Oh! I suppose, before I eat anything, I should determine the price."

"Funny you should mention that," the helpful fellow said.

He wiped at his shirt, which had received a liberal splash of the water, then revealed a hefty weighted leather sack with a wooden handle. "It'll be all of that silver of yours."

"Oh? Rather a steep price," she said, pushing the pouch across.

"And hand over that fancy necklace."

"The pendant is most *certainly* not… oh. I see. Brigandage."

"What did you call me?"

"I had a feeling you would be trouble. I really must warn you, I am not someone to be trifled with. I vigorously advise against this sort of behavior. There is no reason you can't change your mind right now."

"I'll have the silver and the necklace, and we'll decide what else I want after that," he said.

"Sir, I am a rather skilled water mage. Highest master of water magic, if you'll permit me the boast. As such I have a very high degree of control over water, and there is rather a lot of it running through your veins right now."

"I'll believe it when I see it," he said, slapping the sack against his palm with a leaden thump that hinted at the sort of damage a blow to the head might cause. "The necklace or you'll be missing out on your meal."

"Sir, please, one last chance. And you won't see it, you will feel it."

He moved forward to make good on his threat. Though he motioned for the necklace, his fingers never reached it. His body grew still, while a soft light flickered in the pendant. She let the stillness linger for a few seconds, then gently flicked her fingers toward the door. The man hurled backward and struck the door. There he remained, pinned.

"It is something of a challenge to immobilize you like this while keeping your blood moving properly, so I'll let you free now, but please consider being a proper gentleman when you are able."

She released her influence, and he slid to the ground. Rather than mind his manners as she'd recommended, he took an equally wise course of action and fled the tavern.

Calypso clapped her hands and huffed a breath. "That was a bracing bit of defense magic. It has been *ages* since I've had to do something like that. I'll tell you, I didn't miss it one bit. Now then, if someone would kindly inform me of the *real* price for this meal, I'm eager to dig in and work my way through my notes."

"I-it's free of charge, ma'am," the tender said, eyes wide.

"Don't be absurd. You deserve a fair price for your work. Here. I shall leave three nuggets of silver on the table, and if you need more, say so."

She scattered the payment and tore a bit of bread to chew on. It wasn't the finest meal she'd had, but it was better than nothing.

"Ma'am," said the man in the corner.

She turned. "Oh, please, Calypso. How may I help you?"

"You said you were after information, yes? About the strange things that have been going on?"

"Oh, yes. It is crucially important I know all I can."

"Well, I used to… that is to say, I *know* a guy who used to keep watch over the Territal archives. I'm fresh from the road, heading up from there, but he said a couple weeks ago something weird happened, and then a couple nights ago something *weirder* happened…"

#

Myranda and the others paced around the war room. The rest of her staff had been sent to their quarters. Now that the king was known to have, at the very least, begun acting erratically, Myranda had decided discretion was called for. They had worked their way through the latest messages delivered via the pads and proposed a dozen different theories that through either observation or deeper thought were abandoned. In light of the concerning events, Myranda had decided to keep Leo by her side rather than risk him

165

befalling something Sadie couldn't handle. The boy was having the time of his life being bounced between Myranda and Ivy while each of them turned their attention toward or away from the task at hand. Even Ether had reluctantly taken the role of babysitter on occasion, at least until Ayna had returned with sufficient knowledge to cast the spell the elder had sent. Since that moment she had been seated silently in the corner. Her eyes were shut, soft glimmers of light dancing around her as she was treated to what the elder had prepared.

"Pad!" Leo crowed, clapping wildly as the Entwell pad began sketching out a message.

Ayna buzzed over and watched the message trace itself out.

"It is from Calypso. Rather rambling, as tends to be the case… She has a dubiously credible claim that there was an event… more than a week ago in Territal. 'Things seemed to happen that had already happened.' This was followed far more recently by a theft, by Deacon. Some manner of item from a general?"

Myranda hurried over and snatched up the pad. Ayna took the opportunity to place a marker in the indicated location, as Territal had previously been absent from the list of places that were affected.

"Why wouldn't we know about that already?" Ivy asked.

"This is Ulvard. Perhaps King Terrance and Queen Tanya wished to keep their affairs to themselves. More likely they weren't aware. It seems both the theft and the time echo were late at night and in a remote portion of the capital." She gazed at the map. "I wish the dates were more precise. If this account can be trusted, that would make this time echo a very early one. It could predate even those Caya described. And the timing of Deacon's appearance would have made his theft very shortly after whatever happened in the Cave of the Beast. This could have been the first place Deacon went."

"But the timing doesn't make sense. If the time echo Calypso has uncovered happened that long ago, it would have been *well* before Deacon started doing this." Ivy tapped her chin. "Unless he's been doing this since before he left."

"No," Myranda said. "I would have noticed, and even if I missed it, he would have written about it. There was plenty in those notes that was worth hiding if he'd been planning this from the start."

"Then why would this newly discovered echo be so long before?"

"This is crucial information," Ayna said. "It means the effects of whatever he's doing are reaching farther back than we'd realized." She buzzed out over the map. "It means the timing of these echoes don't mean what we think they mean. They don't come after he arrives in this place or that to do whatever he believes he needs to do, they come before. As we'd already supposed. But now we know that they come *well* before," she finished.

"Except they don't always," Ivy said. "Deacon came here and fought me *after* the army showed up to the south, but it wasn't four days after." Ivy pointed. "And there are so many little echoes. Did he cause those? And when?"

Ether stood. "I have something."

All eyes turned to her. She stepped up to the map.

"I witnessed an echo firsthand, here." She pointed. "It did not have the feel of magic behind it. But there *was* something. A twist of the fabric of existence. The elder's spell was a remarkably detailed illusory recording of a similar event in Entwell. I saw everything. Felt everything. And that twist of will was absent."

"Is it possible the elder just left it out by mistake?" Ivy asked.

"Send her a message if you must," Ether said, "but the rest of the illusion was stunningly comprehensive. Every other aspect of the experience was in perfect detail. I cannot imagine a mind sharp enough to record all else would have left it out."

"But what does it mean?" Ayna asked.

"With the D'Karon portals speeding Deacon's travel, he can reasonably be expected to have visited any of the places where events have occurred within the northern kingdoms and Tressor. But he cannot have gone to Entwell."

Myranda nodded. "Yes… It means first that these effects are spreading beyond places Deacon has traveled in the past few days, and it gives us a solid example of a place he has visited versus a place he hasn't. The places he has directly visited surely have a place in his plan, whatever it is."

"More to the point, because the echoes come *before* he arrives to do whatever is causing them, the events that bear this distinction may not simply let us know where he has been, but if we move quickly enough, where he *will* be," Ayna said.

Ether stepped back and shifted to flame.

"I must investigate the field to the south. If there is a residue of this twist there, we will have something."

She whisked away. Myranda paced back and forth. Gods willing, Ether would soon return with a way of determining where Deacon was going and when he had been or would be going there, but there still remained the most crucial questions. What was he doing, and why? The answers were there, somewhere. She could feel them just beyond her grasp. She turned over other pieces of the recent information.

"A theft involving one of the generals… if he *is* in the control of Epidime, it would make sense he would seek something from Bagu or the others. Even something of Epidime's own. But if Deacon is still himself…" She shut her eyes. "The major events happen in places where significant moments in the life of a Chosen One happened. We've seen them in places where the Chosen were held, where they were found. Where they spent years of their lives. Where they died… But Trigorah was Chosen as well. She was disgraced, tainted by her allegiance to the D'Karon and her opposition to the rest of us, but she was Chosen."

She leaned on the map table. "He stole something relating to one of the five generals. It could have been her. But why does he need them. What is it about?"

Myranda fixed her gaze on the table. She flicked her eyes back and forth between the markers they had placed and the notes associated with them. The answers she sought remained elusive, but the edges of the facts began to weave together.

"The timing…" she mused.

"What about it?" Ayna asked, darting down to stand atop the map.

"If Calypso's account can be trusted, then the early echo in Territal preceded Deacon's arrival there by a considerable amount of time. But the echo here and his tampering that may have caused it were much closer together." She compared the notes. "We don't know much about what Deacon has been doing, nor precisely where. We don't even know which of these echoes are in places he directly influenced. But we do know that the more potent events are happening more rapidly as time goes on."

"And what does this imply to you?" Ayna asked.

"Nothing solid… but if Deacon *does* have a goal, and all of this is echoing back from it, it could be that the goal is drawing nearer to completion. And if things are becoming more intense as we approach that point… we may have a very trying time ahead."

The air crackled with power and Ether's fiery form returned. "Shut your eyes and open your mind." Ether turned. "All who have the capacity to focus mystically should do the same. I have found something, but I am uncertain of how much value it will be to us."

Myranda nodded and called her casting staff to her hand. Ayna flitted over and landed atop it. Both closed their eyes. The frustration and uncertainty of their investigation made proper focus difficult, but Myranda had more experience than most in enduring such madness with a still and steady mind. As the world around her dropped away and the luminous threads of the astral plane replaced them, Ether's voice filtered into her thoughts.

"What we seek is undeniable, but subtle," she whispered. "Seek it south of the city, in the fields where the attack seemed to originate."

Myranda coaxed her focus in the direction Ether indicated.

"It is easily missed. Not a point of light and power like a soul or a working of magic. And it is not the absence of such, as is so often the mark of

D'Karon works. It is a scar. A healing wound, getting smaller by the hour. A disruption. I cannot make it any clearer than that."

Myranda scoured the shadow of the landscape. She could feel her mind drawn onward by Ether's will, guided toward something that remained elusive. When her mind finally latched upon what Ether had detected, it was both painfully clear what it was and entirely understandable how it could have been missed. What lay at the center of the bygone disruption was less a defining characteristic and more a disruption of a pattern. Myranda would have had as much luck spotting a single misaligned brick in the palace walls. Once it was before her, it was clear as day, but without knowing precisely where to look, she might never have found it.

"This, or something quite like it, was present in the field when I witnessed a time echo. It was larger. And I noticed it only because it seemed to curl more tightly at the moment of the event."

"I am not certain this will provide us with any aid," Ayna said. "Our combined focus could easily stretch our search from one coast to the other, but a broad search will not be enough."

"No… No, this is one part of the key. This will let us know if we are searching in the correct place. What remains is for us to locate those places worth searching. It doesn't solve the puzzle, but it gives us what we need to know if we are on the trail of the solution. And that is more than we had."

#

Calypso paced out of the tavern. Her belly was full, and for the moment the messages had stopped flowing to and from her pad. Her mind felt fuzzy and unfocused in the way it tended to when she'd gone far too long without genuine rest. If the circumstances were different, she would have sought out someplace that could provide her with a warm bath and doze in it for half a day to restore the energy expended in her very taxing journey. Things were moving far too swiftly for that. If she was going to be prepared, she was going to have to resort to a technique she'd not had to call upon since her earliest days in magic. And to do that, she would need some peace and solitude.

"Miss! Miss Wizard!" called a voice from the doorway.

She slumped a bit. Clearly she would not be finding either of them here. "Yes, sir. How may I help you?" she said, summoning up the most genuine smile she could manage.

"I… er… you seemed like you might be heading someplace. And I don't think I saw any carriage or horse for you. I thought you might need some help."

"How very kind of you, but I—"

"I have a horse right there. A good strong one. You could ride in front of me. I'd take you anywhere you need to go."

169

"I am not much of a horseback rider, and as it happens I have my own means of transportation."

"I could make sure you don't fall off. I'm good and strong," he said.

Calypso sighed. "Tell me, sir, would you say that this establishment is representative of the north? Would you go so far as to say it is representative of the entirety of the continent?"

"Er. I don't suppose so. There's nicer ones."

"I'm not concerned with the building, mind you. I'm concerned about the patrons. Is this a particularly unsavory establishment? I ask because, through either your actions or your gaze, the vast majority of the people I've encountered within seemed to be motivated primarily by my appearance or by the silver I am carrying. By virtue of my recent arrival in this kingdom… Ulvard, I suppose you would be calling it now? Regardless, by virtue of my recent arrival, that means that most of the people I've met in the whole of the continent have been similarly motivated by lascivious desires, greed, or the assumption that I am likely to be easily bamboozled. It is not encouraging."

The man stammered for a moment. "We're a pretty bad lot," he admitted.

"That is a refreshing and encouraging bit of honesty, sir. That you would have the means to make such a determination suggests you are aware of venues with clientele more likely to behave in a civil and acceptable manner?"

"I've been to a few places that probably weren't too happy I'd been there."

"Excellent. I find myself rather pressed for time, but when the urgent tasks at hand have been seen to, I am hoping to open diplomatic relations between my adopted homeland and yours."

She swiftly jotted down a message on a slip of parchment. "Be a dear and deliver this to someone with the ear of your king or queen," she said. "And have some silver for your trouble. A bit more if you'll promise to do so swiftly."

"I don't… folks like me don't get an audience with the king and queen."

"You are holding a dispatch from a powerful kingdom that shares a border with your own. A wise leader will be receptive. Now, if you will excuse me."

She touched her fingers to the amulet about her neck. Heavy, wet snow sprang to life at her feet. Runners of crystal-clear ice formed. Elegant filigree of sparkling white traced out the form of a small but capable sleigh. She took a seat. The ice and snow ahead of the improvised vehicle smoothed itself. Behind the sleigh, it reared up into a low, rolling wave. It was enough to propel the sleigh forward, easily a match for the speed of a horse-drawn counterpart.

Her hair ruffled and fluttered in the breeze. Smoothing the snow ahead meant she could bridge small gaps or ease her way over obstacles, granting something of a personal road between herself and her intended destination. It was enormously taxing, but she was able to ease the load somewhat by letting her conjured legs transition back into a tail.

The journey was a mercifully brief one. All she required was a measure of distance from those who might interrupt her and a ready source of water. Within a few minutes she'd slipped deep enough into the countryside to have the former, and the latter presented itself soon after in the form of an icy stream.

Calypso eased her conjured vehicle to a stop and willed the ice on the shore of the stream to part itself. She drew her mind together into a net of spells that would ward off the worst effects of the cold, then slid into the stream. She braced herself against the bottom, eyes shut and mind open. Gradually the stresses on her mind and body eased away. Meditation calmed her mind. It calmed her spirit. The subtle power of the stream flowed into her and through her. When the time came, she would be restored. She would be ready.

#

"And finally, the valley," Myranda asserted.

They had worked swiftly, sweeping through Deacon's notes from the past few days and his records of the last few years. Myranda recounted every conversation she could recall on the subject of the Chosen and their greatest moments. If Deacon was seeking out such places now, it stood to reason they would be places he'd mused about in the past. With each new suggestion, the mystically adept combined their efforts to determine if it was marred in the same way that the field outside the city had been. Several were. But three of them thus far had showed something subtly different. There was a hint of the same disruption, though larger and more diffuse. But it felt important. And so they had continued.

"This valley. Here. This is where Trigorah died. And it is where the rest of us were captured."

Ayna and Ether, eyes shut and minds focused, murmured among themselves.

"Strange," Ether said.

"A place of power," Ayna said.

"There is something…" Ether continued. "Yes. There is a sign of the same blurred, softened distortion."

Myranda nodded and placed a marker on the map.

"Then that makes five. We need someone in each of these places as soon as possible. Each must carry a means to deliver a message to the rest of

171

us. We need to know if there has been some sort of an event there. If not, the lookout needs to stay there and alert the rest of us the *moment* one seems to be occurring. Even if there seems to have recently been an echo, we need to know. The disturbances happen where Deacon *will* be, not where he has been. These are places that fit the pattern he's traced across the landscape. We may just catch him before he arrives."

"I'll go to the farmhouse," Ivy said. "It's nearby. If I bring my violin and keep my strength up, I can make it there on foot by tomorrow."

"I'll go to the mountains in Tressor," Ether said. "I doubt any but me could reach it in time."

Myranda shook her head. "No. Not fast enough. I think you and Ether should go to the same place. Even if it means keeping track of fewer places, I'd prefer we stay close and nimble. Considering the tension at the border, it is likely best not to send someone south. I'll send a message to warn them."

"But what if they discover it is Deacon?" Ivy said.

Myranda took a breath. "I don't know. But we won't avoid that going there to wait for him. Our very journey there will raise suspicion and draw attention." She tightened her fist. "There is no right way to do this. The man I love is doing something I don't understand. Something that is endangering his people. What are the possible reasons? That he has lost his mind and I will have to subdue him? That he has been subverted and is the puppet of a dark will that is even now trying to maneuver us into killing him? But we have a job to do. I serve this world. And if Deacon were here, he would want me to do what it takes to protect his family and preserve the good we've done for this world. If you think you know better than me, then speak up. I am desperate for a better option. But I don't know that a good one exists."

The others looked to one another, then to Myranda again.

"Ivy and I will go to the farmhouse," Ether said. "It is the potential location with the least logical reason for him to visit and may be a low priority for him."

"I should be able to reach the cave in the Rachis Mountains in no time at all," Ayna said. "Calypso will be heading in that direction. I can coordinate to rendezvous with her."

"Good. That is midway along the Rachis Mountains. You can speed Myn and I along for the first half of our journey."

"Of course."

"Then the plans are made."

"What about Leo? Are we leaving him here alone?" Ivy asked.

"My father and Sadie will see to him. Right now the world needs us more than he does. We know what we all must do. Remember, everyone. This is Deacon. Remember what he has done for us, and what he has done for this world. We have to stop him from doing any damage, but our goal is to bring him to his senses, *not* to kill him. Now let's go do what needs to be done."

# Chapter 9

Ether flapped her wings and gazed down at the landscape below. Her favored form when tasked with transporting someone was that of a silver-feathered griffin. She'd assumed it often enough and for long enough that maintaining the shape required little additional effort, despite its size. This left enough of Ether's mind and spirit free to conjure winds to help speed her along more swiftly than a natural beast could achieve.

Ivy held on tightly to her back and matched her gaze. "This seems familiar now. We must be close," she said. "You're faster than I remember."

"Recent trials have caused me to hone my skills."

"Impressive for a creature who believed herself to be perfect."

"My primary flaw has been underestimating my own formidable capabilities," Ether said.

"Uh-huh," Ivy said flatly. "There, that's the place!"

The malthrope held a little more tightly as Ether wheeled toward the farmhouse nestled between two large fields below. As much as Ivy enjoyed the flight, she still hated the landing, something that Ether became acutely aware of as the grip about her neck became uncomfortable. She fluttered to the ground and allowed her form to ease back to human. Ivy stumbled a bit as the shape beneath her slipped away. Ether caught her arm and steadied her.

"Oh, wow," Ivy said, shaking herself a bit to chase away the jitters of the landing. "I remember this place so well. Right there is the barn where Myn slept. It was right after we found her. Right after she got big. And that's the farmhouse! Oh, do you think Sandra is home?"

"There is smoke from the chimney. I should say she is."

Ivy squealed and hopped in place. "I can't wait to say hello again!"

"We are here with a task, Ivy," Ether said.

The malthrope put her hands on her hips. "Is this the right place? Do you feel the scar or whatever on the landscape?"

"It is, and I do."

"Then the 'task' we have to do is wait and see if Deacon shows up or if something out of place in time happens. Between my ears, my nose, and your magic, we can do that easily enough while visiting with Sandra." She grabbed

Ether's hand to pull her forward. "Come on!"

Ether stubbornly refused to speed her pace to match Ivy's enthusiasm.

"Oh, the cabbage is doing so well," Ivy said. "Isn't it amazing how it can grow even through the coldest months? I wonder how much Sandra knows about it. I'll bet she'd love to talk about it."

The shapeshifter stopped for a moment. Ivy turned to face her.

"Is something wrong?"

"You do understand that we are on the fringe of what might well be a horribly destructive arcane event, don't you?"

"I can't say I understand it, but I'm aware of it."

"And yet you are giddy at the thought of discussing the particulars of growing cabbages with a woman you've met once before."

"Three times! She was invited to some of the ceremonies over the last few years."

"That is not the aspect that puzzles me, and you know it."

"Ether, I haven't exactly had a normal life. None of the Chosen have, if you get right down to it. Sometimes it feels like I've spent more of my life dealing with things that might end it than I've spent actually *living*. You've got to steal the happy moments any way you can."

"But the moments are simply moments. Fleeting."

"That's not a very challenging notion, Ether."

"How can you enjoy something knowing that someday it will be gone?"

"How can you *not*? That it is fleeting makes it all the more precious. And besides. The nice thing about life just being a bunch of moments strung together is that the bad times are just moments too. They'll pass by just as surely as the good ones do. And then there's the next chance for something nice."

Ether gave Ivy a measuring look.

"How could so simple a creature with so few years in this world have attained such wisdom?"

Ivy grinned and gave Ether's shoulder a shove. "You want to know the secret?" She leaned forward and whispered in Ether's ear. "I knew I didn't know much, so I listened to people who did."

She backed up and took Ether by the shoulders. "Your problem was you knew too much from the beginning and thought you couldn't learn any more. If you don't move forward, eventually people will pass you, no matter how slow they are. Now come on. If you want to learn a little something about stealing happiness in the moments between adventures, follow me. I smell apple pie, and if I know Sandra, she'll be willing to share a slice."

#

Ayna buzzed in the mouth of an unremarkable cave in the Ravenwood face of the Rachis Mountains.

"A cave…" she muttered, eying the darkness ahead. "I agreed to come to another cave."

She flitted forward a bit, then pulled back. Even a few yards into the maw of the cave gave her the terrible sensation of enclosure and captivity.

"The return to Entwell is going to be unpleasant."

She buzzed back and landed on an icy branch and shut her eyes. The wind from the mountains curled about her wings. She should have felt at home here, just as much as she did in Entwell. All the wind was connected. When she focused, she could even feel the familiarity of this breeze, as though she had sat in this very spot before. And though she didn't feel cut off, as she had inside the jar, she still felt lonely. What worried her wasn't that feeling but the slow realization that the loneliness was a return to normal. She wasn't any *more* isolated and alone here, in the middle of a vast world she'd left behind long ago, than she was in Entwell, the place she'd called her home for longer than most fairies could hope to live. Ayna tried to set her concerns aside. She came here for a reason, after all. But the odd, creeping anxiousness remained. Fairies were *not* solitary creatures. Yet somehow she'd cut herself off from the others.

"It doesn't matter," she grumbled to herself. "Such has been the way of things for *years*. Why should something that has been perfectly acceptable for so long suddenly concern me?"

The swirls of wind brought the distant hissing slide of ice on snow. Almost more confounding to her than the feeling of loneliness was the buoyant feeling that came with the realization that Calypso was approaching. After decades of being completely self-reliant, she found she craved companionship. It was unpleasantly like discovering a nutrient that once meant nothing and now she couldn't live without.

"Ayna!" Calypso called out, her gleaming sleigh grinding to a stop on the jagged debris at the foot of the mountain.

"Calypso," Ayna said with calculated aloofness.

The water master stepped up to the base of the tree where Ayna was perched. She was dressed differently from when they'd parted ways. Most notably, she had donned a long fur-lined coat.

"What is this all about?" Ayna asked, gesturing to the clothes.

"I suppose life in Entwell has spoiled me a bit. The temperatures were grating on me, and rather than squandering my strength keeping myself warm, I encountered a lovely traveling market on the way here that had quite a selection of warm clothing. Nothing for fairies, I am afraid."

Ayna crossed her arms and threw her head back. "They *wouldn't* have anything for fairies. We get no respect here." She buzzed down and perched on Calypso's shoulder, shuffling into the furry fringe of the hood.

"Has the time echo occurred yet?"

"I… haven't made that determination yet."

"Why not?"

Ayna narrowed her eyes and glanced to the darkened mouth of the cave.

"Oh! Oh, I see." Calypso smiled sweetly. "It was very kind of you to wait for me. With your speed, I was worrying I wouldn't have the opportunity to investigate at all. Would you like me to go first? Perhaps you could stay here and watch from the outside?"

"No. We should combine our expertise," Ayna said.

"Splendid."

The mermaid paced inside. She fished out the pad and flipped to the appropriate page. Ayna focused enough for her glow to light the way.

"According to Myranda, this cave is where she found Myn. If we are watching for an event, it will likely be a clash of dragons." She closed the pad. "Exciting."

Ayna muttered uncomfortably as Calypso paced deeper.

"How has the outside world been treating you?" Calypso asked.

"It hasn't been treating me at all. We have a job to do."

"But you've been to Kenvard already. I've only heard stories about it, and all of them are from the days before the massacre. When our task is through, I look forward to seeing it."

"I don't imagine we will find anything out here that is more impressive than what can easily be found in Entwell."

"It's not about being impressive. It's about being unique."

They paced deeper. The wind outside howled at the mouth of the cave. Ayna slipped a little deeper into the ruffle of the hood. She sniffed the air.

"Do you smell that?" she asked.

"Fresh char," Calypso said. "And if there was a dragon here, I suspect we would be aware by now."

"So we've missed the time echo."

"It would appear so. But the prevailing theory is that the echoes precede Deacon's appearance. He may yet be coming along. We should investigate as best we can and await word from the others."

She crouched down. Ayna peered down from her shoulder.

"Can you feel it?" Calypso asked.

"Faintly. An odd twist of existence, but not of magic. The only distinctive aspect of this place but still quite easy to miss if we'd not been told to look for it."

"Mmm… It feels… stable. If this *is* the sort of thing that changes with time, drawing inward until the point that Deacon causes it, I would expect to notice the shift."

"Agreed. I believe he has come and gone."

Calypso tipped her head aside. Her hair dangled down beside Ayna.

"I feel something else."

"I do not."

"It is weak. One moment…"

"Deacon…" Ayna murmured. "I never would have believed it. That he could bring about something like this. That he would be capable of it, not just from a competence standpoint, but in terms of wisdom and judgment."

"You were never very fond of him. You spoke quite passionately against him just days ago."

"I am not fond of anyone. And he broke our rules. I stand by my assessment. But he was of Entwell. His area of study may have been a pointless endeavor, but he pursued it with dedication. He should have known better."

Calypso revealed the dagger she'd been entrusted with. She placed it down on the point in the cave where the odd twist of the fabric of the place was most prevalent. "Do you feel it now?" she said.

Ayna shut her eyes. "I can't… yes. Yes, I can feel it. There is a force between them. They repel each other."

Calypso picked it back up and looked it over. "It's a good sign. Azriel knew what she was doing when she provided it." She shut her eyes. "If we use it, it may well work. I only hope we don't have to."

"Do you have the package that Deacon left?" Ayna said.

"I do."

"And what was inside?"

"I do not know. I haven't opened it."

"Calypso, it is clear by now that Deacon is at fault for potentially ruinous events. His privacy is undeserving of consideration."

"Whether or not that is so, he has taken steps to protect it."

"Let me see it," Ayna demanded.

Calypso retrieved the small bundle from within her things. The fairy darted down and quickly set about tearing it open. She failed miserably. A tight, potent swirl of magic ripped at the package but did little more than blast the pair of wizards with kicked up ice and dust.

"I don't understand it. This is a bundle of *canvas*."

"It is a bundle of canvas enchanted by a peerless gray wizard. If it is to be opened, it won't be opened by *us*."

Ayna stewed angrily.

"Get that bundle out of my sight. The sooner we find and stop Deacon, the sooner I can put his frustrating mystic workings behind me…"

\#

Myranda stood on the rocky shelf overlooking a valley in the Rachis Mountains. This place brought back chilling memories. Of all the times the Chosen had nearly fallen to the forces of the D'Karon, this was the nearest they'd come to total defeat. The wind howled as visions of that day flashed through her mind. Myn huddled around her, wings raised against the wind and puffs of flame replacing the warmth the icy gales stripped away.

She placed a hand on Myn's side. It felt strange to have nothing more to do than to stand here and wait. The evidence of history repeating itself had been fresh when she arrived. Boot prints. Black blood. All far too recent to have been anything but a recurrence of the battle that had just a few years prior made this valley infamous. It felt important that she had arrived so near to the event yet late enough to miss it. Like fate was sending her a message, sparing her the pain but leaving her the certainty. Deacon would come here. The only question was when. Time, once so reliable, was now an unknown. With the echo so recent, would Deacon come here next? Some of the other sites the Chosen and their allies had been dispatched to were similarly disturbed. Would Deacon reach them first? Or had they missed him entirely?

She kept her mind in a high state of focus, constantly listening and feeling for any of a thousand things that might suggest she or one of the others had found him. She could feel the barely detectable scar on the fabric of this place. She could feel the dull mystic thrum of a place where a disgraced Chosen One had lost her life. But none of the things she sought. No glimmers of Deacon's soul. No messages from the others.

Myn was the first to see it when it finally happened. Her head darted up. "There!" shouted the faithful beast.

Myranda followed her gaze to a point tucked in a nearby crevice of the rocky cliffside. A gleam of ragged purple energy appeared. It swirled and spread. Within the churning indigo tendrils, a deep black circle formed. It widened until it was man-sized, then clarified until she was looking upon a window to another part of the world entirely. The badly damaged black stone of a D'Karon fort became visible. Myranda's heart froze in her chest as Deacon stepped into view.

The days had been unkind to him. There was no longer any doubt that the affliction had dug its roots deep into him. Far deeper than she'd imagined. He stepped through the portal with his gem in the chaotic hand. No longer content to simply change from one form to another without notice or regard for reality, now his arm sought to be many things at once. Through his sheer force of will, it remained recognizably human most of the time, but multiple other potential forms fought for control of it at the same time. They were ghostly overlays atop reality, simultaneous afterimages trailing his arm as he moved. Wretched, semisolid mockeries of his arm flickered into view and out again. Feral claws. Stone gauntlets. Skeletal spikes. Pure, porcelain-white flesh. And they didn't stop at his hand. The chaotic visions claimed much of his arm. Veins of shifting discoloration had reached his neck. The many potentialities of form came and went, all secondary to his true self, but in constant struggle for dominance.

His eyes set upon Myranda. At first sight of her, a powerful wave of shame and regret claimed his face. The intensity of it chased the chaos from him, leaving Deacon briefly as she'd always known him.

Myn uncurled from around Myranda and stalked closer to Deacon. She spread her wings and, with a pained expression, let a wisp of flame curl from her nostrils. Though she could now speak, the posture was far more efficient at delivering her feelings and intentions. She didn't like it, but she could and would attack if needed. Myranda took her place beside the beast, her own expression similarly pained.

"Myranda," he said. "I should have known you'd work out a way to find me."

"You've tracked me across the world to help me when I needed it. What sort of a woman would I be if I didn't do the same?" she said.

She released her staff, leaving it to drift beside her, and pulled two pads from her things. "In the valley, now," she scribbled onto each.

"Two pads?" Deacon said. He took a step forward.

Myn lowered her head and bared her teeth. "Stay back," she warned.

"Why do you need two pads?" he asked.

"Because the people of Entwell have pads as well now. Ayna and Calypso have come to help."

"They have? I thought I felt them, but I… I can't always trust my instincts at the moment."

"They came to help you. They were worried about you."

"Worried about me, or worried what I might do?"

"At this moment, both are valid concerns, Deacon, you aren't right."

"I know. I know I'm not right." He held up his hand. "It is getting more difficult to keep myself intact. But I need this now. I can't find my way to the root of things without it. I can't cast the spells that need to be cast without it."

"I've read your notes, Deacon," she said.

"I imagined you would. I wanted you to. I would have protected them, otherwise. Do you see the brilliance of them?"

"All I see is a man coping with his own slipping sanity."

"All revolutionary ideas appear to be madness at first. Myranda, there is a deeper truth to the world. Deeper than elements. Deeper than raw magic. We never had the means to access it before because there is more to magic than the words and the forces. There is the one *casting* the spells. You cannot effect change in a world that you are not a part of. A character in a play cannot change the world of the audience, because they are of a different kind. The people of this world cannot manipulate the most fundamental and abstract elements of existence, because, compared to the gods, we are no more real than the characters on the stage. But there are those who walk among us that are born of the gods. The Chosen, Myranda."

Both pads flipped open again. Styluses jotted down messages from the others, acknowledging Myranda.

"They're coming," Myranda said. "Listen, Deacon. I don't want to see you hurt. My love for you might stay my hand if the time comes that nothing less will stop you. But you know as well as I do that Ether will not hesitate. Ayna will not hesitate. You need to stop this insanity before they arrive."

"No! Please, listen. If you could understand, you would agree with me. It is alchemy, just at a higher level! Even someone devoid of mystic skill and power can do works of magic with the proper ingredients. Mix together the right components, each with their own effects, and you can produce the effects of your choosing. The Chosen, combined, have the power to change fate. It is why you exist. And if you can change fate, you can change other things as well."

"We won't help you do whatever it is you are trying to do."

"Of course not! I wouldn't want you to. If this goes wrong, I don't want the stain on your hands. And that's why I need this!" He held up his disorderly hand. "It isn't just in my arm. It is in my mind. I am seeing things from different angles, thinking in different ways. I can do what needs to be done. I just need the ingredients. And if you want to change reality, it isn't enough to simply sample from objects. It isn't just things to sprinkle into a cauldron. Artifacts are necessary, but I also need to collect moments, experiences, places…"

He slipped his healthy hand into his pocket. Myn and Myranda tensed, but he revealed what appeared to be a simple coin. Myranda's eyes locked upon it. There was nothing physical that suggested it was remarkable, but the mere presence of the coin made the valley seem like a reflection. Insubstantial and illusory in comparison. He released coin and gem, willing each into the opposite hand. The moment he was no longer clutching the gem with his monstrous hand, it ceased to behave itself. The flickering potential forms started to twist his flesh. He gripped the coin and crouched.

"What are you doing?" she demanded.

Deacon pressed the coin to the ground in the precise point where the supernatural scar had marred this place. There was no light, no crackle of energy or flex of arcane might. But from the moment the coin touched the ground, the form of his arm writhed and boiled. He struggled, eyes shut tightly and face twisted in pain. Myn was able to bring herself to action before Myranda could. She surged forward and butted him. He was thrown back, sprawling on the ground a few yards away. His gem flared. He shakily rose to his feet, coin still in hand. No damage seemed to have been done, but the coin was imperceptibly more significant than it had been before.

"Look, see?" he said, swapping the gem and coin again. "The valley is intact. I've done what I must, and no harm is done. The coin is only a focus. I am close. I just need a little more. Somewhere down there is the place where Trigorah Teloran died. Surely you feel it. That may be enough to complete what I've started. The blue moon is tomorrow night. If I have the pieces by then, I will succeed, I know I will."

"The blue moon… that *is* when you will cast the spell, isn't it?"

"Of course. Something so powerful could succeed on no other day. It will be perfect, you will see."

"Perfect? Deacon do you know what is happening? Things that were gone and buried are digging themselves back up. Soldiers who died decades ago are marching to the front again. And it is getting worse! If things continue as they have been, who knows how many lives could be lost before the blue moon tomorrow night? Do you understand what sort of horrors could fall upon the world? The Kenvard Massacre nearly happened again."

He shook as if struck. "Has anyone been hurt?"

"Not that we know of, but it is only a matter of time. The Northern Alliance and Tressor spent more than a century at war. Land that was fought over a hundred years ago has been reclaimed for towns and farms. People might awaken tomorrow to find themselves in the middle of a battle."

A horrid pain swept across Deacon's face. He held the coin in his palm. The dancing images of chaos claiming his arm rattled and trembled. Deacon shuddered. He turned his head away and his expression changed.

"It is worth it, Myranda," he said through clenched teeth.

The voice was almost not his own, cold and disconnected.

"Worth it? How many people need to be hurt before it stops being worth it, Deacon? How many people need to die for the price to be too high?"

Deacon did not answer. His gaze drifted to the ground. Myranda's grip on her staff tightened.

"You shouldn't have to think, Deacon."

The wind was starting to kick up. Help was on the way.

"That was a D'Karon portal you used to come here," Myranda said. "Desmeres is concerned Epidime may have gotten his claws into you."

The mention of the D'Karon general's name snapped him back to reality in a way that his own name failed to. He looked up, desperation in his face.

"No! No, Myranda, I assure you, Epidime remains where I left him. Take my hand, I'll show you."

He stepped forward. Myranda stepped back. Myn thrashed the ground with her tail and huffed a rolling puff of flame, just shy of a full attack.

"Your mark! I… here, look." He flipped the Kenvard coin in his hand, such that the mark struck his palm. "The mark spares me! I haven't been taken by Epidime."

"Then there is still a chance for you to stop whatever this is, to tell us what you've done and how to keep it from tearing apart the world we've sought so hard to save."

He closed his hand tightly around the coin. Again he was silent, grappling with Myranda's words. He slumped a bit, fatigue and anxiety showing through the cracks in his certainty.

"I think… I think…" He shuddered, shutting his eyes tightly again.

Pain wracked him. The churning mass of half-substantial arm spasmed. When he opened his eyes, he looked like a cornered creature watching the walls close in on him. "I think I've spoken to you for too long."

He took a step back. His crystal flashed with a brilliant light. Myranda and Myn flinched away from the brightness. When it subsided, where Deacon had once stood, there was now a crowd of precise duplicates.

"Leave me to my work, please," they said in unison.

Myranda and Myn dashed forward. Myranda reached out with her magic, dispelling two and three of the illusions at a time. Myn lashed with her tail and swatted with her claws. None of the things they targeted were the true Deacon. A dozen of the figures leaped from the cliff, surges of magic controlling their descent. Myn spread her wings and leaped into the air. Myranda dashed for the edge and wrapped her will about herself, controlling her drop.

The dragon managed three wheeling passes, each time singling out one of the false Deacons. Only five of them reached the ground. Myranda landed hard. She raised her staff and brought it down. The ice and snow rolled in a wave. Four of the images of Deacon stumbled and fell as the wave passed them. For the final one, the wave split around him.

"That's him, Myn!" Myranda called.

Deacon was running for the only distinct portion of the valley, a ring of five enormous trees that flanked a narrow, icy stream. The dragon landed and charged at him, ready to snatch him up.

He raised his gem. A fresh swirl of D'Karon magic curled in the air. It swelled, opening into a fresh portal in a blur of motion. The portal widened. Myn dug her claws into the icy stone, but her momentum was too great. She tumbled through the portal with an angry roar.

For a moment, the roar was in two places at once. The portal snapped shut with a soft burst of untamed energy. A far more furious second roar rang out, now from the top of the cliff. All he'd done was transport Myn to the top of the cliff again, but it was enough of a delay and distraction for him to cross the threshold of the ring of trees.

Myranda sprinted for the trees. Deacon was already among them. But as she approached the edge of the ring, she felt something deep in her core that was enough stop her pursuit. She could see what lay before her. It was nothing more than a patch of ice and snow. But something inside her insisted there was a yawning abyss before her. Something vast, endless, labyrinthine. Everything in her mind and spirit screamed for her to remain where she was.

Deacon continued forward, heedless. He passed behind a tree but did not emerge from the other side. Myranda neither saw nor felt any sign that he had truly vanished. He was still very much in the valley with them. But somehow he was also impossibly far away. He may as well have leaped into a bottomless pit, still very much within the confines of this little hidden piece of the mountains but miles away and moving farther by the moment. The feelings were conflicting, confounding, and yet she knew that they were genuine. There was something very wrong with this ring of trees.

Myn struck the ground beside her and held her ground.

"You feel it too," Myranda said.

"What is it?" Myn muttered.

"I don't know… But I need to find out."

Myn curled a paw around Myranda to haul her away from the trees and close to her. "Do not," Myn pleaded.

The wind was whipping now. Ether was nearly here.

"Listen. I don't know what will happen to me, but Deacon has gone in there. If he can still be saved, I have to follow to save him. If he cannot be saved, I have to follow to stop him. Either way, I have no choice. Stay behind. Tell Ether what happened. Tell them to keep watch elsewhere. Tell them that the blue moon is the key. That is the moment all of this is heading toward. And in case it is dangerous, make certain no one else enters this ring of trees. One way or another, I'll be back."

Myn's jaw tightened. She raised her head, shut her eyes, and let Myranda go. Myranda gave her friend a pat on the leg and dashed into the circle of trees.

Joseph R. Lallo

# Chapter 10

The first steps between the trees sent a wave of vertigo through Myranda. She stumbled a bit but continued. Ten long strides. Twenty. After she'd taken fifty paces into the ring of trees, she'd yet to reach the opposite side of the ring. From the outside, the edges of the ring looked to be only a dozen or so paces apart, but no amount of running brought her any closer to the far side.

Myranda stopped to catch her breath. She turned her head to see how far she'd gone. There should have been just two trees behind her, but now a thickening forest lay there. Hundreds of trees clustered more and more densely until their interlocking branches cast the ground in total darkness. She turned back and found the valley had been replaced with more forest, sprawling onward into a shadowy void.

"What is this place?" Myranda breathed.

Her eyes swept across the darkness as she listened. There was only silence. Even the howling wind had faded away. Then, a steady crunch of snow underfoot. She squinted in the direction of the sound. A shadowy figure stepped into the light of the clearing. He was old, with a short, well-kept white beard and a clean white blindfold across his eyes. His clothes were simple brown robes.

"Welcome, Myranda," he said. "It has been too long since we last spoke."

"Oriech…" she said. "Is this place your doing? Is this real? Or have you pulled me from the world to offer more cryptic advice?"

"You ask many complex questions, Myranda. Is this place my doing? No. It has been here for as long as the valley has. To my knowledge none of the gods has taken credit for it, though I have my suspicions your patron is to blame. It has a mischief to it. Is it real? Not quite. But real enough to have consequences. And I did not bring you here, for advice or otherwise. You entered freely, which I am sorry to say carries a price."

"A price! Oriech, there are lives at stake. I am trying to stop Deacon before he does any more damage."

"On that point you can rest at ease. He will do no more damage for as long as he is here. Nothing he does here can affect the outside world, and he will leave this place only after he has paid the same price as you. Follow me, please."

Oriech turned and took a few steps. Myranda lingered.

"Oriech, explain yourself," she demanded. "I don't have time for this."

He turned back. "You will leave this place precisely twenty-four hours from the moment you crossed the threshold. As will Deacon. That will place you mere seconds behind him. Until then, you have all the time in the world. Now follow. I will explain along the way."

He continued. Myranda reluctantly matched his pace.

"We call this place the forest of Spirit Oak. All times here are one. If you have ever come to this place, you will always *be* in this place, even after you leave."

"That doesn't make any sense."

"It doesn't make sense by the rules that govern the rest of existence, but it is perfectly in keeping with this place. When you have spoken with me in the past, pulled aside from the world, you were pulled here. When I do not walk among you in the guise of a jingoistic man of the cloth, or a wise and put-upon old slave, or a grumpy curator in Territal's archives, I am here."

"Why didn't I know of this place?" she asked.

"Because it isn't *for* you. You were never supposed to come here. The way isn't even supposed to be open to the living. It would appear Deacon's tinkering has changed that."

"Who is it for, if not the living?"

"The Perpetual War was not the only dire time this world will ever face. And, lest we forget, we have already lost a Chosen One. It was decreed that there should be a means to purify even the most tainted of Chosen."

"Purify… Then can you cure Deacon?"

"We can. We can do most anything. But that will be his choice, not ours. All who choose to enter this place are tested. For each test you pass, no matter how long it takes, a single hour passes in the outside world. When you pass the final test, you reach the center of the forest and you are granted one request. Within certain limits and our own discretion, virtually any request can be granted, so long as it only applies to the one making the request. We will not change the world. We will only change *you*. For most, that request will be to leave the forest. You may make another request, but you will be forced to prove your way to the center again to be permitted to leave, at the cost of another day, and a far more strenuous trial."

As they walked, the darkness of the forest grew deeper. The crackle of ice and snow changed to the crunch of grass and leaves.

"You are Chosen, and you are pure. Your tests will be mild. Those who have been badly tainted will face harsher tests and more of them. I suggest you take your time on them. Here, at least, you can have a respite from the weight you've taken upon yourself."

"Just get it over with," Myranda said.

"Very well. Your first test. Why did you enter this place?"

"I entered this place because Deacon needs to be saved from himself, and the world needs to be saved from him."

He nodded. "Selfless. Devoted. A proper reason. You have passed your first test. Continue forward for your next test."

"How will I know I've found it?"

"Everything here is a test, Myranda. Good luck to you."

"Do I need luck?"

"This place was not meant for the living. You may. You'll find out along the way, but for some tests, the consequences for failure could be dire."

"Why would you do this?"

"I do this for the same reason I do everything, Myranda. Because it is my purpose, and because I have no choice. Now, let us begin. Because you are pure, and because you have proved yourself time and time again, I will give you the only piece of guidance you should need. Just move forward. You'll know when you are through."

#

Myn stood, eyes trained on the ring of trees. Her nostrils flared. Her tongue flicked at the air. Every fiber of her being and every instinct and sense available to the formidable hunter scoured the valley for some semblance of the two humans she cared for above all others. All that remained of either of them was the fading scent of their trail as they'd entered.

The first sound she heard beside the whistle of wind through the leaves of the terrible trees that took her friends away was the crackle of flame far above. She turned her eyes to the sky. Ether's fiery form dropped down from above.

"Where are they? What has happened?" Ether demanded.

"Myranda and Deacon are inside," Myn said.

"Inside where?"

"The trees. They stepped between and were gone."

"And you did not follow? Come, quickly!" Ether said.

Myn lashed her tail around to block Ether as she motioned to enter. "No. Myranda said to wait."

"She could be in need of our aid."

Myn's expression hardened. "She *said* to wait. And there is more."

"What? What have you learned?"

"Deacon will cast his spell during the blue moon."

189

"The blue moon. That is tomorrow night." Ether looked aside. "Yes… The way things are worsening… it *would* make perfect sense if it aligned with the new moon. If something needs to be done about Deacon before then, and we know precisely where he is, we should follow him."

"Myranda said to wait," Myn said.

More wind whistled. A tiny, gleaming point darted down from the sky. Ayna buzzed to a stop beside the others.

"We were summoned?" Ayna said.

"Myranda is in the ring of trees, which has some manner of mystic significance. Deacon is there too. We now know that he has been preparing for the blue moon to cast whatever spell he is seeking to cast."

"Then what are we waiting for?!"

"Myranda said wait," Myn repeated.

"I will not do something foolish simply because Myranda wants us to. I was given to believe there was a degree of urgency."

Ayna darted up to enter the ring of trees. Myn reared up to block her.

The fairy gave a defiant look. "I am not afraid of dragons. One of my colleagues is a dragon and far more powerful than you. I intend to follow Myranda and solve this problem once and for all."

"Myranda. Said. *Wait,*" Myn stated, punctuating the final word with a curl of flame.

Even once she'd learned a language besides that with which she was born, Myn had remained a creature of few words. But rhetoric tends to take on a different meaning depending upon the speaker. When a dragon speaks emphatically, it makes an impression.

Ayna flitted back a bit. "How *long* do we wait?" the fairy asked.

"Until she returns," Myn said.

The dragon settled down and trained her eyes on the ring of trees again. Ayna glanced at Ether uncertainly, then darted down and perched between Myn's horns to grudgingly join the vigil.

#

Deacon paced through the forest. Eyes wide and crystal held high. Unlike Myranda, he'd not been met by a familiar figure when he had entered the place. He'd simply been treated to the odd and unexplained disappearance of the valley and appearance of an ever thickening forest for what felt like ages. When Oriech finally deemed the moment right, he came first as a voice.

"I didn't expect you to come this far, Deacon."

The wizard slowed and looked more warily about but didn't stop his purposeful journey.

"You knew what you would find here. That is reason enough not to enter," Oriech's disembodied voice remarked.

190

"I knew of Gilliam's teachings, and I theorized this was the place to which he had been referring. A place of power and trials. But Gilliam's words could seldom be taken at face value," Deacon said.

"You can make that claim. But your mind and intentions are clear here. Perhaps you have convinced yourself of that fact, but I know the truth. You will be tested."

"I am no stranger to tests. How many shall I face?"

"Twenty-four."

"I see. I would have assumed five. That seems to be the number of this world. Five Chosen. Five tests."

"That would hardly be the first mistake you have made."

"Quite true. Mistakes are evidence of effort. If you aren't making mistakes, you aren't learning." Deacon twitched and flinched. He felt a hot bolt of chaos curl through his spirit and stir his thoughts.

"We speak a great deal of rules," Oriech said. "Life is governed by such things. At a certain level, rules are all that matter. Rules *form* the game."

"And a wizard's place is to learn the rules and utilize them to produce the desired effects."

"You are playing at a level that was never meant for you. You are attempting to rewrite the rules."

"Every game has flaws. We should not be prisoners to the mistakes made by those before us. Or above us."

Oriech stepped out of the woods ahead. "That you came here, as you are, is regrettable. Now this version of you, as you are, shall exist as a record within this place. Not the best face to put forward to history. And more to the point, not the best mind to tackle the tests I have for you. Fortunately, my service to fate has afforded me a bit of latitude. Hold still."

Deacon took a step back. "You cannot take the chaos away. Not yet. I need it."

"Not that you have any say in the matter at this moment, but I do not intend to cure you. I merely wish to render you stable enough to know that I am testing *you* and not some errant twist of a tumultuous mind."

Oriech touched the shoulder of the shifting, tainted arm. The struggle to keep it in shape eased. After a moment, Deacon found that the effort he had been expending to tame the affliction was unnecessary. It was as though his crown and ring had been returned. His restless mind was tamed, though very much still under the influence of the chaos to a diminished degree. His expression changed. The clarity that returned to his mind was unwelcome. It cast some of his recent acts and motivations in a stark light. He did not like what he saw.

"You came here seeking contact with a fallen Chosen. You wished to sample that essence for your spell. Your spell has been devised to violate the laws set forth by the very beings responsible for your world. Suffice to say that is *not* a virtuous reason for entry. You have failed your first test."

Deacon rummaged in his bag and revealed the coin. He pressed the marked side of it to his palm.

"You haven't betrayed your world yet. Your crimes are of a different kind. The world is feeling the echoes of what you have *yet to do.* You have done something no wizard before has had the capacity or the inclination to even attempt. You have created a fixed point in history. An inevitability. There is nothing anyone can do to prevent what you've set out to do. All we can do is learn if there is enough wisdom and integrity left in you to solve the problem you will soon create."

Oriech paced ahead toward a clearing that had not been present moments earlier. "Your trials will be particularly difficult. That much I can assure you."

#

Myranda stepped into the next clearing. In a life that had been defined by absurd and impossible events, she should have become accustomed to unexpected obstacles between herself and her goal. This forest was testing her patience. Deacon's fate, and quite likely the fate of the world, hung in the balance. Yet she was being asked to prove her worth through puzzles and trials. Perhaps her time as first a duchess and then a queen had spoiled her somewhat, but she could feel her temper flaring more than it had in years.

The clearing before her gradually populated with what would clearly be her next test. A wide river of icy water rippled through the forest ahead of her. At first glance, it looked entirely impassible. The flow was rapid, and there was no bridge in sight. A dense fog had rolled in across the water, shrouding everything more than a few yards from shore.

"Move forward…" she muttered.

Thus far the tests had been minor. Bits of forest that tried to turn her around. Dead ends with puzzles or riddles that would part the trees when solved. This was the first obstacle for which the proper course of action was not immediately clear.

She paced along the shore, eyes scanning the hazy distance. The first clue of what was to be done came in the form of a stout rope strung a few feet above the water. A vessel of sorts sat beneath it with a short tether connecting it to the rope via a loose loop. Unlike most of the ferries of this sort that she'd encountered, the vessel itself was barely larger than a one-person raft. It looked terribly rickety, but she imagined if it were sturdy and reliable, then this wouldn't have been a test.

## The Coin of Kenvard

Myranda stepped shakily onto the ferry. She shut her eyes and focused, but her magic refused to obey her. That was hardly a surprise. Myranda had imagined that her time here might mirror her experiences in the crystal arena, but the truth was much more frustrating. There, her magic was not only available to her, but enhanced. Here, the sorts of spells she could cast and the proficiency with which she could cast them varied from test to test. At the moment, she may as well have never learned a scrap of magic for all the good it was doing her.

"Very well. At least the way forward is clear."

She secured her staff behind her back and hauled at the rope. Tug by tug she slid away from the shore. It was hard work. The current was quite strong, and sliding the loop along the rope required a tremendous amount of force. Throwing her weight against the rope caused the raft to shift about beneath her feet, constantly threatening to pitch her into the water or leave her dangling by the rope itself. She gritted her teeth and fell into a rhythm. Somewhere out there, Deacon was facing similar tests. If she wanted to reach him, she had to solve them just as he did.

The rope creaked. The water splashed and dragged at the raft. Myranda tried to stay focused on the task, if only to keep her mind from dwelling upon what Deacon had done, what he was doing, and what might be happening beyond this place. The fog had swallowed the shore she'd left behind. She was entirely surrounded by gray mist. The far shore had yet to become visible. The isolation and disorientation wore upon her mind.

A mote of darkness loomed into view ahead. Each tug of the rope dragged her closer. Gradually, the indistinct darkness resolved into a rocky outcrop sticking up from the water. It was little more than a few large stones, one of which stuck up sharply above the others. The spire of stone had an iron ring set into it, through which the rope had been anchored and steadied. It continued onward into the endless gray, but for the moment Myranda's eyes lingered on something else clinging to the tiny foothold in the rushing river.

At first it wasn't clear what she was looking upon. It only seemed to exist at the edge of her vision. Any attempt to look at it directly caused it to fade away. She dragged herself closer and attempted to draw her mind into some semblance of focus. While she'd been stripped of the capacity to cast any spells, steadying her mind and deepening her concentration served to sharpen her view of whatever lingered upon the stone.

What held on to the stone tightly was not a thing of flesh and bone. Indeed, there was no solid form at all. She saw highlights and shadows, but not the structure that the tricks of the light traced out. The ghostly figure was broadly human in shape, slender and lithe of build.

"Hello?" Myranda called as she neared the outcropping. "Who are you?"

The spirit raised its head. For a moment it flickered to solidity.

"Friend or foe," the figure replied.

Its voice was as insubstantial as its appearance, an echo without the sharpness of its original sound.

"Friend, until you give me reason to be otherwise," Myranda replied. She pulled herself the final few feet to the outcrop and placed a boot on the slick surface. "You are the first creature I have encountered here. Are you being tested as well?" she asked.

"Tested. Always. This is a strange one. Different from most."

"Why can't I see you?"

The figure flickered again. "Nothing to see," the stranger replied. "I don't believe there is much left of me."

Though the figure couldn't maintain visibility or solidity for any amount of time, its voice became more distinct. It was a woman's voice. She had a frazzled tone that somehow maintained a degree of nobility, as though this place had worn her down but not yet broken her dignity.

"Who are you?" Myranda asked.

A wry laugh echoed around her. "That was the first to go. Not much use for identity here."

"Do you need help?"

She crouched down and cautiously reached for the figure. As her fingers approached the arm gripping the stone, the limb shifted to visibility. The mere proximity of Myranda's body loaned substance, the light of a torch pushing back the darkness. The swirling solidity spread to the rest of her body. The finer details of her face remained elusive, smoky and blurred like a half-remembered dream. Rather than clothes, the figure wore armor, too eroded and disheveled to be identified. Myranda was able to grasp her arm and pull her to her feet.

"How long have you been here?" Myranda asked.

The unknown woman paused. "I do not know how to answer that question. But you sound familiar to me."

"I wish I could say the same. Your voice sounds so far away. How did you get here? On this rock. Are you trying to get to the other side?"

"I don't know. I just… have been here. Waiting for something." Her ill-defined face turned aside, then back to Myranda. "I don't think you are part of one of my tests. I think I am part of one of yours. What are *you* trying to do?"

"They just told me to go forward."

The figure nodded. "Your first time through. Yes. The trials are so *clear* the first time."

"You've been through more than once?"

"More than once. More than twice. More than I could hope to count."

"Why? Why haven't you left?"

"Something about… I… Ah, yes. I recall now. Because I am dead. It seemed unwise to leave in such a state. I have a notion that death is more troublesome outside this place than in. So I need to reach the center to return to life."

"But you've been to the center more than twice. Why didn't you leave?"

"I have the unfortunate habit of dying again before I reach the center." She leaned closer. "Things become more difficult the more often you pass through. A word of advice? Don't die. It complicates things tremendously." She straightened up. "Though to be fair, the first death is always the most difficult. … The burning…"

Her voice became sharper. A steam-like hiss and acrid scent filled the air. The flesh of the arm visible through a tear in the armor gleamed brightly. When it faded again, a blackened shape marred the pale skin like a fresh brand. The Mark of the Chosen.

"You… Trigorah?"

A flicker of elven features resolved themselves. Her expression was stricken and confused. "That name is so familiar."

"You were Trigorah Teloran. You were my godmother. You fell to Epidime, and—"

"*Epidime,*" she hissed viciously.

For a moment, the face Myranda had last seen years ago in this very valley asserted itself in the half-defined figure. It was twisted with rage.

"Where is he?" she demanded.

"He has been defeated, but Deacon has felt his touch. Deacon is here too. Have you seen him?"

Trigorah shut her eyes. "Memories don't last long here. I may have…" The fallen Chosen stood, her features fighting to remain sharp and distinct. "I need to reach the center again. I need to leave this place. Epidime… Epidime needs to pay."

"We'll go together. The way things have been going, we may well need every hand we can get."

Myranda stepped back onto the raft. She pulled the spiritual remnant of Trigorah with her. Together, they hauled at the rope and continued on their way.

"How long has it been out there?" Trigorah asked. "Since I died."

Her expression was complex as she worked at the rope. She seemed to be searching, lost. Like the entirety of her mind was a fleeting thought that she had to work to keep hold of before it slipped away.

"About three years."

"What's become of the world?"

"Peace. The Alliance is three kingdoms again. I am the queen of Kenvard, and Deacon is the king."

Trigorah shut her eyes tightly. "For decades I tracked the Red Shadow and the war raged on. I die and the world heals… If I'd known that was all it would take, I would have died sooner."

They pulled themselves onward. With two more arms at work, the ferry moved along far more swiftly. The tiny stone island that had held Trigorah vanished into the fog. Once again, Myranda was in the center of a gray void, no shore in sight.

Water lapped at the edge of the raft. Then slowly crested over its edge. The work of dragging it through the water compounded as each new pull scooped water along with it.

"We'd best hurry," Trigorah said. "This raft won't last much longer with two of us on it."

"We'll make it," Myranda said.

They redoubled their efforts. The cold water of the river washed over their feet and curled about their shins. Trigorah's eyes drifted down to the water.

"You were surprised to find me…" she said.

"I was."

"They didn't mention me when they gave you your task? It was just 'move forward'?"

"That is all."

"Of course they didn't…" Trigorah shook her head. "They pull this trick often. We aren't working toward the same goal."

"What do you mean? We both need to reach the center."

"We do. But the way toward the center isn't a *direction*. It's a sequence of tasks. Your task is to move forward. They've stopped telling me what my tasks are. Part of the puzzle is figuring it out. And I think I have. My puzzle, anyway."

The raft was fully beneath the surface of the water now. If not for the tether connecting it to the rope, it would have likely sunk to the bottom.

"What do you mean? What are you meant to do, if not take my help and reach safety?"

"This place is about your flaws. Giving you a chance to correct them. I am your godmother. I could not have failed you more in that regard. It's time to correct that."

Trigorah smiled serenely and released her grip on the rope. Myranda took one hand away and grabbed her wrist before the current could wash Trigorah free.

"What are you doing?!" she cried.

"The raft is only sturdy enough for one. Take it. Go. I'll find my way."

"You barely *existed* when I found you. It wasn't until I helped you that you even remembered who you were. I can get you to the center. I know I can."

"Myranda, I'm already gone," Trigorah said.

She held on tightly, but the tether holding the raft to the rope was beginning to fail. Everything in her heart demanded she hold on. It was the right thing to do. But the words echoed in her mind. Oriech's words. *Just move forward.* Trigorah was a part of her past. Was it really so simple? Was it really so cruel?

She loosened her fingers and let her past slip away. Trigorah was swallowed by the rapids. The raft lurched back to the surface. Myranda trembled with anger as the image burned itself into her mind. Around her, the fog dissipated. The water slowed. The distant shore came into view.

Myranda took a breath. "You were never one to make your points lightly, Oriech," she said.

"Just because you came here without a stain on your soul doesn't mean you can't stand to learn some important lessons," Oriech replied.

She turned. The shore was much closer than it had been when she last looked, and Oriech was standing there, waiting for her.

"That I'll have to make sacrifices to succeed? Do you honestly think I haven't learned that time and time again?"

"It's a lesson that bears repeating. Onward, Myranda. Not much further now."

#

Deacon marched through the forest, awaiting his next trial. Oriech had kept his promise. Several tests were behind him, and they had been alternately confounding in their complexity and savage in their physical demands. Despite the travails, his time here felt almost like a reprieve. Oriech's influence had calmed the roiling chaos in his mind without stripping it away. He was thus free to view this unique aspect of his world with the wonder and fascination of his thoroughly analytical self while still cursed with the slanted insight of his affliction. It was enlightening, and were the circumstances less dire, he would have relished the opportunity to test himself against this place.

He shut his eyes and allowed the power of Spirit Oak to wash over his spirit.

"Astounding…" he murmured. "Not even the crystal arena coaxes arcane energies into so skillful an approximation of reality. I can still *feel* myself within the valley, and yet all of this, this endless forest, seems as real as my own body."

"It is far more real than that," remarked a voice from the forest.

Deacon opened his eyes and looked to the source. The darkened depths of the forest surrounded him. "Who is there?" he asked.

"A fine question. If I'd not been reminded, I might not have known the answer. This place has a way of scouring the mind clean. Have you felt it yet? The searing clarity of stripped-away sanity?"

A figure stepped from the darkness, though it remained barely a whisper of form. Curls of light traced out vague details. A pair of lips pulled into a wry smile. "Oh, no. I can see it. The patina of reality is still clouding your mind. First time through as well. So I suppose that would make you Deacon."

"Again I ask you, who are *you*?" he asked.

The figure stepped closer. It spoke in a far clearer voice. "I am the one you came here to find."

Deacon sharpened his focus and allowed a thread of his power to curl out toward the figure. Like a handful of dust blown into the rays of the sun pouring through a window, his power swirled and became illuminated, tracing the form more vividly. "Trigorah... I knew I would find you here."

"You'd *hoped* you would find me here," she said. "And by most measures, you *haven't* found me here. My body, and the better part of my soul, are long gone. The one you came in search of is no more."

"No. You cannot lie to me. This place does not destroy. It is a crucible. It has rendered away the impurities. Your essential nature, that which I have sought, still remains."

"Well, you are the fool who came here knowing what you would find. And so you've found it. What do you intend to do now?"

Deacon reached into his bottomless satchel and withdrew the coin. "I need the barest whisper of your essence. Just a sample of your nature," he said. "I believe it may well be the final ingredient to a ritual that will permit me to literally change the world for the better."

"Change the world. And by who's authority do you do such a thing?"

"By my own."

"I sense no mark upon your skin. No divinity in your soul. Indeed, I sense quite the opposite coiled about you." The half-seen eyes flashed with anger. "Something familiar. Something unwelcome."

"Please. All I ask is that you touch the coin. I shall do the rest."

Trigorah approached. Her ghostly hand, little more than a dull glow given vague form, reached forward. The fingers closed about the coin. For a heartbeat, there was nothing. No surge of power, no flicker of intensity. Then came the torrent. Threads of light spilled into the form standing before him. It was as though Trigorah was little more than a vessel, and the coin was pouring golden, shimmering light into it, filling it to bursting. The curves and shapes of her body became brilliant and vivid.

Deacon shut his eyes and spared himself the glare, putting his mind to work. As he had at each mythic site, each meeting point of the Chosen, he poured his mind and focus into the coin. He unraveled its physical and mystical form ever so slightly, allowing the merest notion of Trigorah's aspect to entwine with the other sampled moments, places, and people. Just as two simple metals can combine to become an alloy that is greater than the sum of its parts, the reality of the coin was enhanced. Trigorah loaned it a measure of her importance, of her once crucial role in her world.

As the raw power of the moment subsided, so too did the blinding light that composed the form before him. The details of Trigorah's body coalesced again, solid and whole. Her ragged but formidable armor, her fierce and determined gaze. She was, for the moment, herself again.

"There…" Deacon said, letting his focus ease. "It is as complete as I am likely to achieve. I thank you."

"Say nothing of it," Trigorah said.

In a startling motion, her grip on the coin tightened and she wrenched it from his hand.

"What are you doing?" he demanded.

"You are being *tested.*" Trigorah dropped the coin into a pouch at her belt. "You didn't suppose I would loan you even a sliver of what the gods gave me without being satisfied it was in the right hands, did you?"

"Oriech is the one testing me. The *forest* is the one testing me. Not you. Give me the coin."

"Wielding the power of the divine? Daring to wrench fate and reality from its stated course? Those are the tasks of the gods and their surrogates. You are neither a god nor Chosen. If you can assign yourself the task of reweaving reality, I can assign myself the task of judging your worth." She gave him a defiant look. "And as it stands, I will require some convincing."

"Give me the coin," Deacon demanded again.

"Do you believe you can take it?" she said.

"I have no desire to hurt you."

"I am already dead. And even if I still lived, I doubt you could do so."

His fingers tightened around his crystal. A flex of magic curled out from his mind. Before it could take hold, or even take form as a proper spell, Trigorah's form blurred and vanished. He tensed his mind, ready for some manner of mystic assault from the powerful spirit.

What he received instead was a punishing physical blow to the midsection. The wind rushed from his lungs, and he dropped to one knee. Trigorah took a deep breath and released it in a glorious, contented sigh.

"Flesh and bone," she said reverently. "A rare gift for me in a place like this."

She set her boot on his shoulder and kicked him to the forest floor. It could have been a cruel or crass motion, but the way she delivered it, it simply seemed efficient.

"Why a coin, Deacon?" she asked. "What is so special about the coin?"

Deacon fought breath into his lungs and tried another twist of magic. Trigorah knelt down, her knee on his chest, and placed a hand on the side of his face. Her touch was like ice, though he knew the sensation well enough to know it had nothing to do with true temperature. The penetrating cold was a function of the soul not the body. It plunged past his flesh and into his mind, muddling his thoughts and fouling the spell he was attempting to concoct.

"You…" Deacon said. "How are you doing this?"

"If Myranda can be believed, three years have passed out there. Three years. In this place, only the completion of a test advances time in the world beyond the valley. Some puzzles take mere minutes to solve. But each time through, the trials become more difficult. They can take weeks… *years* to complete. And for each one, a *single hour* passes in the world beyond. I don't have much of a mind for figures these days, but I think you can appreciate the *eternities* I have called this place home. I have seen and endured many lifetimes of mind-rending tests. It is a wonder I have any sanity left. But while I maintain my wits, I assure you, you cannot best me."

"It must… it must be torture…" Deacon said.

"It is what I deserve. It is what is necessary to wipe my crimes clean. So I know a thing or two about what it takes to be *worthy*, Deacon." She placed her hand on the pouch at her side. "Why a coin?"

Deacon sat up. "The ritual needed a focus. A hub to bind the elements. It could have been *anything*. I just needed something separate from the artifacts."

"You don't make it this far in an endeavor that is effectively at odds with the desires of the powers that be without being extremely well-measured. This coin was a conscious choice."

"It was the first thing that seemed suitable."

"I don't mind you lying to yourself, but please don't lie to me." Trigorah leaned lower. "I recognize that stain on your soul. You aren't passing *my* test until I'm convinced *you* are the one who is in control. What is so special about this coin?"

Deacon shut his eyes. Words began to form in his mind. He took a breath and made ready to defend his statement, that the coin meant nothing at all. But the words rang hollow. For the first time since he'd selected the fateful bit of metal, he considered why he had chosen it.

"It… it isn't what the coin *is*. It is what the coin represents. That coin… it is *everything*. It is renewal. Its very existence is a testament to a kingdom reborn. It is progress toward the goal of reclaiming our world from the damage, the *poison* of the D'Karon. It is everything that matters. Myranda's face. The name of the home we have made for ourselves. Our ideals, written plain and clear. Wisdom. Courage. Honor. And it bears the mark."

"It bears the mark," Trigorah repeated.

"I needed it. I need *something*. Something to assure me…"

"To assure you that you haven't crossed the line. Something to assure you that you are still pure?"

"Yes."

Trigorah pulled the coin from the pouch and considered it. "Doubt… You doubt yourself."

"I am as sure as I have ever been that what I seek to do *must* be done," Deacon said. "But I can never be truly certain. I'm only human."

Trigorah flipped the coin and caught it. She held down her other hand to help Deacon to his feet. "You speak with heart and vulnerability. Two things that *he* never could. I am satisfied." She handed him the coin.

"Two things *who* never could?"

"You know precisely who," Trigorah said, pacing once more into the darkness of the forest.

Her substance, so recently restored by her contact with the coin, unraveled and faded. Soon she was little more than a vague suggestion among the trees. Before she vanished entirely, she turned, a glitter of challenge in her fading eyes.

"And when he shows his face again, you tell him I haven't forgotten. I'll *never* forget…"

With that, she was gone. A path through the forest opened before him. Another trial gone. Another step closer to his goal. He held the coin firmly in his grip. It felt heavier than before. The mark was cold against his skin. He had to press on. He had come too far. Soon it would be over.

#

Myranda marched forward. She'd done all that had been required of her thus far. Time here was curious and uncomfortable. On one hand, it felt like days had passed. On the other, she'd never once felt fatigue or weariness.

"You've done well, Myranda," Oriech said, emerging from the forest beside her. "Not that we expected anything less. Now you must face your final test. Against the advice and wishes of my colleagues, I have successfully argued that you should be permitted to collaborate on this test."

Ahead, a table not unlike the one in her war room loomed out of the darkness. Beyond it, another figure stepped toward her. It was Deacon.

"He has had more to answer for than you," Oriech said. "But he is clever, resourceful, and determined. This is his final test as well."

Deacon's face was stern and steady. He looked as though it was taking everything he had to keep himself from losing control of the chaos wrapped around him. So close to him, and with the benefit of time and patience, she finally got a clear view of what had become of him in both body and spirit. Without the crown and the ring, he was different. Fundamentally so. It wasn't that Deacon was gone. He was still there, still in some measure of control. But his spirit looked fractured. Twisted. He wasn't a single mind anymore. There was his core self, and clinging to it was a jagged, splintered tangle.

For now, Deacon seemed stable. His body looked very much his own, but there was an artificiality to it. She could see the effort it took to maintain the appearance that should have been natural.

Oriech approached the table.

"This final test should be familiar to you. What you have here is a world. Land, sky, sea, and people. Created just for you, for you to oversee."

Myranda peered down from one side of the table, Deacon from the other. At a distance, the table had seemed to be a map. But now that she was close, she saw that it was a whole, genuine continent in miniature. Clouds drifted over the surface. Tiny waves lapped at the shores. Myranda found that when she focused upon any part of the map, though it didn't appear to grow larger, she could nevertheless see with greater and greater detail. A mottled patch of green mountain resolved into a forest and then individual trees, and finally to a mouselike creature with clever eyes and cunning paws huddled beneath the tree.

"Fascinating..." Deacon said, looking over the world.

"I will set your minds at ease—this is not a *true* world. It exists only for the purpose of this test. But for that purpose, it will behave in every way like a real one. With one small exception."

He held out his hand. An illuminated golden orb rose out of it. Its light poured across the table like the rising sun at dawn.

"You have control over a single day. You may choose at any time to return to dawn. The rising of the sun will return the world to this same state. Your task is to see the world safely through the day. When the sun sets, your test is done, and you shall be judged. Until then, I leave you to your task."

Oriech vanished. Myranda paced around the edge of the table to

Deacon's side.

"Deacon…" she said, touching his arm.

He shut his eyes. "I know… I know, Myranda. You can see it in me. You can see what's become of me. I'm sorry… I thought I was strong enough. I thought I could use it, use the chaos in me, without losing control."

"It isn't too late, Deacon. There's got to be a way. We can heal you. We can fix what you've done."

"We can't…" He turned to her, tears in his eyes. "Myranda, we can't do both. I've had time here. Time to think, just as you have. You say that history has been repeating itself, time has been echoing."

"Yes. With worsening intensity."

"I haven't *done* anything to cause that. I've traveled the world. I've gathered the ingredients, but I haven't turned my mind to time at all. Either it is happening because something else I've done has caused time to begin to unravel, or it is happening because something I *will* do will cause time to unravel. "

"If it is unraveling, then we will fix it. If it is something you have yet to do, then you just have to choose not to."

"You don't understand," he said. "You act as though time is a thing that happens gradually. It is not. It is gradually *revealed* to us, but every piece of it is already in place. These echoes are happening, and that means I won't choose not to. I can't choose not to create them, because in the fullness of time, I already have. What's done is done. And what will be done will be done. To suggest I could repair this problem by simply choosing to avoid creating it is to suggest I could repair ahead bridge by patching the ground beneath my feet. The problem already exists. We simply haven't reached it yet."

"Then we can change things."

"The ritual I have been endeavoring to complete was supposed to be *about* changing things, about rendering the unalterable fabric of being soft enough to be manipulated. If time has been broken, then it is a result of me changing things. And if it can be fixed, it can be fixed only *because* of the same ritual. Somehow I've created my own prophecy. I've set something in motion that I have to see through to completion, because the very act of mysticism I hope to achieve is also the only act that can prevent further damage."

He turned his eyes to the table. "Something is happening," he said.

Myranda turned to the world they were to protect. The sun had already reached midday. Smoke rose from a section of the forest. As their attention drew it more sharply into focus, they saw beasts similar to the mouselike residents of the world, but a shade more feral. There were many of them, and they were sweeping like a wave across the landscape. The mouse creatures were no match for them, and the ferals were merciless.

"We should stop them," Deacon said.

He held his hand over the table. Myranda felt him cast a simple spell to draw the monstrous creatures away from the table. The spell did its work, but as the monsters were torn from the ground, the ground was torn asunder as well. Faults split the continent. Fires consumed forests.

"I… I didn't intend that. I cast the spell as precisely as I could."

The miniature sun continued its path, shining upon a crumbling, imagined world. Myranda reached out and drew it back, reeling time back to dawn.

"We must be gentler next time," Myranda said. "Deacon, they say they can cure you here, if you request it."

"There is only one way through this," Deacon said. "I need the affliction."

"You don't. It is *killing* you."

"It is making these spells *possible*," he snapped. "The spell I used to reach you all those years ago. The spell that left me with this curse clinging to me. I manipulated the probability of things. It was chaos magic. I thought I could control it, and to a degree I did. But you can never completely control chaos. By its very nature, chaos defies control. It is the counterpart to order. But it is also one of the very fundamental, underlying truths that I'd been trying to uncover. Chaos is change. Chaos magic is what allowed all of this to occur. Whatever I've already done, and whatever I will do, it is possible only because of the chaos that his plaguing me. I need it."

He revealed the coin. "Here. This ritual required a single point around which I could gather the power. It could have been anything. I chose this coin. This coin is the focus of it all. This coin is the key to my intention," he said.

Myranda took it from his hand. With it in her grip, her mind was awash with sensations she doubted she would have been able to comprehend if not for her experiences with magic. It was a simple coin, the same as any other. But he had done something to it. Through his magic he had turned a common bit of metal into something humming with the power of change itself. The coin felt like an anchor. It felt like the hub around which the surrounding world rotated. It felt like a tool, designed for precisely one task. It was as he said, it was a key. But just as it felt as though it was central to all that surrounded it, Myranda similarly knew at a primal, spiritual level that the lock for which this key had been created didn't exist. This was a solution with no problem. An answer with no question. It was out of place.

"You can feel it too. You can feel that it has a power, an aspect that does not belong. It feels the same to me. But when I place it in the afflicted hand, I can feel the shape of it. The missing ingredients of the alchemy of reality. And I can feel it drawn toward the final piece. I need the affliction,

Myranda. I need its influence on my mind to concoct the spells, I need its presence in my spirit to cast the spells. If something has been changed, I will need the chaos in me to change it back."

"I read your notes. Even in your wildest musings, you made none of these claims."

"I've earned a tremendous amount of insight in the last few days."

"How? This plan seems to have leaped from your mind fully formed in the time between when you left Kenvard and when you left the Cave of the Beast."

The sun rose over the miniature world again. They turned their eyes to it. Sure enough, it was whole, returned to the state it had been during the previous dawn. They both focused their attention on the section of the world where the violence had begun before.

"If you wish to accuse me, accuse me," Deacon said.

"You say you haven't been taken by Epidime, and I don't feel his presence in you. But you *did* encounter him, didn't you?"

"I encountered him. I spoke to him. I learned from him."

Myranda felt a flare of anger. She forced it away and tried to keep a closer watch on their world. "He doesn't need to be in control of you to manipulate you."

"He is a repository of knowledge. He told me things I never could have known. The story of our world will be *complete* because of him. And with the knowledge he provided, our world will be *safe* because of him."

"There are some things we are better off not knowing."

"That is simply not true."

On the world below them, the attack they had witnessed the previous day began again.

"I don't have the control to fend off the foes gently enough," Deacon said.

"Let me try."

She set her mind to the task, curling the merest whisper of power into the world. It still struck the land like a hammer. It didn't rend the earth asunder as before, but it was as destructive against those Myranda sought to protect as it was against their foes. It still ended in a rout. She pulled the sun back and awaited her next opportunity.

"We are being too direct," Myranda said.

"How are we to protect this world if we don't take a direct role in doing so?" Deacon asked.

She gazed at the sun as it climbed into the sky. "The gods do not protect our world directly. And it is for this precise reason. They have too much power to do so safely."

"Mmm… Yes, of course. The world needs Chosen."

They waited for the dawn to come again, and they each swept their attention across the world. Though these beings were not real, mere flickers of will, Myranda could feel their virtue, their bravery. Not as true traits, but as though they were simply colors of paint used to render them. She picked the most virtuous of them and shut her eyes. The merest thought in the direction of the creature stirred it to greater power. Deacon selected another, the one he deemed to be the wisest and sharpest of mind.

With their avatars selected, they watched and waited. The battle began. It quickly became clear that something was wrong. Those they had chosen were far from the early attack.

"We need to get them where they need to go," Myranda said.

Deacon touched a hand to her shoulder. "We need to *learn* where they need to go. And what they need to do. For now, let us observe."

The battle raged. It consumed the world. When it finally reached their warriors, the battles began to pitch against the evil, but it was too little, too late. A handful of the creatures survived, but by the time the sun was sliding from the sky, it was clear this world belonged to the ferals. Deacon pulled back the dawn, and together they selected new Chosen. They chose those nearer to where the first battles were fought. Perhaps in that way the war would be ended before it began. Alas, such was not the case. Deacon's Chosen lacked the courage to fight until it was too late. Myranda's fought bravely but lacked the strength.

They began another day. Again they tried. Again the world fell. The balance of the battle was so delicate. If they empowered too many, the Chosen would end up fighting among themselves. If they empowered too few or the wrong ones, they did little good. For victory to come, the proper creatures had to be in the proper places. And things never unfolded as they needed to in order to provide the besieged creatures with victory.

"A prophecy," Deacon realized, just as the sun was rising over a new world. "It worked for our world. We need the Chosen to know their purpose. We need them to know where they need to go."

Myranda nodded. She leaned low over the brightening world and whispered of the coming battle. She spoke of the threat and where it would begin. She spoke of those who had the tools to succeed. She spoke of their need to stand up for their fellow creatures.

With avatars selected and messages delivered, Myranda and Deacon stepped back to watch and wait. The battle began, as it always did. But the Chosen had found each other. They fought for the people and rallied them to the cause. The sun crept across the world. The battle raged on. Many fell. For a time, there was a stalemate. Clouds curled over the field of the most intense battle. Rain began to pour. The feral beasts shrugged off the weather, continuing their vicious assault. The other creatures faltered.

Myranda struggled with the desire to reach out, to turn the tide herself. But she already knew how that would turn out.

"They can't win if we help," Deacon said, voicing her concerns. "And they cannot win without our help."

"It's all been about a gentle touch," Myranda said. "As little as we can do. We've gotten them this far…"

"Then we need to do something, but magic will be too much."

Myranda nodded. She leaned low and pursed her lips. With barely a breath, she blew upon the clouds. They curled and drifted. The setting sun shone upon the battlefield. Freed of the weather, the Chosen led their forces valiantly. Finally, the foes were beaten back. The day was won. Myranda looked down on the battlefield.

She knew these were not real creatures. She could feel the magic that fueled them. They were little more than puppets, illusions. But for an undefinable amount of time, she and Deacon had worked to save them. Seeing the battlefield scattered with their fallen was troubling. As the sun neared the end of its arc, Myranda reached out to it. She was already thinking of the ways she would push and prod things, to try to lead them to victory more swiftly, more certainly. She was trying to find ways to save more lives. Deacon caught her hand.

"Don't," he said.

"That was not a proper end. So many of them died. We can do better."

"The world is safe. The battle is over."

"But we didn't save everyone."

"We can't always save everyone."

Myranda grappled with his words as she watched over the false world she had been charged with protecting. When the sun set, the table vanished.

Oriech appeared beside her. "You did the job well. Your puzzle is solved. And so, with your trial passed, the time has come for you to make your requests. I shall remind you that if you wish to leave, that must be your request. If you request anything else, you will have to earn your way back to the center of the forest for a second request. The return trip will be far more trying and will take no less than one full day in the outside world."

"Can we request that the disturbances outside be stopped?" Myranda asked.

"You cannot request anything that changes the outside world. Your change is limited to you."

"Then I request that Deacon be cured," she said.

"Again, the request is limited to you."

"It is no good," Deacon said, shuddering as a wave of chaos swept across him. "We could request a thousand things. We could request the knowledge of how to solve this problem that has been caused. We could request the tools to achieve the desired goal without making the error. But it will delay us by a day. The blue moon will have passed."

"There will be other blue moons," Myranda said.

"No… There won't. There is no other choice for me to make. Time is unraveling, and the only thing powerful enough to cause it is the very concoction I have been building and its proper application at the proper time. That time is breaking down means I have already performed the task. I have a date with destiny."

He shut his eyes. Another, more vicious wave swept over him. When he opened his eyes again, it was with apology and regret.

"We have one chance, Myranda. I have to leave. Twisted as I have become, I am the only one in this world with the knowledge to understand what is happening and the power to stop it."

"Deacon, no. Let us think this through. We have time here. We can—"

"The affliction is progressing. The longer I wait, the deeper the claws sink. I am sorry. I've created this disaster. I have to fix it. Oriech, I wish to leave."

"So be it," Oriech said.

Branches overhead spread apart, revealing a path leading to the iciness of the valley.

Deacon clutched the coin. "I need some time to prepare, but I am nearly ready to do what I set out to do. I am going back to where it all began, Myranda. That seems a fitting place to end it. I'll do my best to set things straight and leave the world better than I found it. But if I fail, or you truly believe there is no other way, I trust you to do what must be done."

Deacon marched for the opening. As he crossed the threshold of dry undergrowth to icy snow, he faded from the forest. Myranda squeezed her staff. The enchanted wood groaned under the viciousness of the grip.

"Is there a way out of this, Oriech? Or is this all just another one of the games fate has chosen to play with us?" she asked.

"I can't answer that without sending you back for more trials," Oriech said. "But in your heart, and your mind, you know the answer. Trust them both."

"Then send me out there."

"Go. And make us proud, as you always have."

#

208

Myn stood with her wings spread and her claws crackling the icy ground. Ether stood before her, with Ayna buzzing back and forth. Each had arrived not long after Myranda's call for aid went out. Since then, Myn had been discouraging them with ever increasing firmness from entering the ring of trees.

"It has been more than a day, dragon," Ether fumed, her human form heaped with furs to ward off the chill. "I do not care what Myranda told you. She would not remain in that place for so long if she didn't need help. She'd demanded immediate help. Ivy agreed to be left behind so that I could travel more quickly, and now I have squandered a full day of precious time waiting."

"She will return. And you are not to enter," Myn stated.

Ayna buzzed aside to look upon the trees. Myn raised her wing a bit more.

"It is a genuinely fascinating place. I've never felt its like," the fairy said. "The nearest thing to it in my experience is the crystal arena, but this is *more,* somehow. The crystal arena feels like the product of whatever wills are occupying it at the time. This feels like a legion of wills, all piled atop one another."

"Yet another reason to enter it," Ether said.

Ayna shook her head and flitted back to Ether. "By no means. You will find that one of the *many* ways that I am superior to Deacon is my own quite secure knowledge of when something is not to be trifled with. Though I *am* somewhat fascinated that *you* do not seem aware of this place. You *were* watching over the world as a more general consciousness before my associates and I summoned you during the blue moon ritual, were you not?"

"I was."

"So shouldn't you have a *comprehensive* awareness of things of profound mystic importance such as these?" Ayna asked.

"My attentions were focused upon the other Chosen, if and when they should arise."

"Curious. I suppose even one of the original intended Chosen isn't perfect or infallible."

Ether glared at Ayna. "I am as near to perfection as any being can ever hope to be. Indeed, I *exceed* perfection in all ways that matter, in that I can adapt to any challenge."

"Mmm. But you quite literally spread yourself too thin. Perhaps you would have been better served by focusing yourself upon a single pursuit, as I have. After all. You claim to *exceed* perfection. That means you are, by definition, *not* perfect. I, on the other hand, would never make that claim."

A flash of violet colored the valley. Myn, Ether, and Ayna turned to the ring of trees. A portal had already opened on the north end of the ring. Ether and Ayna darted toward it, but before they could reach it, Deacon's form tumbled through and the portal vanished with a clap of energy. The fairy bobbed in place where the portal had been, then pivoted and pointed a tiny finger at Ether.

"Where is your perfection *now*!" she said. "You had to keep focused on a single point in the world for scarcely a day, and you failed at the very moment it was needed. My point is made."

"You were distracting me with your blather!" Ether countered, swirling into the air as flame.

"Mere *words* are sufficient to foul your fabled vigilance? Hardly a sign of quality."

Myranda's voice cut through the exchange. "What is going on?"

Ether and Ayna turned. Myranda was standing beyond the ring of trees. Myn pounced, pulling the wizard tightly against her and rumbling in relief and joy at her appearance.

"I'm fine, Myn. I'm fine," she said softly, stroking the dragon on the brow. "Ether, Ayna. Did you see Deacon?"

"Briefly," Ether said.

"They were arguing," Myn said.

"Some things never change, I suppose," Myranda muttered. "Listen closely, everyone. I know where Deacon is going. We, every last one of us, need to get there as soon as possible. He is convinced that because he caused it, he is the only one who can stop what is happening. Whether he is right or he is wrong, we need to be ready. Ayna, where is Calypso?"

"Still on the other side of the mountains. She cannot travel as quickly as I can. I don't suppose we could expect to have her here in less than a day unless Ether or I fetched her."

"No, we don't have a moment to lose. She will meet us when she can. We have until the blue moon rises."

# Chapter 11

Hours later, Myranda and Myn touched down in an icy field. When Myranda had last been here, she could scarcely imagine a more terrible place. A day's travel by foot from the nearest town to the north, and another day's travel to the nearest town to the south. It was a forsaken, barren stretch of ice. At the time, the only thing to differentiate this patch of earth from any other in the field had been the frozen remains of a beast she now knew as a dragoyle and a warrior she now knew as Rasa. Now a small memorial stood, a marble plinth marking this as the place where the swordsman had fallen.

She hopped from Myn's back and held her staff tightly. The sky was darkening. The blue moon was rising. Even without focusing her mind, she could feel that this place was wrong. It was humming with power. The very air and earth seemed to be anticipating what was to come. It created a tension, a fragility. This place was thin ice over a deep lake, ready to shatter at any moment.

Myn's head lowered, her eyes shut. She sniffed the air and flicked her tongue. Myranda took notice and sharpened her focus. It was difficult to pinpoint, with the whole field quivering with mystic energy, but there was certainly a point of disturbance. She turned her attention to it. Before she could attempt to dispel the magic in place, the illusion fell of its own accord. Deacon stood before them.

No longer in the forest, and thus no longer buoyed by its unique nature, the chaotic effect upon him was even more pronounced. His arm was no longer a shifting accumulation of ghostly forms. It was solid now, constant, but wrong. The flesh had the translucent and faintly luminous appearance of something carved from some manner of milky crystal. Veins of the afflicted flesh striped up his neck and left streaks of white hair where they curled across his scalp.

"Deacon… Look at you…"

"I know. An affliction created when I transported incorrectly seems to feed upon further transportation. Fascinating. Not to worry, though. I shan't need to transport any longer." He took a breath. "You can feel it, can't you? You can feel that *something* is going to happen here. Not something may happen. Not something should happen. Something will happen. The seams of reality are straining and separating. It can't be stopped. Either I find the flaw and correct it or these echoes, these disturbances, just keep happening. Time won't matter anymore. And to a degree, neither will space. Chaos of every kind will reign."

"Do you even know how to stop it?" Myranda asked.

"I don't. Not specifically. It will be interesting to see how it plays out."

"*Interesting,*" Myranda said. "You are talking about the fate of the world."

"I take this perfectly seriously, Myranda. But I cannot help but be fascinated."

His voice was chillingly calm, and his tone terribly familiar, though Myranda for the moment refused to allow herself to dwell upon it.

"We should wait for the others," he said. "Ether is on the way, I assume? And Ivy as well? It would be unwise to face a moment like this without the full complement of the Chosen."

"They will be here soon."

Myranda felt a tremor shake the field. Thin lines of curling light began to weave jagged patterns around them. It was not her doing, nor could she feel Deacon weaving a spell. It was happening on its own.

"I hope they hurry," Deacon said. "I'm not certain how much longer reality will keep its present form if we don't get started. The moon is nearly in place. Even the clouds have separated to mark the occasion. Portentous."

"How can you be so calm?" she asked.

"There's something comforting about inevitability. Whatever will happen will happen. We will do our best. We will succeed or fail. But by the end of the night"—he gestured to his hand—"this? This will be over. It taught me much. But I look forward to the peace."

He pulled his pack from his bag and dumped it out on the ground beside the memorial. Most of the goods seemed completely random: a few lengths of bandage, a piece of blue enameled armor, a scattering of dried bones. The largest piece, and one that by rights shouldn't have fit into the bag, was the Sword of the Chosen.

A speck in the sky to the south moved with unnatural speed.

"Ah. Ether is here. Right on time."

As she drew nearer, Ether's present form was revealed to be a silvery-feathered griffin. A streamer of blue suggested Ivy was atop her back and, evidently, unhappy with the speed at which the shapeshifter was traveling. A brilliant yellow second streamer of light revealed that Ayna was present as well.

Ether set down in the field, Ivy clinging tightly to her neck with eyes squeezed shut. The elemental shifted to wind, dumping Ivy to the ground.

"What has he done?" Ether demanded, eyes sweeping over the widening lines of light splitting their surroundings.

"Nothing yet," Deacon said.

"Deacon," Ivy said, climbing to her feet. "What happened to you?"

"I shall explain after. Because time is of the essence now, and it very likely won't matter for much longer."

Another tremor shook the field. The jagged lines of light lengthened, now meeting at a point not far from Deacon's feet.

"Nearly time. Listen closely, everyone. I've heard a great many tales where this has been done, but not until this moment has it ever made any sense to me. I am going to tell you precisely what I planned to do, because some part of it *will* cause this whole mess. I need you all to understand, as best you can, what I was hoping to achieve and how. There is something missing, some flaw. It must be corrected, or there is no telling what will happen."

Another tremor shook the ground. It didn't fully subside, merely weakening to a low rumble.

"The D'Karon came to this world and nearly destroyed it. If not for you all, our people would still be killing each other on their behalf, weakening the world to eventually be subsumed by them. And there is nothing to stop them or those like them from coming again. Dark worlds, perhaps some even worse than the ones from which the D'Karon hail, can open a door to this place. But it shouldn't be that way. And I realized it didn't have to be."

The ground shook.

"Get on with it, Deacon!" Ivy shouted.

"Chaos, order, time, space. All the building blocks of a reality. What if they weren't abstract? What if we could manipulate them just as we do earth, fire, wind, and water? The more my mind was torn and twisted by the affliction, the more I saw there may well be ways. But not by mortals. It needed to be done by the gods. Or someone with access to the same traits and natures of the gods. The Chosen."

He knelt and began arranging the items at his feet.

"I needed to sample the Chosen. And just as a physical or mystical formula needs physical or mystical things, an abstract formula doesn't need something as simple as a lock of hair or a drop of blood. It needs moments, places, proximities. I scoured the world for samples of every Chosen and their exploits. Not only the five, but the fallen as well."

"But what are you trying to do?" Myranda said.

He picked up the sword and pulled free its covering. After a moment of hesitation, he touched the handle, placing one of the many Chosen emblems firmly against his flesh. There was no sizzle. No flash. He'd yet to be declared a traitor to his world. He palmed the coin and gripped the sword tightly with the same hand. Some semblance of the odd weight and significance of the coin bled into the already potent sword.

"I want to remove something from creation. I want to make certain that no one can ever enter this world from the outside again. And because such a trait of existence is abstract, and thus beyond my influence, I had to change that."

The rumble was growing stronger. The moon approached its zenith. There was no longer any question. Whatever this disaster truly was, it was already happening. It would not be enough to simply stop what Deacon had set in motion. The solution, if it existed at all, rested within the spell itself.

"This is the moment, everyone. Be ready." Deacon raised the sword over the meeting point of the lines of light.

"Are you certain this will work?" Myranda asked, flaring the gem of her staff.

"I am certain it won't. Not the way I intended. But now we shall find out why, and lay bare the broken workings so that we may repair them."

He plunged the sword into the ground.

#

The plunge of the sword was felt around the world. From Castle Verril to the deepest reaches of the Southern Wastes, from New Kenvard to the Crescents. The tension that had grown to the point of catastrophe in that frozen field had been creeping up throughout the many kingdoms. Mystics had felt it as a distant, troubling pressure. Even untrained minds could detect it as an unplaced anxiety gnawing at them. Then, in that moment, when the sword found its place—

Silence.

All was calm. All was as it should be. But to have so constant and potent a feeling pulled away all at once was enough to bring people from every corner of the world to a stop. People stood in place, brows furrowed, eyes shifting. Every person in every kingdom was struck at the same moment with a sensation they could not identify.

#

Deacon removed his hands from the Sword of the Chosen and took a step back. The coin dropped to the ground, seemingly drained of its uniqueness and gravity. The trembling around them had ceased, but the lines of light hadn't vanished. Their jagged paths straightened, leading out from the sword's position like a starburst. One by one, they curled and split. The architect of this spell took his place beside Myranda and watched it unfold.

His assortment of artifacts drifted up around the sword. The filaments of light curled out from them and wove upon themselves. They traced out sigils in the air, forming an orbiting galaxy with the sword as its center. Each sigil was deceivingly simple. They symbols were barely larger than dinner plates, yet they resonated not only with meaning, but with power.

"It worked…" he said.

"What are we looking at?" Ivy asked. "They're beautiful."

"These are the abstract elements of existence," Deacon said, stepping forward. "Time. Space. Chaos. Order. Love. Hate. Music. Drama. So many more. I never imagined there would be so many."

"Keep your distance," Ether said. "The world is restored. The damage undone. Put an end to this now."

"It isn't that simple," he said. "I'd devised the spell such that these wouldn't simply be revealed, they would be made *real*. *Physical*. I wanted to remove an element. Disable it. And that isn't what's happened. They're simply present. The spell isn't whole, so it cannot be completed."

"So what do we do?" Ivy asked.

"We try to figure out what the missing piece is. Once that piece is brought into proximity, the formula is complete, the spell is complete. These will become physical. We can alter them, separate them from reality. Or simply remove the sword and they recede into abstractness again. Whatever we do, we must do it very carefully."

Ayna flitted to Deacon's side. "You are quite literally playing god, Deacon. This is unacceptable."

"Unacceptable? This is why we study magic!" he said. "This is everything."

Ivy stepped forward, eyes set upon a curling emblem orbiting the sword. It was crescent-moon shaped, with dozens of filaments stretching from one side to the other. From the right angle, it looked like a harp made entirely of filigree.

"This one… this one is music, isn't it?" she said.

"It is."

She shakily held up a hand. Ever so lightly, she brushed it. The filaments trembled, producing a tone that was beauty distilled. Ivy shut her eyes and drank in the sound.

"Amazing."

As joyous as the sound was, a gleam in Deacon's eye suggested there was something else that Ivy's action had produced.

"They can be manipulated…" he said. "They aren't fully physical, but they can be manipulated. We are closer than I thought."

"Steady, Deacon," Myranda said.

He turned to the others. "Listen. Do you know why there were five

Chosen?”

"Because that is what was determined necessary to defend this world," Ether said.

"Precisely. No more, no less. But we do not have five Chosen here. I've cobbled together as many elements of the Chosen as I could, but only four of you have been brought into proximity of the spell in flesh and blood." He turned to one of the sigils. "We are missing the fifth."

Myranda and Ivy both saw what he was planning. They motioned to stop him. Deacon raised a mystic shield. As powerful as Deacon was, his shield was no match for Myranda. But it didn't have to last more than a few moments. He drove his healthy hand into the space sigil. His chaotic hand thrust into the time sigil. He curled his fingers and focused his mind. The field around him shattered. It would have been enough if the earth had been broken, hurling the others to the ground. What truly happened was far worse. The very fabric of existence around them fragmented like a broken mirror. Shifting, irregular-shaped windows of reality orbited the sword. A glimpse of a green field slipped past Myn. Her claws sank into the soft grass, and when the sliding window continued on, she was nowhere to be seen. She had been left behind in whatever warm glade Deacon had conjured up for her. One by one, he willed them away. Ayna was banished to a sandy slice of desert. Ether was dropped onto a rocky mountainside. Myranda was dropped into the throne room of New Kenvard. A sun-dappled stretch of forest attempted to claim Ivy.

The nimble malthrope, the last to be targeted, sprang back and away from the roving bit of displaced landscape. Another drifted and sliced toward her. Flares of blue colored her panicked attempts to avoid them. Though none were able to capture her, each pushed her just a bit farther away from Deacon, leaving him to his task.

He twisted his hand in the time sigil, turning it in sequence with the space one. A new fragment of reality split the increasingly patchwork field. This one revealed a howling, frozen place. Stones seemingly exempt from the forces of gravity danced in an impossibly complex pattern of orbits and clashes. Gradually, one stone in particular came into view. It was small with a flat top. A black silhouette of an inhuman form was burned like a charred shadow into the gray rock. On either side, a footprint looked to have been carved into the stone itself. And driven into the heart of the silhouette was a sword of intricate, unmistakable design.

A subtle adjustment to the time sigil caused the windswept snow to slow to a stop, then reverse. Faster and faster the time reeled back. Days, months, years. The passage of time was almost imperceptible. Then came a single, dazzling moment. An impossibly intense light flashed, dousing the field in a heat that singed Deacon's robes and sizzled the snow from the field around him. Deacon squeezed his fingers more tightly in the space sigil. The jagged shape tightened, masking out the worst of the powerful glow. Just before his final manipulations isolated only his intended targets from the roiling power of the white wall, a tendril of energy lanced through and struck him, hurling him away from the sword.

#

Ivy took another desperate dive to avoid being swept to what looked to be a small island in a vast sea. She was barely able to keep hold of her senses, on the verge of a fearful transformation. A window burst into view ahead of her, far too close for her to react. She shielded her face with her hands and dug in her heels, sliding to a stop. Though she wasn't certain what being banished to a distant part of the world would feel like, she was quite certain it wasn't simply the same icy chill of a frozen field. When she was confident she'd somehow been spared, she lowered her arms and opened her eyes.

The window was right there ahead of her, and two more had come within inches of boxing her in, but all of them had frozen in place. She crouched and sprang into the air, clearing the smallest of the windows. When she landed, she was presented with a field littered with similar angular shards showing random pieces of the world. They were arranged like the exhibits in some sort of haunting art gallery, stationary and monolithic. She wove between them, approaching where the sword had been driven into the ground.

When she reached Deacon, he was motionless and barely breathing. The energy that struck him had seared his skin in places. The blighted flesh of the affliction crackled and darkened to a smoky gray.

"Deacon..." she said, crouching beside him. "Deacon, I don't know what you did, but we need to fix it. We need to..."

Her voice trailed off as she looked to the sword. It would have been enough to see what had become of the sigils. Where once they had been stunning designs of pure light etched into the air, now they looked to be sculptures crafted from the very essence of reality. They were real. Solid. Gleaming with metals far brighter than gold and silver. Sparkling with fragments of what Ivy imagined all gems were striving to be. It was a sight no mortal had seen before. And it was meaningless in the face of what waited beyond it.

Huddled down, frozen in time, was a robed malthrope. His teeth were bared. His eyes wild and unseeing. Like a statue locked in his final moment. It was Lain, driving his sword into the unspeakable form of the thing that had once been called General Bagu. The light was already gone from the black thing's eyes, but even locked as he was in the space of a single instant, Lain was clearly still very much alive.

Deacon groaned. His afflicted arm shuddered.

"Deacon... you did it, Deacon," Ivy said, wiping tears from her eyes as she tried to fight through the emotions of seeing her dear friend, if only in this momentary echo. "We've got to get this fixed now. I don't think I can just pull the sword out while everything is in bits and pieces."

The stricken wizard was too dazed to answer. Ivy turned to the orbiting sigils.

"Why did I have to be the one here for this part…" she muttered.

With the sort of respect normally reserved for chained attack dogs, Ivy crept toward the sword and its many shapes.

"Don't break the world, Ivy," she whispered.

Deacon seemed quite capable of identifying what each of the shapes did. There were dozens of them, slowly orbiting the sword. Ivy decided her first step was to bring the others back. If she could bring Myranda, Ether, or Ayna, they might have the wisdom to solve the rest of the problem. But which was the space sigil?

The shape she selected first was a perfect circle embedded with concentric rings of colored gems. Even approaching it sent jolts of raw, vibrant power through her. She touched a finger to the sigil. Images and knowledge flooded into her mind. She saw every hue, every shade, every combination of colors the world had ever seen. And more. She saw colors that had never existed. Colors mortal eyes couldn't hope to process. A slow slide of her finger made white snow and gray earth come alive with bright blues and rich browns. Through the jagged gates to other parts of the world, she saw similar effects intensify the colors there. A glide in the other direction caused the tones to cool and deaden.

She returned the colors to what they had been. Tempting as it was to leave the world quite literally a little brighter than she'd found it, she wasn't here to toy with nature.

Ivy tugged at her fingers and watched the drifting sigils go by. They were things of such beauty, such deceiving complexity. For things like color and music, she could see the symbolism. But what sequence of shapes was meant to imply space? The answer dawned on her not when something of clarity and beauty slipped into view, but when something random and discordant did. There were only two of the sigils that seemed wrong, with elements shifted out of place. They must have been the ones that Deacon had manipulated.

She held her breath and pressed her hand to one of the two. In a rare stroke of luck, she selected the one she'd been searching for. Images flowed into her mind, layering one atop the other. Every part of the world, all at once, forced its way into her thoughts. It was dizzying, far more than her untrained mind could sift through. Fortunately, she didn't need to. The merest hint of a notion caused the images to scatter and refocus. She wanted her friends by her side, and instantly she saw each. They were running or flying, desperate to return to the place where Ivy now stood.

Ivy slipped her fingers across the surface of the sigil. Impossibly intricate elements of the design slid and slipped. The jagged windows around her aligned themselves. The sizzling heat of the window with Lain's frozen echo of time mercifully vanished. Though the motions necessary to produce the effects she desired were feeding themselves into her mind, it was hardly a simple thing to achieve them. It was like being taught a new language or art form all at once. She had the knowledge in her mind, but accessing it with the subtlety and precision that was called for was at the very limits of her ability. If she'd not had an artist's hands, she very much suspected the windows into other parts of the world would have plunged down into the ground or off into the sky. As it was, one of them dipped far enough into a warm tropical sea to send a wave of saltwater gushing across the field.

One by one, she was able to maneuver the windows such that she could see, however distant, each of the Chosen. They hurried toward her. For good measure, Ivy attempted to open windows near a handful of other allies. It never hurt to have a few extra friends.

"Close enough is close enough," she said.

"No," Deacon said.

She turned. The wizard was on his feet. His afflicted flesh was near black now, with feathery fractures running across the skin. "I came this far. I did this much. It would be a crime to subject the world to the dangers and risks that I have conjured in error and not complete what I started."

"Deacon, it's over. We just need to—"

"*It isn't over!*" he barked. "Not until we learn all we can from this. Not until we test it and experiment. Not until we've made the change we seek to make."

The tone wasn't his anymore. The kindness, the duty that flavored Deacon's voice even in his darkest moments was gone. He was cold. Hollow. Vicious. He summoned his gem to his afflicted hand. In his grip, the same thin lines of light curled across its surface.

Ivy could feel him beginning to weave some manner of spell. She looked about. The nearest of the Chosen to the window she'd conjured was Ether, but she wouldn't arrive before Deacon did whatever he was aiming to do. She narrowed her eyes and hissed a breath.

"I really hope this isn't a terrible idea..."

She turned and grasped the space sigil. Ivy didn't try to manipulate it. She doubted she could use it with the same finesse Deacon managed, and thus she doubted she could banish him. Instead, she tugged at it. After only a moment of resistance, she hauled the entire sigil free and dashed into the open field. When there wasn't a world-ending destruction of the fabric of reality, she knew its removal was at least not the *worst* thing she could have done. With it in hand, he couldn't keep the others from arriving. All she had to do now was keep it away from him until someone better equipped to deal with magic could set things right.

She felt power crackle behind her. Instinct and panic served her well enough to dodge the first three lancing bolts of arcane energy.

"Ivy, you are forcing my hand," he said. "The longer the facets of existence remain physical, the greater the risk something irreparable occurs. You are my friend, my ally, but my loyalty is to the world, not to you."

Ivy didn't bother turning back or replying to him. He was beyond the point of reason. And from the sound of the wailing wind, Ether would very shortly make any argument a moot point.

"Very well then. I shall have to improvise," he called.

The tingle of magic directed at her dropped away. Rather than relief, realization struck her like a blow to the stomach. She'd taken the sigil that would allow him to keep the others at bay, but he had *every other sigil* at his disposal.

She slid to a stop and turned. Ether's fiery form was screeching toward him like a comet. Deacon placed a hand on one of the sigils. The whole of the field lurched and twitched with his influence. Whatever he was doing, the air above the sword was luminous with power. White light curled and sculpted into an angular, dragon-like form. The light cracked away like a cocoon to reveal a dragoyle in midstrike. He had reeled time back to the moment many years ago when, in this precise place, a dragoyle had clashed with the swordsman named Rasa. On that day, the swordsman had fallen and the Sword of the Chosen was left for Myranda to find. Right now, the thing was simply frozen in the air. Another tweak by Deacon allowed it to roar to life and swoop forward.

The thing was not under his control, but it was a beast of D'Karon creation and, thus without other instruction or control, would strike at any and all of the Chosen it could detect. Right now, that meant Ether.

The elemental struck the horrid beast. For a moment, the monster battled her to a standstill. Ether was a force to be reckoned with. After three fiery blows, she'd already ruptured the beast's hide. Ivy's gaze shifted to the air above the sword again. A second dragoyle was forming, and when it was released, a third was summoned. Deacon had yet to put his hands to anything but the time sigil, and he'd already worked out a way to conjure an unlimited quantity of dragoyles to occupy the Chosen.

This battle would be dire.

#

Myranda charged toward the window before her. Already she could see that pure chaos had claimed the field ahead. She held her staff tightly and brought a series of spells to mind, then dove through the portal and landed in the field. A dragoyle's attention turned to her. She raised a shield to deflect the monster's blow and summoned a lance of fire to sear it.

"Deacon! Enough!"

"Not enough!" he called, a demented glee in his voice. "Never enough! Look at it all. Think of the possibilities!"

She warded off another monster. "You've unleashed works of the D'Karon on the world again. It is precisely what you sought to *prevent*!"

"It is simply an echo. Again, and again, and again. And they exist or cease to exist at my whim." He paused. "Echoes…"

He inspected the sigil he had influenced to summon the dragoyles.

"Yes… I see… Subtle changes, stretching backward. The source of the time echoes. And so it is solved. So long as the sigil is repaired when I am through, the echoes will cease. Best that I be left to my work, then."

Two of the beasts collided in the air above Myranda. They scrabbled against one another, fighting for the chance to be the one to reach her. Neither would get their chance, as a burst of flame and a flash of claws signaled Myn's arrival to the battlefield. She smashed them from the air and trampled them into the earth.

Myranda dashed for Deacon. She made it no more than three strides before it seemed that the ground itself was tipping beneath her. She felt like the level plain was becoming a steep hill. Myranda drove her staff into the earth to steady herself.

"There," Deacon said, poking at another sigil. "A force I've never conceived of manipulating. The very thing that holds us to the ground, freely manipulable."

A third dragoyle struck Myn, knocking her to the ground. Its jaws yawned wide and a plume of caustic black miasma belched forth. Myranda focused her mind into the wind, but found a will already in place. The breeze whipped into a gale, first whisking the black stuff harmlessly away, then ripping the beast itself from Myn's back. A piercing point of yellow light marked where Ayna had entered the battlefield, hands raised and potent mastery at work.

Myranda fought the force trying to pull her and the others away from Deacon as he continued to intensify whatever effect he was working at. She heard something touch down beside her and felt something firm and slick form beneath her feet. She looked down to find something akin to an icy staircase was rising out of the field.

"Steady there," Calypso said from beside her. "Was it you who brought me into this fracas? I'm more than a bit cross with Ayna for leaving me behind when she heeded the call."

"It wasn't me, but I'm glad you're here. We've lost Deacon, he's toying with the forces of nature."

Ayna darted down beside them. "If those symbols control aspects of reality, he's too close to them for us to risk attacking him directly."

"Mmm… The least we can do is clear the field a bit," Calypso said. "Leave the Chosen to the greater tasks. Can you get these beasts out of the way, Ayna?"

"Simplicity," she said.

The fairy landed atop Myranda's staff, borrowing it as a focus. She swirled her wings and raised her arms. The air around them followed her motions like she was conducting an orchestra. Dozens of identical black monstrosities, their great leathery wings caught in the gale, were ripped skyward. The warriors themselves were spared, as was a wide swath around Deacon lest the wind disturb the sigils.

"It was nice of fate to pitch me into my first legitimate battle with a ready supply of water all around. And already frozen!" Calypso remarked.

She waved her hands, and the snow obediently rose to her command. Globs of it formed into cones and condensed into spikes. She fluttered her fingers, and the spikes whisked into the screeching wind. Icy shards peppered the struggling dragoyles, shattering their hides and reducing them to broken rubble to rain down over the surrounding field.

#

Ivy tried to dig her toes into the ground and fight the force dragging at her. The same mysterious influence Deacon had summoned to keep Myranda and the others away from him was working to pull Ivy toward him. She was slipping. Flickers of blue light marked her mounting terror. For years she'd been keeping her emotions in control, but something about seeing her friend turn upon her and the others had pulled the rug out from under her. A part of her wanted to give in to the fear, to let it carry her far, far away. But she was clutching an object of profound power, and letting herself lose control with it in her clutches could do just as much damage as Deacon could.

Finally, she lost her footing and went sliding toward Deacon and the sword. She tucked the sigil under her arm and scrabbled against the icy ground, but she couldn't regain her footing. When she was near enough to him, Deacon pulled his hand from the sigil he'd been manipulating. The force tugging at her vanished, but before she could attempt to escape again, she felt Deacon's will curl about her and pull her closer. She fought against it—and began to make headway. But he rushed toward her and grabbed the sigil in her grasp with both hands.

"Give it to me. Things are getting out of hand," Deacon commanded.

"You're getting out of hand!"

"I'm doing what I need to do to keep the world safe."

222

"You're tearing the world apart. You're attacking your friends."

"You'll understand when it's done."

He focused a spell about her. Tendrils of light coiled around her arms, wrenching them away from the sigil. With a flick of his mind, she was thrown to the ground beside the sword. Deacon began to manipulate the space sigil. The still-open windows to other parts of the world started to shift. Ivy looked to the orbiting array of abstractions just above her. Then she looked to the ground, where the expended artifacts had fallen. Among them was the seemingly innocuous object that Deacon had focused all of his power into to make this madness possible, the Kenvard coin.

"Deacon!" she shouted. "You want proof? Test yourself!"

She grasped the coin and threw it to him. Deacon raised a hand and caught it. Savage flares of light sizzled between his flesh and the coin. He recoiled and dropped it. When it fell to the snow, the Mark of the Chosen on its tail face was still incandescent with heat and power.

Grim realization twisted his expression. True clarity, for the first time in too long, gleamed in his eyes. He'd abandoned his friends. He'd attacked them. His mind was no longer his own, and it had made a traitor of him. In that moment, he might just have had the strength to pull himself from his obsession. He might have had the strength to put the sigil down and allow the others to undo what he had done. But alas, for all that had gone right to allow the instant of clarity, there was one thing that had gone very, very wrong.

Deacon was holding the sigil in his afflicted hand.

A tremor shook him. His fingers clenched. The sigil fractured. And then…

Nothing…

#

Myranda's eyes opened. She didn't recall closing them. Whatever had happened, it had happened swiftly and forcefully enough to rob her of her wits. Her vision was blurred, and there was a brilliant white light before her. She tried to blink her vision clear, but no matter how she tried, she saw only white. Slowly, she realized that it was not a light, it was all there was to see. The world had vanished. She was alone in a white void stretching out in all directions. Despite the fact that she felt as though she was lying on a surface with the texture of polished marble, even beneath her was nothing but white.

She took stock of her condition. She was weary, but her spirit was still strong and she was uninjured. Her staff was still in hand. Her mind and her mystic focus had always been enough to see her through before. And this was hardly the first time she'd awoken in a situation she didn't understand. There was nothing to do but climb to her feet and press on.

"Hello?" she called.

Her voice didn't echo. Though there were no walls, the sound seemed tinny and stifled. She shut her eyes and focused. Her mind beheld a landscape nearly as featureless as the one she had seen. There was but one vague notion, something distant and difficult to focus on. With nothing else to do, she marched toward it.

This wasn't death. She was no stranger to death. By most measures, she had already experienced it. And she doubted this was oblivion. In oblivion there could be no thought, no action. What chilled her wasn't the thought that she had been killed or that she had been wiped from existence. What struck her to her very soul was the possibility that she was precisely where she had been when Deacon had broken the sigil. This might well be what had become of the world.

#

Ivy struggled to stand. As had been the case for Myranda, the world she'd awoken in was not the one she knew. But she had been nearer to Deacon when the sigil was damaged. What shreds of existence were still hanging together clung more closely to this point.

Fragments of the field remained. They scattered around her, bits of snow, land, and sky spread thin in her vision. They were faint, like half-forgotten images of a strange dream. She stumbled along the ground toward a stone twisting in front of her and reached out. Her hand passed through it. It wasn't real. She could see it, and in her heart she knew what it was and where it belonged, but there was no place for it to be. Deacon had broken the sigil that allowed for such things.

"There must be something," she murmured. "I'm still here. I'm still real. There must be something here. Something I can use. Something I can do."

She continued forward. In her mind, she was walking toward where the sword had been plunged into the ground. For all she knew, direction had no meaning anymore. But moving toward something, even something imagined, was better than staying still and giving up hope.

And there *was* something there. An insignificant speck in the distance. It may as well have been a mote of dust, but it was solid. In the midst of the half-reality she was lost in, anything genuine and unmistakable loomed large as a mountain.

She quickened to a run. The thing approached with aching slowness, but time was as unreal here as distance. She could have been running for an hour, she could have been running for a heartbeat. It was all meaningless in this place. The only thing that mattered was the fragment of reality she was dashing toward. Its color became visible, gleaming gold and silver. Then its shape. She recognized it.

"Of course…" Ivy said, reaching out to it.

Ivy had manipulated only two of the sigils. One had been broken. This was the other. Music. It seemed only right that in this moment, this was what she would find. The very thing that had rescued her so many times before. The thing that had soothed her and brought her comfort when so few things could. The thing she had used time and time again to bring people together. And it would bring people together again.

She took the sigil in hand. Her claws gently raked across it. She coaxed a glissando from the instrument. It wasn't just beautiful. It was beauty. It wasn't just soulful, it was soul. For Ivy, music had so often been everything. Now it quite literally was. She plucked out notes until she understood the voice and feel of the instrument. The melody formed itself, drawn from her mind through her fingers. It was haunting, subtle, solemn.

As she played, she became more familiar with the instrument. She layered more depth into the melody. At the edge of her hearing, something beyond the music reached her. Motion. The click of footsteps. Someone was approaching. She opened her eyes to find Myranda walking toward her. With Myranda's approach, the tone of the music grew stronger. Ivy could feel the tiniest breath of a breeze on her fur. She stirred the song to a livelier tempo. The flap of a dragon's wings came next. Myn set down beside her. Then the crackle of an elemental flame.

Like candles coming together to push back the darkness, each of those who heeded the call of her song brought a bit more reality. Ivy could feel the crunch of snow beneath her feet again as she swayed to the song. Ayna flitted to her side, and a bit of color returned to their surroundings. She put more spirit into the song. By the time Calypso joined them, the melody was soaring and triumphant. She brought it to a final flourish and wiped the tears from her eyes.

The pieces of reality had gathered about them, forming into an island of existence in the middle of the white void like candles gathered in the darkness. Ivy's song hung in the air for a moment. As it began to fade, the vibrancy of the patch of ground surrounding them faded too, and it began to recede into the void. She idly plucked a few more notes, invigorating it again.

"It looks like you'll need to keep the music flowing," Myranda said.

"That I can do," she said, strumming softly with a blissful look on her face.

"I never would have dreamed Deacon could be capable of this," Calypso said.

"And you were in favor of allowing him into the good graces of Entwell again," Ayna said with her arms crossed.

"This isn't Deacon. This is what that sickness has done to his mind,"

Myranda said. "How could he have kept this to himself…"

"We have bigger problems than worrying about Deacon's state of mind," Ether said.

"Considering what he's done, I'm not sure I agree," Ayna said.

"Have we left the world, or has the world left us?" Calypso asked. "And if all of creation has been shattered, why are we still here?"

"If we are still here, then there is something left. And if there is something left, there is still hope," Myranda said. "If the music sigil survived, then the others must have. We survived, and we were at the center of what happened. We must assume the rest of the world fared better."

"A weak assumption," Ether observed.

"It's what we have, and it's enough. Somewhere out there is the center of all this. The sword, the remaining sigils, and Deacon. We have to find them. We have to piece things back together, and we have to put this to an end."

Ether approached the edge of the island of reality around them and crouched. She reached beyond it and shut her eyes.

"It will not be simple. There isn't anything there. We can travel as far as we like, but we will never draw nearer to anything else, because the distance between us isn't real."

"I don't understand," Myranda said.

Ayna and Calypso joined Ether in investigating.

"She's right," said Calypso. "I've never felt such vacancy. The very firmament is gone. If we survive this, there are volumes to be written in trying to work out just how it's possible *we* exist when the world around us doesn't. But we certainly can't go toward something when the very concept of location is fractured."

"We found Ivy," Myn said.

"We found Ivy because she was calling to us. In essence, she created a place for us by drawing upon one of the elements of existence."

Myranda drove the tip of her staff into the snow at her feet. The gem kindled to life. She held out her hands. "Join me."

Calypso paced to her side and took her hand. Ether took her other hand. Ayna landed on her staff again.

"Play with spirit, Ivy," Myranda instructed.

"Gladly."

The malthrope increased the tempo of her song. Wisps of a golden aura wove around her. Ivy's music had always had a profound effect on her, and through her, it had a similar effect on the others. For the first time, Myranda could feel the power of the music itself. It stirred her. Fueled her. She was experiencing music in its purest form. In its *elemental* form. If Ivy felt even a fraction of this beauty and truth when she played, Myranda fully understood her love for the art form.

Their focus and power joined together, widening the reach of their minds and spirits. Each had a distinctive color and texture to their spirit as they pulled themselves to the task. Ether was tight, controlled. Calypso was fluid and elegant. Ayna's mind was a diamond-clear point held viciously in focus almost out of sheer spite.

"What are we searching for?" Ayna asked.

"We'll know it when we find it," Myranda said.

The images that filled their minds were chilling. Not since the earliest days of her training had Myranda felt so little from the world around her. Even when pains had been taken to shield things from her, she'd always felt *something*. But not here. They strained and stretched their focus. Still, there was nothing. Magic was about manipulating the forces around you. There were no forces to manipulate. What little power they had at their disposal came from within, and from Ivy's music.

Myranda shut her eyes tighter. She guided her mind further, choosing a direction based solely on intuition. The others followed her lead. Their minds shone upon the emptiness. Their influence rolled outward like waves. In time, as Ivy's song slid into a soft lull, they felt a ripple in response. It was weak. If the world were still in place, they would have missed it. But Myranda felt it. It was Deacon. She could feel his spirit tugging, struggling as if chained.

"There," Calypso said. "It's him."

"He is far. If we are going to reach him, we'll need a way to travel," Ayna said.

The group let their focus subside.

"We'll need to build a bridge of reality," Myranda said.

"How does one do such a thing?" Calypso mused, fingers to her chin.

"I wish Deacon were here. He'd jump at the opportunity to work it out," Myranda said.

"Plus, if he was here, we wouldn't have to find him," Ivy helpfully added while plucking at the strings.

Ether stepped to the edge of their little sanctuary and gazed out into the void. "Deacon believes that reality is defined by these abstractions, rather than the earth, fire, wind, and water that surrounds us at all times." She turned. "In his meddling, he has shattered reality. This reveals the truth of his belief. But more than one thing can be true. What am I if not a will crafted to harness power and create the elements?"

She planted her feet and set her eyes upon their unseen target. "This will require all my attention. One of you will have to guide me. The rest will have to empower me. But I will build the bridge." Ether turned to Ivy. "Play well."

"If only this were a violin, you would see just how…" Ivy began.

Before she could finish, the instrument in her fingers obliged her. The change managed to be subtle. It was less a matter of the shape of the sigil changing as existence changing its mind about what it had always been. It was still intrinsically, fundamentally, and unquestionably the same embodiment of magic. The actual shape it took was its least important trait.

Ivy didn't question the change. She simply flashed a smile, flourished the tip of a bow that hadn't been in her hand until a moment ago, and raised the violin to her chin.

"This is going to be a song for the ages."

Bow met strings. Joy and triumph themselves leaped from them. The power of it surged through her, radiating like beams of golden sunlight. Ayna flitted in front of Ether, hanging just above the fringe of their little piece of reality. The elemental changed first to wind. She let flame, earth, and water slowly separate until she was a churning mass of each. The flame did not sizzle the water. The air did not scatter the earth. They blended like the colors of the rainbow. It was precisely how Ether had looked on the day Calypso, Ayna, and Myranda had helped to summon her. But now, rather than coming together out of those elements, she was splitting apart, returning them to the world around her.

Streamers of the elements curled out, weaving into earth and snow. Ayna drifted forward slowly. The icy field that should have occupied this place formed beneath her. Ether wasn't creating the ground out of whole cloth. The way it appeared felt less like it was being crafted and more like it was being revealed. This place was a vessel that had been emptied of its contents. Ether poured fragments of herself into it, and those fragments filled the vessel and took its shape.

The music and the wills of the wizards behind her replenished Ether's strength, allowing her to craft more of the elements and continue.

"Onward," she said. "Quickly."

#

Elsewhere, the effects of the magic had taken their toll. The world had, for most of its inhabitants, ceased to be. The subjects of the northern kingdoms found their homes, their places of business, the very ground beneath their feet torn away. Like the Chosen, they found themselves afloat in a vast, featureless sea of white. Unlike their defenders, they knew not why. Most were adrift, isolated. No scrap of land or sky could be seen. Not another soul could be felt. Millions of people, suddenly alone. Single points of life.

Those with stronger wills and steadier nerves managed to keep grasp of some shred of reality. In Entwell, the masters stood atop fragments of their homeland. They could feel the distant flicker of other minds and spirits. Places of power drifted like islands in the void, held together by a sort of self-imposed reality. Wolloff's tower and the clearing around it refused to succumb to the nothingness. The long strip of land at the Tresson border, where so many lives had been lost, clung to existence.

In a tower of the castle of Kenvard, a frightened young servant of the Crown stood with a child in her arms. She gazed in terror at the hazy edge of the floor before her.

"It… it's going to be all right," she murmured to Leo.

She tore her eyes away from the nothingness to offer what little comfort she could to the boy. She didn't understand what had happened, but she had a duty to the child. Yet, when she looked to him, she found no terror, no confusion in the face of her charge. Leo was not afraid. He held out his hand and pointed a chubby digit.

"Go," the boy said.

"There is… there is nowhere to go," Sadie said.

"Go, go, go! Dada, dada," Leo demanded impatiently.

Sadie took a cautious step toward the edge of the island of reality. The void ahead retreated, revealing more of the ground. She turned. Behind, the void had advanced. She'd remained at the center of a tiny speck of existence. It followed her for another step, though the way ahead didn't match what it should have been. As she paced forward at the child's urging, the rug of the palace was replaced by the icy cobblestone of the courtyard, then the packed gravel of a road.

She swallowed hard and looked to the child. He wore a dull smile, but in his eyes was something she'd rarely seen in him, or in any child of his age. There was something approaching determination. Certainty. It was as though he knew what he was doing. What had to be done. He jabbed his finger. Sadie steeled herself and continued on. There was only one way, and that way was forward.

#

A scene opened out before Myranda and the others as they finally approached their destination. She had prepared herself for something disastrous, something horrid. She hadn't prepared herself for this. The sword was still in place, still driven into a piece of ground scarred by heat and battle. A constellation of sigils orbited about it, but there were three glaring gaps. One was the embodiment of music, still in Ivy's hands. The other was the space sigil, which lay in pieces on the ground. The third was nowhere to be seen, and none but Deacon knew which it might be. And though he was present, they knew better than to ask him.

The man Myranda loved, the father to her child, was no longer recognizable. His body had been completely consumed by the affliction.

His form was in vague but perpetual flux, dancing between an assortment of shapes from moment to moment. One was Deacon's own body. Others ranged from a twisted black-as-night silhouette to a featureless white figure. His gem was similarly fragmented. It was broken into dozens of cruel shards that spread about his upheld fist like a swarm of luminous bees. The pieces of what had once been the space sigil lay spread out before him, disassembled like a clockwork mechanism. Deacon poked and prodded at the pieces, fitting them together with a childlike sense of curiosity and experimentation. Whenever a pair of pieces fit together, the void around them trembled, shifted, and produced a slice of landscape. Some lingered, stretching far into the distance. Others came and went in the blink of an eye. It had produced a calico assortment of environments spread around him.

When Ether's carefully woven reality finally reached his, Deacon noticed the fresh patch of earth. He looked up.

"Ah. You are alive," he said calmly. "I had anticipated Myranda and the other Chosen would survive. But Ayna and Calypso are alive as well. Interesting."

There was no relief or joy in his voice. He noted the survival of his friends as something worthy of jotting down in a journal for further study.

"Deacon. We need to set this straight."

"In time. In time. And we have plenty of it. All of it, in fact," he said. "I *did* have a job to do, and I mean to do it. It is genuinely intriguing, the complexity of the underlying mechanisms of our world. I've learned much already."

Ether, no longer called upon to craft the very ground they walked upon, dropped to the patch of reality stretching out from the sword. She was visibly fatigued by the effort, even with the help of Ivy and the others. Myranda and the others spread into a semicircle around Deacon. A handful of the greatest warriors the world had ever known looked upon the wizard as an enemy. He wasn't even concerned enough to pull himself from his puzzle. He raised a hand, coaxing a wheel-shaped sigil into position before him. It was comparatively simple, five spokes leading from an outer circle into a small round hub.

"This is an element of the space sigil. It represents the permeability of our world. While it exists, and is whole, creatures like the D'Karon can find their way in, and we can find our way out. If I could simply destroy it, that would be all. A wall would be built that none could penetrate. We would still have our own threats from within, our own wars, our own troubles. But we would be safe from external forces."

"You can't toy with such things, Deacon."

"That is plainly untrue. I am doing so presently."

"What's happened to the rest of the world?"

"What happens to day when night falls? What happens to winter when it is summer? The world is still there… or *here*, I suppose." He indicated the fragments spread before him. "When the pieces come back together, so too shall the world. The same goes for every sigil. The hard part isn't assembling them. They *want* to be whole. The hard part is getting them to remain apart. But I am making progress."

"So to solve what you've done, we need only gather the fractured sigils together and they will heal themselves?" Calypso said.

"No. *You* can't do that. Only I can." He held up his blighted hand. "Chaos. Only chaos can effect true change. Furthermore, I am devoting a fair amount of my skills to preventing this particular sigil from reassembling, so you would also have to kill me to even allow the pieces a chance to assemble. And that won't happen for a number of reasons. Myranda loves Deacon. As does Ivy. I have my doubts about Myn, but I believe the affection is sufficient to stay her flame. And—"

There was a blur of motion. His words were choked off by Ether's stone hand wrapped about his throat. She raised him into the air. "I have no such compunctions."

"Ether!" Myranda shouted.

It was too late. She hammered him to the ground with a punishing blow. The impact crackled the frozen earth beneath him. Deacon's flickering, chaotic form twitched once and became still. The fragments of gem floating about his fist darkened and fell to the ground. All were silent, shocked.

"Ether…" Myranda said, when she found her voice.

Ether stood, eyes fixed on Deacon's fallen form. "It needed to be done. The man you knew was gone."

"We could have saved him…"

"There was nothing left to save. And he was long past deserving it."

Deacon's body twitched. The gems flickered to life.

"Impossible…" Ether growled.

She raised her rocky foot. Deacon's battered body dragged itself away and drifted up into the air. She tried to attack again, but he raised a shield to deflect the first few blows.

"Don't waste your time, Ether. I've taken precautions." He held his hand out to one of the other sigils. "And if you don't calm down and listen to reason, there is always free will to be toyed with. I would hate to do so. It would make things unbearably dull. And were I to damage my own, I believe that would be the end of things."

Ether, vibrating with rage, backed away. Deacon lowered his hand.

"What just happened?" Ayna demanded.

"I am glad you asked. It is a contingency I am rather proud of. You see I wasn't confident I would be able to hold all of you off, should you arrive before I was through with my work. So I took the liberty of removing the death sigil and breaking it in two. I have had access to the means to create and manipulate reality for a considerable amount of time before you arrived. I feel quite certain you won't be able to find the pieces of the death sigil while I am still alive. And you won't be able to kill me until you find them. In short, I cannot be defeated at the present time. So why not be civil? Let me see to my work. We can all learn so much."

"Deacon, you need to—" Myranda snapped.

"You *must* stop calling me that," he objected. "Ether is right. Does this look like the man you knew? The chrysalis has split. Do not mourn the caterpillar when the butterfly is born."

Myranda began to pull her mind to focus. The others did so as well. Myn widened her stance and spread her wings. One by one, their eyes shifted to the assortment of sigils. The thing that no longer wished to be called Deacon looked crestfallen.

"All of time, all of creation, all of possibility hangs before you to be studied and understood, and this will degenerate to coarse combat and a scramble for shiny baubles?" He shook his head. "Such a waste. But I have planned for this as well."

He fitted a few pieces of the space sigil together. The fractured bits of landscape shifted again, expanding out to consume the area around them. As the island of reality grew, the Chosen and their allies were scattered. The land *between* them was expanding along with the rest, spreading them dozens of yards away from Deacon and away from each other. Where once they had been standing in a broken remnant of reality, now an arena-sized field of frigid ice and snow spread out around them. It was a moment locked in time, and it was easily one of the worst moments in their world's history. The very same moment Deacon had summoned to make the spell work in the first place. This was Lain's End, in the moments before it earned its name.

Horrid monstrosities, products of the D'Karon, flooded the field. They were motionless. Even windblown snow was still. The chaotic Deacon took advantage of the disorientation of having the world around them shift. He touched his hand to the time sigil. A few choice creatures dropped to the ground, freed of the stasis that held the rest of them in check. The simple-minded things assessed their surroundings. They represented a terrible assortment of the D'Karon monstrosities. Blade-mouthed, panther-shaped predators. Great, lumbering behemoths. Deacon's monstrous new form raised his voice and spoke in the fractured, otherworldly dialect of the D'Karon. The things couldn't help but obey.

Monsters clashed with each of the heroes. Now with ice and wind at their disposal, Ayna and Calypso were quite ready to lend a hand. Myn locked claws with a thing twice her size and belched flame. The monsters were skewered, scorched, and pummeled. Most shrugged off the blows. Those who fell to them quickly rose again, either exempt from death as all other things were or restored by the influence of the time sigil.

"Get to the sigils! Nothing else matters!" Myranda called out.

Ayna filled the battlefield with wind strong enough to peel the flesh from bones. Calypso sealed monsters in impenetrable shells of ice. They fought valiantly, the legion of beasts to choose from was nearly endless, and any who were soundly defeated could simply be conjured again with barely a gesture to the time sigil.

"It's no good," Ether called out. "His control over this moment is too great. We need something beyond his control."

"We need to end him!" Ayna said.

"But there is no way to kill him. We simply don't…" Calypso paused. "Wait."

Ayna's wind sent two beasts clashing against one another to give the mermaid some cover. Finally, she revealed an elegant blade.

"We have this!"

"What good will a blade do?" Ether demanded, driving an abomination into the frozen earth. "If I couldn't kill him by shattering his body, stabbing him will be of little worth."

"This blade was augmented in the crystal arena by Azriel. She's always seen more of what is and what will be than anyone short of Hollow. We've got to try. If only I'd taken my combat training in the blade rather than the spear."

Ayna grasped the handle of the weapon and wrenched it away. It was larger than the whole of her body, but she held the grip firmly. "I am quite familiar with bladed weapons. Clear the way as best you can."

The wind master conjured a potent gale and buzzed her wings to a blur. Combined, they propelled her tiny form with arrow swiftness. Lances of ice pinned down leaping beasts ahead of her. Ether smashed and heaved aside a hulk that targeted her. Bursts of flame from Myn, bolts of magic from Myranda, everything that the group could manage was brought to bear.

Deacon must have felt the point of magic streaking toward him. He raised a shield and hurled a bolt of magic of his own. Ayna circled up and away to dodge the bolt. Ivy dashed forward, flares of red in her aura, and clashed with the shield at the same moment that Ayna did. The twin blows weakened it enough for the fairy to break through. The air crackled with spells as Deacon hurled an onslaught of attacks at the fairy. Beasts elsewhere prevented the others from helping, but this close to Deacon the monsters wouldn't dare attack.

Using guile as much as magic, Ayna kept ahead of Deacon's attacks. She harried him, keeping him from the sigils. Deacon, in his right mind, was far from the most skilled of fighters. Blighted by his affliction and distracted by the need to hold the Chosen at bay, it was inevitable that Ayna finally landed a blow. The supernaturally sharp tip of the blade met Deacon's shifting flesh. He growled in rage and managed to strike Ayna with a savage dose of black magic. The blade dropped to the ground. The fairy retreated to regroup. But the damage was done.

Deacon held up the arm that had been slashed by the weapon. The dagger had left an ugly, deep gash in it. It drizzled deep red blood. The flesh around the wound was pink and human. It had wounded him, but in doing so it had pushed back the affliction.

The realization that the weapon might truly threaten the affliction's control over him brought first fear, then fury to Deacon's twisted eyes.

"So be it," he said. "I just wanted you busy before. I didn't want you to suffer. But if that is how it must be, then I'm not holding back any of the creatures. You face them all."

He touched his fingers to the time sigil. The ground trembled as each of the beasts dropped down at once. He barked D'Karon orders at them, and the battlefield was consumed in a sea of slashing claws and bellowing beasts. They closed ranks, winged monsters filling the air, stout abominations blocking the ground. The twisted Deacon watched with vague interest as the Chosen gathered together. Mystic shields rose. Potent flashes and flares of elemental magic roasted foes. But always there were more to replace those that fell.

#

Satisfied they were of no concern for the time being, he broke the space sigil down again, taking pains to retain his recent adjustments, lest they be freed from their battle. He was close. He could feel it. The pieces could be made to fit solidly without the gateway aspect he had removed. If he could make a complete and seamless rune, then he would need only shatter the remnants of the gateway aspect and the task would be complete. An endless sequence of further experiments on improving things still remained to be done, of course, but one solid and inarguable goal would be achieved.

The battlefield, still echoing with monstrous bellows and shrieks, took on a new tone while he worked. Quietly at first, something harmonious and pure penetrated the chaos. Rapid notes and complex chords started to push back the tide of discordant sound. A blue-white light of intense magic shined through the cracks of a mounding collection of monstrosities. Then, all at once, something burst from within the mound. Deacon didn't spare a look, at first. His hands were full. Keeping his army in place to keep them at bay while still manipulating the rest of the sigil was delicate work. There were too many moving pieces for him to risk setting any of them down to take a direct role in the battle. He placed his trust in the overwhelming numbers to keep him safe until he was finished.

Myn soared high and fast, propelled not just by her own considerable flight prowess but by Ayna's wind magic. Ivy, Myranda, and Calypso held on to her back tightly, the former sawing at the violin with a manic enthusiasm. Her gleeful mastery of the music flooded the others with power. Myranda kept a flickering shield in place around them. Calypso ripped up vast sheets of ice from the field to foul, freeze, and ensnare the monsters. Ether swirled windily ahead of Myn's snout, tearing at anything that breeched Myranda's shield. They were unified in their strategy, a single force slicing through the monsters like a hot knife.

Deacon offered the briefest glance. "Impressive. I'd not anticipated this level of synergy with a pair of non-Chosen in the group," he said. "Entwell truly is a wondrous place. I shall have to make it a point to return, once there is an Entwell to return to."

As Myn darted toward him, the legion of dark forms grew denser. Myranda's shield began to fail. Deacon focused more intently on his work. So close. Myn heaved in a deep breath. Ether shifted to flame before her maw. The dragon belched out a column of flame around her. Ayna funneled wind into the inferno. The acrid hide of the D'Karon creatures were consumed by the flames, fueling its intensity all the more. Deacon could feel the heat of it. Still he worked. When the burst of flame finally tapered away, a single swirling point of it remained, Ether's fiery form. Her white-hot body made short work of the last few rows of beasts between her and Deacon.

He tried to peel away a bit of his focus to raise a shield. She shattered it easily. The glow of her body was stinging his eyes now. In heartbeats she would be upon him. But heartbeats were enough. The final piece slotted in place. The space sigil was his to manipulate again. He raked his fingers across the surface, banishing the Chosen and the beasts in a single, monumental wave. They weren't destroyed. The space sigil couldn't manage that. And they weren't far enough away that they could never return. He'd yet to repair reality sufficiently for there to *be* someplace from which they couldn't return. But they would have to find each other again and find him again. And when they did, he could simply banish them again. It would be irritating but manageable, and would give him the opportunity for further experimentation.

"What warrants my attention next?" he murmured aloud. "I think perhaps... Oh... Clever." His gaze settled upon the time sigil. It was slowly rotating. "You weren't after me, were you, Ether? You were just reaching for a sigil. And you reached it. Poor foresight on my part. Such is the danger of distraction."

He crouched before the sigil. "What did you do…" he mused. "It was only time. She could only bring something that had occupied this slice of the space. What am I missing…"

The answer dawned upon him an instant too late. A sword hissed through the air. Deacon pulled his mind together to muster a defense, but it was no ordinary sword, wielded by no ordinary warrior. The defense barely slowed the blow enough for him to roll back. He scrambled to his feet and looked upon his foe. Standing tall, with sword in hand and fury in his eyes, was Lain.

"Who are you and what have you done to the others?" he seethed.

"I don't have the patience to explain it, and there is little value in doing so for an echo of the past. Leave me to my task."

Lain didn't waste breath on further words. He seldom did. The warrior burst forward with a speed Deacon had forgotten could exist in a creature who lacked the knack for magic. The wizard unleashed a flurry of spells. Lain deflected and scattered them with his masterpiece of a blade. It was all that Deacon could do to keep Lain's weapon from tasting his flesh. Death wouldn't linger, of course. It couldn't. But while he was incapacitated, there was no telling what Lain might choose to do with the sigils.

The assassin kept the pressure on, slashing away the spells hurled in his direction. Deacon tried to summon portals to send him away, but the D'Karon magic needed a target, and they had been whisked away with the rest of the world. It was inevitable, but eventually Lain's agility and skill combined with the weapon that could counter his magic proved too much for Deacon. An attack hit home, driving deep into Deacon's abdomen.

It should have been enough to kill him. But the rule of death was presently repealed. Deacon stumbled. He wheezed. But he had enough of his wits left to conjure a blast to knock Lain back. The wizard stumbled. He withdrew the sword. His body felt cold, but he had what he needed to ensure the weapon would no longer be a factor. A swirl of earth magic split the ground beneath him. He dropped the weapon into the crevasse and sealed it away.

"You…" Deacon coughed. "You did well. But you are through now."

Lain's fierce gaze flicked to the sky. Deacon didn't need to look. The others were already finding their way back.

"It doesn't matter," Deacon said. "I can already feel my strength returning. You've lost your weapon. You can't counter my magic any longer. You don't know how to work the sigils. You have no time to try. And death is no concern here. What good is an assassin in a world where no one can die?"

Lain's gaze flicked aside again. "There are worse things than death."

Deacon had trained all his life to think deeply and think clearly. He could maintain maddeningly complex networks of enchantments and spells in his head simultaneously. He could recall deep and nuanced mystic interactions and weave them together in moments. But when it came to thinking swiftly and decisively, he was nothing compared to Lain.

The malthrope dove aside. Deacon abandoned the more potent and more easily dodged projected magics, seeking instead to summon something more direct. His magic began to swirl about Lain as the malthrope's feet struck the ground. After three strides, Lain must have been wracked with pain from the spell already, but he continued on. There was the glint of steel in his hand. Deacon added some hastily hurled bolts of energy. Lain deftly dove between them, rolled, and continued his sprint. Finally, Deacon realized the flash of steel he'd seen was the dagger Ayna had wielded against him. This realization struck him a moment before the blade did.

The force of the blow and Lain's charging weight knocked Deacon to the ground. The blade had found his heart. Under its mystic influence, the twisted, chaotic form Deacon had taken on began to be wicked away.

#

Myranda and Myn and Ivy were the first to reach the island of reality they had been cast away from. Having had to navigate oblivion once already, finding their way back was swift. The others were already visible in the distance. Myranda's hands were trembling as she dropped down from Myn's back. A friend and ally she had lost years before was back. And he had her husband pinned to the ground with a blade. Even the small mercy of the nearly unrecognizable distortion of Deacon's features had finished dropping away. It was simply him. Blooded. Burned. Defeated. And struggling as the release of death refused to come.

"Myranda…" Deacon murmured in a ragged voice. "I… I'm sorry…"

"Don't talk," Myranda said, crouching beside him. She looked up to Lain and touched the grip of the dagger. "I've got him," she said softly.

The assassin nodded and stood. He looked to Ivy. The music sigil slipped from her fingers and reverted to its original form as it crunched into the snow.

"Lain…" she whispered.

She rushed to him and wrapped her arms around him, sobbing uncontrollably. Myranda fought to keep her eyes on her stricken husband.

"I've made a terrible mess of things…" Deacon wheezed.

"You weren't in your right mind."

He shook his head. "No excuses. Listen… to set things right…" He held out a hand. The air beside him rippled, and a pair of semicircular fragments tumbled down. "The death sigil. It needs to be repaired. The spell can't be completed until they are whole again."

"Not before you are healed," she said.

"Listen. Anyone can manipulate the sigils. Control their power. But only chaos magic can alter them. Break them. Repair them. Summon them. That… affliction is chaos. It is how the spell was cast."

"It's gone now."

He shook his head again. "My shadow."

She looked to the mote of black beneath him. It was in his shape, but twisted and ghastly. It had the same unnatural shape and motion that Myranda had long ago learned to distrust. The same sort of cold mockery of form that clung to anyone under the influence of one of the D'Karon generals. The shape was too perfectly, too precisely as Myranda remembered it. The only thing lacking was the cold certainty in its motions. This was Epidime.

"No… It can't be him. You survived the mark until you cast the spell. He couldn't have been in control of you."

"He wasn't. I left him in the cave. But I can feel his mind now. It is him… an empty, wild version of him, but it is him." He smiled weakly. "Perhaps he infected me with a slice of himself. Perhaps chaos itself was what spawned him. I would dearly love to solve the riddle. But time is short. He is still clinging to me. I can still repair the pieces. Bring them to me."

"Can we trust him?" Ayna said, buzzing with Calypso beside her.

Myranda took her marked hand from the dagger and touched it to his face. Though the shadow shuddered and recoiled, Deacon was unhurt. The mark spared him. It meant a great deal. It meant this was truly Deacon, and it meant that the actions that had marked him as an enemy of the Chosen were not his own, but the work of that wretched creature clinging to him.

"So long as that *thing* isn't in control, he can be trusted," Myranda said. "Bring me the pieces."

Calypso gathered up the halves of the death sigil. Ayna swirled her wind to collect the nearly complete space sigil and the entirely intact gateway aspect that was removed from it. Ether crackled up to the island of reality. She looked upon Deacon's stricken body, then turned to Lain. Myn had thrust her head between Ivy and the assassin, great tears rolling down her face as he gently stroked her brow.

"I knew you would find a way," Ether said. "You always did. You always will."

"What is all of this? What has happened?" Lain asked.

"You've been plucked out of time," Ether said. "You've been dead for years. In the moment I pulled you from—"

"I had already decided to give my life to protect you all from Bagu," Lain said.

Ivy pulled reluctantly away. Myn did the same. Ether stepped up and gently caressed Lain's cheek. She couldn't hold back the tide of tears. "I wanted you back. But you aren't. Not really. You are a stolen moment. A memory given form. You can't stay."

"I wouldn't want to. I have a job yet to be done," Lain said.

"Then… then he's going?" Ivy said, sadness coiling about her. "We are going to lose him again?"

"He's already been lost. There's no changing that." Ether had a genuine, heartsick vulnerability in her expression. "But at least this time we can say goodbye."

Ivy tackled him in a tight hug. Ether embraced them both. Myn pulled the group to her in a single-pawed hug.

"Y-you need to know," Ivy said, voice cracking with emotion. "Sorrel! Sorrel and the twins made it. They found more like us, Lain. There are more malthropes. A whole society. They had their trials, but they are still there, and they are strong. It's so beautiful, Lain. And they're your family."

"The war is over," Ether said. "The world is at peace."

"The slaves are free," Myn rumbled.

"It's all because of you, Lain." Ivy sniffled. "You did it."

"Then my life was worth something," Lain said. "No need for tears. This is the best I could have hoped for. It is what I always meant to achieve. All that remains is for me to return to my final task."

Ivy reluctantly pulled away.

"I love you, Lain," she whispered. "We all love you. And we always will. The world will never forget you."

The others released him. Lain looked to Myranda. Each offered a solemn, respectful nod. The moment allowed for nothing more.

"Touch the sigil," Deacon instructed. "It will be enough to send you back."

Lain silently turned and stepped to the sigils circling the sword. As though in salute of his sacrifice, the array rotated to present him with the proper piece. He held out his hand.

And he was gone.

The weight of the moment didn't have time to linger. His job was done, but theirs remained.

Deacon was fitting the fragments of the space sigil together. The landscape around them smoothly shifted from the mountainside to the icy field they had begun their battle in.

"The pieces fit. It is too much of a risk to break the sigil again to restore the gateway aspect. Just"—he coughed—"return it to the sword. Together or apart, it will serve its purpose, so long as it isn't shattered. And do the same when I fit the death sigil together again."

"There must be some other way."

"You remove the dagger and I'll lose control," he said. "You remove the affliction and I won't be able to repair the sigils. It has to be this way, Myranda."

"I'm not letting you go that easily. You have a son to raise," she said sharply. "Do what you need to do. I'll find a way to save you. What good is there in being Chosen if I can't save the father of my child?"

He raised a hand to her cheek. "You can't save everyone. It's fate." He pulled her close and kissed her cheek. "I'm sorry I couldn't have been a better man."

Deacon took the two pieces of the death sigil. He touched them together. The pieces fused. Deacon released a final ragged breath and fell limp.

Calypso and Ether quietly took the restored sigils and replaced them. Myranda remained on her knees, eyes on Deacon's lifeless body. Before the grief could work its claws past the anger and shock, a motion caught her eyes. The shadow, still wretched and twisted, was struggling. It tugged and pulled. With Deacon gone, the chaotic presence began to panic. It was a parasite without a living host. It tore free and peeled away, its form dark and jagged. It moved with the same unnatural motion as Epidime, and like the D'Karon creature, it attempted to seize control of a new host. The blackness curled about Myranda. It contacted her for only an instant before her mark seared it away. This was precisely the sort of otherworldly demon Epidime had been, but it was empty and feral, lacking the cool calculation of the monster she knew.

Abandoning her, it streaked toward the other Chosen. One by one their marks forced it away. Then it came to Ayna.

"The mark. Someone put her in contact with the mark!" Myranda called. "If that thing truly is Epidime, or something like him, it will seize control of her."

Already the fairy was shuddering and twitching. "Epidime..." she whispered, in a voice that was not her own.

Calypso acted quickly. She grabbed the Kenvard coin from the ground again and snatched Ayna out of the air. She clapped the icy coin against the tiny, struggling creature. Ayna shrieked in anger and pain.

Myranda rushed for the still-rotating sigils and pulled the gateway sigil free. It had but a single purpose, to open the door of this world to another. With her fingers wrapped around the spoked wheel, Myranda offered a single flex of her influence. Instantly, a portal opened. The ball of darkness that formed above the sword rippled and roiled.

The black demonic wisp curled from Ayna's tiny body. It tried to worm its way up Calypso's, but Myranda reached out with her marked hand

and caught it like a squirming eel. It squealed in her grip and tried to pull free. She thrust her fist into the darkness she had summoned and released it.

In the brief instant she was in contact, Myranda had felt the tug of the void, as though it were hungry for her. That same otherworldly hunger tore at the squirming black mass. It shrieked as it was drawn toward the darkness. Tendrils and claws burst out of the writhing shape. One of them slashed at Myranda. It struck and hooked the gateway aspect. The other slashed the time rune, setting it in rapid motion. The black void shifted to brilliant white. Ether scrambled to correct the whirling rune. The demon's grip was strong. One moment it seemed that it would pull itself free. The next it seemed that it would pull Myranda after it. Myn wrapped her tail about Myranda and held her tightly. The tug-of-war continued. Finally, with a brilliant flash of light, the gateway aspect shattered in the demon's grip. It produced a final, agonized wail and flailed for something to grab hold of. Its claw made sizzling contact with the Sword of the Chosen, tearing it from its place.

With its removal, the sigils began to vanish. The demon was drawn away. The portal closed. The sword rattled to a rest on the ground.

Ivy stared in disbelief at the fallen weapon. "Is it over?" she said.

Myranda turned to where Deacon lay, motionless and growing cold. She narrowed her eyes. "No. It isn't over yet."

She dropped to her knees and pulled the blade from his chest. Little blood came. His heart was not beating.

"Myranda," Ether said. "It was his fate."

"I'm through letting fate have its way," she affirmed. She placed her hand over the wound and held out her other. Her staff darted to her grip.

"His spirit is gone," Calypso said.

Myranda shut her eyes. Her crystal flared. The wound on his chest slowly closed. She dumped all the strength she had left into him. Gradually, his body became whole, healthy, but vacant. The easy part was done. Next came the hard part. Fortunately, she'd traveled this path before.

"Ayna. Get him breathing."

"He is dead, Myranda," Ayna said.

"Keep air going into and out of his lungs. And do the same for me if I stop breathing. You are the highest master of wind magic. It should be simple. Calypso. Keep his blood flowing, and mine."

"It won't do any good if there is no mind or soul."

"I will provide the soul. Ether, I need you to guide me back."

"I shall make myself visible at whatever distance you require," Ether said.

#

The world washed away as Myranda sank into as powerful a focus

241

as she could muster after the day's trials. Surrounded by such smoldering and intense souls, the vacant shell before her was a chilling reminder of how far gone Deacon was. She knew his spirit better than any other. It had drifted far, but it was not yet beyond her reach.

She stretched her mind and spirit. Her consciousness slipped further and further. The cold, unsettling, and far too familiar sensation of her spirit slipping free of her body followed soon after. She was, once again, on borrowed time. She didn't care. She set her mind on the half-felt point in the distance and pursued. The world lay far below her now, its people little more than points of dim light in an icy expanse. Above, Deacon grew more distant. He became more difficult to pursue. As had happened once before, a golden light and irresistible force swelled above her. It threatened to blot Deacon's spirit out. Myranda didn't allow herself to look away. She wouldn't lose someone like this. Not again.

Myranda forced herself further and further from her physical body. The force above that was separating her from what she was now certain was the weakening spirit of her beloved became more difficult to resist.

"You won't keep him. I won't let you have him. Not yet," she demanded.

She could feel her strength, already taxed by battle, draining away. She knew that if she let that strength dwindle too far, there would be no returning to her body. If that happened, she would have sacrificed her life. If she didn't turn back soon, she and Deacon would both be gone. Righteous fury spurred her forward. She would not fail. She would not be denied.

The force ahead of her relented. She surged up to meet the ember of strength that remained of Deacon. Around them, she felt a presence. More than one. A circle of wills that dwarfed her own. Each was endlessly powerful. Each was needle sharp in its focus. Myranda felt as though she were surrounded by a ring of suns, too bright to look upon directly. Potent enough to threaten to snuff out her meager existence. She took the hand of the afterimage of her beloved. When she tried to pull him back, he would not budge. It was as if he was tethered, chained to this point in the plane. Deacon was their prisoner. They both were on trial.

"Give him back to me," Myranda demanded.

The wills around her remained impassive.

"Have we not done everything that was demanded of us? Have we not protected your world for you? Fought your battles? Drove off your rivals? Haven't we endured endless war while you waited until your rules were broken before allowing us to fight? Haven't we picked up the tattered leftovers of our kingdoms and stirred them to new life?"

She tugged at him. They still wouldn't release him.

"I have served you. We all have. We haven't been perfect, but we've done your will and more. I am not asking for a reward. I am asking you to allow us to have the lives we have earned."

Still there was silence and judgment. She felt a flare of anger well within her.

"I am not one of the original Chosen. I was not crafted by the hands of gods to fill my role like Ether was. I was just a human, touched by the gods in some accident of fate. But I have served you. I have listened to your council. I would have given *anything* to save my world. But the world is safe now. Against all odds I have survived, and I have found a family again. I would die for my world, but for my family, that isn't enough. For my family, I intend to do something far more important. I intend to *live* for them."

The beings around her became more distinct. It was still too painful, too intense to look upon them directly, but she could see something of their shapes, feel something of their nature. And she could feel that the ember of a spirit that remained of Deacon was rapidly dwindling.

"I know what you want. I know you want to take him. Because he defied your will. Because he trod ground that was only meant for you. Or perhaps just because it is blasted *fate* that he should die, here and now. I heard your messages. I understood the meaning of the tests within the forest. I am to let him go. To allow this sacrifice as the price of victory. Of safety. I will *not pay that price*. Not when I know it is your will alone that prevents me from having the life I fought to have. Not when it serves no purpose but to satisfy your whims."

She felt a pressure begin to drive her away. Deacon's weakening form began to slip free. She held tighter.

"*No.* I know you created this world and everything in it. I know you gave me the power to defend it and the wisdom to solve its problems. I fight the battles you dare not fight. I right the wrongs of those beings who would destroy your work. I am Chosen. You *chose* me. And I choose *him*."

She felt something change. The wills began to shift. Without language, she felt their judgments, one by one. With each decision, she felt their force more powerfully upon her. The words of the gods, thrust into her mind.

*No.*

A wave of power pushed her away.

*No.*

Her grip on Deacon weakened.

*No.*

She faltered, slipping back.

*No. No. No.*

…

*Yes.*

Around her, she felt the gathering of gods part until only three remained. Separate from the rest, she could feel more of their nature. One was the embodiment of mischief. One was a roiling golden form of war and battle. And one, so similar to the being of war, was something else. Something familiar. It was a spirit she had known in life, but distilled somehow. Purified by the fires of death.

It was Lain.

Not an echo of the past. Not another lingering spirit. It was, in a way, more purely the creature she had known than he had ever been in life. The mortal part of him was burned away, leaving only the divine. He, and the other dissenters, had spoken. After a moment that seemed to last an eternity, the others listened.

They vanished, and with them the force holding her at bay. She drew Deacon to her and turned her focus to the world below.

The world was dim. The constellation of souls was too far away, or her strength had waned too much for her to sense it. She searched for the pure, intense strength of Ether, her beacon back to her body. She could feel that it was somewhere, but she couldn't follow it. It was too indistinct.

She'd waited too long.

Deacon's spirit beside her shuddered. She drew it close and felt his calm, serene thoughts. At first, it felt like acceptance. Like he was resigned to his fate and content to spend this final moment with the one he loved in life. But as the thoughts became clearer, she realized there was something else. He had been looking for something else. And he had found it.

She turned her focus once more below. She felt it too. Bright, strong. It wasn't where she needed to go. But if she had only one choice of a final spirit to seek in this life, and this moment, it was this one.

#

Ivy stood, hands clutched before her. Myranda had slowly slumped onto Deacon's chest as the minutes of focus passed on. The only indication that Myranda was alive was the glow of her staff. It was all but dark now. Myn's head hung low, great snout nuzzled beneath Deacon's cold hand. Ether watched and waited. Ayna and Calypso worked their craft. Minutes had passed. They'd felt like hours. Ether lowered her head.

"I feel nothing," she said quietly.

"If there is something there, it is weak," Calypso said.

Ivy's ears flicked. She sniffed the air. "How…" Her head snapped around. "Where?" She squinted into the distance. A shivering figure was plodding toward them.

"It doesn't matter how. If anything will work, this will." She dashed toward the figure. "Just keep them alive! Just a little longer."

She reached the woman approaching. It was Sadie, Leo still in her arms.

"This way, fast!" Ivy urged.

She rushed Sadie toward the others.

"What happened, Miss Ivy? Where are we? I was in the palace, and everything went white, and then I was walking through places that I knew I couldn't have reached."

"If there are answers, you'll have them later, just hurry. Lives depend on it!"

They reached the others. Ivy tugged Leo from Sadie's arms and set him on the ground beside his parents. Leo toddled forward and nestled between them. There was no flash of magic. There was no glimmer of power. Leo simply cuddled closer to the cool bodies of his mother and father and sat with a look of calm and serenity.

The moments dragged on. Slowly, Ether's expression changed. "Stop," she said. "Leave them be."

"Are you certain? I feel nothing at all," Calypso said.

"If they are to live, they must live on their own. Leave them be," she said.

The wizards obeyed. Their wills eased. Seconds passed.

"Come on, Myranda," Ivy begged.

Seconds more. Slowly, imperceptibly, her chest rose and fell. Ivy crouched down and pulled her aside, resting her on the ground. A second breath came and went, too cold to even curl as vapor. Now Deacon took a reedy breath.

"We need to warm them up," Ivy said. "Myn!"

The dragon tenderly slipped a paw beneath the trio and raised them to her. She curled her wings around them and held them tightly against her body. A soft puff of flame curled from her nostrils. Warmed blood surged through her veins. Myranda shivered. Her eyes fluttered open. Myn set them down again. Myranda groped for Deacon and Leo. Ivy guided their hands together. Leo gripped Myranda's hand. Myranda's fingers tightened around Deacon's. A moment later, Deacon weakly gripped hers in return.

Ivy laughed gleefully and threw her arms around Ether. The shapeshifter reluctantly hugged her back. Myn lowered her muzzle until her nose was nearly touching Myranda's.

"Never again, Myranda," she stated.

Myranda raised a shaky hand and patted the dragon's snout. "Never again. Now let's go home."

Joseph R. Lallo

# Epilogue

The months that followed were tense for the world. Deacon's mystic tampering had been felt in every corner of it. Little true damage was done, but some effects still lingered. In a world so recently held hostage by the whims of dark wizards, casting so sweeping an unexplained and potentially apocalyptic wave of magic across the many kingdoms was not something that could simply be dismissed and forgiven. It had taken great efforts by Myranda, Deacon, and Caya to quell the fury of the crowned heads of Ulvard and Tressor. War most certainly would have erupted again if not for the still-fresh memory of the price of the Perpetual War.

A day earlier, the final discussion had ended. Assurances had been given. Treaties had been signed. The troops that had gathered at the borders stood down. Travel resumed, and not a moment too soon. Some things simply would not bow to the slow grind of diplomacy.

"Ah, finally, the cave," Ayna said. "I never thought I'd be happy to see the blasted, confining, mystically stifling nightmare of a place."

While Anya had avoided as many as she could manage, Calypso had proved indispensable in the discussions. Deacon's near catastrophic use of magic had stoked an already simmering fear of the mystic arts. Having a peerless wizard without an allegiance to any particular kingdom served to provide what most of the other diplomats perceived as an unbiased point of view on the arcane.

Of course, the revelation that there was a previously unknown village with a legion of incomparably skilled wizards may have influenced the shifting attitudes of the Ulvardians. A wise leader does not issue a blanket condemnation of magic while sharing a border with the greatest concentration of mystic expertise the world had ever known.

The pair of wizards were traveling courtesy of Calypso's magic. The icy sleigh the water mage had conjured was a good deal slower than what Ayna could manage on her own, but the need to carry some significant cargo and the unspoken desire for company during the trip had persuaded Ayna to hitch a ride.

Calypso flipped open her Entwell messenger pad. There were eight such pads now, not counting the one within Entwell itself. All five of the kingdoms on the continent had one, in addition to the personal one kept by Calypso. At present, two of them were en route across the Crescent Sea to be presented to the people of North and South Crescent. Once they were in place, Entwell would well and truly be a part of the world that it had so long been hidden from.

"According to Deacon, the falls relented two days ago. They've never been silent for less than three days, to my knowledge. You know the way better than anyone, and you can fly. You ought to be able to clear it in hours."

"Alone, certainly. But I have to drag *you* along, in all of your flopping, land-bound fishiness." She grumbled. "At this rate you'll have to stuff me into that blasted jar again. The flood is sure to start before we reach Entwell."

"Er. Yes. About that. I have some rather good news for you in that regard," Calypso said.

"What possible good news could you have for me with the prospect of a days-long plunge into the heart of a mountain with the slenderest thread of a breeze connecting me to the proper wind of the outside?"

"You won't have to drag a flopping, land-bound fish with you."

Ayna turned to her, face stricken with poorly hidden dismay. "*What?*" she said. "You aren't actually thinking of remaining among these backward, uncultured clods."

"I would counter that they are neither backward, nor uncultured, nor clods, but I do believe I will spend a few months more in the greater world. My role of ambassador is not entirely complete. There are still the Crescents for me to tour. By virtue of their distance and the borders closed by the Perpetual War, we've not seen newcomers from those lands in ages. I am rather looking forward to seeing what has become of the land I've only heard secondhand stories about."

"But… you…" Ayna shut her eyes and shook off the flustered tone. "You would send me through that blasted cave alone?"

"You rose to the challenge on the way out. I think the cave is no match for you now."

"Well—wh… *naturally*, this is so, but we have traveled as a pair for so long. I… what of *you*? Hmm? How will *you* return, when the time comes? I suppose you'll expect me to come and fetch you. Not to speak ill of my kind, but I know the other fairies of Entwell well enough to know none of them have the fortitude to make the journey alone."

"Visiting the Crescents will take me across the sea. I can simply return through the seaward passage when the time comes."

"I… but that's… we could have discussed it."

"I would have thought you would be happy to be rid of me."

Ayna crossed her arms and gritted her teeth. "Long past time for it," she said with little conviction.

Calypso eased the sleigh to a stop. The mouth of the Cave of the Beast was just ahead. A ragged and ruddy figure crouched in the darkness of the cave's mouth, sheltered from the wind while a small fire crackled at his feet and cast him in its dim glow. The man stood and stepped into the brighter light of day. It was Desmeres.

"Ah! I am pleased to see I timed my journey properly." Calypso stepped from the sleigh, which slumped into the snow it had been conjured from. "I trust you have not been waiting long."

"A few hours," he said. "I moved as swiftly as I could. I have had quite enough of that cave for one lifetime. Are you the one who will be escorting me back?"

"I did indeed volunteer for that duty."

Ayna gave Calypso a hard look and buzzed in front of her. "You what?! Just how long did you have this extended sabbatical from your Entwell duties planned?"

"If you would have attended a few more of the meetings with the nobles, you would know, wouldn't you?" Calypso jabbed playfully. She turned to Desmeres. "I have something for you that I was told you would be eager to have."

Calypso pulled open a pack by her side. She withdrew a dagger in a freshly made sheath.

"Ah…" Desmeres said, accepting the weapon as though he were being reunited with an old friend. He slipped it from the sheath and looked it over. "You've had a few more chapters added to your story, haven't you?" he said. "At the center of a catastrophe. Used to strike down a king who had made himself into something of a god. Used to ward off a demon. Wielded by a fallen warrior pulled from history itself."

Desmeres turned the blade to watch the gleam creep across the edge. "My first true collaboration, and it is a god-killer of a dagger with not a nick or scratch to show for it." He slipped it back into the sheath and hung the weapon at his side. "And it isn't even my best work. I'm rather looking forward to how the next collaboration comes out."

Ayna buzzed behind him and pointed. "Is that what this hideous weapon of war is destined to be?" she said.

Desmeres reached back and slipped an unfinished sword from its place on his back. "This? I suppose you could call it that. The last work of my father. If would be a crime to make it less than the absolute finest example of my craft when I am through with it, but in light of recent events, that is a *rather* high bar to cross. It'll take some time, but I believe I am up for the challenge."

A clacking sound drew their attention to the mouth of the cave. Calypso took a step back as another familiar, but altogether more unnatural, form emerged from the darkness. It was the mismatched and stitched-together tapestry of an animal known as Mott.

"Ah… so *that* followed you," Calypso said.

Mott took a few skittery steps back. Its head and tail sagged a bit as it sheepishly looked away, clearly remembering the less than courteous impression it had made upon Calypso during their last meeting.

"Evidently he decided he wished to return to his post, guarding Epidime's cavern, at least until a more formal solution can be found." He looked at the creature. "Not that he did a particularly good job last time."

Mott eyed him irritably.

"I suspect he will do fine," Calypso said. "He's certainly threatening enough. And it won't take much to keep people from wanting to explore this particular cave. Despite my best efforts, I am getting the distinct impression that the people of the northern kingdoms and Tressor are growing wary of magic and its practitioners. I wouldn't anticipate a rush of hopeful apprentices, even knowing what waits on the other side."

The fairy buzzed to the mouth of the cave and paused. An almost imperceptible shudder ran through her little body at the prospect of continuing. Calypso smirked.

"You know, Ayna, I'm sure you're welcome to join me as I finish up my tour."

"No… This cave is… I have something to prove to myself regarding this cave. And I don't have the same taste for these kingdoms as you." She darted back and jabbed a finger in Calypso's face. "But you hurry back, do you understand? You have an obligation to the people of Entwell."

"Of course," Calypso said.

The fairy nodded, took a deep breath, and buzzed into the cave. Calypso turned to Desmeres.

"And what about you? Shall we wait here until you recover? Or are you eager to be on your way?"

He held out his hands. One of them was weathered and toughened. The other was strangely pale and pristine. Both were flesh and blood.

"I believe I have achieved the recovery I was after. If you are able, I would much prefer to return as swiftly as possible."

"By all means," Calypso said, raising her fingers and stirring the snow to rise to a larger, sturdier sleigh. "I imagine, as you are still technically meant to be in the custody of Queen Caya, it would be appropriate not to delay."

Desmeres considered her words. "I suppose you are correct, but that did not even enter my mind."

"Then why the hurry?" she asked, putting the finishing touches on the sleigh.

"There is a woman at home. I know she never truly needed me, but I hope after these last few months she still has use for me." He stepped into the sleigh beside Calypso. "I miss her terribly. And as I've said, I find myself quite optimistic about beginning a new collaboration."

Calypso laughed. "Well then I'll be sure to get you there as soon as I can."

#

The journey home had taken several days. Worsening weather had slowed them such that Myranda and Deacon hadn't reached the palace until long after Leo's bedtime. Deacon cradled the sleeping boy in his arms as Sadie prepared his room.

"I'm surprised Ivy wasn't here to scold us for being so late," Deacon whispered.

"She's off with Ether. It's Celia's birthday, remember?" Myranda said.

"Ah. Yes. I never would have dreamed they would spend so much time together."

"That's what family is about."

Deacon gazed down at his boy. "He's already grown so much," he whispered.

"Soon he'll be ready to start taking on his princely duties," Myranda said. "Frankly, I think bringing him along to Ulvard helped smooth over some of the tensions. He's a born diplomat."

Sadie took the boy. Myranda gave Leo a kiss on the forehead, and the nobles left Sadie to put him down for the evening.

As they paced the short distance to their own room, Deacon was uncharacteristically distant.

"Is something bothering you?" Myranda asked.

"I don't think I should be a part of future diplomatic trips to Ulvard."

"That's absurd. You are the king. You will be expected."

"King Terrance and Queen Tanya don't trust me. And with good reason. I nearly shattered the world."

"What's done is done."

They stepped into their quarters.

"It is all well and good to say that, but what's done is going to echo through generations. You must have heard the latest from Ravenwood. Wolloff's tower still hasn't returned to normal."

"I wouldn't call it a hardship, having a tower that exists in perpetual spring."

"Hardship or not, it is seemingly permanent. It is a scar my actions left in the world."

"You weren't yourself." She set her crown on its pillow. "Now that the stain on your mind is gone, we won't let something like that happen again."

Deacon removed his crown but hesitated. He surveyed the gleaming masterwork. To any but the palace staff, there wouldn't have been any reason to imagine it was anything but the one and only crown of Kenvard's king. The truth was made clear only on close inspection. It was grander, more precisely and elegantly crafted. In that way it was a match for the queen's crown.

Deacon had not worn a crown for most of the last few months. The people of Kenvard believed the previous one had been lost during the chaos that had consumed the world and had only just been found and returned. There was no telling how the rumor started. Myranda had her suspicions Ivy had dreamed it up to keep people from asking unpleasant questions. In truth, this was a new piece. It had been finished in just the last few weeks. The more exquisite design was due in part to the fact that this crown had no purpose but to stand as a symbol of status and power. Its predecessor was enchanted and needed to bear runes and weave in mystically attuned gems and metals. Without such restrictions, the new design needed only serve the whims of dignity and grace. But there was another, far simpler reason for the subtly different design. The original crown had not been available to duplicate.

He set the new crown down and shifted his gaze to a sturdy chest on the display beside it. "I wasn't myself..." he murmured.

Deacon opened the chest. Myranda stood beside him as he looked down into the dim interior. A ragged bundle was nestled into the bottom of the chest. It was the very package left at the mouth of the Cave of the Beast and delivered by Calypso when the worst of the crisis had passed. It had not been opened. He tugged the package from inside.

"I think it is time," he said.

He set the bundle on his desk. The thick cloth it was wrapped in still bore the faintly sparkling silt of the Cave of the Beast.

"You seemed rather insistent that the package not be opened," Myranda said.

"When I'd prepared the package, I didn't expect... well, I suppose that will become clear."

He shut his eyes. A flicker of magic dispelled whatever sorcery still clung to the bundle. He pulled it open. The bulk of the contents was, perhaps predictably, the original crown of Kenvard. It was dingy from its time in the cave and badly marred from having clacked and clinked its way down a long tunnel. His ring lay beneath it. The mad rush to restore peace and order to the world in the time since the crisis had consumed their attentions such that they had yet to replace the ring. It was no longer needed to treat an affliction, and neither Deacon nor Myranda needed to be reminded of their love and devotion to one another.

The final object within the bundle was a tightly folded piece of parchment. Deacon plucked it up. He took a breath and handed it to Myranda.

"For Myranda and Leo, if I am lost." She handed it back. "Are you sure you want me to read this?"

He nodded.

She opened the message.

*Leo,*

*I write this in the darkness by the dim light of my fractured crystal. It is cold here. My hands are unsteady. The future is uncertain. I pray this note finds you in a place of light and hope. I do not know what will have become of me by the time you read these words. I may have fallen for nothing. I may have succumbed to forces beyond my control. But I could not bear a future in which you did not know the truth. First, you must know that what I do today I do for you. Second, and of far greater importance, you must not blame yourself for my actions. In a few moments, I shall seek the wisdom and council of the last vestige of the D'Karon in our world. The trials of our world and the route to safety are a puzzle, and the one called Epidime holds the final pieces. He is weak, and I shall take what precautions I can, but I cannot guarantee he will not get the better of me. What I do now, I choose to do because I believe it is right, because I believe it is necessary. I may be wrong. This may be the latest, and most disastrous, of my many lapses in judgment. But I know that whatever becomes of me, you are protected by beings of wisdom and honor. You will grow into a great man. Know that my last clear thoughts were of my love for you.*

*Myranda,*

*I am sorry. I am sorry for the weight I have placed upon you. Even if I succeed, I am sorry that my rash decisions have left you with the weight of the world on your shoulders. I am sorry that I have left you to raise Leo on your own, but I know you will rise to this challenge as you have to all others. And, if the worst has come to pass and my life has been lost to you or the other Chosen, know that I understand what you had to do. I forgive you. And I will always love you.*

The queen blinked tears from her eyes and folded the message. She searched her mind for the proper words for the moment. Deacon saved her the trouble.

"I meant all of those words, and I still mean them. But you need to understand something. I wrote that message, I abandoned the crown and the ring, and I communed with Epidime. My thoughts were clear. For all that came after, I was addled by the affliction and blinded by the knowledge that Epidime had given me. But in that moment, when I made the choice to take the first steps down that potentially disastrous road, my mind was my own. I did this. Me."

"The world survived, Deacon."

"But at what cost? I damaged the fabric of our existence. I angered the forces that govern us. And in my defense, you stood in opposition to them as well. Everything that happened was because of me, in order to take away the gateway that might allow the D'Karon and those like them into our world. If this chapter of our history has a villain, it is me. And though the world survived, it is *changed*. Changed in the very way that I sought to change it. The villain *won* this time. And what of Epidime? I have locked the door that allowed the D'Karon to invade, but in doing so I have trapped him here with us. He may be locked away in the cave, but he still lives."

He tightened his fists. "And most treacherous of all, even in giving me what I asked of him, he has found a way to deny it to me. I wanted the answers. All of them. I wanted to know what events had shaped the world that I'd yet to record. I wanted his point of view. And I have it. I have every conversation and memory he had with the Chosen, with the other D'Karon. I know the depths of D'Karon magic so intimately it will take me years to unravel it. But after all that has happened, I only have *more* questions. As best as I can determine, the affliction that gripped my soul when I first made my ill-advised escape from Entwell was a thing of pure chaos. And yet, by the time it was torn from me and cast away, it had grown into something that could only be Epidime. We cast it out, the last being to pass through the doorway before it was sealed for good. It was hurled from this world, and in its throes it set the time sigil in motion. I can only assume it was cast back, far, far into the past. Did it grow in exile, only to return, to attack, and to tell us its name? Where did the name come from? And Epidime's arrival with the other D'Karon is what spurred the Chosen to action, which endangered your life, which inspired me to cast the spell that caused the affliction that created Epidime. Where does the loop begin? Where did Epidime really come from? Was my affliction truly the seed from which such an evil was formed? Was Epidime an inevitability, a thing that is its own beginning and end? The answers aren't even in the blasted creature's own mind."

Myranda placed a hand on his shoulder. "Deacon, if we cannot find the answers, we learn to embrace the mystery. There are more than enough challenges ahead to keep us busy through the rest of our years."

He nodded. "That, I suppose, is the greatest wisdom of all."

"Come to bed. There will be much to do tomorrow."

Deacon took a seat at the desk near the bed and summoned his stylus to hand. "I shall join you shortly."

"What are you planning to do?"

He flipped open his book. "As I've said, Epidime was able to fill many of the gaps in my record this momentous time. I began recording the adventure long ago. I'm very nearly through. I think the time has come to finish the tale…"

# From the Author

Thank you for reading! If you liked this story, or perhaps if you found it lacking, I'd love to hear from you. Leave a review, or contact me directly on social media or via email. You can find the relevant links (as well as my newsletter sign-up) at bookofdeacon.com/contact

**Discover other titles by Joseph R. Lallo:**

**The Book of Deacon Series:**

Book 1: *The Book of Deacon*
Book 2: *The Great Convergence*
Book 3: *The Battle of Verril*
Book 4: *The D'Karon Apprentice*
Book 5: *The Crescents*

**Other stories in the same setting:**

*Jade*
*The Rise of the Red Shadow*
*The Redemption of Desmeres*
*The Adventures of Rustle and Eddy*

**The Big Sigma Series:**

Book 1: *Bypass Gemini*
Book 2: *Unstable Prototypes*
Book 3: *Artificial Evolution*
Book 4: *Temporal Contingency*
Book 5: *Indra Station*

**The Free-Wrench Series:**

Book 1: *Free-Wrench*
Book 2: *Skykeep*
Book 3: *Ichor Well*
Book 4: *The Calderan Problem*
Book 5: *Cipher Hill*

## Collections:

*The Book of Deacon Anthology*
*The Big Sigma Collection: Volume 1*
*The Free-Wrench Collection: Volume 1*

## Other Stories:

*Between*
*Fallen Empire: Rogue Derelict*
*Structophis*
*The Other Eight*